Cookies and Scream

"This novel has all the right baked-up ingredients for an awesome mystery . . . I love how creative Lowell is with the story line . . . Will keep you hungry for more." —*Fresh Fiction*

"Lowell is great at storytelling and she has built a world of very enjoyable characters." —*Lily Pond Reads*

"Well-written . . . An enjoyable read . . . Nothing better than a good book and fresh baked goods." —*Open Book Society*

"Sentiment, humor, and cookies blend together in this sweet mystery that shines with characters who genuinely support one another and appreciate the eccentricities that make them all so unique." —*Kings River Life Magazine*

"An enjoyable read that entertained and kept me engaged from beginning to end with a good mystery that quickly became a page-turner." —*Dru's Book Musings*

One Dead Cookie

"This is such an enjoyable series . . . [*One Dead Cookie* is] a fast and fun read." —*MyShelf.com*

"Scrumptious descriptions of baking, extensive details about the history and technique of baking cookies, and a considerable cast of surprisingly well-developed characters all make this a fun, enjoyable, and tasty pleasure for readers."
—*Kings River Life Magazine*

"There's never a dull moment in Chatterly Heights, and once you come, you may never want to leave again."
—*The Reading Room*

continued . . .

When the Cookie Crumbles

"Cozy fans will enjoy the third delicious Cookie Cutter Shop Mystery."
—*Genre Go Round Reviews*

"An enjoyable book with believable characters and situations. Fans of Laura Childs, Joanne Fluke, or Jenn McKinlay will savor this delightful mystery."
—*The Season*

A Cookie Before Dying

"An entertaining investigative thriller . . . Fans of cozies will enjoy this Maryland small-town whodunit."
—*Genre Go Round Reviews*

"A great combination of wit and mystery."
—*Fresh Fiction*

"What a great read. This well-layered, page-turning mystery kept me on my toes . . . I can't wait to read the next book in this enjoyable series."
—*Dru's Book Musings*

"Virginia Lowell does it again . . . This excellent offering will satisfy your sleuth tooth (and make you hungry for an iced sugar cookie). Well done, Ms. Lowell! Long may you bake up delectable books with toothsome plot twists and tasty characters."
—Sherry Ladig, *Irish Music and Dance Association* magazine

Cookie Dough or Die

"It's always a joy to find a new series that . . . contains such promise."
—*CA Reviews*

"Virginia Lowell made me a cookie cutter convert with her cleverly crafted *Cookie Dough or Die* . . . The writing is strong, the story line engaging, the characters ones you'd like to be your friends. This is what makes a good cozy mystery a special read. I look forward to more cookie adventures—with sprinkles and chocolate icing on top."
—AnnArbor.com

Berkley Prime Crime titles by Virginia Lowell

COOKIE DOUGH OR DIE
A COOKIE BEFORE DYING
WHEN THE COOKIE CRUMBLES
ONE DEAD COOKIE
COOKIES AND SCREAM
DEAD MEN DON'T EAT COOKIES

Dead Men
Don't Eat Cookies

VIRGINIA LOWELL

BERKLEY PRIME CRIME, NEW YORK

BERKLEY
PRIME
CRIME

An imprint of Penguin Random House LLC
375 Hudson Street, New York, New York 10014

DEAD MEN DON'T EAT COOKIES

A Berkley Prime Crime Book / published by arrangement with the author

BERKLEY® PRIME CRIME and the PRIME CRIME design are trademarks
of Penguin Random House LLC.
For more information, visit penguin.com.

ISBN: 978-0-425-26071-5

PUBLISHING HISTORY
Berkley Prime Crime mass-market edition / July 2015

PRINTED IN THE UNITED STATES OF AMERICA

10 9 8 7 6 5 4 3 2

Cover illustration by Mary Ann Lasher (B&A Reps).
Cover design by George Long.
Interior text design by Kristin del Rosario.

Penguin
Random
House

In memory of my father

Chapter One

Olivia Greyson opened a kitchen cabinet and reached for a bag of flour that wasn't there. With an impatient sigh, she reminded herself that she was working in an unfamiliar kitchen. She and her business partner, Maddie Briggs, had organized the kitchen, which was twice the size of their own cozy little kitchen back at The Gingerbread House. This kitchen, with its state-of-the-art appliances and many cabinets, felt less homey to Olivia. She loved to lose herself in the pleasures of baking decorated cutout cookies, such as the feel of a cutter as it slid through the dough and the warm, sweet aroma of the cookies. She loved to watch a colorful design emerge as she squeezed royal icing through the tip of a pastry bag. To Olivia, having to stop and hunt for baking ingredients felt like hearing the doorbell ring as she drifted into a cookie-filled dream.

Olivia shut the cabinet door with more force than she'd intended, though the new magnet kept it from bouncing back at her. "This is very irritating," she said as she swiped at a lock of auburn hair that flopped over one eye. "I could have sworn we had another bag of flour. There's no more sugar, either. I'd so rather be back at The Gingerbread House, baking in our own simple, well-stocked kitchen. Maddie, remind me why we agreed to work here, and make it convincing."

Maddie, Olivia's best friend since age ten, tousled her curly red hair over the sink to shed a dusting of flour. "Because, my cranky friend, we solemnly promised your mom we would help her achieve her dream of transforming this disreputable dump into an arts and crafts school. As I recall, you were all gung-ho about the idea. I believe you hoped it would keep Ellie too busy to pressure you into taking yoga classes." Maddie straightened and tossed back her hair, which appeared to have ballooned by several inches.

"Well, it's a reason, though I doubt Mom will ever give up pressuring me to take yoga."

Wielding a pastry bag, Maddie piped a burnt orange outline around a baked and cooled cookie shaped like a saw. "Our delectable cookies are sorely needed to energize those hungry workers upstairs," she reminded Olivia. "It's tough work, transforming this old place into a structure capable of passing a housing inspection." Maddie piped burnt orange polka dots on the saw-shaped cookie.

"Those dots look like rust spots," Olivia said, nodding toward the cookie.

Maddie's pale eyebrows lifted haughtily. "Thank you," she said. "That's the look I was aiming for. It's a subtle yet tasty reminder not to leave tools out in the rain."

Olivia snickered, awakening Spunky, her little Yorkshire terrier, who'd been snoozing on a soft blanket in the corner of the kitchen. Hoping for food, he yapped and flapped his tail.

"Not a chance, Spunks, my little con artist," Olivia said fondly. He trotted over to her, and she scooped him up for a cuddle. "I must admit, I'm glad Spunky could come with us," Olivia said as she rubbed his ears. Unlike the Gingerbread House kitchen, this was still considered private property. Since they weren't preparing food to sell to the public, they were safe from the threat of a Health Department inspection.

Maddie finished decorating the last baked cookie, a wrench, with burnt orange candy stripes. "By the way," she said, "if you were thinking about starting another batch of cookie dough, I put the flour on the bottom shelf of the refrigerator, shoved toward the back, behind the bread and lunchmeat. The sugar is in there, too. It's for their own protection." Maddie glanced up at the stained ceiling. "I don't want to be around when the workers rip down that ceiling. I'm still not convinced those mice have vacated the premises."

"Yet another reason I'd rather be baking in the lovely kitchen of our own little shop." Olivia opened the door of the newly installed refrigerator to retrieve the bag of flour.

"Point taken." Before the refrigerator door slammed shut, Maddie reached inside to grab a disk of chilled cookie dough from the top shelf.

Olivia opened the fresh bag of flour and measured enough for one batch of dough. "I'll feel more cheerful once I start another batch of cookie dough," she said. "Besides, you and I usually bake all Sunday and Monday, while The Gingerbread House is closed. *Where* we bake isn't really important. It's the rolling, cutting, and decorating I truly love."

"And the cookie sampling," Maddie said.

"Can't argue with that." Olivia lowered the mixer beaters into the bowl, where sugar and butter waited to be creamed together. "Tomorrow we'll be back in our own sweet, low-tech kitchen. Although I have to admit, it's fun to watch those workers upstairs devour our cookies. I wish I could eat like that."

"They will be renovating all those old rooms," Maddie said. "They need sugar." Her freckled brow furrowed as she assessed the cookies she'd finished decorating. Apparently satisfied, she said, "Personally, I think it's fun to test out a newly renovated kitchen, especially when someone else is paying for top-notch equipment. We should get one of these silicone rolling pins for the store kitchen. I used hardly any flour to roll out the dough, plus this is so easy to wash." Maddie held the rolling pin by one handle and pointed it toward the ceiling like a drum major's baton. "This isn't solid wood, but it might make an effective weapon should we ever again have to protect ourselves from a murderer."

"When it comes to confrontations with killers, we have more than fulfilled our lifetime quota." Olivia nestled the unopened bag of flour in a cloth sack to be carted back to The Gingerbread House.

Maddie applied the rolling pin to the center of the chilled dough and began to roll it out. "I do get a kick out of making cutout cookies in the kitchen of an old flophouse."

"This place didn't start out as a flophouse, you know," Olivia said. "Mom told me it was a boarding house built in the 1920s for single workers aspiring to middle-class status. Respectable single women could live here alone, as long as they had jobs. Then the Great Depression hit Chatterley Heights, not to mention the rest of the—is that your cell phone blasting? It can't be mine, because I left it charging in my own humble kitchen, where it is safe from your compulsion to mess with other people's ringtones."

"Ha! I knew it," Maddie said. "You've been forgetting your phone on purpose, just so I can't spice up your boring taste in ringtones." When her cell phone blared again, Maddie said, "My hands are covered with flour. Would you see if that's someone worth talking to, like my sweet, hunky husband or my aunt Sadie?"

Olivia reached toward the kitchen counter and scooped up Maddie's cell phone. "It probably isn't Lucas or Aunt Sadie," Olivia said as she checked the caller ID. "It's a local number, though. I don't recognize it. Maybe one of the workers upstairs is calling you for some reason. I suppose we'd better answer."

Maddie grabbed a towel and wiped the flour off her hands before she took the cell phone from Olivia. "Hi," Maddie said.

"Who are you?" Her forehead crinkled in puzzlement. "It's your mom," she whispered to Olivia. "Ellie, why are you . . . ? Yeah, I know, Livie is always forgetting her phone. It drives me crazy. But what happened to yours? Did the poor, ancient creature finally die? Maybe now you'll consider getting a smartphone. I could help you set it up." Maddie's frown deepened as she listened. "Ellie, slow down, I can't understand you. Is that pandemonium I hear in the background?" Maddie glanced at Olivia and shrugged. "All right, ours not to question why. We're on our way upstairs." Maddie hung up and slid her phone into the pocket of her jeans. Spreading a clean towel over her partially rolled dough, she said, "Our instant presence is required upstairs in room eight."

"What on earth . . . ? Has one of the workers been injured?"

"I don't know," Maddie said, "but all will be revealed. From the sound of it, your mother was busy coping with someone in hysterics. Maybe several someones. Prepare for anything." Spunky left his blanket and ran to join his human buddies. He barely made it into the hallway before Maddie closed the kitchen door.

"Just an ordinary day in Chatterley Heights, Maryland," Olivia muttered as she followed Maddie and Spunky up the rickety staircase to the second floor. They walked down the dimly lit corridor on stained, threadbare carpet to room number eight. Through the thin wood of the closed door, Olivia heard a jumble of voices. She turned the knob, but the door cracked open before she could give it a push. Olivia recognized her mother's hazel eyes, or at least one of them, peeking out at her. Ellie Greyson-Meyers's small, yet remarkably strong arm snaked out, clutched Olivia's wrist, and yanked her into the room. Maddie and Spunky followed.

At first, Olivia saw nothing to explain her mother's urgent summons. The room was littered with stained and splintered boards, along with equipment she couldn't identify by name. No one appeared to be working. Five workers clustered together in a corner of the room, near a bare window with a northern exposure. Their spirited discussion halted abruptly when they noticed Olivia and Maddie. Through the window behind the workers, Olivia saw a small forest of overgrown trees.

Olivia's tall, gangly younger brother, Jason, stood apart from the group. For once, Jason wasn't cracking jokes. As he stared down at his feet, a lock of brown hair fell across his forehead. He ignored it. When Spunky trotted toward him, Jason's sober expression brightened.

A woman huddled on the floor against the west wall. Long, wavy chestnut hair fell forward as she hid her face in her hands. From the distressed skinny jeans that clung to the woman's slender legs, Olivia guessed she was fairly young.

One worker broke ranks to join the young woman. Olivia did a double take as she recognized her stepfather's cousin, Calliope Zimmermann. She was in charge of the work crew, in addition to providing substantial funding for the project. In work boots, jeans, a loose sweatshirt, and a hardhat, Calliope looked indistinguishable from the male workers. As usual, her long, plain face was free of makeup. A fringe of gray-tinged brown hair showed beneath her hardhat. Calliope slid down the wall next to the young woman and handed her a wad of tissue. "Steady on now, kid. Blow your nose. When the police finally show up, they'll want to ask you some questions."

"I've told you over and over, my name is Alicia, not kid. Besides, I'm nineteen years old." With a sulky frown, Alicia snatched the tissues from Calliope's hand.

"Yeah, I know." Calliope removed her hardhat and ran her fingers through her matted hair. "I just wanted to make you mad. Mad is better at a time like this. Believe me, I've been through it, and I was a lot younger than you. Why don't you go home? You only work half days, anyway."

"You're only saying that because I don't do anything but fetch stuff," Alicia said. "You never let me do any real work. I need the money, you know. I won't make enough waitressing."

Calliope sighed loudly. She was not a small woman, but she hopped to her feet with no apparent effort and ambled back toward the other workers.

"Mom, what the heck is going on here?" Olivia asked Ellie in a low voice. "Why were the police called?"

Calliope heard the question and joined them. "It looks like we've got ourselves another murder here in Chatterley Heights," she said.

Alicia wailed into her wad of tissues.

"I'll go comfort Alicia." Ellie glanced toward the east end of the room, where a sheet of plywood leaned against the wall. "I've already seen what there is to see. Come on, Spunks, we are needed." The little Yorkie followed her eagerly.

Calliope motioned to Olivia and Maddie to follow her across the room. "Alicia is convinced it's her father in there," Calliope said, nodding toward the plywood.

"Her father is inside the wall?" Maddie exchanged a quick glance with Olivia. "Is Alicia . . . I mean . . ."

"Sane?" Calliope shrugged her broad shoulders. "She's emotional, that's for sure. Won't stop bawling." When they were a couple of feet away from the wall, Calliope signaled them to stay where they were. Olivia glanced back at her mother, who was sitting on the floor next to Alicia, an arm around the girl's shaking shoulders. Spunky gazed at Alicia, his head tilted, as if he were trying to puzzle out what the sobbing sounds meant.

The workers had begun to chat among themselves. Jason broke away from the group and crossed the room to join Calliope, who spoke softly to him. Jason nodded. He positioned himself at one end of the plywood. Calliope took hold of the opposite end, and together they eased it away from the opening in the wall. Olivia assumed they were trying not to disturb the site any more than necessary. When the plywood scraped against the floor, Olivia heard a cry from across the room. Probably Alicia, Olivia thought, but she didn't turn around to check. She couldn't drag her gaze away from the wall.

"Livie, dear," Ellie said, "Alicia and I will be downstairs

in the kitchen making sandwiches and coffee. Did I hear you mention you'd finished baking some cookies?"

Olivia answered her mother's question without turning her head. "Oh, sure, Mom, eat the cookies, drink the coffee. There's plenty of both."

"You'll need to move some dough off the table," Maddie said. "Just wad it in a towel and stick it in the fridge."

The workers shuffled closer to the wall to get another look inside. "You guys clear out," Calliope said. "You can take the rest of the day off, with pay. Stop for lunch on your way out. Wait for me in the kitchen and don't leave before I get there." The men whooped. "And if I find out you've told anyone about what we discovered in that wall, I'll fire you on the spot. Understood?"

The workers all nodded vigorously and filed out of the room.

"Everyone in Chatterley Heights will hear about these bones by sundown at the latest," Maddie said. "You know that, right?"

"Sure, I know that," Calliope said. "But I'm betting my threat will slow them down, maybe make them think twice. I'm paying them well, and they need the work."

Jason and Calliope leaned the plywood against the wall, revealing a cavity more than a foot deep. The area seemed generous for a wall, but Olivia knew that walls had often been thicker in the past. No one spoke for a time. There wasn't much to say because there wasn't much to see beyond some bones. Olivia was too embarrassed to admit, at least in public, that she'd envisioned a skeleton more like the plastic one her family had hung on their front door every Halloween.

"Huh," Maddie whispered. "Is that all there is?"

"Jeez, sorry to disappoint you guys," Jason said.

Olivia felt something brush against her ankle. She glanced down to see Spunky sneak toward the cavity. His fluffy tail swished with eager curiosity as he sniffed the air. "Spunky, no!" Olivia grabbed him and lifted his tiny body to her chest. "Those bones are not for you," she whispered in his ear. He squirmed in her arms, clearly not convinced.

Olivia ran her finger over several small holes along the outer edges of the wall. "Are these nail holes? So that plywood was actually nailed to the wall?"

"It was," Calliope said. "Sloppy job. I'd have re-plastered the whole wall. No one would have been the wiser, at least until the site was cleared for development. Even then, the bones might have been crushed by a bulldozer before anyone saw them."

Olivia peered into the wall cavity, taking care not to step inside. "This area seems large for an inner wall," she said. "Shouldn't there be insulation or something?"

Jason snorted. "Inside walls don't need insulation. However, despite the dumbness of your question, I agree that the space is larger than I'd have expected. My guess is this might originally have been a shallow storage closet. It goes along half the wall. There would have been another closet in the room sharing this wall to fill in the other half. For some reason, the closets in both rooms got plastered over to make them into walls. Don't ask me why. Maybe the closets were disintegrating. Anyway, the building was abandoned years ago. Somehow the wall got damaged, and someone covered the whole thing with plywood. That's all I can figure."

"Let me have another look." Calliope peered around the cavity. "You might be right, Jason. I'd say this wall has been through several renovations, mostly on the cheap. It started out good and solid. Then maybe somebody decided it used up too much valuable space and tried to make a closet out of it. Not a very good closet, but by then the inhabitants were probably too poor to need much storage space." Calliope shook her head. "Too bad. This was a decent building once. I hate to see good construction go bad."

"Forgive me for interrupting such a fascinating and poignant discussion of wall design," Maddie said, "but I thought someone said the police were on their way. Did you give them the right address? Won't they be here soon, and shouldn't we put the plywood back?"

"Mom called 911," Jason said. "The dispatcher said it might be some time before someone could get here. I guess there's been a huge accident between here and Twiterton. That's what's occupying all the available police from several towns. The dispatcher decided that finding some old bones wasn't a big emergency, so it could wait."

"I know Del has been in DC at a conference," Olivia said. "Did anyone get hold of him?" Sheriff Del Jenkins was, as her mother put it, Olivia's "special friend." Ellie was a sixties flower child who had once lived in a commune, but when it came to her daughter, she'd turned traditional.

"I called Del on his cell," Calliope said. "He said he'll drive back to town this evening, after he does some talk or other. He warned us not to touch anything, and we haven't, except for removing the plywood covering. Del wants to look at the scene first before he calls in the experts. I mean, this guy's been dead for years. Anyway, chances are he sneaked in here and died of natural causes."

"But then why was he hidden in the wall?" Maddie asked.

Calliope shrugged. "This was a hangout for vagrants. My guess is they didn't want any trouble, so they stuffed the body into a rotting wall, found an old piece of plywood, and nailed him inside."

Maddie grimaced. "Wouldn't it, um, smell?"

"The place probably didn't smell great to begin with," Calliope said. "A passed-out drunk might not care, especially if he had nowhere else to sleep."

"Where is Cody?" Olivia asked. Chatterley Heights' deputy sheriff, Cody Furlow, was an eager investigator, though he could be indecisive at times. Olivia also knew that Del wanted to give Cody a chance to gain confidence and experience.

"Cody's dad had a heart attack during the night," Jason said. "I heard about it from Ida this morning at Pete's Diner. Ida said Cody took off early this morning. She knew that because he'd left a message ordering a take-out breakfast, which he picked up just after the diner opened at five-thirty a.m. He had it half eaten before he got out the diner door. Ida was impressed."

"Ida doesn't impress easily," Olivia said. "Poor Cody. He probably just wanted to get to his dad as fast as possible. So Chatterley Heights is currently without any police protection?"

"Jeez," Jason said, "don't be such a wimp. This town doesn't need 24–7 police protection. Besides, you've got me and Cal."

"So good to know," Olivia murmured. "Why is Alicia so convinced those are her father's remains?" Olivia directed her question to Calliope.

"I'll show you." Calliope squatted down and pointed toward some thin, curved bones that Olivia guessed were ribs. She and Maddie leaned in as close as they could without disturbing the scene.

"Is that a necklace?" Maddie asked. "I think I see a thin piece of chain."

Calliope nodded. "When I mentioned seeing a chain, Al burst into sobs. She refused to come over and take a look, but she said she'd given her father a necklace with a silver chain. That's all it took to convince her these bones were his. Maybe Ellie can get more out of her."

"Mom has a talent for wheedling information." Olivia arched her neck to get a better look at the chain. "I don't suppose someone brought a flashlight?"

"I never leave home without one. Hang on a sec." Calliope returned with a hefty cordless spotlight.

Olivia held her breath as Calliope aimed the spotlight at the narrow floor inside the wall. For an instant, the pile of bones seemed to brighten and stir, as if light were all they'd needed to restore them to life. The thin length of chain, on the other hand, looked dirty and dull. Olivia leaned forward to follow its path over a rib and behind a thicker bone she couldn't name. "I think something might be attached to that chain," she said. "Calliope, can you shift the light a bit to the right so I can see behind that bone? Good, that helps."

"I'm about to explode," Maddie said. "What do you see?"

Olivia craned her neck. "I'm not positive, but I think it's . . . Maddie, you won't believe this. I think it's a tiny cookie cutter."

"Be serious," Maddie said.

"Really, it looks like a tiny cookie cutter with a back."

"Let me see." Maddie nudged Olivia aside.

"I'm five-seven, and I can barely see it," Olivia said. "You're shorter than I am."

"Only by an inch, and besides, I'm more flexible."

"I'm five-eight," Calliope said. "That makes me taller than both of you. Step aside." She left the spotlight on the floor pointing toward the remains.

In the interests of fact finding, Olivia and Maddie yielded to Calliope's superior height. Besides, Olivia reasoned, Calliope knew a cookie cutter when she saw one. Olivia retrieved the spotlight and aimed it directly at the area where she had spotted the tiny object nestled among the sad bones.

Calliope dropped to her hands and knees, her neck muscles straining as her eyes followed the path of the thin chain until it dropped out of sight. "Lift the light higher," Calliope ordered. With a curt nod, she said, "Livie was right."

"A cookie cutter on a chain?" Maddie asked. "That sounds really uncomfortable, especially for a guy. Are we sure these bones belonged to a man? Shouldn't we ask Alicia's mother about what happened to her husband before we leap to conclusions? Not that I don't enjoy speculating, of course."

Calliope sat back on her knees and brushed dust off her hands. "Her mom doesn't care what happened to him, as long as he is gone forever. Anyway, that's what Alicia says. She and her mom don't get along. Alicia is living at home until she can save enough money to afford an apartment of her own. Meanwhile, she tries not to be home when her mom is there. They rarely speak to each other."

"Wow," Maddie said. "You've lived in Chatterley Heights for less than a year, and already you know more about the place than I do."

"Ellie told me," Calliope said. "Once I decided she was worth listening to, I started picking up all sorts of interesting stuff. I don't listen much when she tells long stories, though. I get bored."

"I hear you," Olivia said. "Although there's usually a point to those stories, if you can hang on till the end."

"I'll bear that in mind." Calliope rolled off her knees and stood up, demonstrating an agility that made Olivia feel old, even though she was at least a decade younger. "About that necklace," Calliope said. "It looks like a sappy Valentine's Day cookie cutter shaped like a heart with an arrow through it. I don't think it's a real cutter, though. It's even smaller than a fondant cutter, and it isn't deep enough to cut through rolled dough. I'd say it was meant to represent a cookie cutter but thin enough to function as a charm. I'll bet Jason's farm—for which I hold the mortgage, at least until he pays me back—that the pierced heart shape had a personal meaning for whoever once owned those bones."

"I agree," Olivia said. "Why else would a man, assuming these bones do belong to a man, wear a cookie cutter image of a pierced heart around his neck?"

Calliope leaned against the wall. "Alicia told me something right before she started all that crying. She said her father was 'wearing her heart,' like he'd promised her. Mind you, she hadn't seen the charm. None of us had at that point, but it sure looks like this necklace could be the one her father wore. Of course, for all we know it was her dad who killed the person these bones belonged to, and then he threw the necklace in there to convince everyone he was dead. He might have assumed it was worthless costume jewelry."

"Maybe it is," Maddie said.

Calliope shook her head. "The charm is tarnished, just like the chain, but it has held up well. From what I can see, it looks well crafted. I'm betting the whole thing is made of silver. It isn't gold, but still, he could have gotten something for it, enough to buy a meal, anyway. For a vagrant, that's a lot."

"If those bones really are Alicia's father, whoever nailed his body inside that wall didn't take the necklace," Olivia said. "Why not, I wonder."

"The real question," Maddie said, "is do we wait for Del to get here, like good little girls, or do we start asking questions on our own?"

Olivia grinned. "Do you even have to ask?"

Chapter Two

❧

Before joining Calliope and her crew for lunch, Olivia and Maddie felt they should try to secure room number eight, where the skeletal remains lay as they'd been found, untouched. The lonely bones could rest for another day or so, at least until the police removed them for analysis.

While Olivia held Spunky, Maddie rifled through a satchel slung over her shoulder. "There's no way to lock the door to this room," she said, "so I asked Calliope for a roll of duct tape and scissors. I'll stretch some tape across the door as a warning to stay out. That's the best we can do for now. Hey, when we see Del, we should ask him to requisition some crime scene tape for us. You know, for next time."

"There will be no next time," Olivia said.

"You said that last time." Maddie cut long strips of duct tape and crisscrossed the closed door in three places. "That ought to do it." She stood back to admire her work. "No, wait a minute." Maddie drew a rag from the pocket of her jeans and used it to wipe off the doorknob. "If anyone besides Del breaks through the tape and goes into the room, we'll have their fingerprints."

Olivia arched one eyebrow at her best friend since age ten. "You're enjoying yourself, aren't you?"

"You bet," Maddie said. "Solving a crime is almost as much fun as baking and decorating cookies. This time I don't feel so sad. Those are old bones, so it's not like finding the body of someone who was alive just a little while ago. But, Livie, maybe we've jumped the gun a bit . . . if I may mention a gun or any other weapon, which, by the way, we didn't find with those bones."

"It could have been removed." Olivia paused on the staircase to look up at her friend. "If that was your unique, round-about way of saying this might not have been an actual murder, then I agree we can't be sure. Only it does seem odd that someone would stuff a body inside a wall and nail up a sheet of plywood to cover the hole. The building had already been abandoned. If the death was natural, the body could probably have remained out in the open. To me, it looks like someone wanted to hide the body but didn't have much time."

"I suppose you're right," Maddie said. "Still, even if this was murder most foul, it didn't happen recently, or we would have found a body instead of bones, right? So this feels more like we've stumbled upon an archeological site. It doesn't upset me."

Olivia wasn't sure she agreed. She had felt a rush of sadness when she'd first seen those bones, even though she hadn't known Alicia's father . . . assuming they belonged to him. Discovering a recent murder victim, especially if she'd known the person, would have disturbed her more deeply. Yet Olivia couldn't forget that those bones had once been a living person. At the same time, she had to admit she'd always experienced a surge of satisfaction whenever she and Maddie helped bring a murderer to justice. Okay, maybe a tiny thrill, too . . .

Maddie bounced down the staircase and headed toward the kitchen. Olivia followed at a more conservative pace. On their way up, she had noticed how creaky the stairs were. She had visions of putting her foot through a step, and she didn't trust the wobbly banister to save her. The old boarding house would need a lot of work before it could reopen as the craft school that kept expanding in her mother's fertile imagination.

Constance Overton, owner of the Chatterley Heights Management and Rental Company, had bought the old place for a song, or more like half a stanza. However, Constance wouldn't have taken it for free if she'd thought it couldn't be put to a profitable use. Luckily, she had offered Calliope and Ellie a rent-free year, so they could focus their efforts and resources on yanking the building up to code—if it didn't fall down first.

When Olivia opened the kitchen door, she felt as if she'd barged in on a party. She held on tightly to Spunky. He was used to shoppers roaming around the store, but Olivia kept him in her apartment whenever she and Maddie hosted an event. She was afraid someone might trip over the little five-pound pup.

The noisy room felt crammed, though it was at least twice the size of the Gingerbread House kitchen. Calliope, Jason, and the other workers slurped coffee, devoured sandwiches, and snatched cookies so quickly that Ellie was searching the refrigerator for more food. At the kitchen counter, Alicia slapped cheese and lunchmeat between slices of buttered bread. Sandwiches piled higher and higher, rapidly filling a large platter. On the table, a second platter was emptying fast. When a worker grabbed the last sandwich, Alicia swapped the plate for a loaded one, then began making more sandwiches.

Maddie, who'd beat Olivia to the kitchen, had nearly finished filling the reservoir of a new twenty-cup coffeemaker. She measured ground coffee into the basket and flipped the on switch. "Want a sandwich?" Maddie asked as she joined Olivia.

"Are there enough to go around?" Olivia watched the workers swoop up the newly delivered sandwiches as if they'd worked sixteen hours straight without stopping for food.

"There's plenty, if we act quickly." Maddie snatched two sandwiches from the tray and handed one to Olivia. "Those guys will eat anything they see, but they aren't really starving. Ellie said they went through two trays before I got to the kitchen. She was delivering a third tray to the table as I walked in. Alicia took over for her, and . . . well, as you can see, those appetites know no bounds." Maddie nodded toward the new tray, which now held only one sandwich. In an instant, a beefy hand grabbed that last sandwich.

"Yikes," Olivia said. "Lucky thing Calliope is footing the bill for food."

"No kidding. Your mom said she plans to do some major grocery shopping and restock the fridge this afternoon, so the workers won't starve tomorrow—assuming the police allow them to go back to work, that is."

"They might be able to work in other areas of the building," Olivia said. "After all these years, there can't be much evidence left to find, except maybe inside that wall. But we'll see what Del says."

When Calliope spied the empty plate on the table, she called a halt to the feeding. "All right, you guys, gorge on your own time. I'll call all of you tomorrow if, and only if, the police won't let us into the house. Otherwise, assume we'll be working. Be here at eight a.m. and not a minute later." The worker who had scored the last sandwich stuffed half of it into his mouth as he scraped his chair back from the table.

"Wow, you're a tough boss," Maddie said as the kitchen door slammed behind the last of the workers.

Calliope shrugged. "I know what hard work looks like, and most of those guys aren't even trying. They think a woman boss is a pushover. They'll think differently when I'm through with them."

"You go, girl," Ellie said.

When her mother bumped fists with Calliope, Olivia had to sit down. "I feel a bit light-headed," she said softly to Maddie. "The atmosphere is thin in this alternate universe."

As soon as Calliope arrived in Chatterley Heights after a nomadic life in Europe, she'd moved into the Greyson-Meyers house, Olivia's childhood home. Olivia's stepfather, Allan Meyers, was Calliope's cousin on his mother's side. The living arrangement had not gone well, especially for Ellie. For a time, Olivia had worried that her normally self-contained mother would lose her carefully centered mind. However, fate and building projects intervened. Calliope had vacated the Greyson-Meyers home to move in with Olivia's brother, Jason. Calliope was helping him renovate his new farmhouse and barns, in addition to overseeing the transformation of the crumbling old flophouse.

Once they were no longer under the same roof, Ellie— petite, intuitive, and yoga obsessed—had bonded with the tall, forceful, and blunt Calliope over a dream for a new arts and crafts school in Chatterley Heights. Calliope, who was wealthy and loved to work with her hands, provided and subsidized the materials and workers. Ellie had taken charge of overall planning for the school. She adored learning new crafts even more than she loved her yoga classes, although she had no intention of choosing between them. Calliope had drawn up plans for the building renovation that included a specially designed room for yoga enthusiasts. The two vastly different women had become friends. Olivia, however, continued to hold her breath, because when it came to families, you never knew.

"We might as well clean up the kitchen and get back to The Gingerbread House," Maddie said. "Calliope, I'll put these cookies in cake pans and store them in the fridge. They should keep you and the guys supplied for the week, as long as you dole them out daily and don't let anyone know where they are kept. We'll be working in The Gingerbread House through Saturday. Our own baking time will be devoted to keeping our customers happily in a mood to buy anything from cookie cutters to expensive mixers."

"We'll be fine," Ellie said. "Thanks to both of you for all your work setting up the kitchen. The room looks lovely.

Maddie, once we open the school, you will be available to teach cookie baking and decorating, won't you?"

"Hey," Olivia said, "what about me? I'm almost as good a cookie baker as Maddie is."

"Yes, of course you are, dear." Ellie gave her daughter a gentle smile and turned aside to consult with Calliope.

"I think I've been insulted," Olivia said.

Maddie grabbed her cell phone from the counter and pushed Olivia through the kitchen doorway. Once they were out of earshot, Maddie said, "I think Calliope might be rubbing off on your mother. Either that, or Ellie isn't getting her optimal dose of yoga. However, I suggest we wait and see. Right now the two of them are obsessed with this building project. Once that's completed, your mom will surely revert to her sensitive, intuitive self." Maddie's cell phone rang, and she glanced at the caller ID. "I'll bet this is for you, Livie. I'm getting used to fielding calls for you, though I do wish you would try to remember your cell when you leave your apartment."

"Who is it from?"

"Del." Maddie handed her phone to Olivia and closed the front door of the old building.

"Hey, Del, it's me," Olivia said as she negotiated the cracked stone steps. "Or did you really mean to call Maddie?"

Del chuckled. "Nope. I've adjusted to your forgetfulness. When your cell goes to voice mail, I call Maddie. So I understand we need to touch base about some skeletal remains. I already talked to the crime scene crew about how to handle the evidence. I'm now heading toward Chatterley Heights. I should be back—"

Olivia paused on the sidewalk. "You're driving, aren't you? You know how I feel about that. It scares me."

"Sorry, Livie, but honestly, traffic is practically at a halt, and as I keep telling you—" The blast of a horn came through loud and clear.

"Call back when you are safely parked," Olivia said. "Assuming you're still alive." Without hanging up, she handed Maddie's phone back to her.

"Hi, Del," Maddie said as they turned the corner and headed north on Park Street. "You can talk to me. I deeply believe in the superior multitasking abilities of our intrepid police." She listened for a while. "Okay, we can do that. Are the guys allowed to work on the renovation tomorrow? Yeah, that's what I thought. Calliope installed new locks and deadbolts on all the outside doors. You'll have to get keys from her or Ellie. I put duct tape across the door of the room in question, so it should be all right, assuming the murderer isn't still alive, in town, and willing to break and enter. Was that extended horn blast aimed at you? I take back my compliment about your multitasking abilities. Bye." Maddie hung up and shook her head. "Men."

"Amen to that," Olivia said. "What were you supposed to tell me?"

"Del assured me I did the right thing to tape the door, although I'm pretty sure he was trying not to laugh." Maddie slid her cell phone into her jacket pocket. "When he gets back to town, he'll take pictures of the scene. Then he'll secure the door somehow and put real crime scene tape across it. He said the guys can probably get back to work soon, but he'll let Calliope know when. They will probably have to work downstairs for a while. Del will close off the upstairs until the crime scene folks remove the remains and anything else they will need. The lab is overwhelmed at the moment, so this is a lower priority case."

"Does that mean Del will be in charge of the investigation?" Olivia asked.

Maddie clapped her hands. "Ooh, I hadn't thought of that. If Del is the lead investigator, that means we, through you, will have a front-row seat. I've always wanted to solve a cold case. They always sound so . . . historical."

"Yes," Olivia said, "that would be due to the 'cold' part. But just because Del and I are involved doesn't mean he'll share his investigation with me. A case is a case, cold or not."

Maddie paused as they reached the sidewalk in front of The Gingerbread House. "Remember, Livie, Del did lighten up a bit last summer, after we helped Cody solve a murder while Del was out of town." Maddie drew her car key from her jacket pocket. "I'm parked a block north on Park Street, so I shall bid you adios. Was that Spanish or French? Never mind, the important thing here is that Del will need our help with the case of the bones in the wall. He didn't move to Chatterley Heights until around 2006, right? So he doesn't have a long personal memory of this town and its inhabitants. He'll need our superior insight into the town's many secrets. Anything we don't know, we can wheedle out of your mother or my aunt Sadie. You and I are essential to this investigation. You can start working on Del this evening during dinner." Maddie turned to leave.

"Wait," Olivia said. "What dinner?"

"Oh yeah, I forgot. Del said to tell you that he's treating you to dinner at Pete's this evening. He'll meet you there, but he's not sure what time. He'll call you when he finishes the crime scene stuff."

"I hate to dash your hopes," Olivia said, "but what if Del tells me there's no evidence of foul play at the scene?"

Maddie's windblown locks seemed to bounce with energy as she flashed a bright smile. "Not to worry. Del won't draw his conclusions that quickly. He'll want to do more investigating, which will give us time to do the same. Once we dig into the victim's past, we will find what we need. I can feel it. Foul play will rear its ugly, yet fascinating head."

Chapter Three

A chilly breeze ruffled Olivia's auburn hair as she crossed her own front lawn. She pulled her jacket tight around her T-shirt and held Spunky against her chest. Front door key in hand, Olivia hurried up the front steps of her little Queen Anne house to the wraparound porch. She made a mental note to start dragging out her warmer clothes. The wind was powerful enough to rock the empty chair near the large front window. A shiver snaked down Olivia's back as she recalled seeing a dead man in that very spot. However, this was a different rocking chair. Its predecessor had gone to the crime lab, and Olivia had neglected to reclaim it. Instead, she had visited her favorite antiques mall and found a replacement, a southern country porch rocker. It was a simpler design than the abandoned rocker and, therefore, less likely to hide a body from view.

Olivia hesitated in the foyer, near the door to The Ginger-bread House. The store occupied the entire ground level of her beloved Queen Anne style house. She and Maddie were business partners, but it was Olivia who carried a hefty mortgage for the whole building. The store was always closed Sunday and Monday. Olivia had been so busy helping to set up the kitchen at the old boarding house that she hadn't been inside her own store for two days. She was tempted to check to make sure it was ready for opening the next morning.

Bertha Binkman, their head clerk, had offered to restock the shelves for the beginning of the work week. Bertha was a woman of her word, as well as pathologically drawn to deep cleaning. Surely the store was ready to wow the most critical of customers. Besides, Spunky was due for a good, brisk walk. Except for quick outdoor bathroom breaks, he'd been restricted to the boarding house kitchen for most of the day. His exercise had ranged from begging for cookie crumbs to flopping around on his blanket. He'd be desperate for a run, no matter how short.

Olivia passed by the locked Gingerbread House door and unlocked the door to the stairway that led to her second floor apartment. As soon as she took the first step, Spunky leaped from her arms and hit the stairs running. Olivia heard an explosion of yaps as he reached the landing upstairs. Spunky had a ferocious set of lungs for a five pound Yorkshire terrier.

"Knock it off, Spunks," Olivia yelled up the stairs. "I am a mere human. My legs won't work any faster." Spunky's yaps took on a plaintive edge, as if he hadn't eaten in weeks, although Olivia had brought his food along to the boarding house. The little guy was feisty and brave, but highly manipulative. Olivia loved him dearly. But sometimes she needed to remind him who bought the kibbles and Milk Bones. Not that it made any difference.

Spunky repeated his commands and complaints while Olivia climbed the stairs to the second floor landing. As she inserted her key into the lock, Spunky scratched at the door as if he were helping it open. Olivia felt touched that he wanted to get into the apartment so badly. When she'd first brought him home as a puppy, Spunky had tried relentlessly to escape from the very same apartment. His instinctive desire to flee from confinement had helped him escape the puppy mill where he'd been born, and his fierce intelligence had kept him safe on the streets of Baltimore until a Yorkshire terrier rescue group finally caught up with him. Olivia was relieved that Spunky had apparently decided he was safe with her. It probably helped that she was a pushover when it came to doggie treats.

Spunky managed to squeeze between Olivia's ankles when she opened the door. He hopped inside, paused, then turned around and waited, as if he wanted to make sure Olivia wasn't going to lock him inside and leave. When she entered the apartment and locked the door behind them, he relaxed and headed toward the kitchen.

"Good boy, Spunks," Olivia said. "And you're right, it is your suppertime." Spunky followed his mistress into the kitchen and paced impatiently, nails clacking on the tile, while she filled his small bowl with kibbles. "I owe you a long walk after keeping you cooped up all day," Olivia said. "When we get home from our walk, we can relax on the sofa until bedtime. How does that sound?" Spunky had sunk his head into his bowl, but his fluffy tail wagged his approval.

Olivia decided to start a small pot of coffee for herself. As she opened the cabinet where she kept her favorite Italian roast, she saw her cell phone plugged in behind Mr. Coffee. She unplugged the phone and flipped it open to check for messages. There were three from Del and a recent one from a number with no name attached. "Oh jeez, I forgot about dinner with Del," she said out loud. Spunky whined from the depths of his food bowl. "Sorry, kiddo, relaxing on the sofa will have to wait until later." Olivia punched in her code and listened to all three of Del's messages. "He wants me to meet him at Pete's Diner in . . ." She glanced up at the kitchen clock. "In an hour. That gives us time for a run through the park, Spunks. Then I'll need a quick shower and a change of clothes."

Olivia dropped the phone on the counter and turned away. She took one step and stopped. "No, Livie," she muttered, "do not walk away from that cell phone. You know you'll forget it again." As she picked it up, she remembered there'd been another message, which she had skipped because the number was unfamiliar. Probably a wrong number, but she called her voice mail and listened.

"Um, Livie?" asked the timorous female voice on the recorded message. "It's Alicia . . . Alicia Vayle. We met earlier at the renovation site, remember? I'm sorry to bother you, but . . . Well, Calliope gave me your cell phone number. I hope that's all right." Olivia heard a long, shaky breath, as if Alicia might be trying to suppress tears. "Someone told me that you and Maddie have solved some crimes in town. Well, actually, it was Calliope who told me. So I was wondering . . . The sheriff called and talked to me a little while ago about finding my father's . . . The thing is, I don't think the sheriff believes me. That it's really my dad, I mean. And even if I convinced him, I got the feeling he didn't think they'd ever be able to find out what happened to him. What if his death was—" Alicia halted abruptly as if she'd run out of air. "I have to know the truth. Would you help me find it? Please? You see, I know everyone was wrong about my father. He was a good—" The message ended. Cell phones, Olivia knew, could be unpredictable, so she wasn't too concerned.

Spunky had emptied his bowl of every kibble crumb, so he trotted to the kitchen door, where a leash hung from the knob. He stared intensely at Olivia to remind her that she'd promised him a run in the park. When she didn't respond, Spunky went over to her. He stood on his hind legs and pawed at her jeans, whining. Lost in thought, Olivia reached down and rubbed his ears. Spunky enjoyed the attention, but that wasn't all he'd had in mind. Finally, he resorted to a volley of insistent yaps.

"Oh, Spunky, I'm sorry, I wasn't paying attention," Olivia said. "We'd better do that run in the park pronto, or I won't have time for a shower." She gave up on making coffee and grabbed Spunky's leash.

A few minutes later, they were outside, heading for the park that marked the historical center of Chatterley Heights, known as the Town Square. Unlike many small towns, Chatterley Heights hadn't been nipped too badly by the Great Recession. Tree-lined streets and vibrant small businesses, ranging from quaint to practical, formed a square around a large park. Only two shops stood empty, hoping for new owners. Olivia and Spunky waited for traffic to clear before they jogged across the street and into the park.

Spunky strained at his leash in his eagerness to run, and Olivia was more than willing to keep up. After a day of baking, she relished the exercise as much as Spunky did. "Better enjoy this while you can," Olivia said. "Winter is coming. You know how I feel about jogging in cold winds." Spunky picked up his pace. He didn't slow down until they'd nearly reached his favorite spot in the park—the statue of Frederick P. Chatterley, the amusingly disreputable founder of Chatterley Heights. Spunky halted near a rear leg of the horse that Frederick P. never quite managed to mount.

"Fine, Spunks," Olivia said. "Take your time. I need to catch my breath." Spunky sniffed his way around the horse's four legs, searching for the most inviting scent. Olivia followed him, keeping a tight grip on the leash. "Don't take too much time, though," she said. Spunky obligingly lifted his leg and aimed at the horse's left front leg.

"I think that's really disrespectful," said a petulant female voice behind Olivia's back. She spun around too quickly and lost her hold on Spunky's leash. The little Yorkie had been too engrossed in his task to hear the woman's approach, but he made up for his negligence by yapping ferociously as he lunged toward her. The woman froze and shrieked, "Help, someone help! It's a mad dog. He's trying to kill me!"

"Spunky, stop." Olivia used a low, commanding voice that was supposed to convey authority, or so she'd read in the puppy training books. It had never worked before. This time it did, though Olivia suspected the woman's hysterical reaction had alarmed the little guy. He stopped yapping and stayed where he was, several feet away from the woman. "Spunky, come," Olivia said, hoping not to break the spell. Spunky stood his ground and began to growl softly. Taking slow steps, Olivia inched toward the leash handle until she could reach down and recapture it. "Okay, kiddo, that's quite enough bravado." She scooped him up in her free arm. He squirmed and whined, but Olivia held him tightly around his middle. Finally, he gave up and cuddled against Olivia's chest. "Good choice," she whispered.

"Binnie Sloan was right about that dog of yours," the woman said. "He's a menace, just like Binnie says in her blog. I read it every day, so I know what's really going on in this town."

Olivia didn't bother to defend her hometown or her tiny, adorable dog from the outrageous rumors Binnie Sloan perpetrated in her newspaper, *The Weekly Chatter*, and in her disreputable blog. Most Chatterley Heights citizens subscribed to the paper because it was the best way to find out who had died, the cause of death, and the funeral details. Otherwise, most of them treated the paper, as well as the blog, as dubious entertainment, not to be taken seriously. Binnie's only employee was her niece, Nedra. Ned, as she preferred to be called, was a fine photographer. Unfortunately, she wasted her talent and skill snapping embarrassing photos of anyone her aunt happened to be targeting at the moment.

"I'm sorry," Olivia said to the woman, "but you seem to know me, and I don't know your name."

"Well, of course I know you. Your picture is in *The Weekly Chatter* all the time. You run that little Gingerbread House store with all that cookie stuff. I used to have cookie cutters, but I got rid of them. Silly little things. Anyway, that's where I was going before that vicious dog of yours attacked me—to your store."

"I see," Olivia said, although she still felt confused. She

guessed the woman to be in her late thirties to early forties. She was small boned and slender enough to look good in tight black jeans. No gray showed in her honey brown hair, though the lines across her forehead and around her mouth hinted at a painful past. "And your name is . . . ?" Olivia asked.

"Oh." The woman looked flustered. "Well, my name is Crystal. Crystal Quinn." When Olivia failed to register recognition, Crystal added, "I'm Alicia's mother. I heard about what happened this afternoon at that place where Alicia is working part-time. I know she called you because I caught her doing it. I gave that girl a firm talking-to, believe me. Telling private things to a complete stranger . . . That girl has no sense. We had a big fight, of course. I decided to go right to your store and tell you to mind your own business." Crystal straightened her spine and planted her fists on slender hips. "You don't know Alicia like I do. She's stubborn. She'll keep calling you, trying to get you on her side."

"What is her side?" Olivia asked. "What does she want from me?"

Crystal fiddled with the buttons on her cardigan sweater. "Oh, all right, I'll tell you. I'm quite sure that Alicia wants you to prove I killed Kenny. She hates me that much. That's the real reason I was coming to talk to you. I wanted to talk to you face to face to make sure you understand that Alicia doesn't think straight. Honestly, I don't know what to do with that girl."

Olivia glanced at her watch. She had only half an hour to run back home, shower, and get to Pete's Diner in time for dinner with Del. But Crystal had piqued her curiosity. She also felt a measure of sympathy for Alicia, who clearly had loved her father, and who now lived with a critical, even hostile mother. Olivia really, really wanted to hear what Crystal had to say about her daughter and about the sad pile of bones that might once have been her husband. And she seemed willing to talk.

"I need to make a quick phone call, and then we can talk

more," Olivia said. "It would really help me to know what's going on with your daughter." Crystal nodded.

Olivia patted her jeans pocket and was relieved to find that, for once, she had remembered to bring her cell phone. On the other hand, letting Crystal listen in while she called to delay a dinner date with the Chatterley Heights sheriff sounded like a bad idea. "The Gingerbread House is closed on Mondays," Olivia said. "But we could talk in the band shell, assuming it's unoccupied. We'll have more privacy in there, as well as protection from the wind." There wasn't much wind at the moment, but Olivia did not want to open up the store or, worse, invite an unpredictable stranger into her apartment for coffee, cookies, and a harangue. Besides, she still hoped to get to Pete's Diner on time.

"Why don't you go into the band shell and warm up," Olivia said. "I'll meet you there in a minute."

"I guess that would be okay." Crystal frowned at Spunky, whose melting brown eyes watched her from the safety of his mistress's iron grip. "I've got things to do. I can't take all night."

Olivia smiled and nodded to convey warm understanding, which she didn't feel. When she pulled her cell phone from her pocket, Crystal took the hint and headed toward the band shell. Olivia waited until she'd begun to climb the band shell steps before speed dialing Del's cell phone number. The call went immediately to voice mail. "Hi, Del, it's me. Dare I hope you are driving and wisely decided not to answer your phone? I'll be a bit late for dinner, but don't give up on me." She lowered her voice. "I might have some interesting information for you. And, no, Maddie and I are not breaking into a house or in any way risking life or limb." In case Del hadn't yet heard about the victim's family, Olivia told him about Alicia Vayle and her mother, Crystal Quinn. "Crystal wants to talk to me, in a less than loving way, about her daughter. Might be nothing; might be something. I will tell all at dinner."

Crystal's face appeared briefly at the band shell entrance. "Oops, subject is getting impatient. Gotta go, Del." Olivia slid the phone back into her jeans pocket, tightened her grip on her pup, and hurried to join Crystal. "I expect you to be on your best behavior, Spunks. There's an extra treat in it for you," she whispered as she approached the band shell steps. Spunky maintained silence but made no promises.

Once inside the band shell, Olivia paused to let her eyes adjust to the dimness. A bench encircled the inside of the seashell-shaped structure. Olivia spotted Crystal sitting at the back, in the darkest area of the band shell. *At least no one will overhear us.* Crystal stared at her feet, her arms wrapped tightly around her chest, as Olivia approached and sat on the bench next to her.

"Listen, I'm sorry if I came on too strong," Crystal said. "Alicia is high strung, like her father . . . like her father was, that is. Everything is so serious to her. She gets overly emotional. I keep telling her to take things in stride, but she just rolls her eyes at me."

"If I'd found bones that I believed to be my long-lost father's, I'd be upset, too." Olivia stroked the silky hair on Spunky's head as she thought about her own father's death from pancreatic cancer. It had happened so quickly, but the shock had lasted a long, long time. Alicia's father, as far as Olivia could tell, had been absent, reputedly drunk, for much of his daughter's life, yet Alicia had continued to long for his return. It must be tough to let go when a parent simply disappears. Death is final; Olivia had no illusions that her father would ever again walk through the front door, although she'd often wished for it.

"I don't want Alicia to follow in her father's footsteps, that's all." When Crystal shivered and crossed her arms, her elbows showed through the worn knit fabric of her thin sweater. "That man was weak. I've had to fight for everything that's come to me, but not Kenny. All he ever did was sit and wait . . . and drink. Lord knows why Alicia worshiped him. He could be fun, I'll grant you that. And generous, especially with money I'd earned." Crystal shook her head impatiently, as if to rid herself of bitter memories. "Alicia is convinced it was my fault that Kenny left, but it wasn't. He just disappeared one day nearly five years ago. He never sent his own daughter so much as a postcard, but whose fault was that? Mine, of course. According to Alicia, I'm such a witch that Kenny couldn't take it for another minute. She thinks that's why he left." Crystal's thin shoulders slumped. "Alicia doesn't know the half of it. She doesn't want to know. She's a dreamer, like her father. She wants everything handed to her, without her having to work for it. Yeah, I know she's got a job, but it's just waitressing and a few hours of fetching and carrying at a construction site. Those are barely jobs, but she figures she can quit fast when her dreams magically come true."

Olivia remembered Alicia's concern that she couldn't make enough money waitressing, and she wondered if Crystal had the slightest clue how her daughter really felt. "What are Alicia's dreams?" Olivia asked.

"Oh, who knows. They change from week to week." Crystal sank back against the hard wall of the band shell. "A few years ago, she wanted to be a dancer. She'd put on a skimpy outfit and jump around the house pretending to practice." Crystal wiggled her shoulders in derisive imitation of a dancer trying to look suggestive. "Alicia was convinced that someday a producer would come to town. He'd go for a walk, see her through the window while she was dancing, and beg her to compete on one of those ridiculous dance shows." Crystal snickered. "If any producer ever saw her dance, he'd have a good laugh. She was always crashing into the furniture. She broke my favorite cake plate, the one my mother gave me for a wedding gift."

Olivia stroked Spunky's silky head to keep him calm as Crystal's voice grew harsher. It was more than clear that Crystal found her own daughter irritating. Was that only because Alicia reminded her so much of her despised former husband?

"Crystal, do you have any idea where your husband was going the day he left?"

"Well, I know where he *said* he was going. Had himself a job interview, he said. A really good job that would solve all our problems forever and ever. I just laughed at him. I figured he'd borrowed some money and was heading for the bar again. Even if he'd really had a job interview, he'd have gotten too drunk to show up for it. Alicia believed him, of course. When he didn't come home, Alicia accused me of driving him away by laughing at that ridiculous lie about a job. That man was never good at anything except baking."

"Baking?" Olivia hadn't seen that coming.

Crystal laughed at Olivia's astonishment. "Yeah, I thought you'd be interested in that. His mother taught him to bake just about everything, but he was best at making those fancy cookies like you make at your store."

"Decorated cutout cookies?" Olivia asked.

"Whatever."

"Did Kenny ever work as a baker?"

Crystal's laugh had a hard edge. "Work? Kenny was not familiar with that word. He baked at home sometimes, especially when Alicia was little. He taught her all his baking secrets. Alicia was fourteen when Kenny left for good. By then she was almost as good a baker as Kenny was. She just started working as a part-time waitress at Pete's Diner, even though she could make loads more money as a baker, maybe in one of those fancy bakeries in DC. Lazy, like her father."

"But she does have a job," Olivia pointed out. "Two jobs, in fact, even if they are both part-time."

Crystal shrugged one shoulder, a dismissive gesture. After several seconds of silence, she said, "If anything, Alicia is a better baker than Kenny ever was." Crystal's derisive tone had softened. "She kept at it, too, even when Kenny started getting bored with baking because it wasn't making him rich. I thought maybe Alicia had found a place for herself, a job she could be good at. But she drifted away from it after Kenny disappeared. Oh, she kept on baking for quite a while because she was hoping he'd come back. She would experiment with new recipes, so she could show him how much she'd learned. But after a while, the light went out of her." Crystal went silent and stared down at her hands. With an impatient shake of her head, she said, "Alicia was angry a lot. She was well into her teens by then, and you know how they are. One minute she'd be in a rage, then all of a sudden she'd tear up and sob that life wasn't worth living." Crystal slowly shook her head. "Well, I need to get back. My husband will be home from work soon, and he'll be wanting his dinner. I think I've said what I had to say. I only wanted to warn you that Alicia isn't very reliable, and she gets overemotional. Don't get sucked in by her. She doesn't always tell the truth."

Olivia thought about the cookie cutter necklace. Alicia had identified the bones as belonging to her father based purely on the presence of a tarnished cookie cutter necklace, found amid the bones. The girl hadn't even seen it, but she'd been certain it identified the deceased as her father. That necklace was part of a larger story. Olivia was almost sure of it. She found herself more and more curious about its history and meaning.

"Crystal, do you remember if Kenny ever wore any jewelry?" Olivia hesitated to give away too much information, but her curiosity was growing by the minute.

"Jewelry? Kenny? He wouldn't even wear a wedding ring."

Interesting, Olivia thought. Alicia must not have told her mother about the cookie cutter necklace she'd bought for her father.

Crystal's eyes narrowed with suspicion. "Why are you asking? Did Kenny have expensive jewelry with him when you found him? Because if he did, by rights it should come to me. I supported that man and raised his child practically by myself."

Olivia felt a chill roll down her back, and it wasn't from the cold. Spunky's low growl said he'd picked up on his mistress's discomfort.

Crystal stood up and pulled her sweater tightly around her slight body. "Kenny took everything that was important to me. He left me with nothing. If that man had anything on him when he died, it's mine, and I want it back."

Spunky squirmed to free himself from Olivia's grip, but she tightened her hold on him. "I'm not the one who found the . . . your former husband," she said. "Besides, for all we know, it might not be Kenny, after all." Strictly speaking, Olivia was telling the truth. "The police are in charge of the case. You'll have to check with them about what they found, if anything."

"Oh, I'll do that," Crystal said. "You bet I will." She turned to leave the band shell. At the entrance, Crystal hesitated for a moment, silhouetted against the light of an old-fashioned streetlamp. Her arms fell to her sides. A moment before Crystal strode down the band shell steps, Olivia saw her fingers curl into fists.

Chapter Four

By the time Olivia arrived back at her apartment, after her unsettling meeting with Crystal Quinn, she had eight minutes to shower, change, and walk back across the park to Pete's Diner to meet Del. If she tried to meet that deadline, she'd end up needing another shower.

Olivia called Del's cell and got his voice mail. "Hi, Del, it's me. I'll be late." She checked the time, and added, "I should get to Pete's by about seven. I'll have much to tell you. Long story, though interesting and highly relevant. To be continued." As soon as she hung up, Spunky pawed at her leg and whined. "I hadn't forgotten your post-run snack, Spunks," Olivia said. "Okay, I did forget. However, here we go." Spunky's ears perked with excitement as Olivia opened the treats drawer, took out two small Milk Bones, and snapped them into halves. She tossed the pieces across the kitchen floor, smiling at the sound of little Yorkie nails tapping on the tile.

As Spunky hunted every last crumb, Olivia escaped to the shower. She was in and out in six minutes, which she considered a personal best. Settling on an outfit took about two seconds—Olivia chose the only clean clothes in her closet. Luckily, the light wool slacks, the color of dark chocolate, fit her perfectly. A once-over in the mirror told her the burgundy sweater brought out the green in her blue-green eyes. However, she'd better get serious about doing some laundry.

For once, Spunky didn't make a fuss when Olivia headed toward the front door of her apartment, grabbing her keys from the small hallway table. After finishing his dinner, Spunky had snuggled on the living room sofa for a post-prandial snooze. Olivia wrapped herself in a heavy wool sweater and escaped quickly. Despite her best efforts, she was running behind schedule. If she could make it to Pete's Diner in eight minutes, she'd be acceptably late.

Olivia pulled her sweater tightly around her chest as she headed across the Gingerbread House porch. At the bottom of the steps, she hesitated. She'd planned to cut through the park, which would shave a few minutes off her travel time, but the park was dark except for a circle of light around the old streetlamp near the band shell. She told herself that Chatterley Heights was perfectly safe, but . . . Olivia opted for the lighted sidewalks. If Del got worried, he could call her. As she hurried along the sidewalk, passing stores closed for the night, Olivia reached in her pocket for her cell phone. She found only her keys. The other pocket was empty. Once again, she had left her cell phone at home, languishing on the kitchen counter. Her mother was forever touting the benefits of yoga to undo the effects of a busy schedule. Maybe she was right. Olivia suspected her system needed more calming and centering than her hectic life allowed. Naturally, she had no intention of admitting that to her mother.

Olivia was slightly out of breath when she entered Pete's Diner. She spotted Del at once and waved. When she reached the table, Del made a show of checking his watch.

"I'll have you know that I flew like the wind." Olivia sat across from Del and pointed to his nearly empty tumbler of merlot. "I'm surprised you can even *see* your watch."

"I can hold my merlot, I'll have you know," Del said.

Olivia cocked an eyebrow at him. "With the help of appetizers, perhaps in the form of cheesy muffins?" She pointed toward a bread basket containing only crumbs.

"Pete took pity on me. Besides, we had a bet about how late you'd be. Thanks to you, Livie, I won."

"I think I've been insulted." Olivia picked up a menu as their waitress, Ida, shuffled toward their table. "I no longer feel obligated to enlighten you about what I've been learning."

"Aren't small town traditions fun?" Del drained the last of his merlot.

Ida poured more merlot into Del's empty tumbler, drained the remainder of the bottle into Olivia's water glass, and sighed. "Let's pick up the pace here," she said. "It's the end of my shift, I'm tired, I don't want to trudge back to this table any more than I have to."

Del winked at Ida. "We love you, too." He picked up a ketchup-stained menu. Without consulting it, he said, "I'll have the meatloaf, my personal favorite, with extra sauce."

"Plus potatoes and green beans with bacon," Ida said.

"Absolutely. You know me so well, Ida." Del winked at her again as he slid his menu back into its holder.

"Not much of a challenge," Ida said, though her tone had softened. "And you . . ." She turned to Olivia. "Meatloaf, extra sauce on the side, green beans, no potatoes because you always think you're gaining weight, and more merlot. Plus some coffee for the both of you."

"Um, sure," Olivia said, though Ida had already turned away. She hadn't written down their orders, but she never made a mistake.

Del slid his chair closer to Olivia. "Okay, Livie, let's talk," he said quietly. "I went to the old boarding house and took lots of photos of the scene. I also nailed the plywood back in place. I'm hoping a barrier will discourage folks from messing with the skeletal remains, although it won't stop someone who is determined. Thanks for putting the duct tape across the door, by the way. Nice touch."

"That was Maddie's idea," Olivia said. "She's the creative genius, remember."

"And you are the diligent investigator, which I wish you wouldn't do, but never mind that right now." Del took a small sip of wine. "Tell me everything, including your observations about the people who were there when the remains were revealed."

"I wasn't actually in the room at the time," Olivia said. "You should ask my mother for her input. She was there, and she's good at observing people. From what I saw when Maddie and I got to the room, only one person reacted emotionally. That was Alicia Vayle, who was convinced the remains belonged to her father, Kenny Vayle. Alicia sobbed for quite some time." Olivia spotted Ida approaching their table, carrying a pot of coffee and a pitcher of cream. "To be continued," Olivia said.

As Ida sloshed coffee into their empty cups, Olivia asked her, "I suppose you've heard about what happened today while we were working on the renovations for Mom's new school?"

Ida's thin, gray eyebrows shot up, creating rows of wrinkles across her forehead. "Well, of course I've heard. Who hasn't? All I can say is, at least now we know what happened to that lazy bum, Kenny Vayle."

Olivia glanced at Del, who raised his eyebrows but didn't interrupt. "Doesn't Alicia Vayle work here?" Olivia asked. "Has she talked at all about her dad?"

Ida snatched a clean coffee cup from a neighboring table, dragged over an empty chair, and sank down. "Been on my feet all day. It's time I got a break." She poured herself a cup of coffee and gulped it down. "Alicia's a sweet kid," Ida said. "Not much of a waitress. She's slow, chats too much with the customers. Pete says we should go easy on her, though, on account of her dad." Ida poured herself more coffee and took a big gulp. "Bones in a wall . . . I've been alive more than seventy years, and I never heard of such a thing. Not here, anyway . . . maybe out there in California or New York, but not here in Maryland."

"Why did you say Kenny Vayle was no good?" Olivia asked.

When Ida shook her head, an iron gray curl escaped the confines of her hairnet. She poked it back underneath the net. "Kenny was a dreamer and a schemer. Nearly drove that little wife of his to the loony bin with his get-rich-quick notions. Crystal had no respect for the man. I remember her calling Kenny an idiot because he didn't know what was valuable and what wasn't. That was the day the two of them had a fight right here in the diner. Pete had to break it up. He kicked them out, told them not to come back, ever."

Del's brown eyes darkened. "Did Kenny become violent with his wife? Did you ever witness him hitting her or their daughter?"

"Kenny would never hit his daughter. Crystal, though . . ." Ida began to chuckle. "That day in the diner, those two did come to blows, but it was the other way around. Crystal hit Kenny. Socked him right in the kisser. After he saw that, Pete hated having to throw them both out of the diner. He has a soft spot for a woman who can throw a punch. I told him, 'Pete,' I said, 'that woman's no good.' I had to break it to him that Crystal was having an affair. Pete's got strong feelings against broken marriage vows. He's been married twenty-five years now."

Olivia's interest piqued. "Who did Crystal have an affair with, do you know?"

"Well, of course I know," Ida said. "She did finally marry the guy, or she said she did, but that don't make it right."

"Are you talking about Robbie Quinn?" Del asked.

"Robbie? Nope, he was later. Not much later, mind you, and Crystal was still officially married . . . to somebody. Not clear to me who it was by then." Ida closed her eyes tight while she thought. "I never met the second guy, and I don't remember his name. Just somebody who landed in town during the housing boom a while back. Crystal was still married to Kenny, but he'd left town, or so we all thought."

"I'm confused," Olivia said. "If Kenny had disappeared, how could Crystal marry two more men?"

Ida grinned, an unusual occurrence that revealed a missing tooth. "There was boyfriends, too, before Robbie came along. Most of 'em only lasted about a month before they disappeared. Don't remember any of their names."

"It sounds like Crystal doesn't like to be on her own," Olivia said under her breath.

Ida scraped back her chair and stood up. "Your dinner should be ready by now. Pete said it's on the house on account of the wait, never mind he's not the one who caused it," she said with a stern look at Olivia. "How Pete makes a living, I'll never figure out. Long as he pays me, I guess I won't worry about it." Before turning to leave, Ida said, "Livie, you tell Alicia that Pete doesn't like that boyfriend of hers hanging around the diner. The kid's first name is Kurt. Never heard his last name. I saw Alicia sneak some free food out to him in the alley. If Pete gets wind of what she's doing, he'll put that girl on notice. It's all right if Pete gives away his own food, but nobody else can." Ida shook her head all the way to the kitchen.

Olivia leaned toward Del. "I'm fairly certain Alicia didn't actually see the necklace found with the bones, but she insisted the remains had to be her father's because she had given him a silver necklace. Maddie and I did wonder if Kenny himself might have killed someone and thrown the necklace inside the wall to make it look as if he was the actual victim."

Del frowned in silence as Ida reappeared with their dinners. Once she had wandered off toward the kitchen, he said, "You're thinking about Crystal's second husband, the one who disappeared?"

"I am." Olivia spread Pete's delicious tomato sauce evenly over her two generous slices of meatloaf.

"It's something to investigate," Del said. "By the way, I did manage some decent photos of that necklace. I removed it from the scene before I boarded up the hole and sent it to the crime lab. I've never seen anything like it, though I'm no expert on necklaces. I don't expect enlightenment anytime soon. The crime lab is backed up, as usual, and this is a low-priority case."

"You might ask Aunt Sadie if she has any ideas," Olivia said. Maddie's aunt Sadie had taken her in when she was ten years old, after her parents were killed in an automobile accident. Aunt Sadie possessed remarkable expertise on the subject of cookie cutters, plus she knew the history of nearly all Chatterley Heights residents, past and present. Olivia ate a bite of her meatloaf and sighed. "Best meatloaf ever. I wish I could get Pete to tell me the secret to his sauce. I'm fairly certain Ida knows, but she refuses to rat on him. Mom thinks there are tiny bits of rosemary in the meat and maybe diced shallots instead of onion, but the sauce is a mystery to her."

Del touched his napkin to Olivia's chin. "A dab of secret sauce," he explained. "Unless you were planning to sneak it out for analysis? In which case, you'd probably need a bigger sample. But back to the necklace." Del ran a hand through his brown hair, perpetually creased by his uniform's hat. "If Alicia didn't actually see the necklace, I'll need to find out why she was so sure it was the same one she gave her father."

"I could ask Calliope if Alicia said anything more about the necklace after Maddie and I left."

"I'll be interviewing Calliope as soon as possible," Del said.

"You could ask Mom, too. By the time Calliope, Maddie, and I saw the cookie cutter charm attached to the chain, Alicia was down in the kitchen with my mom and the workers." Smiling at her forkful of green beans, Olivia said, "I'd eat more vegetables if they tasted this good." She knew they were cooked with bacon, but she tried not to think about it.

While Del devoured his potatoes, Olivia told him about her conversation with Crystal Quinn. "By the end of our talk," she said, "it became very clear that Alicia had never mentioned the necklace to Crystal. I got the impression they rarely speak to each other, even though Alicia still lives with her mother and stepfather. Alicia works part-time jobs, so she probably can't afford to live on her own at the moment." Olivia soaked up the last bits of sauce with a roll. "I wish I could tell you about Alicia's stepfather, but Crystal did little more than mention him."

Del pushed aside his empty plate and leaned his elbows on the table. "I know Robbie Quinn," Del said, "although not well. When I first arrived in Chatterley Heights, Robbie would stop by the station to fill me in on what he considered the shady doings of various townsfolk. He'd appointed himself as sort of my trainer and informant."

"Oh dear," Olivia said.

Ida appeared at their table carrying two plates of apple pie and an open bottle of merlot that might half fill their two tumblers. "Pete said this is all on the house," she said. "It's a wonder that man doesn't go broke, giving away food and drink to folks who can afford to pay for it." Ida piled their empty dinner plates on a tray and trudged toward the kitchen.

Once Ida was out of earshot, Olivia asked, "What was your assessment of Robbie Quinn? Just a cop wannabe, or was there something else going on?"

Del emptied the remains of the merlot into their two glasses. "This is all conjecture, and I wouldn't repeat it under oath. Robbie didn't yearn to be a police officer, as far as I could tell. He reminded me more of a tattletale. He seemed to feel superior to pretty much everyone."

"I sense from your tone that you aren't fond of the type." Olivia dug into her apple pie, which was almost as meltingly delicious as Maddie's lemon sugar cookies.

With a rueful smile, Del said, "As a kid, I was more the type that got tattled on. Lucky for me, in fifth grade I had a teacher who realized that punishments like sending me to the principal's office or making me stay indoors during recess weren't having the desired effect. I was becoming more and more rebellious. So she started talking to me, getting to know me better. When she found out my folks were going through a divorce, she told me about her own experience being a kid with divorcing parents."

Olivia's heart gave her a little pinch as she flashed back, once again, to her father's death when she was in high school. His loss had been even harder on Jason, who began to hang out with troubled kids and nearly flunked out of high school. "Your teacher understood your rebellion was really about pain," she said.

Del took a sip of wine and nodded. With a shrug, he said, "The kids who tattled on me had their problems, too. Who knows what was going on with Robbie Quinn. At any rate, I tried to discourage him from gleefully turning in his neighbors for partying past nine p.m. It took a while, but he finally ceased his daily reporting. Underneath it all, Robbie seemed resentful. But that's for a shrink to decide. I'm just glad he isn't my brother."

Olivia thought back to her conversation with Crystal in the band shell. "I'm thinking Robbie Quinn might be an irritating husband, but he seems to be a good provider. And I suppose he is more reliable than Alicia's real father was. When I spoke with Crystal, she struck me as deeply angry. She was openly critical of her daughter and still resentful of Alicia's father. Also, money seems to be a big issue for her. I suspect she'll show up at your office and demand that you hand over anything of value that might have been found with the bones. I'll let you handle that situation, though I'd appreciate hearing about it."

"I'm guessing you'd like me to set Crystal straight, and not in a gentle way?"

"Goodness, no," Olivia said. "That would be unprofessional. I'd like to be kept in the loop, that's all." She attempted a wide-eyed, innocent expression, which made Del laugh. "Anyway," Olivia said, "I doubt we can trust Crystal's perceptions about the people in her life."

"I'll talk to Crystal tomorrow." Del drained the last of his merlot. "It's interesting that she doesn't seem to know about the necklace. I wonder what else Alicia might be keeping from her mother." Del pushed aside his empty dessert plate. "It might be some time before we confirm who those bones belonged to. Maybe it isn't Kenny Vayle after all, but it won't hurt to question the family informally. I don't have much else going on right now, assuming you don't stumble upon another body any time soon."

"Hey, not fair," Olivia said. "This time someone else did the stumbling. Maybe I'll have a chat with Mom. She will almost certainly have lots of long, involved stories about the Vayle/Quinn family, going back decades. The trick will be sorting out what's relevant."

"Patience, Livie. Ellie's stories are always relevant."

"Eventually." Olivia checked Pete's Audubon bird clock. "Well, it's past the red-winged blackbird and approaching the yellow warbler. I'm opening the store tomorrow morning, so I'd better wend toward home."

"And I have a cold case to warm up." Del pulled out his wallet. "Ida deserves a tip."

"Nope, it's my turn." Olivia counted out several bills for a generous tip. "By the way, Maddie is thrilled with this case," she said as she slid her arms into the warm sleeves of her thick sweater. "All the intrigue of a murder investigation without the squeamishness. At least that's what Maddie thinks. I'm not so sure."

Del slipped on his uniform jacket and buttoned it up. "Your instincts are more accurate," he said. "Cold cases have a way of igniting. They can dredge up all sorts of nasty secrets."

Chapter Five

❧

Much as she cherished her sleep, Olivia awakened at six o'clock on Tuesday morning feeling revved up for work. She was well aware that not everyone looked forward to the work week, but not everyone was lucky enough to run a store like The Gingerbread House. Spunky, whose furry little head emerged from a fold in the blanket, looked less enthusiastic. The covers were warm, the bedroom was not.

"Come on, Spunks, it's Tuesday. You can nap all day downstairs in the store. You love your chair by the front window, remember? The adoration, the ear rubs, the extra treats . . ."

When he heard the word "treats," Spunky wriggled out of the bedclothes and hopped to his little paws.

"Good boy." Olivia pulled a long sweatshirt over her pajamas and took her pup downstairs for a quick, chilly visit to the side yard. Spunky finished his business with unusual efficiency and declined a run around the property.

Olivia had intended to return upstairs to her apartment for a shower and change of clothes before unlocking the store, but when she entered the foyer, the aroma of freshly baked lemon sugar cookies floated under the door of The Gingerbread House. "What do you think, Spunks? Should we stop to visit Maddie? Lucky thing I keep a supply of kibbles in the store kitchen." Spunky would want to eat in the kitchen with his two favorite humans, but the health department disapproved. Feeding him breakfast in the sales area would keep him content for a while.

As soon as Olivia opened the door of the store, Spunky slid inside. He headed directly for the cookbook nook, where he usually began his morning inspection. While her little guard Yorkie was happily distracted, Olivia opened the kitchen door to a rush of warm, sweet air. Maddie was in constant motion, as always. She sang snatches of whatever song her earbuds piped into her ears and swayed in time with the music. Somehow, her hands remained steady enough to swirl dusty rose royal icing into a perfect scalloped pattern around the outer edge of a round cutout cookie. However, Maddie's perfect aim was limited to icing—flour dusted her bouncy red hair, and a glob of excess cookie dough rested on her shoulder.

Olivia admitted to herself that her mother was right. Maddie would be the perfect choice to teach the cookie decorating classes at Ellie's future arts and crafts school. Olivia was good, but not that good. Besides, who could resist Maddie's exuberance?

"Hey, girlfriend." Maddie capped her pastry bag and removed her earbuds. "You're up uncommonly early. Although I notice you're still in your jammies, such as they are, and you have yet to brush your hair."

"Or my teeth," Olivia said. "Spunky and I made a brief visit to the side yard. I thought I'd feed him breakfast out on the sales floor, while I go back upstairs and make myself reasonably presentable."

"Not until you've told me about your dinner with Del last

night." Maddie refilled her coffee cup and fixed a cup for Olivia. "Want a cookie for breakfast?"

"No, thanks." Olivia sipped her coffee and felt the warmth flow through her. "I think I'll hold off on sugar for, oh, maybe an hour."

"Such willpower." Maddie hiked herself up onto the counter, from where she could swing her legs. "So, back to your dinner with Del . . . What did he say about the bones?"

"Wait two seconds." Olivia opened a canister and scooped out some kibbles, which she poured into a small bowl. She slipped out to the sales floor and headed toward Spunky's chair, an antique with a padded seat, located in front of the large front window so the vigilant Yorkie could keep an eye on both the store and the porch. However, Spunky wasn't there.

"Spunks?" Olivia called. Spunky slid out from behind the heavy front curtain. "Oh, there you are," Olivia said. "Are the squirrels invading the porch again?" Spunky's nails tapped on the floor as he scurried toward his breakfast. Once his face disappeared into the bowl, Olivia shifted the edge of the heavy curtain and peered out at the Gingerbread House porch. She saw nothing amiss. She told herself that finding one body on the porch didn't mean more would follow. She returned to the kitchen, trying to repress her lingering anxiety.

Maddie was back at work piping scallops on her round cut sugar cookies, this time with violet icing. She paused and glanced up as Olivia closed the kitchen door. "Speak," Maddie said. "Piping this icing design takes no concentration whatsoever."

"I'll take your word for it." Olivia relaxed on a kitchen chair. "I have trouble making perfect scallops time after time. Those cookies look wonderful. Did you tint the dough?"

"Yep," Maddie said without looking up. "Pale yellow works well with violet, don't you think?"

Olivia answered with an extended sigh.

"Oh, for heaven's sake, eat one," Maddie said. "What's

the point of running a store filled with everything cookie if you never indulge?"

"Can't argue with that." Olivia bit into a cookie and sighed again, this time with pleasure. While she nibbled, she told Maddie about her dinner conversation with Del, minus the personal parts.

Maddie glanced up in midscallop. "You left out the personal parts, didn't you? Never mind, I'll let it go this time, but only because I desperately wanted to hear what Del had to say about those bones." As she spoke, Maddie smoothly completed the interrupted scallop curve and began icing another. "It sounds as if he is taking the bones more seriously than the crime lab is. And yes, I do know the lab is always overwhelmed with more immediate cases . . . which is okay with me because it means we can investigate without too much interference from those pesky professionals."

"Except Del is a professional, and he certainly sounded interested in this case," Olivia said. "Although I wouldn't call Del pesky. He does seem more relaxed than he usually is about our avid curiosity. He didn't tell me to back off and mind my own business, though he sort of hinted. Of course, his casual attitude could change quickly if this turns out to be a murder. Especially if living, breathing, weapon-toting murder suspects begin to emerge."

Maddie capped her pastry bag and put it on the kitchen counter. "The cookie decorating is hereby finished for the morning." She stretched her arms toward the ceiling, then checked the clock above the sink. "It is 7:23 a.m., which gives us at least an hour to begin our investigation. Now, don't argue, Livie. You can shower later, and I can open the store. Tuesdays are usually slow, anyway."

"Are you sure you can stand being in the same room with me before I shower?"

"I'll try, in the interests of the murder investigation." Maddie gathered up the tiny bottles of gel food coloring she'd used for the icing. "I'll simply focus on the lingering aroma of lemon sugar cookies."

"Such dedication," Olivia murmured.

"Why don't you tidy up the kitchen, while I power up the laptop. I have a couple ideas for online searches that might help us."

"I'll clean up in a minute," Olivia said. "First I need to check on Spunky and retrieve his breakfast bowl, which I'm sure is empty and licked clean by now." When she entered the sales floor and headed toward Spunky's chair, the little Yorkie opened one eye. He closed it again when he noted the absence of doggy treats in her hand. "Wise choice, Spunks," Olivia said as she massaged his soft, sensitive ears.

Spunky sighed.

"Sleep while you can, little one," Olivia said. "Your adoring fans will arrive in about an hour, and they will expect you to be perky. It takes energy to be adorable."

The kitchen door opened, bringing with it a hint of lemony sweetness. Maddie's head peeked around the edge of the door. "Livie? Is that you muttering to yourself?"

"I do not mutter." Olivia gave her pup a final pat and picked up his empty bowl. She headed toward the kitchen, dodging display tables as she navigated the sales floor. "I was merely conversing quietly with Spunky. He has sensitive hearing." A strip of light from the kitchen sparkled off a cookie cutter mobile as it stirred in the air currents. "I love this time of morning," Olivia said. "The store feels magical, as if we were in the middle of a fairy tale."

"Luckily, I've turned off the oven," Maddie said, "so we won't be trapped with Hansel and Gretel in the evil witch's kitchen. Now I think of it, most fairy tales felt dark and disturbing to me when I was a kid. I wasn't always tough as over-baked cookies, you know. Aunt Sadie used to ask me to read fairy tales to her—you know, to make it fun for me to practice reading—but she stopped because they gave me nightmares."

As she followed Maddie into the kitchen, Olivia asked, "Was that soon after . . . ?"

"After my parents died?" Maddie's forehead puckered in thought. "Now that you mention it, you're right. Right after the accident, I went through a quiet, sensitive phase. You and I had just met."

"I remember, though." Olivia poured herself a fresh cup of coffee. "You seemed shy at first, but eventually the boisterous Maddie emerged. At ten, I didn't think much about it."

Maddie sat at the kitchen table and opened a laptop Olivia had never seen before. "Time for some fun," Maddie said, "which is something we boisterous folk do especially well. And before you ask, yes, I splurged on a new, faster laptop. Let's see what we can dig up on the not-so-recently deceased and his less-than-loving family."

While she waited, Olivia checked the icing on Maddie's freshly made decorated cookies. It hadn't hardened. She arranged a single layer on a large platter. Later, if the icing had hardened enough, she would pile the plate high with cookies, which would disappear soon after she placed them next to the coffee urn on the treats table.

Olivia dug through the stuffed freezer to locate the container of ground coffee. She was about to measure enough for the store's large coffee urn when Maddie let out a whoop.

"I am so very good at computer research," Maddie said.

"And so very modest, too," Olivia murmured.

"Okay, here's what I've found out so far." Maddie turned her laptop sideways so Olivia could read the screen, though she had no clue what she was seeing. The print on the screen was unusually small and faint. "I know this isn't your favorite activity," Maddie said, "so I shall interpret for you. The person who posted this piece is sort of an electronic age version of the old-fashioned neighborhood gossip . . . an underappreciated role, in my humble opinion, and not to be confused with the nasty editor of a certain small town newspaper. I will say no more."

Olivia topped off her coffee and pulled a chair next to Maddie. "Why is the print so small?"

"I'm not sure," Maddie said. "Maybe she—or he, I suppose—is trying to create a blog that looks like whispering. You know, sort of like a neighbor whispering gossip to someone over a fence. Or, more likely, it's meant to discourage casual readers. The posts are hard to read, and the blog link is just a string of nonsense, so outsiders probably wouldn't drop in to read posts, let alone take the time to enlarge the print. This is probably aimed at a select group of visitors who have shared the link with each other. Although if I found it, so can others. Of course, I am not just any Internet explorer." Maddie zoomed in on the post, which made it more readable.

"Wow," said Olivia as she read through the post. "This makes Binnie Sloan look like an amateur. It says here that Crystal was already involved with Robbie Quinn, her second husband, before Kenny Vayle's disappearance. And Kenny was still living at home, trying to stay sober. According to Ida, Crystal was seeing *another* guy in between Kenny and Robbie." Olivia summarized Ida's story about Crystal's brief second so-called marriage.

"This is making me dizzy," Maddie said.

"All this must have been incredibly painful and confusing for Alicia. Wasn't she in her teens?" Olivia skimmed ahead, looking for some mention of the young woman's age at the time of the post.

"Alicia was thirteen," Maddie said. "It says so at the end of the post. That means Crystal was stringing along maybe three men for a number of years. Incredible."

"Unless these are all lies," Olivia said.

"A distinct possibility." Maddie stretched her arms above her head. "There are several posts following this one, most of which hint at dirt on other neighbors. Months later, the blogger returns to the Vayle family. That one is even more interesting." Maddie scrolled through the blog until she came to a post that contained a photo.

"That looks like a young Alicia," Olivia said pointing at the girl in the photo.

"So that smiling man might be her father, Kenny Vayle. If so, it's the only picture of him I've seen in this blog." Maddie tapped her finger on the screen. "That looks like a hand on Alicia's shoulder. So is Kenny posing for an affectionate father-daughter photo? Why would this blogger include a positive image of them?"

"Kenny may have a smile plastered on his face, but look at his eyes," Olivia said. "Do they look unfocused to you? He seems to be looking beyond the camera."

Maddie leaned closer to the screen. "I see what you mean. It's like he's staring off into space. And his hair . . . part of it is sticking out as if the wind were lifting it up, but Alicia's hair is lying perfectly flat. I'm thinking that man was drunk."

"Or on drugs, I suppose," Olivia said. "Not that I could tell the difference."

"Either way, his brain would have been mush." Maddie hopped out of her chair and gravitated toward the plate of decorated cookies. She picked up a round cookie decorated with violet scallops. "I'll never understand why anyone would turn to drugs when there are cookies in the world."

"I couldn't agree more," Olivia said. "Bring me one of those, would you? The one with peach scallops will do. I'll pretend it's fruit." Maddie delivered the cookie and took her seat facing the computer. While the two friends munched on their cookies, they studied the photo on the screen.

Kenny must once have been an attractive man, Olivia thought. His medium brown hair had a reddish tinge, brought out by the sun, and his fine-boned facial features reminded her of Alicia. Olivia found her gaze riveted to the vague, blue eyes behind his wire-rimmed glasses. A tiny glint of light sparkled off the metal. Olivia's gaze lowered to the front of Kenny's neck, where she saw a second point of light.

"Maddie, look." Olivia pointed to the spot. Kenny was

wearing a button-down shirt, as if he had dressed up for a special occasion with his daughter. His shirt was unbuttoned at the top, perhaps due to the warmth of the day.

"Whoa, that's the necklace. It's got to be." Maddie zoomed in again to enlarge the photo. The image became fuzzy. Maddie ran her finger down the screen, stopping at the middle of Kenny's collarbone. "I see something right there below the suprasternal notch."

"The super-what?"

"Suprasternal notch," Maddie said. "Just something I picked up during my brief stint in chiropractic training."

"Okay, but how on earth did you remember the name? As I recall, your 'stint' lasted less than a month."

"More like three weeks," Maddie said. "Or was it three days?"

"You can't remember how long you studied chiropractics, yet the supernastral bone, or whatever it's called, just popped into your head?" Olivia crossed her arms and raised a skeptical eyebrow.

"Yep," Maddie said. "And the word is pronounced suprasternal." With a happy sigh, Maddie added, "Thank you. You're always laughing at my French, so it feels good to correct your pronunciation for a change."

"Glad to be of service," Olivia said. "So, what are we looking at here?" She squinted at the computer screen. "Ah, I see what you mean. There must be something shiny around his neck, catching the sunlight." Olivia touched the screen with her fingernail. "See right there where the top button of Kenny's shirt is open? I can just barely see something sticking out. It looks pointy. I wouldn't bet the store, but that could be the point of an arrow."

"Eureka!" Maddie bounced on her chair. "I *would* bet the store, except you own it. Kenny must be wearing the cookie cutter necklace. He might have worn it all the time, under his shirt, but most people wouldn't see it. Maybe the killer didn't know that . . . or he was in a hurry when he stuffed Kenny into the wall, so he didn't even notice the necklace."

"Down, girl," Olivia said. "Even if that is the cookie cutter necklace, it still doesn't prove those were Kenny's bones in the wall. And it doesn't eliminate other possibilities. What if Kenny killed someone else, like another drifter, maybe in a drunken fight? If he wanted to disappear, he might have tossed his necklace inside the wall along with his victim's body."

Maddie's shoulders sagged. "It also doesn't prove Kenny killed anyone, or that anyone killed anyone. The bones might have belonged to some drunk who just up and died. Kenny could have found the body and decided that closing him into the wall would be a perfect way to disappear forever. Or the chain might simply have broken while Kenny was moving the body."

"I'm not sure that makes sense," Olivia said. "It takes time for a body to skeletonize. How could Kenny be sure the body wouldn't be found right away? The police would suspect Kenny at once."

Maddie frowned as she cleared the screen. "Maybe the bones were already in the wall. Maybe Kenny threw in his necklace to make people think he was dead."

"Assuming Kenny knew nothing about DNA analysis," Olivia said. "Speculation isn't getting us anywhere. We have too many unanswered questions. What we do know is that someone was interested enough in Kenny Vayle—or disliked him enough—to showcase him on a gossip blog. I'd really like to find out the identity of the blogger. Meanwhile, my friend, we have a store to open soon, and I need to make myself presentable. *Andiamo!*"

"Okay, Livie, I get the point," Maddie said. "You're using French to get back at me for using a word you don't know."

"Nonsense," Olivia said. "It wasn't French. *Andiamo* means 'Let's go!' in Italian."

Maddie threw a cookie at her.

* * *

Olivia hopped in and out of the shower in record time. Her dark-chocolate wool pants were still clean, so she topped them with a cherry red sweater. Maybe her outfit would trigger a longing for sweet treats among the Gingerbread House customers. It certainly had that effect on Olivia as she entered her own kitchen and went straight for a frozen cookie. For dessert, she had a slice of toast and a hardboiled egg, washed down with extra strong coffee.

By some miracle, Olivia remembered to fetch her cell phone, which had been charging in her bedroom. When she picked it up, she discovered a message from a number that looked vaguely familiar. Someone must have called while she was eating breakfast, because there had been no message when she'd selected her outfit. Olivia checked her watch. Eight forty-four a.m. She'd better listen to the message on her way downstairs.

Olivia left her breakfast dishes on the table. She wasn't worried that Spunky would lick the crumbs off the plate, since he was already snuggled on his chair downstairs in The Gingerbread House. She locked her apartment door behind her and punched her voice mail message code as she bounced down the stairs. Her foot hit the edge of the third step. Olivia grabbed the railing with her free hand and sat down hard. As her mother never tired of reminding her, multitasking was best left to those who possessed coordination and a sense of balance. Luckily, her mother wasn't there.

Despite nearly breaking her neck, Olivia had managed to keep her cell phone near her ear. She realized she was listening to Alicia Vayle's tremulous voice saying good-bye. Olivia sat on the stairs and began the message again.

Alicia's message began, "I'm really sorry to bother you, Olivia, but I didn't know who else to call. I don't have any friends left in Chatterley Heights. They've all moved to Baltimore or DC or anywhere, just to get away from . . . well, there aren't any jobs here, so . . ." Alicia sniffled and cleared her throat. "Robbie is going to throw me out of the house, and my mom isn't even here. Robbie's always doing that, being mean to me when my mom isn't around. Not that she'd have protected me. She probably left the house because she didn't want to deal with me. Anyway, I know Robbie was waiting for an excuse to get rid of me." Alicia's voice quivered as she added, "Robbie hates me, and he's making my mom hate me, too. Maybe he got Pete to fire me, because there wasn't any reason. I mean not a *real* reason. I liked my job, and I was good at it. Pete was going to let me bake cookies." Olivia heard Alicia take a shaky breath before saying, "So I was wondering . . . Would it be okay if I crashed with you for a while? I could sleep on the sofa, and I'd cook and clean for you, and stuff like that. Please? I don't have anywhere else to go." With a final sniffle, Alicia ended the call.

Olivia sat on the step for several minutes. Life in Chatterley Heights, she thought, was getting more and more complicated. She was quite certain that Alicia couldn't stay in her tiny apartment; that was out of the question. However, Alicia had turned to her for help, and she couldn't ignore such a plea. Having Alicia around might make it easier to find out more about the Vayle/Quinn family . . . no, it would never work. Olivia had to wonder if the troublesome boyfriend had gotten Alicia fired. The last thing she and Maddie needed was an angry, aggressive boyfriend hanging around The Gingerbread House, demanding to see Alicia. Olivia checked the time on her cell phone. The store would be opening momentarily. As if on cue, her phone vibrated in her hand. It was Maddie.

"Livie, are you coming down soon?" Maddie paused, and Olivia heard her speaking to someone else. "Okay, I'm back," Maddie said. "Livie, we have sort of a situation here. So don't dawdle, okay?"

Chapter Six

On a normal Tuesday morning, The Gingerbread House awakened slowly. It was rare to find a customer waiting when the door opened at nine a.m. Customers tended to dribble in one or two at a time to replenish supplies after a weekend of binge baking. They rarely lingered. Unless an event was scheduled, Bertha didn't report to work until ten a.m.

The moment Olivia entered the store, she sensed this would be a different sort of Tuesday. She saw Maddie peeking through a slit in the thick curtain covering the large front window. Next to her, a fluffy tail protruded from underneath the curtain. When Olivia joined Maddie to look outside, she saw at least five customers lounging on the porch. Two more were walking up the steps. Everyone appeared to be talking at once. Spunky began to yap and growl, as if he weren't sure whether he should welcome the intruders or chase them away.

"As you can see," Maddie said, "word has spread, and the curious have been gathering outside. I guess we should have seen this coming, although I'm a bit surprised those workers would blab about finding bones after Calliope threatened them with eternal unemployment. Now I wish we'd asked Bertha to come in early."

"We'll have to make do," Olivia said. "At least a third of those folks are men, which means the cookies will go fast. However, we aren't likely to sell much. I suppose we'd better open the store and take it as it comes. "

"I'll keep an eye on the plate and try to keep it filled." Maddie turned away from the window to check the Hansel and Gretel clock hanging on the wall. "I do love that clock," she said, "but I never know what time it is. If I open the store now, we could be anywhere from ten minutes early to five minutes late. I think. I could check my cell phone, but I left it in the kitchen, and I know better than to ask if you remembered to bring yours."

"Mine is in my pocket, smarty-pants," Olivia said. "I vote we wait for about five minutes before opening. Might as well get it over with. Meanwhile, I'll call Bertha to ask if there's any way she could get here a bit early. I'll offer her time-and-a-half. Heck, I'll put her in my will, if I ever have time to make one."

"I'll draft it for you," Maddie said.

"Maybe I'll call her from the kitchen, so I can throw together an extra tray of cookies at the same time." Olivia speed dialed while she hurried into the kitchen. She hoped Bertha would answer quickly when she saw who was calling. Bertha's sense of responsibility was legendary. However, Olivia was sent to voice mail, where she left a quick, desperate message. Then she thought of her mom. Ellie had helped customers before; maybe she could . . . *What the heck, this is an emergency.* Olivia speed dialed her mother and waited through Ellie's lengthy voice mail spiel touting the benefits of yoga and announcing the birth of her beloved arts and crafts school. Finally, Olivia was allowed to leave a message. She explained that the store was about to be invaded by rabidly curious gossip seekers, both male and female, and she begged Ellie to come help.

Olivia attempted a deep, centering breath. Her mother

would be so proud. *Well, Maddie and I will simply have to deal with the situation by ourselves. We've had plenty of experience.* Olivia told herself that their customers' ravenous curiosity about those bones was perfectly understandable. She, too, wanted information, mostly about Kenny Vayle. Maybe she could turn the situation to her advantage by questioning her own customers. Perhaps some of them had known Kenny. Or maybe she'd simply listen and say as little as possible. Years had passed since Kenny's disappearance. Memories dim. Details turn to vague impressions or evaporate altogether. After so many years, would the truth even be recognizable? Any information that did emerge would undoubtedly spread through town like flood icing, changing shape as it flowed from person to person.

Olivia checked the time on her cell phone. Eight minutes past nine. Maddie would already have opened the store. Olivia took a deep breath and marched herself through the kitchen to the sales floor. At first glance, she felt reassured. The store was far more crowded than was usual for a Tuesday morning, but the general mood felt low-key. Customers roamed around the store and chatted with each other as if this were nothing more than a special store event. A few even examined cookbooks or baking equipment.

Unfortunately, Olivia recognized one of those browsers as Binnie Sloan. For once, Binnie's photographer niece, Ned, wasn't with her. Olivia remembered Maddie mentioning, with joy, that Ned had just left town to take yet another photojournalism class in DC. Olivia noticed an old plastic tape recorder in one of Binnie's hands and two rapidly disappearing cookies in the other. Her mouth full of cookie crumbs, Binnie appeared to be interviewing a customer. Before Olivia could deposit her plate of cookies and lose herself in the crowd, Binnie spotted her. Abandoning her interviewee, who was still speaking, Binnie headed straight for Olivia. There was no escape. To deliver the cookie plate to the treats table, Olivia would have to walk toward Binnie, who slithered through groups of chatting customers like a plump snake after a rodent snack.

When Binnie reached her, Olivia held the plate between them. "Have another cookie, Binnie," Olivia said. "They won't last long."

Binnie eyed the plate with greedy suspicion. Her hesitation passed quickly, however. She grabbed three more cookies with one hand and shoved her small recorder at Olivia with the other. "So, Livie, I hear you've discovered yet another dead body," Binnie said, her tone heavy with sarcasm. "Quite a talent you have, wouldn't you say?"

Olivia decided it was time for a cookie. She selected one with magenta scallops and smiled while she nibbled on it.

When Olivia failed to rise to her bait, Binnie tried again. "There's no point denying your personal involvement in this new investigation. You were observed having dinner with Sheriff Jenkins yesterday evening, and my sources tell me you've already interviewed the victim's ex-wife, who is a prime suspect in his murder."

"There's no clear evidence of murder," Olivia said before she could stop herself. She took a big bite of her cookie.

Binnie smirked. "I think my readers are well aware that if Livie Greyson finds a body, it was murdered. The fact that you're already investigating is proof enough. Does your boyfriend know you're playing Miss Marple again?"

A familiar voice intervened. "Why, Binnie, how nice of you to drop by for a visit . . . and for several cookies. It must be a slow news day." Ellie was barely visible behind Binnie's taller and far beefier body.

Startled, Binnie teetered as she spun around. Ellie's small, yet strong arm reached out to steady her. Olivia grinned at her mother from behind Binnie's back. However, the self-styled journalist recovered quickly. Stepping to the side so she faced both women, Binnie held out her tape recorder, and said, "Livie, Ellie, both of you were at the scene where the remains were discovered. What items were found with the deceased?" With a snide grin, Binnie added, "Was there any clothing, for example . . . or perhaps a piece of jewelry that positively identified the victim as Kenny Vayle?" Binnie poked her recorder close to Olivia's face. "What did Kenny's widow reveal to you yesterday evening when you interrogated her inside the band shell? I have photos of that interview, by the way."

"Really? How interesting," Ellie said. "I thought your photographer was out of town."

Binnie hesitated no more than a second before thrusting her recorder at Ellie. "So, as Chatterley Heights' foremost gossip, Ellie, what do you think? Is Crystal Quinn guilty of murdering her drunken, wife-beating husband so she could marry Robbie Quinn, the man with whom she was having an affair?"

Olivia's hand was itching to slap the smug grin off Binnie's plump face. It was clear that she perceived Olivia's anger and relished it. Binnie aimed her tape recorder toward Olivia. "So tell us, Livie, what does the sheriff have to say about your involvement, once again, in a brutal case of—"

A low growl issued from behind Binnie's back. Startled, she leaped aside, revealing an agitated Yorkie in Maddie's arms. Maddie had a firm grip on Spunky's collar but she made no attempt to calm him.

"Get that nasty creature away from me," Binnie shouted.

"Spunky? Don't be silly," Maddie said. "He's such a sweet little tyke." Spunky followed up with a volley of yaps.

"He's a vicious attack dog," Binnie said. "He should be put down."

This was too much for Spunky, who wriggled to escape from Maddie's tight grasp. He freed one front paw and reached toward Binnie's face. She hopped backward, right into the treats table. The room hushed as the coffee urn teetered. Olivia rushed to steady the urn, but she couldn't reach the cookies in time. The plate slid across the table and seesawed on the edge. Finally, it slipped off, shedding cookies in a sparkling, multi-colored waterfall. As it hit the floor, the glass plate shattered.

The cookies cracked into pieces which slid across the floor. Maddie thrust Spunky into Olivia's arms and rushed into the kitchen.

Startled customers froze in place, like full-size action figures preparing to leap into the air. The tableau dissolved when a woman's voice said, "I do hate to see cookies wasted." A second woman added, "Some people should watch where they are leaping." The spell had broken, and the room filled with chatter. After all, there were more cookies piled on plates scattered around the sales floor. Ellie sighed as she began to pick up chunks of broken glass. Maddie returned, bearing a broom, an armful of old kitchen towels, and a full roll of paper towels.

As Olivia cuddled and comforted her over-stimulated pup, she heard a woman say, "Oh, look, Struts, it's a Yorkshire terrier. Isn't he adorable?" The lilting voice belonged to a tall, willowy blonde approaching the treats table. Olivia guessed her to be somewhere in her mid to late twenties. Struts Marinsky, the statuesque, female owner of Struts & Bolts Garage, followed behind the young woman. Struts shot an amused glance toward Olivia, while Binnie, her round face contorted with anger, strode past them, heading toward the front door of The Gingerbread House.

The young blonde only had eyes for Spunky. She reached out to caress the hair on the little Yorkie's head. "So silky," she murmured, gazing into his soft brown eyes. "I'm Dolly, by the way," she said, more to Spunky than to the mere people around him. "Dolly Fitzpatrick."

Olivia felt a prick of envy when she noticed that Dolly's eyes were cornflower blue. Olivia had always wanted cornflower blue eyes, rather than her blue-green eyes that darkened to gray on overcast days. Although Del did seem to like them just fine.

Dolly's short, golden hair fell in perfect curls around her head, and her slim, muscular body hinted at regular workouts. Worst of all, Spunky seemed besotted by her. Olivia felt as if she were a jealous thirteen-year-old again . . . only this time the coveted boy was a five-pound Yorkshire terrier.

"Struts has told me all about you and this amazing store." Dolly smiled, revealing perfect teeth. "I made Struts bring me here, so I could meet you. I've been away from this area for years and just recently moved back. Struts said I could stay with her until I find a place of my own." As Dolly stroked his fur, Spunky slumped in Olivia's arms. His head fell against her shoulder, as if he were too relaxed to hold it upright. Olivia was fairly sure she'd heard him sigh.

"Did your family leave Chatterley Heights when you were quite young?" Olivia felt certain she'd remember a little girl with golden hair and cornflower blue eyes.

Dolly's light laugh tinkled like a cookie cutter mobile catching a breeze. "Oh no, I left right after high school. You know, to see the world . . . I actually grew up on a farm outside of Chatterley Heights, but I went to school in Twiterton, so there's no reason you'd remember me."

"To be precise, Dolly grew up on the farm next to ours," Struts said. "She was just a kid, but we met while I was dating her oldest brother, who turned out to be a jerk. No offense intended, Dolly."

"Absolutely none taken," Dolly said. "Frankie was definitely a jerk, though it's worth noting that he completed a stint in the Peace Corps and humanized considerably."

"Good to know," Struts said. "Wish I could say the same for my youngest brother, the one Dolly dated later. He joined the financial industry and profited from the Great Recession. So you dodged a bullet there, girl."

Dolly nodded as her translucent eyes gazed around The Gingerbread House. "Oh, sparkling sugars," she said, pointing to a shelf along the wall. "I love sparkling sugars." As she stepped toward the display, Struts grabbed her by the arm.

"Focus, Dolly," Struts said. "You had something important to ask Olivia, remember? You ordered me to risk leaving

Jason in charge of the garage, so you could come here and get properly introduced."

"Oh, I wouldn't worry about leaving Jason in charge," Dolly said. "He'll do fine. You'll see." Dolly's eyes strayed toward a cookie cutter display on a nearby table.

Something about the way Dolly defended Jason caught Olivia's attention. Was this lovely creature actually interested in her brother? How could that be? Olivia glanced at Struts with raised eyebrows. "You left Jason in charge of the garage?"

Struts grinned. "Dolly is persuasive. However, I'd rather not leave him on his own all day."

"Fond as I am of my baby brother, I second your concern." Olivia touched Dolly's shoulder to get her attention. "Struts mentioned that you wanted to ask me something?"

"Oh, sorry, I'm just so entranced by your store. Yes, it has to do with cookie cutters." Dolly's eyes strayed toward a nearby display of cutters in classic shapes, such as stars, hearts, and circles. She picked up a heart shape. "I've made some cookie cutters, you know. I love working with metal. Jason is teaching me more about fixing cars. He's such a skilled—"

Struts cleared her throat.

"I'm getting to the point, Struts," Dolly said cheerfully. "This is just a bit of background for Livie." Dolly gently placed the heart cutter on the edge of the sales counter. A customer picked it up and walked off with it. "When I first tried to make cutters," Dolly said, "I worked with aluminum. It's cheaper. I didn't feel so bad about messing up. As I became more skilled, I moved on to copper, which really is much more elegant, don't you think, Livie?" Without pausing for an answer, Dolly said. "When I felt confident enough, I got hold of some thin silver and made a few cutters that people actually wanted to buy, so I kept doing that for a while. I got a bit bored—you know, just doing one thing—so I branched out and tried other ideas, like little fondant cutters." Dolly's voice grew increasingly animated. "That gave

me the idea of making charms shaped like tiny cookie cutters. I figured those little things would take less silver, plus
I could charge more for them because they were jewelry. It's
not that I'm mercenary, you understand, only I needed
more—okay, Struts, stop glowering at me. I'm getting to my
point, I really am."

"Just for the record," Struts said, "I do not glower."

Dolly ran her fingers through her hair, which only made
the curls more perfect. "You see, I heard a rumor . . . Well,
Ida mentioned that a silver necklace with a cookie cutter heart
was found with those bones everyone is talking about.

Olivia tried not to roll her eyes. "Of course she did." *I
must learn never to discuss confidential information when
Ida is anywhere nearby.*

"Well," Dolly said, "one of the pieces I sold was a silver
necklace with a cookie cutter heart. You know, the kind that
looks like it has an arrow going through it? A young girl
bought it. So I'm wondering, could that girl have been the
daughter of the murdered man you found?"

"Now that's a very interesting question," Olivia said.
"Although I didn't actually find the remains myself." Olivia
found herself hoping that her brother wouldn't let this one get
away. Although why Dolly would be interested in Jason . . .
aside from their mutual affection for handling metal, that is.
Focus, Livie. "How many years ago did you sell the necklace
to this girl? Any chance you could describe her? I'll certainly
understand if you can't."

"It was about eight years ago," Dolly said. "Not long before
I moved away from this area. However, as it happens, I have
an excellent memory for faces. I find faces fascinating, don't
you? They reveal so much, especially when they're trying not
to reveal anything, you know?"

"I do." Olivia scanned the sales floor, which had emptied
considerably. Maddie and Ellie could handle the few remaining customers. "Dolly," Olivia said, "I want to hear everything
you remember about the girl who bought the cookie cutter

necklace. In fact, let's go into the kitchen. We can have coffee and cookies while we talk."

"Oh, how lovely." Dolly levitated up on her toes with joy. "I've always wanted to see the baking equipment in a professional kitchen."

Somehow that did not surprise Olivia.

"You two have fun," Struts said. "I think I'll head back to the garage to see if Jason has left it still standing." She turned to leave. On her way to the kitchen, Olivia glanced back to see her mother intercept the tall, muscular figure striding across the sales floor. Struts had to bend over to hear what Olivia's four-foot-eleven-inch mother had to say. Maddie stood nearby, chatting with a customer. Olivia caught Maddie's eye from across the sales floor and gestured to indicate she would be in the kitchen. Maddie answered with a quick nod.

Olivia ushered Dolly into the Gingerbread House kitchen and closed the door behind them. "I'll make a fresh pot of coffee," she said. "I could use a jolt. We're not used to a crowd of customers so early on a Tuesday morning."

While Olivia fired up Mr. Coffee, Dolly explored the kitchen with childlike awe. She opened cabinet doors, peeked inside the oven, and examined the well-used cookie cutters drying on a clean towel. "I notice the cutters are all drying with their cutting edges down," Dolly said. "Is that to let water drain from the hem so the metal won't rust?"

"I'm impressed. You are the first visitor to this kitchen who has noticed that detail," Olivia said. "You're very observant."

"Oh, I don't know about that. It's just that I'm so interested in metals. I love their different sheens and how malleable they can be. Working with metal is such a pleasure." Dolly rubbed her hands together as if she were imagining the smoothness of silver. "All metals have their sensitivities, though. Sort of like people, don't you think?" When Olivia hesitated, Dolly laughed. "Oh, I'm being silly. Don't pay any attention to me."

"I don't think you're being silly," Olivia said. "I've been told that I think of cookie cutters as little people with individual personalities. There's some truth to that observation, although I'm fairly certain no one has meant it as a compliment. When I hold an antique or vintage cutter, I can't help but wonder about the people who used it." Olivia picked up a cutter shaped like a gingerbread girl. "I use this little cutter all the time, and so does Maddie. It makes us think of being little girls. This one belonged to my own mother, who handed it on to me when I turned sixteen."

"Oh." A sudden tear ran down Dolly's cheek. She wiped it away, and said, "Now I really am being silly, but I can't help it. You see, my mother died a month ago. That's why I came back here . . . to be with her. I was planning to go back to DC afterward, but you know how it is. There was a lot of stuff to sort through, and I began to . . . well, to meet people."

Ah, Olivia thought. *Meet people . . . like, for instance, Jason?*

"Like Jason," Dolly said. "He's such a sweet guy. You're so lucky to have him for a brother."

Jason? The one who calls me Olive Oyl in public? "I try to tell myself that same thing," Olivia said. *Okay, that was lame.*

"I really enjoy working on cars with Jason," Dolly said with a wistful smile. "He is so good with metal, and with engines, and just about anything. And he's easy to talk to. The only problem is . . . well, I don't think Jason likes me as more than a friend."

That's because Jason is dense and also an idiot. "It hasn't been that long since my brother broke up with his girlfriend," Olivia said. "They were high school sweethearts. Things didn't end well, so he's taking his time. My advice, for what it's worth, is that you simply go on with the metalworking and car repair thing for a while. Let Jason get to know you."

Dolly's lovely face lit up. "Oh, I'm so glad to hear that. I will!"

Olivia took clean cups and two small plates from the

dishwasher. She put a cookie on each plate, half-filled the cups with coffee, and delivered everything to the table. "Help yourself to cream and sugar." Olivia pointed toward the kitchen counter. While Dolly added both to her cup, Olivia said, "You mentioned earlier that it was a young girl who bought your silver heart necklace?"

"Oh, yes, she looked like she was in her early teens. I can describe her for you." Dolly sat beside Olivia at the kitchen worktable. "In fact, I could draw her for you, if you have some paper and a pencil."

"Even better." Olivia scrounged through the drawer of the little desk where she usually sat while she reconciled the day's receipts. She found a blue pen and an old sheet of notepaper that was wrinkled but unused. "This is all I could come up with on short notice." Olivia delivered the items to the kitchen table. "We do so much on the computer these days."

"I know it's old-fashioned," Dolly said, "but I love to write and draw by hand. I guess I'm an artist at heart." She drew an oval on the paper and began filling in two eyes. "Jason is very artistic, too, don't you think?"

"Uh, well . . ." Olivia noticed that Dolly kept her fingernails short, which made her seem less inhumanly perfect.

Dolly centered a pert little nose on the emerging face, then shaded in cheekbones. "I watch Jason as he works on that wonderful 1957 Ford Fairlane he's been restoring. He wants every detail to be perfect."

Olivia didn't respond, hoping Dolly would be too absorbed in her drawing to notice her silence. Artistic was about the last word that came to Olivia's mind when she thought about how to describe Jason. Obsessive, maybe . . . especially about that vintage car Struts had bought for a song and given to him to restore. Not that Olivia didn't love her brother . . . she certainly did, although often in a barely tolerant sisterly sort of way. Occasionally, Jason surprised her and behaved as if he might become a mature adult. It didn't last long.

Dolly's quick, sure strokes began to form a recognizable

face. Even though the drawing presented a younger girl with shorter hair, the features belonged to Alicia Vayle. "Her hair was wavy and sort of reddish brown, and her eyes were light brown," Dolly said. "Does that help?"

"Wow," Olivia said. "You've got an amazing visual memory. Yes, this helps a lot. Did this girl talk to you at all?"

Dolly wrinkled her nose, a fetching version of a grimace. "I'm not so good at remembering words. When I was in school, I forgot most of what I read as soon as I finished reading it. Sometimes I drew little pictures in the margins to help myself remember the important stuff for tests."

"I remember Jason doing the same thing," Olivia said.

"I know," Dolly said. "That's one of the reasons I liked him right away. We have so much in common. I really admire how much Jason knows about cars and metal working, plus we both had trouble in school until we learned to do things our own way. Also, he's really cute."

"I'm glad you think so," Olivia said, trying not to sound sarcastic. In fact, she truly was glad that Dolly was smitten with her brother. She sincerely hoped Jason wasn't too dense to recognize a promising relationship.

Dolly gazed at her own drawing with a troubled expression. "So this really is the girl whose father was murdered?"

"Possibly." Olivia sipped her coffee as she considered how much information to reveal. "But we don't really know much yet. The police will have to establish whether it was murder or if someone simply died of natural causes." Rumors were inevitable, but Olivia saw no reason to encourage them.

"I understand." Dolly took a generous bite of her purple-scalloped sugar cookie. "I won't say anything to anyone. Rumors get started so easily."

The kitchen door cracked open and Maddie poked her head inside. "Livie, we've got a problem. Your mom is handling it pretty well, only . . ." Maddie glanced back at the store. "I'd feel better if you came out here. Ellie is strong, but she's so tiny."

Olivia scraped back her chair and jogged through the doorway, leaving Dolly to finish her coffee and cookie alone. "Is Mom in danger?" Olivia asked as she followed Maddie past the sales counter.

"Don't panic," Maddie said. "No sign of fisticuffs yet, and even if there were, I'd put my money on Ellie. That guy looks like he'd be easy to topple."

"Topple? What man?" Olivia scouted the sales floor. At first she saw nothing out of the ordinary. A few customers stood near the locked cabinet that held the more valuable vintage and antique cookie cutters. They appeared to be discussing the contents in a reasonably calm way. Olivia's peripheral vision took in Spunky's favorite chair, from which he received admirers and policed the store. A fluffy pile of fur opened one eye but didn't move.

Maddie nodded toward the entrance to the cookbook nook. "That's where they are. It sounds awfully quiet, though. Maybe Ellie convinced him to leave. Or maybe she decked him. That would be so cool."

Olivia took off at a moderate pace, hoping not to spook the customers. She was ready to throw a punch, if necessary. However, when they reached the entrance to the cookbook nook, Olivia hesitated. Ellie occupied one of the two roomy armchairs nestled in a corner for customers who wished to peruse a cookbook or enjoy a chat over coffee and a cookie. Her legs curled under her elfin body as she gazed serenely at a large man occupying the second armchair. The man shot to his feet when Olivia and Maddie entered the cookbook nook.

"Livie, dear, do come in," Ellie said, as if the cookbook nook were her parlor and Olivia an unexpected visitor. "Mr. Quinn, let me introduce my daughter, Livie, and her friend and business partner, Maddie. Oh, Maddie, would you mind getting Mr. Quinn a cup of coffee and perhaps a cookie? I'm afraid I never gave him a chance to get near the refreshments table."

"Um, okay." Maddie flashed Olivia a confused glance as she exited the nook.

Robbie Quinn held out a powerful hand for Olivia to shake. She steeled herself, anticipating crushed fingers, but his handshake felt loose, almost perfunctory. "Everyone calls me Robbie," he said, his voice a shade too hearty.

Olivia shifted from concern to curiosity. If this man was Crystal Quinn's husband, he was not what she had expected. Well over six feet tall, Robbie would tower over his slender, petite wife. He wore oil-stained jeans, heavy work boots, and a sweatshirt with "Quinn Construction" written across the chest. Robbie pushed up his sleeves, revealing elaborate tattoos on both forearms. Olivia recognized a snake slithering along the top of his right arm, but the other shapes intertwined in a complex, confusing pattern.

Olivia declined Robbie's offer of his chair. "I should get back to my customers soon," she said, "but I'd be interested in knowing why you decided to drop in on us."

Robbie nodded but showed no inclination to retake his seat until Ellie said, "Livie, dear, Bertha is on duty now. She and Maddie can handle the customers for a while. Come sit with me. There's plenty of room." Once Olivia had settled on the soft, wide arm of her mother's chair, Robbie sat down again.

"Robbie was just telling me about his concern for his stepdaughter, Alicia," Ellie said.

Robbie stretched out his long, muscular legs and stared at his boots. "I guess I came on a bit strong," he said, "but I worry about Alicia. Her dad was a no-good drunk who left her and her mom to fend for themselves, but Alicia doesn't see it that way. She blames her mom for everything. She thinks Crystal drove Kenny away, but the truth is Kenny probably went off on a bender and never returned. I'm at the end of my patience with that girl. Alicia is a burden to her mother. She won't listen, refuses to obey her elders . . ." As he shook his head, Olivia noticed what looked like an indentation, perhaps from a hard-hat, circling his curly red hair.

Robbie's voice deepened with anger. "Alicia refuses to pay us rent for her room and board, just expects us to support her, even though she is perfectly capable of working. I won't put up with it, so I've asked her to leave. She needs to grow up and take responsibility for her own life. A few months on her own, and she'll soon find out the world won't be as tolerant as we've been." Robbie's weather-roughened face tightened. "Alicia is lazy and takes advantage of her mother."

One quick glance at her mother told Olivia to keep her mouth shut. She was more than willing to do so. She felt sad for Alicia. However, angering Robbie might only make him clam up.

Maddie reappeared at the cookbook nook entrance with coffee, cookies, and a cheerful smile on her freckled face. As she placed the tray on a table at the far end of the nook, Maddie sent Olivia a silent message. Olivia joined her, ostensibly to help pour and serve.

"Did you hear?" Olivia whispered.

Maddie nodded. "Don't worry about Dolly's drawing. She gave it to me before she left, and I hid it in the desk drawer."

"Good."

"Also," Maddie said, "Lenora is on her way to the store. She has a brilliant plan. Her words, not mine."

Olivia suppressed a groan.

Maddie turned and called to Robbie, "Mr. Quinn, I forgot to ask. Do you take cream and sugar?"

"Never," Robbie said. "That stuff pollutes the system and drains your strength."

Maddie said nothing as she arranged the cookie tray with her usual artistic flair. The icing colors, mostly shades of blue and green, blended to form a design that resembled an aerial view of lush countryside. Olivia carried the cookie tray over to Robbie and offered him first choice.

Robbie barely glanced at the tray. "Ladies first," he said. "Always."

Olivia felt a swift rush of shame and anger, which told her how Alicia must feel on a daily basis. With an effort, Olivia faked a smile and offered the tray to her mother. Ellie selected a teal blue and forest green cookie from the edge of the tray. Her signature smile, benign and faraway, seemed farther away and less benign than usual.

Maddie carried two cups over to a small table between the armchairs. She placed the pure, unadulterated black coffee near Robbie Quinn. With the faintest of grins, Maddie handed the evil milky-sugary stuff to Ellie.

Ellie sipped her coffee at once. "Delicious," she said. "Thank you, Maddie, dear. Everything you create is always so lovely and tasty. Such a gift . . ."

"Thanks, Ellie." Maddie said. "Livie, I'd better get back to the sales floor. Things have settled down considerably, but you never know. Take your time, though. Bertha and I can handle it." She flashed Olivia a look that said, *I expect you to tell me everything the moment this guy leaves.*

Once Maddie had disappeared, Olivia settled back onto the arm of her mother's chair. "Mr. Quinn, I—"

"I told you to call me Robbie." His tone gave the impression that he wouldn't tolerate any more disobedience.

"Okay then, Robbie," Olivia said. "I just wanted to say that I understand how hard it is to be a stepfather to teenagers. When I was an older teen my own father died. My brother was a few years younger. Although I was grown when Mom remarried, it was hard for me to accept someone else in my dad's place. Jason had an even harder time. Didn't he, Mom?"

With a slight nod, Ellie said, "Indeed he did. Poor Jason felt bereft without his father. When I married Allan, Jason was quite rebellious for a time. He wanted life to be as it had been before his father died."

"Kids," Robbie said with a derisive snort. "They don't know when they've got it good. They want everything handed to them. You know, Alicia's father was once a buddy of mine. We worked construction together right out of high school.

We'd go out for a beer now and then. I've got nothing against
the occasional beer, but Kenny, he started going to bars every
night, having three or four beers. He'd pour them down his
throat like they were water. I stopped hanging out with him
about that time." Robbie gulped down his coffee as if he were
demonstrating the speed at which Alicia's father had con-
sumed alcohol.

"May I refill your cup?" Olivia asked.

Robbie shook his head. "Can't stay," he said. "I only came
here to make it clear to everyone, especially you, that Alicia
is a troubled girl. Very troubled. She lives in that silly, empty
head of hers, where she thinks she's a poor, unloved child,
and everyone is treating her badly. She's always making things
up. You can't believe a word she says. I keep telling Crystal,
Alicia should be put away someplace where she can get treatment, but I'm not paying for that. She's nineteen. She's old
enough to be on her own."

To hide her discomfort, Olivia slid off her perch and
headed across the nook toward the coffee and cookies. While
she dawdled over the cookie tray, she heard her mother clear
her throat, a sound that still sent an automatic shiver down
Olivia's spine. When Ellie cleared her throat, it meant someone was about to be skewered. Olivia grabbed a cookie and
turned around to watch. Ellie sat on the wide arm of her chair,
her slender back ramrod straight. Even from across the nook,
Olivia could see her mother's flushed cheeks and narrowed
eyes. Olivia knew that look. It transported her back in time
to age thirteen, when she'd announced that she and a girlfriend planned to take the bus to Baltimore for an evening
rock concert. She had added defiantly that her mother couldn't
stop them. Of course, Ellie had quickly stopped them with
but a few well-chosen words and those flashing eyes. Olivia
had learned a lesson that day. When her mother's eyes narrow
and her cheeks flush, it is best to find cover at once.

Robbie stood when Ellie did, but he seemed oblivious to
her reaction to his criticism of Alicia. "Well, I've said what I

needed to," Robbie said. "I need to get back to work. My company is building a new house a few blocks north of the Chatterley Mansion. I stand to make a bundle on that job. Can't sit around all day sipping coffee and nibbling cookies." He handed his empty cup to Olivia, as if she were a servant.

"Before you leave, Mr. Quinn . . ." Ellie paused until she had Robbie's attention. Olivia held her breath.

"Yes?" Robbie checked his watch. When Ellie did not immediately respond, Robbie frowned at her.

Ellie's hazel eyes regarded Robbie's face with a steady, unblinking stare that made Olivia squirm. A steady, unblinking stare from her mother was even worse than narrowed eyes and flushed cheeks. Olivia realized she was holding her breath. She jump-started her lungs, telling herself that Ellie's wrath was not directed at her. However, this was likely to be a memorable moment.

"Mr. Quinn." Ellie paused a moment.

"I told you, call me Robbie."

"Mr. Quinn, when you married Crystal, you surely realized she had a daughter. You became a stepfather, responsible for a young girl's welfare and well-being. Alicia was vulnerable. Her beloved father had disappeared, and she missed him terribly. She felt lost and abandoned. You could have helped change all that."

With an impatient shake of his head, Robbie said, "Look, I'm sure you mean well—your type usually does—but you haven't a clue. Alicia was a lost cause the moment she was born. It's genetics, plain and simple. If Crystal had married me in the first place, our kid would be a go-getter. He'd be making us proud instead of moping around waiting for life to give him everything his heart desires."

Ellie opened her mouth to speak, but Robbie barreled ahead. "I came here to warn you, all of you"—he glanced across the room toward Olivia— "not to believe a word Alicia says. That girl lives in a dream world. She makes up nonsense and sheds those crocodile tears just to get everyone else to take care of her." Robbie fixed Olivia with a hard stare, as if she, too, were a troublesome teenager in need of firm control. "Make sure the sheriff understands that."

Before Ellie could respond, Robbie charged out of the cookbook nook toward the Gingerbread House entrance. After she heard the door slam, Olivia said, "For what it's worth, Mom, you sure impressed me. That man's blustering made me start to think about how to help Alicia. Assuming she didn't murder her father, that is . . ."

"Oh, I doubt she did, dear," Ellie said with a sigh. "Although one never knows, does one?"

Ellie's wan smile worried Olivia. "You look draggy, Mom. Are you feeling . . . you know, uncentered? Shall I call your yoga instructor for an emergency session?"

"That's sweet of you, dear. Ever so slightly denigrating, but still, I'm sure you meant well. I do have a yoga class in an hour, and I think I can survive until then." Ellie's smile warmed up a notch. "However, there is something you could do for me that would lift my spirits."

"Anything." Olivia hoped her mother wasn't about to request grandchildren in the near future.

"I could use a cookie."

Chapter Seven

❧

By eleven-thirty a.m., The Gingerbread House had settled down to its usual Tuesday afternoon slump. The few customers in the store had declared themselves to be "just looking," so Olivia slipped into the cookbook nook and settled into an armchair to give Del a quick call.

Del answered on the first ring. "Hey, for once you've got your cell phone."

"I'll have you know I've only forgotten it once this week," Olivia said.

"It's only Tuesday morning," Del said. "There's still plenty of time to break your all-time record. What is your all-time record?"

"I have no idea," Olivia said with what she hoped was a good-natured laugh. "So what's up? Any new forensic information about those bones?"

Del dropped his teasing tone as he said, "Very little, but the lab is really backed up, so all they've done is a quick review of my notes and photos. Any chance you can get away for a quick lunch? I haven't yet spent my entire paycheck, so it's my treat. How about the Chatterley Café?"

"That's an offer I can't refuse," Olivia said. "Tell me about the 'little' progress on the case."

"I thought we could cover that later," Del said.

"If it's little, what's wrong with now? Business is slow today, so this is a good time." Olivia glanced quickly at the time on her cell phone. "It's a whole half hour before my lunch break. I'm not a patient woman."

Del chuckled. "But if I tell you everything now, lunch with me might seem less tempting. Sometimes I wonder if you only let me stick around because I'm your best source of information about local crimes."

"Are you kidding?" Olivia hesitated, just a moment, before she added, "After all, you are *paying* for lunch . . . at the *Chatterley Café*. Besides, I have information for you that might even be more interesting than—"

Maddie peeked around the cookbook nook entrance. "Livie, our customer population is growing. Bertha took an early lunch to run an errand, and she won't be back until noon. Can you come help?"

Olivia nodded. "My public clamors, Del. Gotta go to work. I'll meet you at the Chatterley Café in half an hour. If I'm a bit late, you can order the most expensive item on the menu for me."

Olivia slid her cell phone into her pants pocket and followed Maddie into the store. She saw five customers on the floor. A sixth person was making a dramatic entrance, though Olivia doubted she was there to buy anything. Lenora Bouchenbein— stage name, Lenora Dove—rarely spent her own money, even on personal essentials. When she did, it was only because she couldn't con anyone else into subsidizing her. To be fair, Lenora had very little income of her own. After a short stint as a Hollywood starlet, Lenora had married the late Bernie Bouchenbein, who was, at the time, a well-known Hollywood producer. The couple managed to burn through the substantial number of pennies Bernie had earned over the course of a long career. Since Bernie's death, Lenora had subsisted on her husband's Social Security income, which wasn't nearly enough to support the lifestyle to which she felt entitled. So Lenora left Hollywood and deposited herself on the doorstep of her nephew, Herbie Tucker; his wife, Gwen; and their toddler son. The Tuckers, both veterinarians, owned an ever-expanding no-kill animal shelter. Chatterley Paws already housed dozens of homeless cats, dogs, horses, rabbits, and other strays, so Lenora fit right in.

Maddie shot Olivia a look that said, *Lenora is all yours.* With a silent sigh, Olivia accepted her assignment. She had no choice. Lenora was already heading in her direction.

"Livie, my dear." Lenora's bony arms flew out in a theatrical gesture that nearly decked a nearby customer. "Isn't it all simply too exciting for words?"

Olivia waited, certain that Lenora would find those words without difficulty.

"*Bones* in the wall." Lenora shivered with delight. "So thrilling! I feel as if I've entered a *Thin Man* movie. Myrna Loy is gone now, poor dear, so naturally I would be playing the role of Nora Charles." Lenora closed her eyes and wrapped her arms around her own thin chest.

Intuition and experience warned Olivia to jump in before Lenora could begin reciting dialogue from a *Thin Man* movie. "Lenora, how kind of you to drop by. Let's have a cookie and a cup of coffee, shall we?" Olivia grabbed Lenora by one sharp elbow and steered her toward the treats table.

Lenora's eyes widened. "Oh, I really shouldn't," she said. "I must watch my figure for the sake of my acting career."

"But you mustn't become too thin," Olivia said as she piled three cookies on a plate and handed it to Lenora. "It's important to have a *feminine* figure. I'm sure Myrna would agree with me."

Lenora accepted the plate of cookies. "Myrna did have a lovely figure," she said, "though she was, of course, bigger boned than I, so she could afford to eat more heartily. Which reminds me, Livie, perhaps you and I ought to have a little chat about this topic with Maddie, don't you think?"

"With Maddie?" Olivia's cookie hand halted on its way to her mouth. "I don't understand."

"Oh, surely you've noticed," Lenora said. "Doesn't Maddie's outfit seem rather tight today? I'm afraid she has been putting on weight since her marriage. Marriage can be so damaging to the figure. I escaped only because I was blessed with such a tiny appetite."

Olivia bit into her cookie to give herself time to think. She glanced across the sales floor at Maddie, who looked stunning in wool pants the color of raspberry-tinged chocolate, a thin matching sweater, and an emerald green scarf that reflected the color of her eyes. The outfit gently hugged her curvy body. Earlier that morning, several men, curious about the discovery of bones in an old flophouse, had accompanied their wives or girlfriends to The Gingerbread House. Olivia had noticed at least one of those men following Maddie with his eyes.

"Oh well," Lenora said, "Maddie is lucky. She isn't an actress, so she doesn't have to worry about looking plump in publicity photos. The acting life is terribly demanding, you know." Lenora heaved a sigh as she finished off her third cookie. "Yet the theater is so essential to the development of true culture, as I'm sure you agree. And that, my dear, is why we must talk."

"Talk?" Olivia found herself scanning the store for escape routes. "Well, I do have to work, but perhaps later . . ."

"We'll have a private little chat," Lenora said as she swept the last cookie crumbs from the treats plate and popped them into her mouth. "This needs refilling, anyway." She picked up the plate and marched into the kitchen.

Olivia checked the time on her cell phone. She had about twenty minutes before she needed to leave for the Chatterley Café to meet Del for lunch. The Gingerbread House was nearly empty. Olivia waved across the sales floor to Maddie, who had just finished helping a customer.

Maddie nodded and joined Olivia at the treats table. "I assume you're volunteering to replenish the cookie supply," Maddie said. "Or was Lenora so desperate for more free food that she decided to do it herself?"

"Lenora has something on her mind," Olivia said. "She ordered me to follow her into the kitchen."

"Scary."

"I'm thinking of escaping while I can." Olivia glanced around the sales floor. "Our last customer is heading for the door . . . Maybe I could—" She cringed as she heard the kitchen door swish behind her.

"Livie, my dear, I'm waiting," Lenora said.

"I'll mind the store." Maddie smiled as she patted Olivia's shoulder.

"Lucky you. Promise you'll come get me in fifteen minutes," Olivia whispered, "or I swear I'll—"

"I won't let you miss lunch with Del," Maddie said. "Now grit your teeth and go."

Olivia opened the kitchen door to find Lenora teetering on a chair as she reached across the top of the refrigerator for a covered cake pan filled with cookies. As she lifted the pan, Lenora twisted her head toward the kitchen door and began to wobble. Olivia rushed over to steady her, saving the pan as it slipped from Lenora's hand.

"You were taking such a long time," Lenora said with a petulant frown. "I decided to prepare refreshments for our chat.

"Let me help you down." Olivia cupped Lenora's elbow to steady her.

"Oh dear," Lenora said, "I do wish a strong, kind man were here to assist me." As Lenora stumbled her way down, Olivia caught a whiff of alcohol on her breath. She remembered at once that Maddie, in a burst of creative enthusiasm, had added sherry to some drop cookies they'd baked for a recent special event. They had stored the opened sherry bottle on top of the refrigerator, toward the back, and forgotten about it. As everyone in Chatterley Heights had learned by now, Lenora was a bit too fond of wine.

"I'll make us some fresh coffee," Olivia said. "Meanwhile, help yourself to a cookie."

"Oh, I really shouldn't." Lenora opened the cake pan and selected two cookies. "Now, Livie, while you prepare the coffee, I will explain the plan to you."

The plan? Olivia braced herself.

"I'm afraid we must take your mother in hand, Livie," Lenora said.

My mother? The epitome of empathy, competence, and tranquility? Olivia filled Mr. Coffee's basket with fresh ground coffee.

"Ellie is a dear, of course," Lenora said, "but I'm afraid she lacks an expansive vision. Her little plans for a craft school are so . . . well, little. It isn't her fault, poor thing. She has lived too long in a small town. The imagination becomes stilted in such a limiting environment. I've offered to help her think on a grander scale, but she doesn't seem to grasp my meaning. So sad."

Olivia clamped her mouth shut as she carried two cups of coffee to the kitchen table. She placed the cream and sugar next to Lenora's cup.

"Thank you, Livie, my dear. Of course, I use only the merest hint of cream and sugar," Lenora murmured as she added a heaping teaspoon of sugar to her cup, followed by a generous dollop of cream. "I am so tiny, I must be careful to keep my calories to a minimum."

Olivia eyed the kitchen clock, wishing time would move faster. "You mentioned a plan, Lenora? Does it concern the craft school?"

Lenora arched her thin, penciled eyebrows. "Really, Livie, I thought you would understand. We simply must stop calling it an arts and *crafts* school. I've settled on a more descriptive and elegant name. I will call it The Chatterley Heights

Academy for the Arts. Naturally, the school will showcase the highest and most essential of the arts—which is, of course, acting. The *theater*. The entire ground floor of the building will be devoted to a state-of-the-art theater, one that will attract the greatest performing talents in the nation, perhaps even the world. I know many of them personally, so I will have no trouble enticing them to come here to perform."

Once again, Olivia checked the clock. She still had time to knock some sense into Lenora. "The arts and *crafts* school is my mother's dream," Olivia said. "We, by which I mean *all* of us, must understand and respect that."

"Of course I understand, Livie. You feel loyal to your mother. But really, it's such a *little* dream."

Olivia gulped her coffee and swallowed her anger. "Lenora, what you need to grasp is that my mother is in full charge of the project. Calliope is fronting the entire cost of renovating the building and is paying the workers from her own private funds. Mom and Calliope are a team. I'm afraid you and I don't really have a say in how the building will be used. Neither of us can offer anything of substantive value to the project."

With a light laugh, Lenora touched Olivia's arm. "Dear Livie, of course we can offer something of value, enormous value. Or rather, *I* can, although you and Maddie have certainly provided . . . well, kitchen help. And lovely cookies, of course. Now, Livie, you haven't yet heard the best part of my plan. As a well-known star of stage and screen, I am able to attract the most talented actors to Chatterley Heights. Audiences will flock to our little town, and the proceeds will quickly pay for the building and the renovation, so no one will feel beholden to Calliope. You must admit that woman is rather odd." Lenora took a delicate sip of coffee, and said, "I've already begun the process by writing a play."

Olivia couldn't help herself. "You've written a whole play?"

"Well, I sketched it out," Lenora said with a dismissive wave of her hand. "I felt inspired. The discovery of those bones gave me the brilliant idea of basing my play on our very own

Chatterley Heights mystery. There really isn't much to writing a play, anyway. It's the actors who truly bring life to a story." With a graceful flick of one bony finger, Lenora brushed a cookie crumb from her arm. "Don't you see, Livie? Those bones may have historical significance. People will be so curious about them. I've come up with a scintillating title—*The Bones in the Wall*. Doesn't that send a chill down your spine? My play will become known far and wide. It will make our little town the talk of Hollywood."

Lenora, Olivia thought, must have listened in as scores of eager writers pitched ideas to Bernie Bouchenbein, her deceased husband.

Lenora sighed happily. "I'm so certain my play will be a worldwide success that I've put out feelers for investors. Several have already responded."

Olivia noticed she did not mention whether those potential investors, once they'd heard more about the project, had expressed genuine interest.

Lenora clasped her hands together like an overexcited child. "Just think of the eager crowds—"

The kitchen door opened, and Maddie's cheerful face appeared. "Time for you to take off for that appointment, Livie. Bertha is back, so we're covered here."

Olivia nearly knocked over a chair in her eagerness to escape Lenora's persistently delusional presence. At the same time, she knew that Lenora wasn't about to give up. Maybe her mother could be more persuasive. If that failed, there was always Calliope. "Thanks, Maddie," Olivia said. "Sorry, Lenora, gotta run."

"Oh, but we have so much planning to do," Lenora said. "Can't your little errand wait?"

Olivia didn't trust herself to respond without snarling, so she said nothing and left the kitchen with Maddie. They walked in silence across the sales floor to the Gingerbread House door. "I sense all is not tranquil," Maddie said as she followed Olivia into the foyer. "What is Lenora up to this time?

You'd better tell me," Maddie said. "I intend to encourage her to vacate the premises, and I might say the wrong thing."

Olivia paused with her hand on the doorknob, in case a customer might be outside on the porch. "Lenora wants to take over the arts and crafts school and turn it into a theater. She is writing a play, or she thinks she is. The title includes the words 'bones in the wall.'"

"Catchy," Maddie said.

Olivia rolled her eyes. "Lenora, bless her greedy, self-obsessed little heart, has already put out feelers to potential investors for this future fiasco. She thinks she can pull in enough money to buy the school building right out from under my mom."

"Wow, that sounds . . . disastrous." Maddie leaned against the foyer wall. "On so many levels . . . including the one where Ellie finally loses her centered self and kickboxes Lenora through a window."

"No kidding. I don't want to be around if Lenora goes ahead with this plan and Mom finds out about it. Oh, and FYI, Lenora discovered that opened bottle of sherry we left on top of the fridge."

"Thanks for the warning." Maddie opened the unlocked front door and pushed Olivia toward the porch. "Go have lunch with Del and do your best sleuthing to find out whatever he knows about those bones. I'll tell your mom about Lenora's grandiose plans. Ellie and I will hatch a strategy for quelling Lenora, even if it requires locking her in the attic with the rest of the bats."

Olivia imagined Lenora hanging upside down from a rafter, which made her feel better.

O livia arrived at Del's favorite booth near the back of the Chatterley Café. She slid onto the seat across from him, leaving her cell phone on the table in case Maddie or her mom called.

Del looked up from his menu. "You're only five minutes late! And look, you remembered your cell phone. Who are you, and what have you done with Olivia?"

"Not very original," Olivia said, "but nice delivery. I'd try for a punchier insult, but you're buying lunch."

Del gave her a lopsided grin as he leaned across the table for a quick kiss. Olivia gave up her plans for retaliation. Almost. She scanned the menu, and said, "How about that, the special today is lobster." Olivia peered at Del over the top of her menu. "You did say you just got paid, right?"

"I was thinking of paying the electric bill this month, but I'm sure they will understand." Del slapped his menu shut and drooped against the back of his seat. "And I suppose it wouldn't hurt me to skip a few meals. I could space them out during the month . . . you know, to avoid passing out from hunger while I'm chasing a mugger."

Olivia rolled her eyes. "What I go through for a free lunch." She pushed her menu aside. "You lucked out this time. I have a hankering for tuna salad, even though it's the cheapest item on the menu." Olivia glanced around and lowered her voice. "For my selflessness, I think I deserve to hear what you've learned so far about those bones we found yesterday. I promise not to share your information with Lenora, lest she fictionalize it for personal fame and profit."

"What has Lenora done now? Never mind," Del said as their waitress, a petite redhead named Peg, materialized at their booth.

"Hey, Sheriff." Peg grinned at Olivia. "Hey, Livie. Are you going for the lobster today? It's great, well worth the exorbitant price tag."

"Regretfully, no," Olivia said. "Del is footing the bill. I'll have the tuna salad."

"Ah." Peg winked at her. "Going easy on him, huh? Well, there's always next time."

"Tuna for me, too," Del said. "And two coffees."

Peg nodded. "With lots of cream and sugar. Found out

anything about those old bones yet, Sheriff? I'm hoping they belong to a certain former boyfriend of mine who walked out on me a couple months ago."

Del shook his head. "Sorry, Peg, a couple months ago would be too recent. It takes longer than that for a body to skeletonize."

"Oh well, a girl can dream." Peg shrugged one shapely shoulder and left.

"You aren't usually so free with information about a case," Olivia said. "Normally you ask a lot more questions than you answer."

Del shrugged. "Right now I don't have much information to pass on. Besides, mentioning the skeletonization process usually discourages further questioning . . . except from you or Maddie, of course."

Peg returned with two mugs, a pot of steaming coffee, and a pitcher of cream. "Sugar is on the table, as always. Holler if you use it all up." She hurried to another table.

Olivia stirred two spoonfuls of sugar into her coffee. "I'd better warn you up front about Lenora's newest delusion, her most grandiose to date. She has devised a maniacal scheme to turn the discovery of those sad bones into a play. She thinks it will bring fame and fortune to Chatterley Heights and, especially, to herself."

"That's scary." Del tasted his coffee and added more cream. "I'm guessing Lenora is all hype and no productive work."

"Hard to say." Olivia added a bit more sugar to her cup. "Lenora claims to have 'sketched out' the play already. She has already contacted potential backers, and now she plans to send out feelers to her Hollywood friends . . . assuming they are still alive and remember her name. Anyway, I have done my duty by warning you."

"For which I thank you," Del said. "I'll try to carve out time for a little talk with Lenora about the dangers of interfering with an ongoing police investigation."

"Good luck with that," Olivia said. "Now about that ongoing investigation, have you found out anything interesting?"

Del smiled and said nothing.

"There's still time for me to cancel the tuna salad and order lobster," Olivia said. "And I might enjoy it so much that I'll forget to tell you what I've learned so far about potential suspects."

"We police take a dim view of withholding evidence."

"Okay, put away the rubber hose. I'll talk." Olivia drained her coffee cup. "This morning, Robbie Quinn visited The Gingerbread House and issued a forceful warning not to believe a word Alicia said about anything. Robbie clearly dislikes and resents Alicia."

Peg appeared at their table to refill their cups. "Tuna salad has been in great demand, but it shouldn't be too much longer." She smiled and left.

"Where was I?" Olivia asked. "Oh yeah, Robbie went out of his way to convince us—Mom was there, too—that Alicia isn't pulling her weight in the household. Robbie threatened to throw her out if she didn't start paying room and board. Alicia may not be in a position to . . . Wait a minute." Olivia grabbed her cell phone off the table. "Things have been so hectic, I totally forgot that Alicia left a message on my cell. I didn't even tell Mom." Olivia found the message and handed her phone to Del. "Here, listen to this."

Del frowned as he listened to Alicia's tearful plea to come and stay with Olivia. "Sounds like Robbie has already made up his mind to throw her out," Del said as he returned Olivia's cell phone. "That's a nasty thing to do to a kid who just lost her job, but I'm not too surprised. Robbie always struck me as a self-righteous jerk."

Olivia frowned at the phone resting in the palm of her hand. "There's something odd about the timing, though. I know I'm right about this, although I suppose there might be an explanation."

"Livie, fill in the blanks, okay? What are you right about?" Del asked.

"Sorry, Del. Alicia left this message for me *before* the store opened this morning. I know because I listened to it as I was coming down the stairs to help Maddie open. That was well before Robbie came to the store, which means that by the time he talked to us, he had already decided Alicia had to go. Yet when he spoke with Mom and me, he made it sound like he hadn't quite made his decision."

Del shrugged. "Robbie probably didn't know Alicia had called you. He didn't want to look like the bad guy."

Peg appeared at their booth bearing a large basket filled to overflowing with a variety of fresh rolls and breadsticks. "Compliments of the chef," she said as she deposited the basket on the table. "I guess the price for the lobster scared our customers. We had a major run on tuna salad, so the chef is making a fresh batch. He didn't want anyone to starve to death in the meantime." She scurried off to another table.

"Something tells me Peg is tired of complaints about the slow service today," Del said. "But back to Alicia. I suppose it's possible she was exaggerating her situation in order to gain your sympathy."

Olivia nodded in silence. She remembered how upset Alicia had sounded in her phone message. On the other hand, she did seem prone to tearful outbursts. Well, time would tell. "I've done my duty by telling you about Robbie's visit," Olivia said. "Now tell me how your investigation is going. I promise to keep it to myself."

"Sure you do," Del said. "Well, this is still a coldish case, so I guess I can share. I showed Alicia Vayle my photo of the cookie cutter necklace found with the bones, and she swore it was the same one she'd given her father. She sounded certain, but Alicia struck me as possibly too emotional to think straight."

"I might be able to help with that issue. First of all, Maddie and I found a photo online of Alicia with her father. Kenny was wearing what looked to us like a shiny silver necklace. And second . . ." Olivia relayed the information Dolly had revealed to her about selling a handmade cookie cutter necklace to a young girl. "Dolly drew a picture of the girl, and it sure looked like a younger Alicia to me."

"I'll need that drawing," Del said. "And I want to talk to this Dolly Fitzpatrick. I've never heard of her."

"She's newly back after some years away from this area," Olivia said. "I should warn you that Dolly is gorgeous, but her heart belongs to my brother. Don't ask me to explain it. Jason hasn't caught on yet, although he seems to enjoy her company while he is working on that old Ford Fairlane of his. I advised Dolly to take it slow with him. Between you and me, I'm afraid she might lose interest in him."

"Why? Is she one of those arrogant princess types?" Del selected a soft garlic breadstick and bit into it.

"Not at all," Olivia said. "Dolly is sweet and genuine and perfect for Jason, who probably doesn't deserve her, but he will be nice to her, in his own way. I'm already picking out my bridesmaid's gown. However, Jason can be slow and dense, plus it hasn't been all that long since he broke up with his last—and only—long term girlfriend." Olivia selected a crescent shaped roll and bit off the tip. "Cheddar cheese . . . yum," she said. "The Chatterley Café makes the best rolls on earth. Anyway, Dolly has a remarkable memory for faces, and she draws quite well."

Del gave her a puzzled look. "And Dolly is perfect for Jason because . . . ?"

"Because she likes him. And because she loves to work with metal."

"Ah," Del said.

"Your turn," Olivia said. "Have you heard from the crime lab?"

"I wish our crime lab worked as fast as the ones on television, but no such luck," Del said. "A cold case takes even longer. As far as I know, they haven't done anything besides glance at my photos. They are working overtime on higher priority cases. I'll let you know when construction on the school can begin again."

"Calliope is working on Jason's house while she waits for the boarding house to be available," Olivia said. "Mom, however, will be impossible to live with."

Del tore the last breadstick in half and handed one piece to Olivia. "I did have a chat with Crystal Quinn," he said. "I wondered if she would repeat any of what she'd told you, but she was more guarded with me. She certainly never mentioned that Alicia wanted to implicate her in Kenny Vayle's death. All she said about her daughter was that she was going through a rebellious period. I sensed Crystal wasn't a happy woman, but she refused to complain about her husband."

"Crystal knows which side her cookie is decorated on." Olivia was glad to see Del smile at her new twist on an old cliché. When he ran his hand through his sandy hair, she noticed it needed a trim. Del looked tired to her. With his deputy out of town, he was handling everything from traffic accidents to murders. "When I talked to Crystal, she seemed angry and a bit scared," Olivia said.

"I certainly picked up on Crystal's anger," Del said, "although she seemed as if she were trying not to give anything away. Living with Robbie Quinn can't be easy."

Peg reappeared bearing two generous plates of tuna salad with chunks of fresh bread. "Here it is, finally," she said before hustling off toward a customer who was signaling impatiently.

Olivia scooped out a spoonful of tuna salad. "This looks scrumptious." The spoon was halfway to her mouth when her cell phone, which she'd left on the table, began to vibrate. "Rats." Olivia glanced at the caller ID and answered. "Hi, Mom, what's up?"

"The complexity of life," Ellie said.

"Are you saying that something has happened to complicate your life?"

"Doesn't it always?" Ellie asked.

"Could you elaborate on that while I take my first bite of tuna salad?"

"That sounds utterly delicious," Ellie said. "By all means, eat. I'm alone in the Gingerbread House kitchen. I'm sure I can unearth a cookie for lunch." Olivia heard a scraping sound. "Ah yes," Ellie said, "here they are, a whole cake pan nearly full of cookies." The line went silent for a short time. "Much better," Ellie said. "Livie, did you know you have an empty sherry bottle on top of your refrigerator?"

"Oops. I'm afraid it doesn't surprise me," Olivia said. "Lenora was alone in the kitchen for a while. Twice, in fact," she added, remembering that Maddie had walked her to the door as she was leaving for lunch.

"Oh dear," Ellie said. "I wonder where Lenora is now."

"She isn't still in the store?"

"I'll look around in a bit," Ellie said. "Bertha let me in through the alley door."

"Why did you call me, Mom?"

"A moment, please." Ellie sounded as if she had a mouth full of cookie. "I came here looking for you. Livie, do you remember getting a frantic call from Alicia Vayle?"

"Yes, I'd forgotten all about that," Olivia said. "It was a message on my cell. It was so busy in the store, I didn't remember to call her back."

"You forgot about a desperate cry for help?" Ellie asked.

"I forgot about it, okay? Life gets complex, like you said." Olivia rolled her eyes, and Del smirked.

"Well, let me remind you, then," Ellie mumbled. "Sorry, my mouth was full. Alicia's family, specifically her stepfather, the lovely man we met today, ordered her to pack her bags and find somewhere else to live, and to make it snappy. Poor Alicia lost her job at Pete's, so she has no money to pay for so much as a room. When you didn't respond to her urgent phone message, she left home with no place to go. She was dragging a suitcase over to The Gingerbread House when I intercepted her."

Olivia sank against the padded back of her seat. "Mom, you know how tiny my apartment is. I only have one bedroom. I mean, I'd love to be able to talk with Alicia about . . . you know, the bones, her father, and so on. But have her stay with me? Where would I put her, on my living room sofa? I don't suppose you and Allan could . . . ?"

"I'm way ahead of you, Livie. I called Allan right away. He dusted your old room and put fresh sheets on the bed, while I helped Alicia transport her worldly possessions to our house. She can stay with us as long as necessary. I'm looking forward to having a young person around the house again, at least for a while."

"Mom, I'm over there all the time, and I'm not exactly a senior citizen yet," Olivia said.

"Of course not, dear. Neither am I. But you know what I mean." A crunching sound traveled across the connection. "Livie, the lemon cookies are so good I can't stop myself from taking just one more. Luckily, I ran three miles this morning."

"I hate you," Olivia said without rancor.

"Yes, dear, I know." There was a smile in Ellie's voice. "I must go soon. Alicia should be settled in at home, and she will be hungry. I'm so glad she brought some belongings with her, so she needn't face that bully of a stepfather again for a while. Before I leave, I'll just check in with Bertha and Maddie, who are minding the sales floor. Oh, and Livie, I have an idea I think you'll like. Why don't you come to dinner this evening? I'll invite Maddie and Lucas, too. You see, I have a tiny scheme."

"Is that like a plan, only smaller?" Olivia asked.

"Exactly, dear. I want to create a warm, safe, family atmosphere for poor Alicia."

"And the scheming part would be . . . ?" Olivia raised her eyebrows at Del, who was listening intently as he worked his way through his tuna salad.

"Isn't it obvious?" Ellie asked. "I'm hoping Alicia will feel relaxed enough to talk openly and honestly about her father. It would be so therapeutic for her, don't you think?"

"Therapeutic," Olivia said with a quick glance at Del. "Yes, I agree completely. Very thoughtful of you, Mom. Can I bring anything?"

"These cookies are remarkably good," Ellie said. "I'd ask you to bring Del, too, but I'm afraid his presence might make Alicia feel threatened."

Olivia chuckled. "He'll survive the rejection. And I think we can rustle up more cookies. Maddie keeps churning them out so we'll always have plenty on hand for last-minute crises. Assuming you haven't cleaned us out, that is."

"I've put the pan back on top of the fridge, Livie. And now I need to go for another run, or I'll never shed that extra pound. Bye!" The phone went dead.

"How's your mom?" Del asked. "And were you discussing what to do with Alicia Vayle?"

"Mom has ballooned up to one hundred pounds, and yes." Olivia stuffed a forkful of tuna salad into her mouth. She had some catching up to do. Del had almost finished his meal.

"So I'm guessing Ellie and Allan have invited Alicia to stay with them, right? Which means you, Maddie, and the rest of your family intend to pump her for information about her family. Honestly, Livie, sometimes I wonder why Chatterley Heights even bothers with a sheriff."

Olivia took another substantial bite of tuna salad.

"I guess I should feel relieved," Del said as he opened his wallet. "If you are spending the evening with your family, at least you should be reasonably safe from harm for a while."

Olivia grinned. "I love you, too," she said, although a mouthful of tuna salad rather spoiled her delivery.

Chapter Eight

❧

After lunch with Del, Olivia returned to The Gingerbread House feeling energized and ready to tackle whatever the
afternoon might toss at her. Or so she thought. She hadn't
expected to find a small group of customers clustered near the
opening to the cookbook nook, whispering and giggling as they
peered inside. Maddie and Bertha were supposed to be minding
the store, but Olivia didn't see them on the sales floor. Even
Spunky had abandoned his favorite chair in front of the window,
where he normally accepted ear rubs and secret treats from
customers.

Olivia joined the enthralled group at the cookbook nook
entrance. At five foot seven, she could peek into the nook
over the shoulders of other curious onlookers, all of whom
were women. Olivia couldn't see much at first. The lighting
in the cookbook nook was normally kept fairly low to create
a cozy ambience. A floor lamp stood between two roomy
armchairs. Usually, the lamp was left lit for customers who
wished to relax and peruse a cookbook. Now the lamp was

switched off and pushed away from the chairs. Olivia soon realized why . . . to keep it from toppling.

It took Olivia several moments to process the full tableau. Her mother stood—balanced, as always—on the seat of one armchair, while Bertha, who was taller and heftier, stood on the floor next to her. Maddie wobbled on the seat of the second chair. All three women faced the wall, their arms reaching up toward the narrow ledge behind the chairs. Olivia's heart did a flip as she saw a petite figure, partially hidden in shadow, teetering close to the edge. For a moment, the light caught the unmistakable features of Lenora Bouchenbein. With a sinking feeling in her stomach, Olivia realized the elderly woman was tipsy.

Olivia reminded herself that the ledge was actually the top of a sturdy knee wall. Olivia had added it to the room for display purposes, rather than structural support. However, she knew it was stable and wide enough to support Lenora's small frame. Unfortunately, the ledge was halfway up the wall, and Lenora seemed unaware that she might easily lose her balance and fall. She waved with both arms, as if she were facing a large, enthusiastic audience.

Olivia snaked through the onlookers until she reached Ellie's chair. "Let me take your spot, Mom," she said. "I'm taller."

"Gladly, dear." Ellie hopped off the armchair. "There was quite a bit of sherry left in that bottle, wasn't there?"

"Yep," Olivia said. "It was nearly full." She stepped up onto the chair's soft seat and stabilized herself as best she could by wedging her legs against its wide arms. As she reached up, Lenora threw out her arms as if she were about to take a bow. She closed her eyes, bowed her head, and began to fall forward.

"Lenora." Olivia tried to imitate her mother's 'don't argue with me' tone, which she remembered so well from childhood. "Lenora, open your eyes and focus on my face."

"Who is it?" Lenora sounded frightened. She opened her eyes and flailed her arms, like a tiny bird caught in a crosswind. "Oh! The stage is too bright," she cried. "The light . . . it's blinding me."

"There's nothing to worry about, Lenora," Olivia said. "It's me, Livie. I'll help you get away from the light." She couldn't quite reach Lenora's waist, so she gripped the frail woman's bony hips. "I'm going to help you down off the stage. Don't worry, I'm holding on to you. I'll catch you if you slip." Olivia fervently hoped that was true.

"But I haven't finished my speech," Lenora wailed. "It's the dramatic high point of the story." She veered to the right, as if she were heading for a new spot on the stage.

"You can finish later, dear." Ellie scrambled onto the arm of the chair, in case Lenora fell sideways. "After the light has been adjusted, you can pick up where you left off."

"The light, too bright." Lenora sounded like a frustrated child. "I have to *test* it, you see. It's about verishim . . . verishiml . . ."

"Verisimilitude?" Ellie put a supporting arm around Lenora's waist. "I understand perfectly, dear. It's quite true that a scene must seem real to the audience."

Lenora nodded once and went limp, slipping from Olivia's grasp. Ellie staggered as Lenora's dead weight fell against her. Olivia quickly grabbed Lenora by the waist and, with Ellie's help, lowered the limp woman down to a chair, then to the floor. Olivia and Maddie slung Lenora's arms around their shoulders and carried her toward the Gingerbread House kitchen. Olivia was aware they had provided what Lenora longed for—an avid audience. Olivia glanced back at Bertha, who nodded as if to say *I'll handle things out here.* As Ellie opened the kitchen door, Olivia and Maddie dragged Lenora inside and lowered her on to a chair. Gently, Olivia placed Lenora's head on the kitchen worktable.

"Should I call 911?" Ellie asked.

"I think not," Maddie said.

"But she's unconscious." Ellie reached for the kitchen phone.

Exchanging a glance with Maddie, Olivia said, "While we were carting Lenora to the kitchen, we distinctly heard her snore."

As if on cue, Lenora lifted her head and opened her eyes. "The show," she said, "muth go on."

"Yes, Lenora, dear," Ellie said. "You carried on despite everything."

Olivia noted that while Lenora's pale blue eyes might be open, they weren't focusing well. Lenora reached toward a cooling rack on the table and tried to grab a cookie. Instead, she picked up an empty saucer. Olivia took it from her as she tried to take a bite out of it.

"You are too thin, Lenora," Ellie said as she put a cookie in Lenora's outstretched hand. "You don't eat enough to keep a bird alive."

Olivia squelched a giggle as she recalled her ornithologist father telling her that some birds eat five times their own weight every day. Much like a bird, however, Lenora stayed slender despite her habit of stealing food off any plate within snatching distance. Olivia was jealous of her metabolism, if that explained her thinness.

Ellie sidled up to Olivia and whispered, "I've seen Lenora down numerous glasses of wine without a problem. If she drained the better part of a bottle of sherry into an empty stomach, no wonder she was so affected. This is quite worrisome."

Maddie poured a cup of coffee and brought it to Lenora, who had finished her cookie. As Maddie wrapped Lenora's hands around the mug, she winked toward Olivia and Ellie. "Have a drink, Lenora," Maddie said. "It will make you feel better." Lenora smiled happily as Maddie guided the mug to her mouth. She drank obediently, then accepted another cookie.

Ellie pulled Olivia aside, and said, "I ran into Gwen at the grocery this morning. She was stocking up on cat food. She mentioned to me how excited Lenora was about the . . .

you know, about the discovery yesterday. Anyway, Gwen said that Lenora stayed up most of the night, pacing and talking to herself about the bones in the wall, as if she were acting in a play."

"She thinks she is writing one," Olivia said.

"Oh dear. Perhaps she became so absorbed in her creative work that she simply forgot to eat."

"If you say so, Mom." Olivia could not imagine forgetting to eat.

Maddie joined them. "This is all my fault, Livie," she said. "After you left to have lunch with Del, I let Lenora stay in the kitchen by herself. She insisted she needed to work on her play, and I didn't see the harm. The sherry bottle had already slipped my mind. After a time, Lenora showed up in the cookbook nook. She said she needed to 'sit in the twilight and create.' A group of women from the Twiterton Cookie Cutter Collectors Club had just arrived by van, so Bertha and I were distracted, and, well . . . The next thing we knew, Lenora was standing on that ledge in the cookbook nook, reciting something that I might have recognized as dialogue if I were fluent in gibberish. I guess Lenora thought the women from the Cookie Cutter Collectors Club had come to watch her perform."

"Maddie, you couldn't have known," Olivia said. "We're too busy to police Lenora. I'd have forgotten about the sherry, too, even though Mom had reminded me about it. However, we will never again leave alcohol in the store kitchen. At least Lenora wasn't injured, so no permanent harm was done."

With a troubled glance toward Lenora, Ellie said, "I'm not so sure, Livie." Her hazel eyes seemed to darken as a row of worry wrinkles gathered between her eyebrows. "You see, Binnie was here."

Olivia felt her stomach begin to churn. She and Maddie exchanged troubled glances. "Oh great, that's just what we need now," Olivia said. "Binnie Sloan and her wretched little recorder."

"I wish it had been a recorder, Livie," Ellie said. "With her niece-photographer out of town, Binnie broke down and got herself a smartphone."

"So Binnie has photos. That is troubling." Olivia glanced over at Lenora, who had fallen asleep face down on her crossed arms. "At least Binnie wasn't around for the grand finale."

Ellie began to braid a lock of her long, gray hair.

"What is it, Mom?" Olivia asked. "You're doing that nervous thing again."

"Oh, am I?" Ellie tossed the partial braid over her shoulder. "I was just remembering . . . I'm afraid Binnie's timing was rather unfortunate. Before you arrived, Livie, Lenora tried to fly off that ledge. I think she believed she was playing the role of Peter Pan. In Lenora's version, though, Peter Pan had come back to life after being trapped inside a wall for decades."

"Really? So she'd already fallen once before I came along? I'm amazed she managed to climb back up there." Olivia glanced at Maddie. "Or did you catch her?"

Maddie shook her head. "Believe it or not, Lenora managed to right herself by waving her arms madly. I grabbed her ankles, and Bertha tried to steady her. I don't know if Binnie caught that maneuver on her smartphone, too. She seemed in a hurry to make an exit."

"We are doomed," Olivia said.

Maddie patted Olivia's shoulder. "Now, Livie, perhaps it will all work out for the best. When Lenora sees herself acting crazy, maybe she'll be so shocked she'll lay off the booze for a while. Or is that just me being unrealistically hopeful again?"

"I'm afraid it's worse than that," Olivia said. "Once those photos hit Binnie's infernal blog, which should be any minute now, everyone within a wider radius than Chatterley Heights will know that Lenora is writing a play about those bones.

What if there's someone out there who thinks he or she got away with murder, and now this elderly actress is determined to dredge up the mystery by turning it into a play?"

"I wouldn't worry about that," Maddie said. "Lenora isn't a very good sleuth. She'll just make up some wild, improbable fantasy."

"*We* think that," Olivia said, "but what about someone with a very guilty conscience . . . or no conscience at all?"

Chapter Nine

After Lenora's dramatic afternoon performance in the cookbook nook, the rest of the workday felt anti-climactic to Olivia. As closing time approached, The Gingerbread House felt more like a cookie cutter mausoleum than a thriving business. Maddie had slipped out to buy more baking supplies, and Olivia had sent Bertha home early. She began to wonder if her customers dropped by only when they anticipated entertainment . . . and Maddie's cookies, of course. Would anyone notice if the store closed early? Probably. Knowing Chatterley Heights, an early closing would trigger rumors that business wasn't going well, or that she and Maddie were losing interest in cookie cutters. Like that would ever happen.

Olivia began rescuing errant cutters that customers had plucked from their displays and then abandoned far from home. She came to the grouping of classic cutters and realized the heart shape was missing. She remembered watching Dolly pick it up, probably because it reminded her of the tiny pierced heart cutter charm she'd made for Alicia. Olivia found the wandering heart on a nearby ledge. She held the cutter in her palm and thought about the necklace Alicia had given her father. If those bones once belonged to Kenny Vayle, then he had died wearing his daughter's gift. But if he had thrown the necklace into the wall to make it look as if he were dead, then he wasn't worth his daughter's adoration.

Who was Kenny Vayle? What had he really been like? It seemed he was either loved or despised. Other than that, Olivia hadn't learned much about him. Del would be investigating to some extent, of course, but he'd wait for word from the crime lab before committing too much of his time to the case. If there was a case . . . For all Olivia knew, those bones had belonged to an itinerant vagrant. Perhaps someone stuffed him into the wall simply to avoid trouble. Yet that didn't explain the cookie cutter necklace found with the remains.

Olivia's cell phone vibrated. She answered with a cheerful, "Hey, Maddie. Still shopping? There's nothing to do here, so you might as well head home. I'll be closing the store in about five minutes."

"So did you hear the news?" Maddie asked.

"Are we talking local or national?" Olivia returned the heart to its display and checked for other orphaned cutters.

"Local, of course. Is there any other? Wait, hang on, I have to pay for the groceries." A few moments later, Maddie said, "I still love debit cards, even though I get up in the middle of the night to check my bank account."

"You're up in the middle of the night, anyway." Olivia locked the Gingerbread House door from the inside. "Again I ask, what news?"

"Alicia's boyfriend, Kurt, got arrested," Maddie said. "I heard it from one of the clerks at the grocery store. She and I lived next door to each other before my folks died. Anyway, it turns out Kurt is a lot older than Alicia. He's got a record, mostly for breaking into cars when he was younger. Now he spends his time online. And he definitely has anger issues."

"What has he been charged with?" Olivia closed the

curtains and dimmed the store lights, which was her signal to Spunky that it was time to head up to their apartment. Spunky stretched, hopped down from his chair, and ambled toward the store's front door.

"One could argue that he was arrested for extreme stupidity," Maddie said. "The kid took a swing at Pete sometime earlier today. He missed, of course. I can't believe we didn't hear about it before now, but I guess Pete wanted to downplay the incident. For a former prizefighter, he is remarkably slow to boil. Ida finally broke down and told Polly, and that was that."

Olivia paused at the door leading up to her apartment. "So did Pete fire Alicia before her boyfriend tried to hit him? That doesn't sound like Pete."

"There is undoubtedly more to the story, and rest assured I will hunt it down," Maddie said. "I stopped at the diner, but Ida wasn't there, and I didn't see Pete, but I will persevere. When I do find out what happened, you will be first on my urgent contact list. Meanwhile, I'm heading to the store to dump these groceries in the kitchen."

"I'll be upstairs feeding Spunky," Olivia said. "Are you and Lucas coming to dinner tonight? Mom said she invited you. We should talk about how to handle Alicia. I'd love to pepper her with all my questions, but she seems fragile."

"I'll be there, but Lucas has to work. I doubt we'll ever get much information from Del, so we'll have to find a way to wheedle it out of Alicia. Hang on again." In a few moments, Maddie's cheerful voice returned. "Sorry, I had to hoist the grocery bag. I got a bit carried away with the shopping. We already have plenty of cookies to bring for dessert tonight, but I also picked up some fancy decorated cupcakes from that new bakery. I'll have a bit of free time before we need to leave for dinner. Shall I fire up the magic computer fingers for some online research?"

"I have a better idea," Olivia said. "Dinner isn't until eight, so I wondered if we could pay Aunt Sadie a quick visit? Would we be interrupting her own dinner?"

"I just happened to pick up some of Pete's meatloaf during my shopping excursion. The stuff is irresistible. I can bring that along for her."

"Good idea." Olivia took her keys from her pocket as Spunky, impatient for dinner, whined and pawed the door to the staircase leading up to Olivia's apartment. As the door opened, Spunky squeezed through and bounded up the steps.

"We can spare some cookies and a cupcake for Aunt Sadie's dessert," Maddie said. "She has a hard time baking these days. I can't wait till Lucas and the guys finish building the mother-in-law addition to our house. Wait, why are we dropping in on Aunt Sadie?"

"Because Aunt Sadie knows everything about Chatterley Heights." Olivia followed Spunky up the steps to her apartment. "I'd like to know more about the boarding house. Why would Kenny Vayle end up there?"

"I'm unlocking the alley door as we speak," Maddie said. "I'll wait for you in the kitchen."

The instant Olivia opened her apartment door, Spunky rocketed toward the kitchen. "Maddie, I have to feed a starving dog and then take him outside. After that, I'll meet you in the kitchen. I'm thinking we should bring Spunks along this evening. He might be able to charm Alicia."

"Good idea," Maddie said. "See you soon."

After Spunky had devoured his kibbles, followed by his Milk Bone dessert, Olivia accompanied him to the doggie bathroom, also known as the side yard. By then it was six forty-five and dark. "Okay, Spunks, let's go say 'hi' to Maddie in the kitchen, just for a minute. Then you can guard the sales floor until we leave for dinner." Olivia led her pup to the back of her Queen Anne, where the Gingerbread House kitchen opened to an alley. Usually, a motion-detector lamp over the alley door switched on automatically. This time it did not. The darkness heightened Olivia's vigilance as she flashed back to her years in Baltimore. With her now ex-husband in medical school, Olivia had taken business courses during the day and had a job that sometimes kept her working until well after dark. Since the job was only two blocks away from their apartment, she used to walk home. Her heart still raced whenever she passed a stranger under a darkened streetlamp.

However, Olivia reminded herself, now she had Spunky. Her fierce protector was trotting confidently toward the alley door to the Gingerbread House kitchen. No sooner had she begun to relax than Spunky stiffened, his ears perked. Olivia froze as she watched those sensitive Yorkie ears shift position, trying to pinpoint and identify a sound that Olivia could not hear. Spunky growled in the direction of the Gingerbread House garbage can. The trash collector must have deposited the can in a dark area a few feet away from its usual place near the alley door. With the motion detector out of commission, Olivia could barely see the outline of the can.

Spunky bounded into the air and unleashed a torrent of yaps. Olivia tightened her grip on his leash. Though she couldn't see into the darkness behind the garbage can, she was certain nothing as large as a person had leaped out of hiding and escaped down the alley. Spunky had probably heard a squirrel foraging for food. The little guy considered squirrels his mortal enemies because he could never catch one.

Yanking on Spunky's leash, Olivia edged toward the locked door to the store kitchen. She heard the sound of a latch releasing. The door opened, and Maddie's face appeared. "Hey, you two. Are you trying to scare the life out of me? Now I'll need an extra cookie to calm my nerves." She opened the alley door wider to allow Olivia to enter. Spunky seemed to have lost interest in whatever he'd heard behind the garbage can. He ran joyfully into the forbidden kitchen, but his leash kept him from getting very far.

"Sorry, kiddo." Olivia scooped the pup under her free arm. "Back in a sec," she said. While Olivia released Spunky from his leash, Maddie held the kitchen door open. She pulled it shut in time to prevent Spunky from sneaking back into the kitchen.

"What happened out there?" Maddie filled a cup with leftover coffee and handed it to Olivia. "I noticed the motion detector light was out when I arrived. Should we call Del and ask for backup?"

"It was probably just a squirrel," Olivia said, though her hand shook as she poured cream into her coffee. "Spunky has more acute hearing than I do."

"If you say so." Maddie turned off Mr. Coffee and rinsed the residue from the bottom of the carafe. "All the same, I'm glad we're taking that noisy little critter with us this evening. And I suggest we leave by the front door. I'm all for good lighting."

"No argument here." Olivia drained her coffee cup and left it in the sink. "We'll only have about forty-five minutes with Aunt Sadie before we'll need to head for Mom and Allan's house. Let's take my car. It's parked near the corner of the square."

"Time to roll." Maddie slid a covered cake pan off the top of the refrigerator. "I'll carry the cookies and the goodies I picked up for Aunt Sadie. You grab the mutt."

In just under ten minutes, Olivia's distinctive PT Cruiser pulled up in front of Aunt Sadie's home, where Maddie had lived from age ten until she'd married Lucas Ashford. Olivia parked under a streetlamp, mostly for security but also because she loved showing off her car's paint job: a colorful depiction of The Gingerbread House festooned with somersaulting gingerbread figures.

"I'll run up and ring the doorbell," Maddie said. "Then I'll come right back for the food. It takes Aunt Sadie a while to maneuver her wheelchair to the door these days, mostly because she's been sorting through everything in the house. She needs to downsize for the move to her new apartment in our place. Not an easy task when you've lived in the same house for fifty years." Maddie's long, muscular legs carried her swiftly across the porch. She punched the doorbell and raced back to the car. "Reminds me of our evil childhood pranks. Remember, Livie? We used to ring doorbells and hide in the bushes to giggle at the clueless adults."

Olivia chuckled as she handed Maddie the pan of cookies and the food for Aunt Sadie's dinner. "Fun times . . . at least they were until my mom found out what we were doing." Olivia remembered well how mortified she had felt when they had to return to each victim's house and confess their silly crime. It didn't help that several homeowners had rolled their eyes and laughed.

Aunt Sadie's greeting felt far more satisfying. Though she was now confined to a wheelchair, she always seemed vibrant. "Now come in quickly and close that door," she said. "Then we can hug in comfort."

Maddie bent down to wrap her arms around the woman who had taken her in after her parents—Aunt Sadie's younger sister and her husband—died in a car wreck. "I love this afghan you are knitting," Maddie said. "Peach and deep red . . . I'll have to try that color combination with royal icing." She kissed the curly gray hair on the top of her aunt's head. "We brought cookies, a cupcake, and Pete's meatloaf. I'll go get you a plate."

"Don't bother, Maddie, dear. I have a fork underneath my knitting. I'll eat the meatloaf right out of the box. Oh, and I happen to have a spoon so I can get every last bit of Pete's special sauce." She opened the take-out box and took a sniff. "That man is a genius. Now, while I eat, you two girls sit right there on the sofa and tell me what you want to know. Am I right to assume that this concerns those sad bones you found in the old Chatterley Boarding House?" Aunt Sadie wheeled herself into her living room, while Maddie and Olivia settled cross-legged on the roomy sofa.

"Was it named after the Chatterley family?" Olivia asked.

"It was named by a Chatterley." Aunt Sadie smiled. "That was back in the 1920s, when the building was first built. It was considered quite a genteel place where even a woman could live alone and maintain her respectability. That changed in the thirties, of course, after the stock market crash."

"Who owned the building?" Olivia asked.

"Now that's an interesting story." Aunt Sadie handed her container of meatloaf to Maddie, and said, "I can finish my dinner later. Right now I'd rather have Spunky on my lap while I nibble on dessert and talk about the old days." Spunky heard his name, went right over to Aunt Sadie, and jumped up to her lap. Maddie handed her a small plate holding a star-shaped cookie decorated with lilac icing and dark red sparkling sugar. "Who could ask for more?" Aunt Sadie murmured before she bit a point off the star.

Olivia forced herself not to check her watch. Would it really matter if they were late for dinner? Aunt Sadie's stories were always worth hearing.

With her free hand, Aunt Sadie massaged Spunky's silky neck, while she made quick work of her cookie. Accepting Maddie's offer of another cookie, she said, "I know you are both in a hurry, so I'll answer your question before I indulge in another of your delicious treats. Although . . ." She picked up a pink and purple rose shape. "Perhaps just one bite, for energy." After a tiny nibble, Aunt Sadie put the cookie on her plate. "Now where was I? Oh yes, the Chatterley Boarding House . . . It was a lovely building in the beginning, which is hardly surprising since it was conceived and built by Horace Chatterley, a direct descendant of our own town founder, Frederick P. Chatterley."

"Horace," Maddie said. "I remember that name. Wasn't he notorious for something or other? I once heard my mother and a couple of her friends discussing Horace Chatterley in hushed, giggly voices. Was he a ladies' man, like Frederick P.?"

Waves of wrinkles spread across Aunt Sadie's plump cheeks as she grinned. "Oh my, yes, but Horace was even worse. Say what you will, Frederick took good care of his wife and family. Of course, everyone knew about his indiscretions, but family always came first for Frederick. Horace, on the other hand, behaved as if he had no family. He attended gala affairs in the company of other women, while his wife stayed home. His children barely knew him."

"I suppose his wife suffered in silence?" Olivia knew that time was passing, but she was hooked.

"Not precisely," Aunt Sadie said. "No doubt she suffered, but not in silence. She turned all five of her children against their father. After all, Horace ignored them, too, while he lived the good life. In the end, it was the Chatterley Boarding House that finally brought him down. You see, he became involved with a lovely young woman named Imogene who wasn't at all like his previous companions." Aunt Sadie paused, her eyes straying to the cookie she had barely begun.

"You're killing me, Aunt Sadie." Maddie handed the cookie plate to her aunt. "Please tell us that Imogene ground Horace into cookie crumbs." Spunky's head snapped up as the cookie changed hands, but he lost interest when no tasty tidbits fell within snatching distance.

Aunt Sadie closed her eyes as she enjoyed a big bite. "Now," she said, "I feel as though I can go on with the story. Yes, Maddie, Imogene proved to be Horace's undoing, as they used to say. She was smart and, in her own well-intentioned way, ruthless. You see, Imogene was a reformer. She despised rich, selfish men like Horace, but she was more than willing to play his companion in order to separate him from his wealth. She strung him along to keep him interested in her. She even managed to convince him to fund the construction of a boarding house for worthy, yet disadvantaged workers. Don't ask me how she did it, but she got Horace to believe that the venture would be wildly lucrative for him. Imogene knew full well he would barely break even, but she was determined to provide good, inexpensive housing for young workers, men and women both, who might have a chance to escape poverty. And it worked, for a while."

"And then the Depression hit," Olivia said.

"Yes, then came the Great Depression." Aunt Sadie put down her cookie. "Horace had invested heavily in the stock market. Ultimately, the Chatterley Boarding House failed, of course. The residents could no longer pay for their rooms, though many of them stayed until they were forced out. In later years, a succession of owners tried to revitalize the building, but it never took off again. It was abandoned many years ago. If Chatterley Heights were a city, these abandoned old buildings would be torn down for new ones, but no one here has shown much interest in the property. So the building sits there, crumbling, waiting . . ."

"Not to worry, Aunt Sadie," Maddie said. "Calliope and Ellie will soon have the place renovated and living a new life."

"I'm so glad." Aunt Sadie checked her watch, and said, "Now, you two must run along or you'll be late for dinner. I didn't mean to keep you so long listening to my silly old story."

"It's an intriguing old story," Olivia said. "I'm curious, what happened to Horace Chatterley's family? It was always my impression that the Chatterleys managed to stay more or less solvent through the centuries."

Aunt Sadie nodded. "Yes, all but poor Horace. His family, however, did just fine. Horace's eldest son, Henry, had realized quite young that his father could not be depended upon to support the family. So Henry decided he needed a trade. He settled on law. Henry was a bright lad, took after his mother in that respect. He convinced his father to turn over to him a portion of the family fortune, which he withdrew from the stock market right before it crashed. He used the money to take care of his mother and siblings while he slowly established his law practice in Baltimore."

"A most satisfying story." Maddie kissed her aunt on the forehead. "I'll put your meatloaf on a plate and heat it up in the microwave before we leave." In less than a minute, she returned from the kitchen bearing a plate of warmed meatloaf, which she handed to her aunt. "By the way, what finally happened to good old Horace?"

"Oh my, such a sad ending. His wife and children wanted nothing to do with him and sent him packing. Poor Horace ended up living in his own boarding house for a time. Finally, he simply disappeared and was never heard from again."

"Why didn't I know this story?" Olivia asked. "And I've certainly never heard a word about Henry Chatterley."

"Oh, there are so many stories about the Chatterley dynasty, and many have been forgotten. I suspect Henry Chatterley has faded from memory because he changed his last name to Jones. Most folks don't know that. Now you two, off you go or you'll be terribly late for dinner. I do hope you can help that poor girl, Alicia. Such a sad way to lose one's father."

"Just one more question," Olivia said, "and then we'll disappear so you can eat in peace. What happened to Imogene and her crusade to save the downtrodden? I'm hoping she didn't sink into a life of despair and poverty."

"Goodness," Aunt Sadie said. "I almost forgot the best part of the story. Well, you see, Imogene married Henry Chatterley. Together they continued Imogene's mission to help the poor rise up in the world. So romantic, don't you think?"

"But Henry had changed his name, so she became a Jones instead of a Chatterley," Olivia said as she scooped her pup out of Aunt Sadie's lap. "Most women wouldn't appreciate that, but I suppose Imogene didn't mind so much."

"Oh no, my dear, you have it turned around. When they married, Imogene kept her last name, which was Jones. So you see, Henry took *her* name. It was done, I believe, without fanfare or explanation . . . though his meaning was clear," Aunt Sadie added with an impish grin. "Taking Imogene's name was Henry's way of divorcing his Chatterley heritage."

Chapter Ten

❧

Olivia, Maddie, and Spunky arrived twenty minutes late for dinner at the Greyson-Meyers home. Jason answered the door, holding a half-eaten cheese sandwich. "Jeez, you two," Jason said with his mouth full. "You sure took your time getting here. It only takes like five minutes to drive from your store. Mom won't let me sample the meatloaf until we sit down to eat, and I'm practically passing out from hunger."

Olivia took in a breath to fire a retort, but she changed her mind when Dolly Fitzpatrick appeared behind Jason's left shoulder. "Hey, Livie," Dolly said. "It was so nice of your mom to invite me for dinner." Dolly was slightly out of breath, Olivia noticed, and her cheeks looked flushed. Either she was excited to be with Jason, or the two of them had recently been arm wrestling. If it was the latter, Olivia hoped Dolly hadn't let him win. That wasn't the way to get Jason to notice her.

"Can I hold your sweet little Yorkie?" Dolly held out her arms to Spunky, who wriggled in an effort to reach her.

"Traitor," Olivia whispered in his ear as she handed him over to Dolly.

"I'll bring our dessert contribution to the kitchen," Maddie said, "and offer my services to Ellie. Livie, you stay here and socialize." She wiggled her eyebrows to indicate she expected Olivia to listen, learn, and report back later.

"Jason, your mom wants your help in the kitchen, too." Dolly lightly touched his arm as she spoke. Jason didn't seem to notice the touch. He rolled his eyes and turned to leave. As he ambled toward the kitchen, he stuffed the rest of his sandwich into his mouth. Dolly watched his retreating figure and shook her head. "If I ate like that," she said, "I'd weigh as much as Jason's Ford Fairlane. It's so unfair."

"I'd like to believe that he'll turn into a blimp one day," Olivia said, "but our father was always tall and thin, despite his cookie addiction."

With a shrug, Dolly shifted her bright blue eyes to Olivia's face. "You're probably wondering why I'm here, Livie. I was really surprised when Struts told me your mom wanted me to come to dinner this evening and take a look at a young woman to be sure she's the girl who bought that cookie cutter charm I made. Of course, she was about twelve when I met her, and it was only for about ten minutes."

"Even so, you have a great memory for faces." Olivia glanced toward the dining room to make sure no one was coming their way. "I certainly thought your drawing of the young girl looked very much like Alicia. I wonder why Mom would go to all this trouble."

"I wondered about that, too," Dolly said.

"My mother's ways are often mysterious," Olivia said. "Do you have any idea how many of those charms you sold?"

Dolly frowned in concentration, which only made her more gorgeous.

It's a good thing Dolly is a likable person, Olivia thought. She was surprised by her fiercely protective instincts. She had already watched Jason nearly go to prison for a former girlfriend, and she still didn't trust his judgment. Besides, irritating as Jason could be, Olivia didn't want her baby brother to endure another broken heart.

"I think I sold four of those heart charms," Dolly said. "But I'm positive that three of them sold to adult women. I could sketch them for you, if you like."

"That won't be necessary," Olivia said.

Dolly motioned to Olivia to follow her to a more private spot near a bookcase. "Listen, Livie, about Jason and me," Dolly said. "Please don't worry that I'll throw myself at him. I do like the guy a lot, but I'm not a dumb teenager anymore. Not that all teenagers are dumb, of course, but I sure was. I thought all those guys who were after me really liked me as a person. Ha! They were only chasing after me because of my . . ." Dolly shook her perfect golden curls impatiently. "That's not important. I want you to know that I like your brother because he treats me with respect. I swear, the first thing Jason noticed about me was I changed the oil in my car all by myself. We started discussing auto maintenance, and pretty soon we were talking about classic cars and how to restore them. That was the best conversation I've ever had with a man."

"Okay, then," Olivia said. "I will worry no more. But I do have one little piece of advice. If you ever find yourself in an arm wrestling contest with Jason, don't—"

"Oh, we arm wrestled soon after we met," Dolly said with a lopsided grin. "I used to arm wrestle with my brothers all the time. Believe me, it wouldn't occur to me let a guy win. Jason put up a fight, but I won in the end. Jason took it well. Wait, you don't think he let me win, do you? That would be *so* disappointing."

Ellie entered the living room, followed by Alicia, who stared, wide-eyed, around the room as if she were having second thoughts about entering. "Poor kid," Dolly said. "She's had a rough time. I think I'll wander over for a chat with her."

As Dolly left, Ellie joined Olivia. "Dear Maddie is minding the kitchen while the meatloaves finish baking," Ellie said. "I thought Alicia might enjoy some social time before dinner."

Olivia observed Alicia's animated expression as she chatted with Dolly. "Those two seem to be getting along well."

"I thought they might," Ellie said. "I must say, Alicia has been quite helpful with the meatloaf experiments."

Olivia's antennae perked up. Her mother's experiments usually had an ulterior motive. "Dinner is an experiment?"

"Of course, dear," Ellie said. "Alicia has a remarkably sophisticated palate. Who better to help me discover the secret to Pete's secret meatloaf recipe?"

Uh-oh. "Mom, aren't you worried that spending an evening discussing Pete's meatloaf might make Alicia feel even worse? He did just fire her, after all."

"I am hardly in my dotage, Livie. Naturally I discussed the idea with Alicia before moving forward with it. She lit up like a house on fire . . . such a disturbing analogy, when you think about it."

"Extremely disturbing, but I won't tell anyone you used it."

"How thoughtful of you, dear." Ellie checked her watch. "I should get the rest of the meal ready soon, but let me reassure you that Alicia is looking forward to our little experiment. She told me she adores all types of cooking. She seems to have survived being fired rather well. She confided that Pete spoke to her privately after he'd thrown that sad young man out of the diner. He said he wasn't angry with her, but he owed it to his customers and staff to keep them safe from violence."

"That still sounds like Alicia got fired," Olivia said.

"Yes, Livie, but Pete also expressed concern for Alicia's safety. He suggested she break all ties with Kurt and report him to the police if he bothered her. I suspect Alicia hasn't experienced much kindness from adults—with the exception of her father, poor soul."

Olivia glanced across the room at Alicia as she chatted

with Allan. "Well, I'm glad she is staying with you and Allan. If she mentions anything that might help resolve what happened to her father, you will tell me, right?"

"Of course, dear, just as soon as I've passed the information on to Del." Ellie's expression brightened as she looked over Olivia's shoulder. "She is such a charming young woman, don't you think?"

"Wait, are we still talking about Alicia?" Olivia turned and followed her mother's gaze. "Ah, you mean Dolly. Charming, gorgeous, artistically and mechanically gifted . . . If only she weren't so pleasant, I could happily hate her. As far as I can see, her one flaw is she is besotted with Jason."

"Now, now, Livie," Ellie said. "You give Jason too little credit. Although, to be fair, he gives you even less. The two of you are so different. I can only hope that someday you will both learn to appreciate one another." With the wistful sigh of a long-suffering mother, she added, "I would so enjoy seeing that happen before I die."

Olivia rolled her eyes heavenward. "Nice delivery, Mom. However, you exercise and do yoga a million times a day, while I live on pizza. I suspect you will outlive me." Olivia regarded her mother with deepening suspicion. "Okay, Mom, what's the real reason for this dinner?"

Ellie's eyes blinked too rapidly, or so Olivia thought. "Livie, dear, I don't understand what you mean. How many reasons must I have to host a dinner for my friends and family?"

Olivia stroked her chin. "I wonder . . . Dolly doesn't really need to be here to identify Alicia, does she? I'm guessing that was just a ruse. I'll bet you and Struts hatched the idea to get Dolly here tonight so she and Jason could get to know one another in a casual family setting."

Ellie shrugged but admitted nothing.

"I thought so," Olivia said. "You'd better hope Jason doesn't get wind of your intentions. He likes Dolly, but he'd hate being set up by his mother. As would I, by the way."

"You have no need of my services," Ellie said.

Olivia couldn't help but laugh. "You're right about Jason. He'd never pick up on Dolly's interest, despite the fact that she is perfect for him—though arguably out of his league, but that's just my opinion. Does Dolly know about this little plot?"

"Heavens no," Ellie said. "No woman likes to be thrown at a man, especially when it's his mother doing the tossing. Struts and I discussed the options. It was her idea to tell Dolly that we wanted to be certain Alicia was the girl who'd bought the little charm found with . . . well, you know."

"Ah." Olivia remembered seeing Ellie intercept Struts as she left The Gingerbread House during the impromptu event on Tuesday. "So this dinner isn't really about Alicia or even about Pete's meatloaf, is it?"

Ellie shrugged her slender shoulders. "One might as well take advantage of an opportunity," she said. "Dear Struts is quite the romantic, you know."

Olivia didn't know, but she wasn't surprised. As a mechanic, Struts was the best, but she indulged in regular manicures, and her work clothes always managed to show off her tall, slender figure.

"Of course," Ellie said, "Struts is also practical. She's been watching Jason and Dolly get to know each other. She is worried that Dolly might quit the garage if she feels Jason is rejecting her. You see, Dolly is a promising mechanic, and she definitely attracts business . . . especially from men who usually do their own oil changes. Struts doesn't want to lose her."

When her mother announced dinner, Olivia joined Dolly as she headed toward the dining room. "I just wanted to let you know," Olivia said, "that Jason never *lets* anyone beat him at arm wrestling. Such an idea would never occur to him. So you did good."

"You won't tell Jason we've been talking about him, will you?" Dolly asked in a whisper.

"Not a chance," Olivia said.

"Good, because I like being one of the guys to Jason. For now, anyway."

Followed by Olivia, Dolly entered the dining room and glanced around the table. There were two empty chairs left. One was next to Jason, who gave her a quick wave. Dolly smiled at him and chose the other seat, across from Jason and next to Alicia. Olivia sat next to Jason. At least she'd be able to observe Dolly and Alicia. Also, Maddie was seated on Alicia's other side, so Olivia could communicate with her nonverbally, if needed.

"Before we begin," Ellie said, "I want to tell you all that I have an ulterior motive for organizing this gathering. I'm hoping everyone here has tasted the sublime meatloaf served at Pete's Diner? Good, because I am determined to replicate his recipe. Pete has refused to share it with me. Normally, I would respect his wishes, but . . . well, his meatloaf is the best I've ever tasted, and I am a connoisseur of meatloaf."

Olivia sneaked a quick look at Alicia to gauge her reaction to the mention of her former boss. Alicia showed no sign of discomfort. In fact, she looked more relaxed than Olivia had ever seen her.

From the opposite end of the table, Allan belted out an enthusiastic, "Here, here," in response to his wife's announcement.

"Thank you, dear," Ellie said. "Although Pete has every right to keep the recipe to himself, there's no law against trying to decipher it through trial and error, is there? Naturally, should I be successful, Pete's secret will be safe with me." Ellie beamed at her guests. "Now for the fun part. I've made four meatloaves, all slightly different. As you taste each of them, I'd like you to rate them in comparison to your memory of Pete's recipe. I did not buy any of Pete's meatloaf for comparison. That didn't seem fair because . . . well, I'd feel compelled to tell Pete what I'm doing."

"How do you know one of us won't squeal on you to Pete?" Olivia asked.

"Oh, Livie. That would make me so very sad." Ellie's tone had an edge that Olivia recognized from childhood. "Now everyone, you have small score sheets hidden under your plates, and tiny pencils under your napkins. We will taste the meatloaves one by one, rate each one, and cleanse our palates with salad and steamed broccoli. Once we've finished our ratings, feel free to eat more. Are we ready? Good, then let the feasting begin."

Feeling oddly self-conscious, Olivia tried but failed to catch Maddie's eye. Everyone at the table seemed eager to follow Ellie's orders, including Alicia. Perhaps she hadn't really minded losing her job, now that she had a place to stay. Or maybe she enjoyed the thought that Pete's exquisite and very private recipe might be revealed?

"Livie?" Jason nudged Olivia's arm with his elbow while holding a large pan in both hands. "If you don't want your share of this meatloaf, I'll take it."

"Hand it over," Olivia said. "My brother, the human vacuum." She was pleased to hear Alicia giggle.

"I wish I had a brother," Alicia said.

"No, you don't." Olivia softened her jab with a grin.

After the tasters had marked their score cards, Ellie said, "I can't stand the suspense. What's the verdict?"

"Very tasty, sweetheart," Allan said.

"Yes, dear, but does it taste anything like Pete's meatloaf?" Ellie's gaze fell on Alicia.

"Well . . ." Alicia took a second bite and closed her eyes as she chewed. With a decisive nod, she said, "Your husband is right, Ellie. It tastes great, but it isn't Pete's recipe. Too much tomato sauce, which overpowers the subtler flavors. The meat tastes similar, though. Did you use finely chopped shallots instead of onions?"

An enthusiastic yap from the dining room entrance seemed to support Alicia's analysis. Either that, Olivia thought, or Spunky could smell the meatloaf and was angling for a taste.

Ellie beamed. "I did indeed, Alicia. How clever of you."

Olivia had begun to catch on. Crystal, Alicia's mother, had

mentioned what a skilled baker her daughter had become. Clearly the girl had a gift for discerning subtle taste differences. Ellie, whose own special skills included understanding people, was using Alicia's talents to draw her out, get her talking . . . perhaps to relax her enough to discuss more painful memories?

Alicia appeared more comfortable with each sample meatloaf that made its way around the table. The second experiment, Alicia decided, had too much garlic in the meat. The tomato sauce on the third meatloaf tasted too sweet, and the fourth was closest in taste to Pete's recipe except the sauce wasn't sharp enough. "By any chance, did you use regular mustard in the sauce?" Alicia asked. When Ellie nodded, Alicia said, "I thought so. Pete does use regular mustard in some dishes, but I'm almost positive he uses Dijon mustard for his meatloaf sauce. I've wondered if he sneaks in a pinch of horseradish, too. He won't share his recipe with anyone, not even Ida."

"I'm confused," Olivia said. "Ida has served Del and me lots of extra meatloaf. She always tells us that 'the cook made too much,' and Pete wants to get rid of the leftovers."

When Alicia laughed, she looked like a carefree teenager. Her light brown eyes sparkled as she shook her long, chestnut hair. "That's a little game they play. I figured that out right away." She relaxed against her chair back. "I always wanted to work at Pete's Diner. I was so happy to get that waitressing job, I came in early my first day. I wanted to learn everything as fast as possible because . . ." Alicia lowered her gaze as if she felt shy sharing information about herself. "Well, because I want to be a cook. Not just any cook, but one of the best. I want to open my own restaurant someday and specialize in desserts. My dad taught me how to make decorated cutout cookies. We were going to open a bakery together when I . . ." Alicia stared down at her hands. "When I got old enough," she finished softly.

"Hey, there's no time like the present," Maddie said. "After dinner, I'll be heading back to the Gingerbread House kitchen for some evening cookie baking. How about joining me for a couple hours? I can drive you back here before Ellie and Allan start nodding off."

"Gosh, I'd *love* that." Alicia looked toward Ellie. "Would it be okay? I wouldn't stay too late."

With a wistful sigh, Ellie said, "Oh, if only my own children had been so solicitous."

"Hey!" Olivia protested.

"Yeah, hey!" Jason said.

"I was only teasing, dears," Ellie said. "Alicia, I would like you to be back no later than eleven, so we won't have to worry. Worrying is so exhausting. However, I will give you a key, in case all of you lose track of time. Creating decorated cookies can have that effect." She scraped back her chair and stood. "Now that we've finished our dinner, shall we have coffee and dessert in the living room? Alicia, would you help me clear the table?"

"Sure." Alicia sprang to her feet, nearly toppling her chair backward. Olivia felt sad as she watched Alicia's eager response to Ellie's firm, yet attentive mothering. Remembering her conversation with Crystal in the band shell, Olivia suspected that Alicia was more used to harsh criticism.

While Ellie and Alicia carried soiled dinnerware to the kitchen for washing, Allan led the others to the living room. "Winter is coming, no doubt about it," he said, rubbing his hands together. "Make yourselves at home, while I stoke the fire." Spunky plunked down in front of the fireplace. He knew from past experience that a lit fire meant warmth, and he intended to claim the best spot.

Jason settled on the sofa next to Dolly. "Want me to head out and chop down a tree for firewood, Allan? We wouldn't want the womenfolk to freeze." Dolly jabbed him in the ribs with her elbow, which made Olivia like her enormously. "Hey," Jason said. "You've got a strong arm, for a girl."

Dolly turned her back on him and asked the group, "Does

anyone know what Ellie is up to? Because it looked like she planned that whole dinner scene pretty carefully."

"Ellie's ways are often mysterious," Maddie said. "And convoluted . . . which is probably why I love watching her in action. I'm never quite sure what she'll do or say next. I wish she'd gotten Alicia to talk about her boyfriend. He's the one who got her fired from Pete's Diner this morning, right?"

"Kurt?" Jason snorted. "He's such a loser."

"You know him?" Olivia's eyebrows shot up. "How? And why didn't you say something?"

"You didn't ask, Olive Oyl. Jeez. And I know him because Struts fired him sometime back. Kurt claimed he was an experienced mechanic. We'd lost a couple guys in the previous months, so Struts decided to give him a chance. Big mistake. He didn't know a piston from an air filter."

"Wow," Dolly said.

"I know, right?" Jason said. "Boy, was Kurt ever mad when Struts canned him. I followed him out to make sure he didn't damage anything. I don't know why he thought he could fool Struts and me. You just had to look at those scrawny shoulders and arms to know he wasn't a mechanic, but Struts likes to give people a chance to prove themselves." Jason socked Dolly's shoulder, and she socked him back harder. "See? Dolly is lots stronger than Kurt, and she's a girl."

"By which you mean *woman*, right?" Dolly's voice had grown a sharp edge.

"Uh, right," Jason said. "Slip of the tongue. No offense intended."

Olivia was impressed. Her brother might be salvageable after all. Barely. "Does anyone know what Kurt actually did that got Alicia fired?" Olivia asked. "I'm having a hard time believing Pete would blame her for her boyfriend's behavior."

"For once, I know the answer to that, or at least part of it," Allan said as he lowered to his knees in front of the fireplace. "As it happens, I stopped in at the diner at about six a.m. for a cup of coffee, so I witnessed the whole episode. Pete unofficially opens up early, you know, for folks who need to be at work by seven." Allan paused to light the fire. "There, that ought to do the trick. Nothing like a fire when the wind starts whistling. Now where was I?"

"Allan, we all know about Pete's concern for early risers," Olivia said. "The question is, why were *you* even out of bed at six a.m., let alone having breakfast at the diner? Has a 'morning person' taken over your body?"

Allan's laugh filled the room. As he lumbered to his feet, Olivia couldn't help thinking of her own tall, thin dad, who'd been Allan's physical opposite. Prone to absentmindedness, her ornithologist father had understood the language of birds. He'd perceived their personalities, much the way Olivia saw cookie cutters almost as little people. Allan, on the other hand, was a shrewd businessman and only slightly taller than Olivia's five foot seven, with a hefty build and a booming voice. Like her father, however, Allan was kind.

"Your mother thinks I should exercise more," Allan said. "Something about my chakras being out of whack." He ran a beefy hand through his thinning hair. "Haven't a clue what that means, but it's usually a good idea to do what Ellie tells me to. Besides, I do spend most of my day hunched in front of my computer. Creating Internet businesses is fun, but it can be intense. So now I get up early in the morning and run around the park a couple times. I figure I deserve a cup of coffee after that. And a nap, if Ellie doesn't catch me at it."

"You were going to tell us how Alicia's boyfriend got her fired?" Olivia reminded him. In his own way, Allan could be absentminded, too.

"I sure was," Allan said. "Quite a scene. Pete had just opened the diner, and there were a few customers. Alicia was the only waitress on duty. She was about to take my order for coffee . . . okay, plus a cinnamon roll, which I needed for energy, but keep it under your hats. Anyway, this Kurt fellow barged in and yelled for Alicia. Gave me a chill, I have to admit."

"Was he armed?" Maddie asked.

Allan chuckled. "Armed with attitude, maybe. I didn't see any sign of a weapon, and he looked to me like there wasn't much muscle to him. When Alicia came out of the kitchen, the kid huffed and puffed at her about how she didn't have any right to break up with him. By then, he sounded more whiney than dangerous. Pete heard the commotion and barged out of the kitchen looking like a prizefighter, which, of course, he used to be."

"Wish I'd been there," Jason said.

"I wish I *hadn't* been there," Allan said. "Kurt came on strong. He accused Pete of taking Alicia away from him, which was dumb. He said to Alicia, 'Come on, baby, let's get out of here.' Alicia told him not to be an idiot, and that's when it got really wild. Kurt gave Alicia a look, sort of disdainful and calculating. Then he said to her, 'So this is the guy you've been sneaking around with behind my back. A cook! And you said *I* was too old for you. You must really be desperate for a sugar daddy.' I'll never forget those words." Allan shook his head.

"I'm surprised Kurt is still alive," Maddie said.

"I have to admit, I expected bloodshed and broken bones." Allan pushed to his feet and stretched. "I've never seen Pete so angry. He grabbed the little pip-squeak by his upper arm, dragged him to the door, tossed him out of the diner, and yelled after him that he'd better never come back. Then Pete turned around and told Alicia that Kurt had to stay away for good or he'd have to let her go. He said he couldn't afford an employee with a dangerous boyfriend."

"That doesn't seem fair," Dolly said. "It wasn't Alicia's fault he came to the diner. She did break up with him, after all."

"I can see both sides," Olivia said. "Maddie and I couldn't afford to have someone dangerously volatile show up at The Gingerbread House. It's bad for business. What if he hurt a customer?"

"But Pete blamed Alicia, too," Dolly said. "She didn't deserve that."

"I suspect that was more for show." Olivia hoped that was true. Pete was known for his soft heart. "Customers witnessed the whole scene. Pete had to make it clear he was serious about keeping Kurt away from the diner. Otherwise, word would spread all through town that Pete's Diner wasn't a safe place to be."

"Hey, wait a minute, I'm confused." Maddie ran a hand through her red curls, which expanded like sprung coils. "I just found out this evening that Kurt was arrested for taking a swing at Pete, but Alicia was fired this morning."

Dolly folded her long, lean legs into a pretzel and leaned her elbows on her knees. "I might be able to help clear up the confusion," she said. "Polly stopped by Struts & Bolts this afternoon. I'm amazed by how much gossip she manages to pick up, given how busy she is with the homeless shelter."

"Polly has her sources," Olivia said. "Plus those powerful binoculars."

Dolly snickered. "No kidding. Anyway, Polly was looking for a used beater to cart folks around to job interviews, so Struts assigned me to take her out on a couple test drives. Polly talked up a storm. Ida had called and told her about Kurt getting thrown out early that morning, so Polly kept an eye on Pete's with her binoculars. She saw Kurt hanging around the diner off and on. He stayed out of sight and never went inside, at least not through the front door."

"Wait a minute," Olivia said. "If Kurt never went inside, how and when did he try to slug Pete?"

Dolly shrugged one strong, shapely shoulder. "Polly said she couldn't actually see the back door, but she did watch Kurt enter the alley behind the diner."

Jason stretched his arms toward the ceiling and yawned, as if he were bored. As he lowered his arms, the left one landed gently around Dolly's shoulders. "You womenfolk make everything so complicated," he said. "There's a simple explanation."

"Oh *really*," Dolly muttered as she slid out from under Jason's arm.

Jason took the rejection in stride. "Well, think about it. The diner kitchen opens into the alley, right? Maybe Pete noticed Kurt hanging around and finally figured he had to fire Alicia to get rid of Kurt for good. Kurt, being a hothead, probably fumed for hours and finally confronted Pete and took a swing at him. Which was dumb, of course, because Pete could have killed him with one blow." Jason's grin hinted that he relished the thought. "Pete isn't like that, though. He just called the police." Jason gave Olivia a look of brotherly disdain. "It's simple logic, Olive Oyl. I'm surprised you didn't ask Del to explain this to you."

When Dolly's fingers curled into a fist, Olivia felt intervention might be a timely idea. "Del is pretty busy right now," she said, lowering her voice. "As you may remember, we did discover what might be the remains of Alicia's father. A deputy from Twiterton is pinch-hitting for Del at the moment, so he's probably the one who arrested Kurt."

Jason shrugged. "Oh. Okay. Sorry." Dolly's fingers relaxed.

"I suppose Pete might change his mind and rehire Alicia once he calms down," Allan said. "He does have a soft spot for feisty ladies." Allan paused a moment, as if he were listening for footsteps. "I wonder why those two are taking so long in the kitchen. Probably talking nonstop. At any rate, I've told you everything I can remember. What struck me most about this Kurt kid was his entitled attitude. Alicia reacted like an exasperated ex-girlfriend. Funny thing is, Kurt looked a lot older than her."

"Yeah," Jason said. "Alicia is only like nineteen, right? Kurt is twenty-six. I know that because he filled out an application form for the job at Struts & Bolts, plus he had to show Struts his driver's license. He wrote stuff about his experience, too, and he sounded pretty knowledgeable. Now I'm thinking he just looked it all up on the Internet to make himself look good on the application."

"That's an interesting observation," Allan said. "From what I saw of him, Kurt reminded me of one of those kids who hide out in their basements and spend all their time online. He's got that pasty look and hunched shoulders." With a sheepish grin, he added, "I guess you could say I hang out with my computer for endless hours, too, but I've got Ellie to kick my butt out of my office and into the world."

"And you're a successful businessman with many professional contacts and friends," Olivia said. "Although your shoulders could use some straightening."

Allan gave her a good-natured grin as he put a finger to his lips. "Approaching footsteps," he whispered.

"Dessert has arrived," Ellie announced as she entered the living room carrying a large tray piled with decorated cookies. Alicia followed with a large carafe of coffee. "The cookies are from Maddie and Livie, of course," Ellie said. "Sorry we took so long. Alicia and I filled the dishwasher while we had a lovely talk." Alicia placed the heavy carafe on the coffee table just as Ellie said, "Alicia, dear, would you mind going back to the kitchen? I forgot to prepare a tray with coffee cups, cream, and sugar. Perhaps you could add some spoons, as well. Thank you so much, dear."

Once Alicia had left, Maddie asked, "So? What did you two talk about in the kitchen?"

"Nothing earth-shattering," Ellie said, "though I am happy to report that Alicia and I plan to chat with Pete about rehiring her. We'll wait a bit, I think." Ellie smiled fondly at her daughter and Maddie. "I would feel more comfortable if that former boyfriend of hers weren't around. He might be more bark than bite, but I'd rather not encourage Pete to let her work at the diner again if she or anyone else might be in danger."

As Allan stared into the fire, his normally affable expression darkened.

Ellie reached toward her husband and lightly touched his forearm. "Is something worrying you, dear?"

Allan patted her hand. "I was wondering . . . Does anyone know what Kurt does for a living? Because if he turns out to be a computer geek, he might be able to discover if someone is tracking him. He might even be a hacker." He shrugged, and said, "It's a long shot, but . . . well, I'd stay alert. And don't discuss Kurt on social networks. Just a precaution, that's all I'm—" Allan stopped abruptly at the sound of clattering crockery. Alicia entered the living room slowly, frowning in concentration as she delivered a tray loaded with cups, saucers, spoons, cream, sugar, and napkins. Allan leaped up to help her.

"Whew," Alicia said, once the tray had landed safely on the coffee table. She began to fill cups to the brim and pass them along. Olivia noted that there was no room left in her own cup for the heaps of cream and sugar she preferred, but she kept her disappointment to herself. It wouldn't hurt to cut down. Besides, she had more important issues on her mind. Olivia took a sip of her unadulterated coffee and left it on the end table to fend for itself. "Alicia," she said, "you've mentioned how much you love to bake cookies. Are you interested in cookie cutters, too?"

Alicia's eyes lit up. "Oh yes. I *love* cookie cutters. I wish my mom had given her cutter collection to me instead of selling it online."

Interesting . . . As Olivia remembered their conversation in the park, Crystal had claimed, disdainfully, that she'd given her cutters away. Had she needed money?

"Some of them were lovely antiques," Alicia said. "Mom once told me they'd been in the family for generations. If only she had kept them for me, like her mother did for her. I would have loved them and kept them safe." Tears doused the sparks in Alicia's eyes. She dabbed her eyelids with her napkin. "I'm sorry. I'm acting like a little kid. Mom always says I'll never grow up."

Ellie reached over and patted Alicia's hand. "You are already quite grown-up, dear." Alicia gave her a shy smile, and Olivia began to wonder if she'd acquired a new little sister. She wasn't sure how she felt about that.

"Hey, let's check some online sites like eBay this evening,"

Maddie said. "Maybe we'll find some of those cutters for sale again. Would you recognize them, do you think?"

Alicia practically bounced off her seat with excitement. "I should have thought of that. If there are good photos, then yes, maybe. Each of those cutters had little marks and dents that I'd recognize instantly. I used to play with them when I was a little girl. I caused quite a few of those dents, but mom never said anything. We got along a lot better when I was little."

Olivia surrendered to her need for caffeine and took another sip of her naked coffee. Nope, she'd never get used to it. Now that there was some room in the cup, she stirred in cream and sugar. The next sip tasted much better. Olivia wanted to bring Kenny Vayle into the conversation, but that might trigger a crying jag. Maybe Crystal would be a safer topic for now. "Perhaps your mom wasn't as interested in cookie cutters as you were," Olivia suggested.

Alicia's shoulders drooped. Her voice quivered as she said, "Mom really wasn't . . . It was my dad who truly loved to bake. He taught me how to make cutout cookies using those old cookie cutters. We'd give each cutter a name and talk to them while we baked. I really, really miss him, you know?"

"I do know," Olivia said. "And so does my brother, don't you, Jason?" She made the question into a statement as a signal to Jason to show a little empathy. "He was only in high school when our dad died," Olivia said, "and it hit him hard. Didn't it, Jason?" At the time, the loss of his father and the shock of it had knocked Jason off his rapidly growing feet. He'd lost interest in school, hung out with borderline delinquents, gotten into trouble . . . Once Jason had straightened himself out, he became tight-lipped about those days.

With everyone staring at him, Jason stretched out his legs, jiggled his feet, and stared into the fire. Olivia was about to change the subject when Dolly gently poked Jason in the ribs with her elbow. He gave her a startled look, and said, "Uh, well, yeah. It was . . . you know, hard."

Alicia grabbed a small pillow from the sofa and held it

tightly against her stomach. "My dad disappeared years ago, but it feels like it only just happened, you know? Do you ever get over it?"

Jason's gaze darted toward Dolly's elbow. "Well, yeah, but . . . It takes a while. The thing is, you've been hoping your dad might still come back, but I . . . well, I knew my dad was gone." Dolly touched Jason's forearm with her fingertips, and his shoulders relaxed.

"I guess you're right," Alicia said. "It's tough to let go when you think someone might only be away for a while, but not . . . not dead."

Olivia decided this wasn't the time to mention that the bones they'd found in the old Chatterley Boarding House had yet to be positively identified . . . or that Kenny Vayle, if he was still alive, might be a murderer.

Chapter Eleven

After dinner at the Greyson-Meyers home, Olivia, Maddie, and Alicia returned to the Gingerbread House kitchen, eager to get to work. Maddie reached into the refrigerator and removed a disk of cookie dough wrapped in plastic. She plopped it on the worktable, where Alicia squirmed impatiently in her chair. "Would you like to do the cutting?" Maddie asked Alicia, who nodded eagerly. "I'll roll out the dough," Maddie said. "While you are cutting, I'll search some Internet sites that sell vintage and antique cutters. There isn't time for much else. Ellie set your curfew at eleven p.m., which I think of as late afternoon, but who am I to question? Everyone knows that Livie's mom was Mary Poppins in a previous life—practically perfect in every way. Livie, do you plan to join us?"

"I'd better finish reconciling today's receipts. It's a boring job, but somebody has to do it." Olivia settled at her little desk in a cozy corner where she could watch, listen, and even get some work done.

"And I'm so grateful you are that someone, not me." Maddie picked up the rolling pin and applied it to the center of the dough. "Alicia, why don't you pick out the cookie cutters you want to use. The ones we use most often are over there." Maddie aimed her elbow at a narrow cupboard. "We try to keep them arranged by category, but when things get hectic around here, organization wanders off for a nap."

Alicia opened the cupboard door and gasped. "Golly, there must be hundreds of cutters in here." She peeked inside the nearest box. "Oh, these are some old-fashioned shapes. Let's use them."

"You can't beat the classics." Maddie exchanged a quick glance with Olivia. They kept a cutter in that box, similar to the one Dolly had noticed when Struts first brought her to The Gingerbread House—the heart pierced by an arrow. With any luck, that cutter might induce Alicia to talk about her father, thereby providing some possible leads. They planned to dig into Kenny's disappearance without involving Alicia in an investigation that might cause her pain . . . or harm.

"Why don't you spread those cutters on the kitchen counter," Maddie said. "While I finish rolling out the dough, you can select four or five cutters that are about the same size. Then I'll turn the table over to you. I find it really meditative to cut out shapes. Maybe the process will jog your memory, so you can describe some of your mom's cutters for my online search."

When Alicia didn't answer, Olivia glanced up from her receipts to see the young woman staring down at a cookie cutter in her hand. Maddie's eyes met Olivia's over Alicia's bowed head. "How's it going, Alicia?" Maddie asked. "I'm almost finished rolling out the dough."

Alicia's head jerked up as if Maddie had startled her. "I'm just about ready. I've picked out four . . ." Alicia hesitated, looking at the pierced heart cutter on her palm. She added it to her small pile of chosen cutters, and said, "I chose five cutters to work with, and they are all close to the same size. Could I add one more? My dad would use a little cutter on those small, leftover bits of rolled dough—you know, so you don't have to keep rolling the dough over and over."

"Sure," Maddie said. "We don't usually do that because our customers seem to go for the bigger cookies. Not that our customers are greedy, I hasten to add. I like to think of them as appreciative."

Olivia watched as Alicia scooped up her chosen cutters and carried them to the worktable, where she arranged them in a row. She placed the pierced arrow cutter at the end. As Maddie settled in front of her laptop, Alicia picked up a daisy-shaped cookie cutter, dipped the cutting edge in flour, and applied it to the rolled dough. She clearly knew what she was doing. Meanwhile, Maddie visited several auction sites, including eBay. She paused now and then to quiz Alicia about her mother's cutter collection.

When Olivia joined her at the computer, she quickly realized that Crystal's cookie cutters would be difficult to locate. They'd been common shapes, such as vintage hearts, flowers, Christmas trees, and stars. There were numerous examples available for sale online. The photos rarely showed exactly where the nicks or dents were located.

Alicia had saved the pierced heart cutter for last. Olivia watched surreptitiously as she picked it up. "This is exactly like the charm I gave my dad," Alicia said, "only this one is a lot bigger." She glanced over at Olivia, then at Maddie. "Why did you put this in the box with the others?"

"Oh, it's just a classic design," Maddie said.

Alicia's eyes narrowed to dark slits. "I'm not stupid, you know. I may have been a kid when I bought that charm for Dad, but I remember the girl who sold it to me. She told me she made it herself. That girl was blond and really pretty. She looked a lot like your brother's girlfriend, Dolly."

Behind Alicia's back, Maddie made eye contact with Olivia and silently mouthed, "Oops."

Alicia spun around to face Maddie. "Is this all a big joke to you two? Are you trying to trick me for some reason?"

Olivia's emotions bounced between dread and shame. "Alicia, we weren't trying to . . . I mean . . . once I realized that cutter was in the box, I was hoping the cutter shape would help you talk about your father. Talking about him might make you feel better. We were only trying to help you without hurting your feelings."

"Why? Because you think I'm so fragile I'll fall apart if you say the wrong thing? I'm not, you know." Alicia tossed back her long hair and crossed her arms tightly over her slender ribcage. "It's been tough living in the same house with my mom and that awful man. My mom doesn't like me much because I remind her of my dad, and Robbie hates me. He threw me out of my own house like I was some worthless leech, just because my ex-boyfriend got me fired."

"Kurt is your *ex*-boyfriend?" Maddie reached into the freezer and dug out a plastic container with half a dozen cookies in it. "I am so glad to hear that news. I think a celebration is in order." She began to spread the cookies on a plate. "It won't take long for these to defrost."

"Of course Kurt is my ex-boyfriend. He's a jerk." Alicia grabbed a cookie and took a bite. "I like frozen cookies," she mumbled.

"Me, too," Olivia and Maddie said in unison as they each selected a cookie.

"So I was wondering . . ." Maddie slid the plate of cookies closer to Alicia. "How did you and Kurt get together in the first place?"

Alicia captured a lock of her chestnut hair and wrapped it around her finger. "I was a kid, about twelve, when I met Kurt. He was maybe eighteen or nineteen. He seemed really grown-up to me. I guess I had a little crush on him then. Actually, he was a friend of my dad's, although, looking back, I think Dad might have felt sorry for him. I don't know . . . I was pretty oblivious at that age."

"How long did you date him?" Olivia asked.

Alicia shrugged. "Hard to say. We were off and on a lot." She selected a scalloped cookie with burgundy icing and placed it next to her half-eaten one. "I think Kurt had a falling out with Dad at some point, because suddenly he stopped hanging out with us. Then he showed up again a couple years ago."

"When Kurt showed up again, did he ask about your father?" Olivia asked.

Alicia nodded. "It was a little weird. When I told him Dad had disappeared, Kurt said it sounded like something he would do—just go off and leave me. I was furious. I told him Dad had gone to see someone about a job, so something bad must have happened. Kurt just nodded and never brought the topic up again. I had the feeling he was relieved that Dad wasn't there to interfere."

"Interfere with what?" Maddie asked.

Alicia shrugged one slender shoulder. "I don't know. Maybe he didn't want Dad to object to our relationship? Kurt can be possessive. I guess you figured that out from his behavior at Pete's Diner. I'm sure most everyone in town knows about that by now."

"Oh, yeah," Maddie said with a light laugh. "That was poor judgment on Kurt's part. Pete used to be a prizefighter."

"I know." Alicia giggled. "I was secretly hoping Pete would punch Kurt, but he didn't. Pete is a gentleman."

"But Pete did fire you," Maddie pointed out. "I don't think that was fair."

"Kurt just wouldn't go away, so Pete had to do it. I understand that, although I would really like my job back. Pete was interested in adding decorated cookies to the diner menu, and he wanted me to bake them. That would be absolutely the most perfect job for me." Alicia clasped her hands together as if she were begging Pete to give her another chance.

Olivia felt touched, and found herself saying, "We'll see what we can do to make that happen. It might take a while, though."

"Thank you," Alicia said softly. She picked up her second, uneaten cookie and placed it in the palm of her hand. With her finger, she lightly traced the burgundy scalloped design around the edges. "I love these little guys," she said. "I love the feel of the dough, the colors, the way the royal icing squeezes out into different shapes and designs . . . I even love cleaning up the mess afterward." When Alicia giggled, gold flecks brightened her eyes. Olivia thought of Del, who also had gold-flecked brown eyes. Suddenly, even though she'd just spent time with him earlier that day, she missed him, missed talking and joking with him, discussing cases . . . She especially enjoyed digging up information before he could.

"Sounds like you're a natural-born cutout cookie baker," Maddie said.

"I think so." Alicia smiled shyly. "So I was wondering . . . could I maybe work here in The Gingerbread House? I'd work really hard and do anything you want, even if it means cleaning up the kitchen. Please?"

"I, uh . . ." Olivia hadn't seen this coming, although she probably should have. She glanced at Maddie, who looked as if she, too, had been caught off guard. "Well, that's something Maddie and I would have to talk about. We already have an experienced clerk, Bertha, who also knows how to cut and decorate cookies. Business can be slow at times, and we don't really . . ." Olivia's voice trailed off as Alicia's shoulders drooped. "We'll think about it," Olivia said.

"It's just that I miss my dad so much, and making cookies makes me feel like he is with me." Alicia took a bite of her cookie, then another, apparently lost in her memories. By the time she had swallowed the last lemony bite, Alicia nodded, as if she had reached a decision. Dusting the crumbs off her fingers, she said, "I want to know what happened to my dad. Kurt keeps telling me to forget about him, that he was weak, a hopeless drunk. I knew he had a drinking problem. So what? It didn't make him any less my father. He was trying to get help to stop drinking, but it's hard when you don't have any money." Alicia paced around the kitchen. "I am so tired of being pushed around by men. First, Kurt, then Robbie, and now Kurt again. My dad was better than both of them put together. He was kind. He didn't deserve . . ." Alicia's slender hands tightened into fists. "I *must* find out what happened to my father. If he was murdered, I want to know who did it, and I want that person to pay. I know you two have solved murders before, and I bet that's what you're trying to do now. Let me help you. Please?" She planted her fists on the kitchen table and leaned toward Olivia and Maddie. "Because if you don't, I'll hunt down his killer by myself. I swear I will."

Olivia met Maddie's eyes, which glittered like emeralds in sunlight. Clearly, Maddie felt no qualms about involving a nineteen-year-old in a potential murder investigation. She probably still perceived the case to be so old it presented minimal danger.

"Let us think about it." Olivia realized she was the only one aware of how quickly a cold case could spark into flame. However, one glance at Alicia's tight, determined face, and Olivia knew she had a fight on her hands. There was no way she could justify allowing Alicia to tag along with Maddie and her as they dug deeper into Kenny Vayle's disappearance and presumed death. But if she excluded Alicia, she might trigger an even more dangerous outcome—Alicia might make good on her threat to investigate on her own.

Chapter Twelve

Olivia returned Alicia safely to Ellie and Allan's house by eleven p.m., as she had promised her mother. Their after-dinner baking session had failed to provide much helpful information about Kenny Vayle, but Olivia had to admit they'd gotten to know Alicia far better. That girl was feisty and determined, no doubt about it. Her deeper awareness had left Olivia feeling uneasy. If Alicia tried to investigate on her own, she might put herself in real danger.

It was eleven fifteen p.m. by the time Olivia returned to the Gingerbread House kitchen, where she found Maddie staring at the laptop screen, her hands poised over the keyboard.

"Please tell me you've cracked the case," Olivia said as she hung her jacket on a wall hook near the door. "I'll feel better when we've made some progress. At least, I hope I will."

"I'll need at least five more minutes," Maddie said, "and sustenance."

Olivia went straight to the refrigerator, where she had left defrosted cookies in a covered cake pan. She brought the pan over to the table. Police work required doughnuts, Olivia reasoned, so she and Maddie deserved cookies, right?

"Sustenance coming right up," Olivia said, "with caffeine close behind." She poured water into Mr. Coffee's reservoir and lowered the lid. "I can't wait a whole five minutes. Have you found out anything at all?" Olivia measured coffee grounds into the basket and punched Mr. Coffee's on button.

"Ah yes," Maddie said. "I believe I have indeed found an interesting tidbit. Remember that strange blog I showed you? The one showing a photo of a younger Alicia and her bleary-eyed father?"

"And Kenny seemed to be wearing a necklace . . . yes, I remember." Olivia deposited coffee cups, a carton of cream, and the sugar bowl near the spitting coffeemaker.

"Well, genius that I am, I have identified the blogger as Kurt, and I've found out his last name. Are you ready for this? It's Kurtzel."

"Kurt Kurtzel? Are you kidding me? That's just plain evil. No wonder he has anger issues. Is Kurt really one of those guys who lives in a basement and blogs day and night? How did you find out about him?"

"Good questions." Maddie stood up and stretched. "I will tell all, but first, coffee and a cookie." She poured steaming Italian roast into her cup, leaving plenty of room for cream and sugar. Bearing coffee plus a rose-shaped cookie decorated with baby blue icing and sapphire pearlized sprinkles, Maddie returned to her computer. "I have to admit that finding Kurt wasn't hard. He maintains an enthusiastic online presence, including on Twitter, where his contributions are snarky, though not in a clever, interesting way. He criticizes famous people, rich people, poor people . . . well, pretty much every-one. Kurt's tweets would be totally boring except that some-times he seems to have personal information about people he is unlikely to have met, as well as people he knows. He never comes out and reveals a secret, but his hints contain just enough substance to make him sound knowledgeable."

"Allen might be right that Kurt is doing some hacking." Olivia carted her coffee and cookie over to the table and sat down. As usual, Maddie's fingers tapped the keyboard with a speed and accuracy that Olivia couldn't imagine possessing. "I'll admit that I'm not an expert on the ways of Twitter," Olivia said. "Mom keeps pressuring me to join Facebook, but I'm just too tired at night to hang out on social networks."

"Luckily, you have me," Maddie said. "I could happily tap keys all night, which is a good thing because otherwise this store would have no online presence." Maddie lifted her fingers from the computer keys and glanced at the cookie Olivia was about to taste. "There's something disturbing about a moss green rose with lavender sprinkles," Maddie said. "Not one of my better color combinations. Thank you for eating it."

"I thought you'd want me to make the evidence disappear." Olivia sampled a small bite. "Yum. It tastes much more palatable than it looks."

"Of course it does. When it comes to flavoring, I never err." A red curl bounced against Maddie's forehead as she nodded toward the computer screen. "Kurt Kurtzel does seem to harbor resentments against a significant number of people. Online, Kurt comes across as hypercritical, sometimes in a whiny way. Maybe that's really why Pete threw him out of the diner."

"Pete never could stand a whiner," Olivia said. "He's even harder on men who behave disrespectfully to women, which is how Kurt was behaving toward Alicia. The more I think about it, firing Alicia because of her ex-boyfriend's behavior seems out of character for Pete. I wonder if he knows more about Kurt than we've uncovered so far."

"Not unless he keeps a techie gnome in the kitchen." Maddie reached both arms toward the ceiling to loosen her shoulders. "Given Pete's background as a prizefighter, he might sense when someone is wound up too tight."

"Do you think Kurt might be making up the information he tweets?" Olivia asked.

Maddie leaned back in her chair and stretched out her legs.

"I'll grant you, social networks seem to invite carelessness when it comes to the truth, but you can still get into hot water if you outright lie about someone and they know who you are." She scrolled down the screen to another of Kurt's posts. "I suspect that's why Kurt sticks to innuendo, for the most part, but . . ."

"But what?"

Maddie's freckled forehead puckered as she stared at the screen. "Listen to this one," she said. "*Dirty work at the diner? Don't eat the meatloaf!*"

"Whoa, that's personal. Was that posted today?"

Maddie nodded. "Looks like it was posted soon after Pete chased Kurt out of the diner. So Kurt must have left for a while and then returned later." She closed the lid of her computer. "My laptop is running out of juice. I'd better plug it in." Her gaze swept the kitchen. "Oops, forgot my charger."

Olivia rolled her shoulders and heard a cracking sound. Maybe it was time to join her mom's yoga classes . . . or restock some shelves, which sounded much more stimulating. "I can't remember hearing Pete say even one word about social networks, can you? I have a hard time picturing him glued to a screen, engrossed in Twitter. He never bothers to advertise the diner. It does just fine through word of mouth."

"A customer might warn him about a nasty post," Maddie said. "Pete has loyal fans, and many of them are young and tech savvy. Kurt might not have thought of that. Maybe he indulged in a bit of passive-aggressive revenge, figuring he could hurt the diner's reputation without Pete finding out."

"In Chatterley Heights?" Olivia drained her cup in one cold gulp. "If that's true, it's hard to believe that Kurt actually grew up around here. Anyone in town who reads this post—and understands what it means—would tell Pete at once."

"And Kurt would be dead meat," Maddie said, "figuratively speaking, of course. Pete is careful to avoid physical confrontation, but he finds other ways to protect his reputation. I've heard him slice someone into bits with a few well-chosen words. If Kurt shows up at the diner again, I'd love to be a termite in the wall. Or am I thinking of the wrong insect?"

"I like your version, although you might avoid mentioning termites in the wall and Pete's Diner in the same sentence."

"At least I'm not mangling French." Maddie opened her laptop and began to close down programs. "I think I'll head home," she said.

"Really?" Olivia checked the wall clock over the sink. "It isn't even midnight yet. Are you feeling all right? This is so not like you. Ooh, are you—?"

"No, I'm not pregnant," Maddie said. "Believe me, you would be the first I'd tell. Okay, you'd be the second, after Aunt Sadie. No wait, third. I'd tell Lucas first. Anyway, I'm heading home because my laptop needs charging, and I want to do more research."

"You get to have all the fun." Olivia rinsed out her coffee cup and put it in the dishwasher. "All right, I guess I'll collect my snoozing pup and cart him upstairs."

"Good idea. I'll be back here in about three hours to get some baking done, but you get a good night's sleep. You're older than I . . . Uh-oh." Maddie frowned at her laptop screen.

Olivia froze, leaving the kitchen door open a crack. "What's wrong? Did your computer die?"

"Nope," Maddie said. "But I almost wish it had. Sleep will have to wait a bit. An email arrived as I was about to shut down my email program. It's . . . disturbing."

"Maddie, you're scaring me. What does it say?" Olivia closed the kitchen door before Spunky could slip inside. She heard him whine in protest.

Maddie swept a few disobedient curls off her forehead as she leaned closer to the screen. "This is Binnie's work. She's being even nastier than usual, and that's saying a lot. But not to worry. All we need is a plan, as you keep telling me."

"What has Binnie . . . ?" Olivia peered over Maddie's shoulder. "Oh no, not those photos of Lenora . . ." She pulled over a kitchen chair and sat down. "I was afraid of this,"

Olivia said as Maddie scanned through four photos, all showing Lenora on the knee wall ledge in the cookbook nook. Binnie had captured Lenora in different positions, all humiliating. In the first photo, Lenora's head hung forward as if she were sleeping. The second showed her reaching toward the ceiling as if pleading with the gods. In the third, she bent sideways, her arms flung out as she tried to keep her balance. In the fourth and final photo, Lenora appeared to be falling forward as disembodied hands reached up to catch her.

"Uh-oh," Olivia said. "Some people can't be trusted with smartphones."

"Oh, Livie, Lenora did this to herself. She nearly fell twice before Binnie even showed up."

"How humiliating," Olivia said. "And how nasty of Binnie. We need to alert Gwen and Herbie." She glanced at the clock. "It isn't midnight yet. Do you suppose one of them might still be up tending to the animals?" Gwen and Herbie Tucker, both certified veterinarians, often stayed up late to nurse a sick or injured animal or to feed a litter of orphaned kittens a good Samaritan had dropped off at Chatterley Paws, their ever-expanding no-kill animal shelter.

A volley of fierce yaps, emanating from the sales floor, penetrated the closed kitchen door. Olivia spun around, and said, "What on earth . . ." Spunky quieted down for several seconds, then began again. "That doesn't sound like his normal squirrel alert. I'd better go check."

Olivia entered the sleeping sales floor, where the dim lighting cast eerie, shifting shadows as air currents jostled the cookie cutter mobiles hanging from the ceiling. Olivia spotted Spunky's fluffy tail poking out from under the heavy curtain covering the large front window.

"Spunks," Olivia called in a commanding voice. The tail withdrew under the curtain to be replaced by an equally fluffy Yorkie face. "What on earth was all that racket about?" Olivia pushed the curtain aside and peered out at the Gingerbread House porch. Spunky sat beside her and growled at something only he could see or hear. Two lights illuminated the front section of the wraparound porch, where the rocking chair rested, empty and still, beside a small table. Olivia saw no sign of a recent human presence. "Well, Spunks, either you are seeing ghosts or you're growling at nothing." She let the curtain fall back into place.

Olivia returned to the kitchen, where Maddie sat in front of her closed laptop, nibbling on a cookie. "Spunky must have been hallucinating," Olivia said as she sat down next to Maddie. "Now, where were we?"

"We were agreeing that we should call Herbie and Gwen to warn them about those awful photos of Lenora," Maddie said, "and I volunteer to do so as soon as I get home. If they aren't up with a sick animal, I'll leave a message. But before I leave, there's more you need to know." She lifted the lid of her laptop, and the last photo sprang to life. "Now watch this." She closed the photo attachment, revealing the original email.

Olivia stared at the computer screen. "So . . . those photos came as attachments to a blank email? How odd. Can you tell if she sent those photos to anyone else?"

"No other addresses show up, but she might have used blind copies so we couldn't tell who else might have received these photos." Maddie jumped up and began to pace around the kitchen table. "Binnie is taunting us. She wants to make us feel angry and helpless, probably to punish us for all the times we've made her look foolish. I'll bet she intends to publish those photos on her horrible blog, and she wants us to believe we can't stop her. She knows that everyone in town will recognize our cookbook nook in those photos. It'll look like we got Lenora drunk . . . which we sort of did, but not on purpose. Picking on poor Lenora to get at us is really low." Maddie closed the computer lid with a shade too much force. "I need to preserve what power I've got left, or we'll need to go upstairs and fire up your laptop, which, by the way, you really need to replace with something that doesn't date from the Stone Age. Anyway, Binnie probably sent this email to both our email addresses."

Olivia ran her fingers through her flat, tangled hair, which, unlike Maddie's fluffy curls, inevitably lost energy as the day wore on. "I suspect Binnie has more in mind than mere revenge. This feels like blackmail. Binnie is demonstrating to us how easily she can humiliate poor Lenora. At least, I assume no one else is receiving those photos, though I could be wrong. Binnie wants something from us, but what? When did this message come through?"

Maddie lifted the lid of her laptop to check the arrival time. "Only about fifteen minutes ago. She probably wanted to be sure we would see it first thing in the morning. We'd feel especially pressured then because we'd be rushing to get the store ready to open. Maybe Binnie hoped we'd respond angrily, without thinking. Then she could quote us in her wretched blog."

"Maybe . . ."

"Livie, if you have a clue what Binnie might be up to, tell me."

"I honestly don't know, Maddie. Let me think about it. Are you still planning to come back here to bake after a few hours of sleep?"

Maddie nodded her head. "If I'm able to sleep at all, that is. If not, I'll be back earlier."

"Then scoot," Olivia said. "I'll lock the door behind you."

To avoid the cold, Maddie had begun parking her little yellow VW in the alley behind the store, right next to the kitchen door. She pulled a thick wool sweater over her head before tucking her computer under her arm.

Olivia held the alley door open, and said, "We need to change the lightbulb in the motion detector, so be careful. And remember, your laptop is about to croak. Shut the poor thing down before you drive off."

"Yes, mother," Maddie said.

Olivia stood in the doorway to watch as Maddie unlocked her car, slid into the front seat, and locked her doors. Once Maddie had driven away, Olivia began to feel exposed. She stepped back into the kitchen, then quickly closed, locked, and bolted the door behind her.

Olivia knew she wouldn't be able to fall asleep until she jotted down a few notes. She settled at the kitchen table and drew a diagram of all the people who were connected, one way or another, to Kenny Vayle. The list included Crystal Quinn, Robbie Quinn, Kurt Kurtzel, Alicia Vayle, and a question mark for Crystal's unnamed second "husband."

Olivia stared at her diagram, but no stunning insights jumped out at her. She brainstormed questions, listing them beneath her drawing:

1. If Crystal did have a second husband or companion, who was he, and what happened to him?

2. Is Crystal legally married to Robbie Quinn?

3. According to Robbie, he and Kenny were once friends. Was Robbie telling the truth when he claimed Kenny's drinking had destroyed their friendship, or did Kenny and Robbie fight over Crystal? Was Crystal involved with Robbie before Kenny disappeared? If she was, did Kenny know about it?

4. Is Kurt Kurtzel definitely the author of the blog post Maddie found? Did he take the photo of Alicia and her father, in which Kenny appears to be drunk and is wearing what looks like a cookie cutter necklace? Why did Kurt post that particular photo of Kenny?

5. According to Alicia, on the day Kenny disappeared, he'd said he was meeting with someone about a job. Was this true? Who was that person?

Not much of a list, Olivia thought as she read through what she had written. She had yet to determine how the people on her list might connect to one another or whether they had a specific reason to kill Kenny Vayle—who might not have been murdered, after all. If the bones in the wall belonged to someone other than Kenny, she was wasting her time . . . although there might still be a mystery to pursue. At the top of the page, Olivia wrote *Call Del!* She folded the paper and wedged it inside the pocket of her jeans. It was a start, she told herself. Maybe a few hours of sleep would point her in a clearer direction. She would feel better when she had a plan.

O livia yawned as she entered the foyer and locked the Gingerbread House door behind her. Spunky squirmed out of his mistress's arms and trotted to the front door, which opened onto the porch. He scratched at the door and whined.

Olivia sighed. "Oh, Spunky, must you?"

The little Yorkie turned around to yap at her, then tilted his head and whimpered. He left no doubt that he needed to use the outside facilities before bed. Olivia had run out of puppy pads, so it would be unwise to deny him. "Oh, all right, but no dawdling. You can stay in bed all night, but I have to get up early, so no chasing after nocturnal creatures."

Olivia hooked Spunky's leash onto his collar. He couldn't be trusted to resist the siren call of the squirrels. When she opened the front door, Spunky strained at his leash, pulling Olivia through the door and across the porch toward the front steps. She had no time to do more than toss the door shut behind her. Spunky's little claws slid on the wood floor of the porch as his mere five pounds tried to yank Olivia down the steps. She followed willingly, hoping Spunky would complete his mission quickly. He obliged as soon as he reached the front lawn.

"Good boy," Olivia said. "Now let's go to bed."

Spunky had other ideas. With a hard yank on his leash, he

insisted Olivia follow him. After a few steps, he came to a sudden stop, ears perked up. His rigid stance and intense concentration sent a shiver down Olivia's spine. "Spunks? What is it?" she whispered. His little head tilted to one side, as if he were listening to sounds no human ear could hear. What Olivia did hear was his low, throaty growl, and she took it seriously. In a quiet, calm voice, she said, "Okay, Spunks, let's go inside now. Come on." The plucky little guy stood his ground. His ears shifted subtly as he listened to the darkness. Keeping his leash taut, Olivia crept toward him until she could scoop him up with her free arm. "Gotcha," she whispered in his ear.

Holding Spunky firmly against her chest, Olivia scooted across the lawn. As she climbed the steps to the front porch, she glanced up at the front door. It had blown partly shut, revealing a sheet of paper flapping in the wind. Olivia shifted Spunky to her hip and flattened the paper against the door to get a better look. She could see writing, but she couldn't make out the words in the weak porch light.

The paper had been tacked to the door. Olivia would need both hands to remove it. "In you go, kiddo." She thrust Spunky inside the foyer and slammed the door behind him. He yelped with alarm, and Olivia broke off a bit of thumbnail in her haste to remove the tack from the door. "It's okay, Spunky. I'll be there in two secs," Olivia shouted. She hoped no one but Spunky was nearby to hear her. The tack fell to the porch floor. A gust of wind threatened to run off with the paper, but Olivia grabbed the note in time.

Olivia squeezed through the front door, fearful that Spunky might make a run for it, but he was more interested in making sure his human hadn't abandoned him. Rather than rush through the tiny opening, Spunky stood on his hind legs and begged to be picked up. With her free hand, Olivia lifted him to her chest. "Good, good boy," she murmured as she buried her face in his silky hair. Olivia lowered Spunky to the foyer floor so she could hold on to the mysterious paper while she unlocked the door to the stairs leading up to her apartment. As soon as the door cracked open, Spunky squeezed through and bounded up the steps.

Olivia, on the other hand, could no longer stand the suspense. She sat down on the bottom step of the staircase. Her hand shook as she turned the paper over, half expecting to find a threat. Despite the dim light and the faint, scratchy writing, she was able to make out the brief handwritten message: *If you want to know what happened to Kenny Vayle, follow the cookie cutter.*

Puzzled, Olivia read the note again, then again. Questions jumbled together in her tired mind: *Who might have written such a note? Why leave it for me, rather than the police? Which cookie cutter—the pierced heart on Kenny's necklace? What might "follow the cookie cutter" possibly mean?* Olivia was inclined to suspect she was the victim of a silly joke. It was common knowledge in Chatterley Heights that she and Maddie often found themselves involved in murder investigations, and, as always, rumors about the bones had spread quickly. Someone might have thought it amusing to taunt her with a puzzling "hint" about Kenny Vayle's disappearance. The name Binnie Sloan came to mind.

Loud yapping from the top of the stairs reminded Olivia that a tired, impatient Yorkie was waiting at her apartment door. "We're lucky we don't have any neighbors," Olivia muttered. "Okay, Spunks, I get the point. Now chill, or I might be tempted to skip your bedtime treats." When he heard the word "treats," Spunky yapped and pawed at the door. "I don't blame you for being impatient," Olivia said as she slid her key into the lock. "It's two a.m. We've both been up way too late."

When the door opened, Spunky raced inside and made for the kitchen. Olivia heard his nails clatter on the tile floor. Then she heard the phone ring. *At two a.m.?* She sprinted to the kitchen, almost tripping over Spunky, who had been watching for her from the entrance. He yipped in alarm as she lunged for the telephone receiver. Panting for breath, she said, "Hello? Hello?"

After a moment of hesitation, a tentative voice asked, "Are you all right? Livie, tell me at once if you need help."

"*Del.* Jeez, you scared the life out of me. It's two o'clock in the morning. Has something happened?" Olivia's shaky legs threatened to give out. The kitchen phone, an old model that had come with the house, had a long cord that allowed her to slide down the wall to the floor.

"Livie, I'm so sorry, I know it's the middle of the night, but . . . You're okay, right?"

"Yes, I'm fine, or I will be as soon as my heart returns to my chest."

"Good." Del sounded relieved. "Listen, I'm at home, and someone left a disturbing message on my personal cell phone. The number didn't register on my caller ID, but it had come through at 1:37 a.m." Del hesitated. "You're sure everything is okay? If someone is threatening you, say 'I'm getting ready for bed,' and I'll be there."

"I'm fine, Del, honestly. A bit rattled, that's all. Long story." Olivia rolled to her knees and stood up. Her legs wobbled, but she remained upright. Good sign.

"I want to hear that story," Del said, "because I suspect it might relate to the message I got. I'd raced off without my phone earlier, around eleven thirty p.m., after I got a call on my work cell. Turned out to be a false alarm. The message on my personal cell was waiting for me when I got home. Livie, what's that noise?"

"It's Spunky whining," Olivia said. "He is suffering from serious Milk Bone withdrawal. Give me two secs, and I'll quiet him down." She left the receiver on the counter and threw Spunky two Milk Bone treats, each broken in half. After retrieving the phone, she sank onto a kitchen chair. "Spunky is happily crunching, so tell me what your phone message said."

Del's voice shifted to professional mode. "According to

the anonymous informant, someone had been skulking around The Gingerbread House at about midnight. Said skulker—no hint as to gender—sneaked up to your porch and tried the front door, probably to see if it was locked. Then the person left. The informant hung up without leaving a name or any explanation as to why they'd waited so long to report the incident."

Having crunched his bedtime treats, Spunky gazed drowsily up at Olivia. When she did not reach down to pick him up, he jumped onto her lap and curled into a sleepy ball. Olivia, however, felt wide-awake. "The informant said this was around midnight?"

"Right, but maybe some kid was playing a trick on me. After all, if you haven't noticed anything suspicious, it might just—"

"I might have noticed something," Olivia said. "I can't be precise, but it was around midnight when Spunky started barking up a storm from the sales floor. Maddie and I were in the kitchen. I went out to the floor to check, but I didn't see anything through the front window. If someone had been at the front door, I wouldn't have seen him from the window. Was the informant's voice male or female?"

"I know what you're thinking, Livie. Maybe the informant was also the person who visited your porch. That might explain why he or she waited to report the incident. I know it doesn't make sense to report oneself, but I've seen stranger things. Some folks just get a kick out of confusing the police."

"Del, about this informant . . . You haven't said whether it was a man or a woman. Couldn't you tell from the voice?"

Del's sigh conveyed his frustration. "Not for certain. The voice was hushed and muffled, as if he or she were afraid of being overheard."

"Or recognized," Olivia said. "Listen, Del, there really was someone on the porch, although I can't be certain of the time. About thirty minutes ago, I called it a night and went out to the sales floor to get Spunky. He desperately needed to 'go out,' in the doggie sense. So out we went. Short version, when we went back to the porch, I realized there was a piece of paper tacked to my beautiful front door, for which, if there is justice in the world, someone ought to pay."

"There is precious little justice in the world," Del said. "About that sheet of paper . . ."

"Hang on." Olivia retrieved the paper. "It's a note written in block letters with pencil. It says, *If you want to know what happened to Kenny Vayle, follow the cookie cutter.*"

"I see," Del said. "Not what I expected. I'm beginning to think this is all a strange and inscrutable hoax."

"You may be right," Olivia said, glancing at the kitchen clock. "I'm meeting Maddie back in the kitchen for a baking session in just over an hour. So I'm going with the hoax theory for now."

"You go to bed, Livie," Del said. "I'll feel better if I come over and take a look around The Gingerbread House. Even if this is a hoax, I don't like it. Save the note and give it to me tomorrow. I'll stop by in the morning to pick it up."

"My fingerprints will be all over the note." Olivia yawned. "I wasn't thinking of it as evidence."

"In the shock of the moment, most people don't, no matter how many mysteries they've devoured. I'll test it for prints, anyway. You never know. Do you have any idea what happened to the tack?"

"Nope. Sorry, Del. I was trying to hold Spunky's leash while I was removing the tack, and it dropped. It's silly, but all I could think about was that the lovely finish on the front door might be damaged."

"I wish I'd been there," Del said. "If you hear anything outside, it'll probably be me. You can call my personal cell if you're worried. I'll bring a flashlight and look for that tack, too."

Olivia yawned again.

"Forget everything and go to bed," Del said. "I'm betting this whole setup was somebody's little joke on us. Sleep like a baby."

"I had colic when I was a baby," Olivia said.

"Then sleep like a baby who wasn't you. Let me do the worrying; it's why they pay me the not-big-enough bucks. Love you," Del said a moment before his phone went silent.

"Love you back," Olivia whispered. She hung up and headed toward bed, fully clothed. Spunky followed close on her heels. She felt exhausted enough to fall asleep instantly and stay out until the cursed alarm rang. Del was probably right that the note and phone call were part of a silly hoax. He had experience with such things. He certainly knew the lengths to which Binnie might go to frighten or embarrass Olivia. But somewhere in the back of her mind, Olivia believed this was no hoax.

Chapter Thirteen

❦

When Olivia unlocked the Gingerbread House door at five thirty on Wednesday morning, she expected to be greeted by the sweet, doughy scent of cookies just out of the oven. Instead, she smelled only the faint leftover odor of yesterday's cookies combined with the fake lemon smell of cleaning solution. When the store wasn't hopping with customers, Bertha got bored. When Bertha got bored, she cleaned compulsively.

Olivia switched on the lights, and Spunky sneaked past her into the store. All business, he bustled from corner to corner, sniffing for unwelcome intruders. Olivia left him to his inspection and headed toward the quiet kitchen. Had Maddie overslept? That would be a first. After the shock of finding a note tacked to her front door in the early morning hours, Olivia felt uneasy. She hesitated, her hand around the kitchen doorknob. She could have sworn she'd heard Mr. Coffee spit out the last of his fresh brew into the carafe. Olivia opened the door to a scene she'd thought she would never see— Maddie was sound asleep, her right cheek resting on the kitchen table. She was snoring. Olivia suppressed a giggle. It was a light little snore, but still tease-worthy, especially given Maddie's frequent reminders that she was two months younger than Olivia.

A sudden surge of apprehension brought Olivia back to the present. Maddie regularly shorted herself on sleep. What if exhaustion had caught up with her? She might be ill. Olivia shook her friend's left shoulder. Maddie showed no reaction. When she shook harder, Maddie groaned. Her head popped up and wobbled, as if her neck had forgotten how to function.

"Hang on." Olivia half-filled a cup with fresh, strong coffee, stirred in cream and sugar, and placed it on the table. Maddie put the cup to her lips and drained it. She plunked it down on the table, nodded once, and said, "Okay, then."

"Maddie? Are you really awake? Your eyes look like they're going in different directions. Do you need more coffee?"

"Don't be silly. I'm awake and fully focused, as always." Maddie checked the kitchen clock. "I was only resting my eyes for a few minutes. Working on my laptop made me feel a bit drowsy, that's all. Although I don't remember what I was looking at on the screen, so more caffeine does sound like a good plan." Maddie fixed herself another cup before she lifted the lid of her computer. It flashed back to life. "Ah yes, now I remember . . . research that didn't go anywhere." She opened her email account. "Nothing yet. Livie, how did you respond to Binnie's blank email with those awful photos of Lenora? She hasn't reacted at all, which isn't like the Binnie we all know too well."

Olivia slapped her forehead. "I forgot about Binnie. So much happened after you went home that I never thought about those photos of poor Lenora. I forgot to talk to Del about them, too. We'd better do some quick strategizing and fire off a response to Binnie. I hate to think how she'd take revenge if she believes we're ignoring her."

Maddie's pale eyebrows shot up. "You saw Del after I left?"

"He called right as I walked into my apartment." Olivia

fixed herself a cup of rich Italian roast. It smelled heavenly. "He was worried about my safety." She relayed Del's story about the late night call reporting a prowler on the Ginger-bread House porch around midnight.

"Wasn't that about the same time Spunky made such a fuss in the store?" Maddie asked.

Olivia nodded. "And someone did come up to our front door. Look at this." She drew the folded sheet of paper from her pants pocket and handed it to Maddie.

Maddie's eyes sparkled as she unfolded the paper and spread it on the worktable. "Oh, this is so cool . . . though in a barely believable sort of way. I feel like I'm in a Nancy Drew novel. *"Follow the cookie cutter,"* she read out loud. "Which cookie cutter, I wonder. Does this refer to the pierced heart pendant Kenny Vayle wore, or is there a cutter we haven't even heard about yet? Because the pendant was found with the bones, so how can it lead anywhere else?"

"I can think of a number of ways." Olivia settled in front of Maddie's computer. "But first, let's deal with Binnie and her revolting photos of poor Lenora. If Binnie thinks she is being ignored, I'm afraid she will splash those photos all over the Internet."

Maddie dragged a chair sideways and sat down next to Olivia. "As it happens," Maddie said, "I spent some time last night thinking about how we should handle Binnie . . . aside from putting a stamp on her forehead and sending her to the jungle."

"Oh, so tempting." Olivia clicked on Binnie's email to open it. "I can't understand why she left the body of the email blank. Maybe she just wanted to see how we would react to those pictures?"

"That's way too subtle for Binnie," Maddie said. "She knows Del isn't her biggest fan, so I figure she didn't want to put anything in writing that might get her arrested for blackmail."

"That sounds right." Olivia scrolled quickly through the

offensive shots of poor Lenora, drunk on leftover sherry. "The photos alone might be sufficient evidence to indicate attempted blackmail." Olivia rubbed her eyes, wishing she had managed to oversleep for another hour.

"What if we accuse Binnie of blackmail and threaten to expose her? Maybe she'll back off."

"I'm thinking of a simpler and more direct approach that might stop her cold," Olivia said. "I think we should forward her email to Del, as is. Let it speak for itself. I'll add a short note explaining what really happened in the cookbook nook, and he can draw his own conclusions about Binnie's intentions. He'll know what to do. Between you and me, Del gets a kick out of quashing Binnie. She is forever interfering with his investigations. She knows Del can toss her in jail if she goes over the line. He has done it before, so he might succeed in scaring her off. The sooner we stop that woman, the better I'll feel."

"Amen to that." Maddie hopped up and wriggled her shoulders. "That little nap did wonders for me. I'm ready to bake. Although not lemon cutouts, I think. I need something fresh and exciting to tingle my senses."

"Is there any cookie you haven't tackled before?" Olivia addressed a new email to Del and immediately attached Binnie's email, so she wouldn't forget. After adding a brief note, she clicked the send command. There was no time to waste. Binnie might even now be preparing one of her infamous posts for that detestable blog of hers. As if her weekly newspaper, *The Weekly Chatter*, weren't torture enough, now she blogged daily about the failings and foibles of Chatterley Heights citizens. Though no one escaped Binnie's attention, Olivia, Maddie, and poor little Spunky were among her favorite targets.

"There are undoubtedly hundreds of cookie recipes I haven't tried," Maddie said. "I find that knowledge comforting, since I can't die until I've perfected all of them. However, for now I'll limit myself to a flavor other than lemon. It's possible to overdo a good thing." She opened a cupboard and selected two bottles of flavoring. "I think I'll try combining plum flavoring with almond." When Olivia didn't respond, Maddie added, "And possibly a soup spoon of vanilla . . ."

"Soupçon," Olivia corrected. "It means 'a pinch' in French." When Maddie chuckled, Olivia looked up from the email she had sent to Del and shot a suspicious glance at her friend. "You knew that, didn't you?"

Maddie clapped her hands like a delighted child. "I heard a French chef on the Cooking Channel use that word," she said. "I've been waiting for the right opportunity to mangle it."

"Well, you did a superb job." Olivia smiled sweetly at her friend.

"I'll accept that as a compliment, even though I think I've been insulted." Maddie measured sugar for a batch of cutout cookies. "To get even, I'm assigning the computer research to you. I shall roll and cut cookies while you do the tapping and squinting." She added butter to the bowl and lowered the flat beater. "Time-out." The beater spiraled around the mixing bowl until Maddie stopped it, and said, "I don't know about you, Livie, but I lost sleep over the thought of Alicia getting involved in a possible murder investigation. I know I was all excited about digging up a cold case, but now I'm feeling squeamish. What if those bones really are Kenny Vayle's and it turns out he was murdered? Alicia is so determined to find out what happened to her dad. I can understand, but . . ." Maddie raised a low cloud as she dumped a measuring cup of flour into the mixing bowl.

"I'm worried about Alicia, too," Olivia said. "The crime lab doesn't seem able to give the case priority. I'm very afraid that Alicia will try to investigate on her own. So far, no one other than Kurt has bothered her, but if someone decides she is a threat . . ."

"Exactly what I've been thinking," Maddie said. "We need a list of suspects and questions."

"As it happens, I started one early this morning, right after you left." Olivia produced her questions about the people she knew to be connected to Kenny Vayle. "It's a start, anyway."

Maddie checked the clock over the kitchen sink. "We still have about two hours before the store opens. I'm dressed for work under this apron, so I can open at nine. Clearly, you will need a shower and change of clothes." She cast a critical eye at Olivia's attire—old sweats and lace-free running shoes. "I'll finish this batch of dough and stick it in the fridge. I've got a disk of chilled dough I can roll out and cut while you are doing my bidding on the computer."

"Yes, ma'am," Olivia said. "While you are finishing up, I'll see what I can find out about Crystal's mysterious marital history." She first did a search for information about Crystal Quinn. Olivia couldn't gain access to Facebook accounts— only Maddie possessed such advanced skills, though even she admitted Facebook was tougher to hack. However, Crystal had a fairly extensive presence on the Internet, including her own website. She seemed far more trusting in cyberspace than she was in person. On her own website, Crystal provided numerous links to what Maddie referred to as "venting sites." She vented mostly about men, although her daughter received her share of online criticism. Poor kid.

After fifteen minutes, Olivia had read more than enough about Crystal's ongoing problems with a series of men she'd been involved with before Robbie Quinn. Crystal discussed the men using first names only. She referred to several of them as husbands, though she never mentioned weddings. While Olivia wasn't as skilled as Maddie at computer searches, she did have a friend, Lori, who had been working in the courthouse records department for years. Lori owed her a favor. Luckily, she was also a devoted gossip and an early riser. Olivia shot Lori an email asking if there might be a way to find out how many times Crystal Quinn had legally married and, if possible, the names of her castoffs. Crystal had been born in Chatterley Heights, so there was a good chance her marriages, if they were real, had taken place in town.

Olivia glanced at the time in the upper corner of Maddie's computer. Forty-five minutes had flown by. She lifted her fingers from the keyboard and reached toward the ceiling, which triggered more distinct cracking sounds in her shoulder area. Maybe she should start exercising more, perhaps take up jogging with her mother . . . Nah.

"I see you have returned from your Internet adventure," Maddie said. "Addictive, isn't it?"

"Yet possibly helpful." Olivia twisted around in her seat as Maddie removed her earbuds. Flour had somehow attached itself to her hair, chin, and one shoulder. On the table, several sheets of cutout shapes awaited baking. "Weren't you just starting to mix dough when I saw you last?"

"That was some time ago." Maddie dipped a cookie cutter in flour. "Since then I have finished mixing that batch and put it in the fridge to chill. Then I rolled out a chilled batch of dough, cut several dozen cookies, and cured cancer. Did you unearth anything interesting?"

Olivia relayed her information about Crystal. "I jotted down the names of the men she referred to as husbands and sent the list to my friend, Lori, at the courthouse. "According to my research, Crystal had at least six husbands. From the dates on her posts, a couple of them overlapped. Apparently, marriage laws have been in flux since my divorce."

"It only seems that way because you actually went through a divorce." Maddie managed to deposit a dusting of flour on her forearm as she replenished the supply she used for dipping her cutters. With a happy sigh, she said, "I love to play with flour."

"I can see that." Olivia stood up and freshened her coffee. "What if I do the cutting for a while, and you traverse the Internet. I might be missing important information because I'm not as skilled as you are."

"True," Maddie said. "Let me wash my hands and dust

myself off. Meanwhile, tell me what else you found, and I'll take it from there."

"Crystal complains a lot about men." Olivia joined Maddie at the sink to wash her hands, too. "Unfortunately, she's on Facebook and a few other sites I can't figure out how to access."

"I can give it a try, while you take over the cookie cutting," Maddie said. "It's odd . . . In person, Crystal seems like the suspicious type, but apparently she doesn't dwell on Internet security issues. Not if she is pouring her heart out on the less secure sites." Maddie settled at her computer and wiggled her fingers. "Time for some fun. Let's see what we can dig up about Crystal Quinn's marriage addiction."

While Maddie's hands flew across the computer keyboard as if she were playing a piano, Olivia wished she could sit down at her desk with paper and pen. So many questions swirled around in her head. She needed a way to trigger ideas and organize them in her mind while she cut out cookie shapes. At once, she thought about cookie cutters. Handling those intriguing little shapes always helped her think.

Olivia slipped out of the kitchen to the dimly lit sales floor. Spunky's fluffy head popped up. "Stay on your chair and rest, Spunks," Olivia said. "It isn't time to get up yet." Spunky resumed his nap without objection. Olivia unlocked the long, narrow storage room that shared a wall with the kitchen. She switched on the light and stepped inside. Shelves along one wall held the store's expansive collection of cookie cutters, all organized in labeled plastic boxes. As the more organized of the two business partners, Olivia had assumed responsibility for labeling each box with a category name and a list of contents, which she faithfully updated when necessary.

It took only a few minutes for Olivia to choose the three boxes she thought most likely to be helpful. She piled the boxes on top of each other with their category names arranged in alphabetical order: careers, housewares, and schoolwork. Maddie would laugh at that, if she noticed it, but Olivia found order and precision comforting when too many questions roiled in her mind.

Spunky barely lifted his sleepy head as Olivia, holding all three boxes, emerged from the storage closet and slipped back into the kitchen. Maddie was too absorbed in her computer work to notice when Olivia deposited her burden on the work-table. She opened the boxes and placed them side by side near the rolled dough, so she could read the contents list for each box as she worked.

Olivia began to select the cutters she wanted to use. A hammer shape reminded her of Robbie Quinn, in more ways than one. Robbie was a builder, but he also had a way of hammering those around him. As she cut three hammer shapes from the rolled dough, Olivia considered Robbie as a suspect. He certainly had the strength to kill a man, especially a smaller and perhaps inebriated one. What would have been Robbie's motive? If he'd been friends with Kenny, as he claimed, he would have known Crystal. Had he wanted her for himself? Perhaps he'd written the note that lured Kenny to his death. Robbie would have been aware that Kenny was always looking for that perfect dream job. On the other hand, it was quite a leap from wanting Crystal to murdering the husband she might have been more than willing to leave.

"A *hammer*, Livie? Really?"

Olivia dropped her cookie cutter, which gouged the smooth surface of the rolled dough. "Maddie, you startled me. I didn't hear you stop clicking those computer keys."

"Does one hear the sound of silence?" Maddie peered at the labels on the cookie cutter boxes. "And speaking of inscrutable, why are you using such a weird mishmash of cutter shapes? Where's the fun stuff, like Halloween, Thanksgiving—which is coming right up, you know. And how could you forget Santa?"

"I can always raid those supplies later, if I need them," Olivia said, hoping she didn't sound defensive. "What did your computer journey reveal?"

"I will tell all, but you must promise to explain why you're using these particular cutters . . . because I know you, Livie. You have a plan. Am I right?"

"Well, in a way. It's really more of a brainstorming technique." Olivia picked up a wineglass-shaped cookie cutter, which made her think of Crystal. Might she have participated in a scheme to eliminate her husband? Why not simply divorce him? "But I'll need more actual information," Olivia said as she glanced up at the kitchen clock. "I'll get ready to open the store soon, but first, tell me what you've found online. Maybe I'll be able to formulate something plan-like while I'm showering."

"I'm quivering with curiosity, but all right," Maddie said. "I picked up where you left off with Crystal's online activities. You were right, she's one of those folks who thinks they are invisible on the Internet. She isn't even taking advantage of the privacy features on Facebook. However, I can't report anything earth shattering—aside from knowing when and for how long Crystal's house will be unoccupied, that is. I did learn that her life with Robbie isn't all bonbons and buttercups. She often complains about his temper and says that sometimes she feels like a domestic slave. One interesting tidbit appeared in a recent post—Crystal claims Robbie threw Alicia out of the house without telling her. Robbie sent Crystal to the convenience store to pick up fresh milk. When she returned, Robbie calmly announced that he'd packed Alicia's suitcase and told her she wasn't welcome anymore. Crystal checked Alicia's room and found most of her clothing still in the closet."

"This is all rather confusing," Olivia said. "Remember when Robbie came to the store later that same morning? He told us he might be forced to throw Alicia out? Only by then he must have already done so. He obviously didn't think we knew that."

Maddie's eyes widened. "Ooh, that would mean . . . wait, this is like math. It's making my brain hurt."

"I have a couple ideas," Olivia said. "Robbie likes to be seen as the 'good guy,' the one who does everything right.

Maybe he wanted Crystal to believe it was her daughter who made the decision to leave. Or . . . this is a longer shot, but what if Robbie manipulated Kurt into getting Alicia fired? Maybe Robbie wanted an excuse to get rid of Alicia."

"I see," Maddie said, although she sounded as if she didn't see at all. "So that means . . ." Maddie's freckled face scrunched up as she thought. "Do you suppose Robbie and Kurt might know each other better than we realize? Maybe Robbie gave Kurt reason to think he could have Alicia if he got her away from Pete. Or is that over the top?"

"At this point," Olivia said, "speculation is all we've got."

"Hey, I'm the one who is supposed to come up with strings of elaborate improbabilities," Maddie said with a snicker. "Although I have to say, Robbie does seem manipulative and controlling. But I still don't understand why he would go to such lengths to get rid of Alicia. Crystal hasn't convinced me she is a devoted mother."

Olivia shrugged. "She did say online that she didn't want her daughter to leave."

"Right, and no one ever lies on the Internet," Maddie said.

"Good point." Olivia glanced down at the wineglass cookie cutter, still in her hand. "It's far easier to play 'poor me' online than in person. The Crystal I spoke with in the band shell wasn't nearly as fragile as her name implies. She was angry."

Maddie scooped up the hammer cutter and held it in the palm of her hand. "Crystal doesn't sound happy with Robbie, either, at least online. Bearing in mind the whole reliability problem with the Internet, I have to wonder if Crystal is just as miserable in her current relationship as she was with Kenny." Maddie glanced at the kitchen clock. "Livie, we should get a move on. It will be opening time before we know it."

Olivia nodded absently.

"Earth to Livie," Maddie said. "What profound thoughts are keeping you from a much needed shower?"

"Hmm? Oh, sorry." She dropped the wineglass cutter on

the worktable. "I was following what is probably a far-fetched thread."

"What thread?" Maddie said. "Never mind the shower. *What* thread?"

Olivia shook her head firmly. "No, the thread is too weak. I'll wait and see what comes next." She left the store and hurried upstairs to prepare for the workday. But the question lingered in her mind . . . If Robbie, Crystal, or Kurt killed Kenny, Alicia might be in a great deal of danger. *Maddie and I must tread very carefully.* The last thing Olivia wanted was Alicia's death on her conscience.

Chapter Fourteen

On Wednesday morning, nine o'clock sharp, Olivia unlocked the front door of her Queen Anne to find Sam Parnell, one of her least favorite Chatterley Heights citizens, standing on her porch. As always, Sam wore the official uniform of the United States Postal Service. In deference to the season, he had switched to long trousers, which hid his scrawny legs. A heavy mail sack hung over one shoulder, and he held a package in his hand.

Sam's dedication to the art of gossiping had earned him the nickname Snoopy Sam. Most folks in town indulged in idle gossip, of course, but more out of curiosity than meanness. Snoopy, however, reveled in the vicious kind, especially if it hurt someone he felt had slighted him. If it suited his purposes, he resorted to fabrication. Olivia had learned through an uncomfortable experience to handle him with delicate finesse. Other folks often treated him as a minor irritant, but as Olivia knew, like a viper, Snoopy Sam struck with lightning speed.

"Sam, what excellent timing," Olivia said, forcing a warm smile. "I usually miss seeing you on your route. Is that package for us?" She nodded toward the large padded envelope in Sam's hand.

"Overnight delivery." Sam's nasal voice could make "good morning" sound like a sneer. "These overnight deliveries must cost you two a bundle. Maybe you should pay more attention to your inventory. But I suppose you've been too busy with midnight visitors and so forth."

"Thanks for the prompt service," Olivia said with a bright smile. She held out her hand for the package, but Sam ignored the gesture.

"I heard you had some excitement around here in the wee hours this morning." Sam's watery blue eyes watched her face.

Knowing how skillfully Sam could transform even the slightest twitch into juicy gossip, Olivia remained silent. It wasn't easy. She wanted to snatch the package and shove him out the door.

"Just between you and me," Sam said, "I wouldn't be surprised if Binnie was responsible."

"Binnie?" Olivia stifled a groan as she realized how quickly Sam had gotten the best of her. On the other hand, now she was curious. Perhaps, for once, Sam actually knew something helpful. "What has Binnie done this time?"

Sam relaxed, having won the initial round. "Sounds to me like you haven't read her post this morning. I figure she's getting desperate for stuff to print in that silly blog of hers, so she's going around creating her own news. Of course, once a rumor starts, you need to talk about what really happened, or the rumor just keeps spreading and growing."

Meaning you will keep enhancing the rumor unless I tell you what's really going on, and then you'll enhance and spread it around . . .

The sound of squeaky brakes made Sam twist sideways to see the street. Olivia watched over his shoulder as a light blue van came to a halt in front of The Gingerbread House. Through the windows, she saw several women chattering with each other as they unlocked their seat belts.

Sam's sharp features expressed disdain as he turned back to face Olivia. He missed seeing the older model Toyota sedan—beige, with a distinctive dent in the passenger door—that pulled up to the curb behind the van. It was Del's personal car. He would be dropping by to pick up the note she'd found tacked to her front door in the early morning hours. More gossip fodder . . . Del stepped out of his car, glanced toward the Gingerbread House porch, and slid back inside. He did a U-turn, avoiding the women emerging from the van, and was gone in an instant.

Suppressing a sigh of relief, Olivia said, "Sorry, Sam. I guess we'll have to finish our little talk later," Olivia said. "My first customers are coming up the walk."

Her cheerful warning had the desired effect. Sam hitched his mail bag higher on his shoulder and said, "Well, you might want to check out Binnie's blog post from early this morning. It looked to me like Binnie might have been hanging around your store when decent folks are sound asleep. I wouldn't be surprised if she staged the whole nighttime visitation just to embarrass you. How else would she know what was written on that piece of paper?" Sam gave her a sneery grin and turned to leave. Olivia heard him whistling as he headed across the porch.

"Whew," Bertha said as she watched the last of the Cookie Cutter Collectors Club members climb into their van for their return trip to Clarksville. "I clean forgot they were coming today, or I would have come in early." She squinted at the lovely, yet inaccurate Hansel and Gretel clock hanging on the sales floor wall. "Those ladies stayed nearly two hours. I must say, though, it's always such fun to discuss cookie cutters with them, and they do spend generously." Bertha planted her hands on her slim, yet still ample hips and assessed the condition of the store. "I can handle customers while I do some straightening up," she said. "You two can get back to your own work. My, I do love a busy day."

Maddie grinned at Olivia and tilted her fuzzy red head toward the kitchen door. "I need to finish another batch of cookies before the next customer invasion," she said as she strode toward the kitchen.

"I'll join you for a bit," Olivia said. "Bertha, holler if you need help out here."

Bertha didn't respond. She was already entering the cookbook nook, dust rag in hand.

Olivia reconstructed a display of autumn-themed cookie cutters before joining Maddie in the kitchen. She found Maddie staring at her laptop screen, her fingers skittering around the keyboard. "I told Bertha a tiny lie," Maddie said, her eyes never leaving the screen. "I'm a bit ahead on the baking and decorating, which is a good thing because we just got an email from Polly. She's wondering if she could stop by later this afternoon to buy a couple dozen cookies to take back to the homeless shelter. Several families with kids showed up last night. That's so sad."

"Polly will take good care of them." Olivia opened a covered cake pan filled with a variety of leaf-shaped cookies decorated with deep red and gold icing. Imagining the children's faces when they saw the cookies, she packed several dozen in the store's largest Gingerbread House box. "Polly will try to pay for these cookies, but we mustn't let her," Olivia said. "Agreed?"

"Absolutely." Maddie's hands dropped to her lap as she studied the screen. "Livie, you need to see this. I'm glad you managed to tell me about your strange conversation with Snoopy Sam about Binnie's blog. I'm skimming through it right now."

"How weird is it?" Olivia closed the box of cookies and slid it into a large bag. Before folding the top, she turned the bag around to admire the new design—a quirky, yet recognizable drawing of The Gingerbread House.

"On a weirdness scale of one to ten," Maddie said, "it's about a fourteen. It's unlike any of Binnie's previous blog posts. It's more like an online war. I get the impression someone's responses are making Binnie really, really mad. Livie, do you know if Sam knows his way around the Internet?"

"I believe he does. Why?" Olivia pulled up a chair and sat next to Maddie. She skimmed through the post, and said, "I see what you mean. It looks as if Binnie is responding to comments that aren't on the screen. Maybe they are being sent as emails. Anyway, those comments must be pushing her buttons big time. Oh my, she insulted the United States Postal Service. I'd say that's a clue."

Maddie stretched out her legs and smiled. "Is it too much to hope that Binnie and Snoopy will feud with each other till the end of time? That would be such a relief for the rest of us."

"From the tone of Binnie's contributions, I'd say there's a good chance." Olivia got up to make herself a cup of coffee. "What does she say about the note I found tacked to the front door?"

"Let me go back to the beginning," Maddie said. "I started at her most recent post, and I've been working my way backward. Okay, here it is, the first post of the morning. Hm, very vague about how the note got tacked to the front door."

"Sam makes it sound like she saw the whole scene and either read or wrote the note herself," Olivia said.

"Sam is such a liar." Maddie clicked away without comment for a couple minutes.

Feeling impatient, Olivia selected a daisy-shaped cookie with pink and red petals. She dunked one red petal into her coffee and managed to chomp it off before it dissolved, which induced a feeling of well-being.

"Ah, I see what happened," Maddie said. "Binnie says '*a mysterious stranger*' attached the note to your door and '*disappeared into the night*.' According to her, the note warned you not to investigate the bones in the wall because it might cost you your life."

"Which isn't what the note said." Olivia bit off a pink petal.

"Right. It isn't clear that she saw who tacked it up, either." Maddie leaned back in her chair. "Hand me one of those daisies, would you? I'm pretty sure computer work burns lots of calories."

"That sounds right." Olivia handed her friend the last cookie in the pan, a blue and green daisy.

"So what I'm concluding," Maddie said, "is that it's more likely someone else told her about the note."

"And it sounds like the unknown tattletale didn't get a good look at the person who defaced my beautiful door," Olivia said. "Nor did he or she have the courage to sneak up onto the porch to read the note. We're lucky Binnie's niece is out of town. Ned would have marched up those steps and taken a zillion photos of the note."

"No kidding," Maddie said. "Also, Ned would have followed the poor jerk, and by now his or her photo would be all over the Internet. Come to think of it, I wish Ned *had* been there."

Maddie skimmed to the bottom of the screen. "Well, at least Binnie hasn't posted those photos of poor, soused Lenora teetering on a ledge in our cookbook nook."

"Maybe Del managed to scare her into silence," Olivia said. "The question is, for how long?"

"That reminds me . . ." Maddie stretched her arms toward the ceiling, "Del left a message for you to meet him at Pete's for lunch. Bertha and I can cope with the noon crowd, which will likely be a gossip fest with few actual sales. I already confirmed the lunch invitation for you."

"Of course you did."

"But, Livie, it's for your own good. No one trusts you to have your phone with you, so I have to handle your email. What choice do I have?"

"By handle, you mean hack." Olivia slid the soiled cake pan into the dishwasher. "Besides, I haven't been forgetting my phone much lately."

"Small-town memories are retentive," Maddie said. "I can't wait to find out how Del prevented Binnie from publicizing those photos. Ooh, and maybe he'll have forensic news about the bones in the wall."

"I can't believe I'm asking this," Olivia said, "but when you invaded my privacy this morning, did you see an email from my friend Lori? She works at the courthouse." Olivia pulled over a chair and sat next to Maddie. "If not, let me check."

"Nothing this morning, but hang on a sec." Maddie opened Olivia's email account in a matter of seconds. "Yep, Lori just emailed you. I'll be magnanimous and let you read it yourself, while I finish stuffing the dishwasher. But tell me what she wrote."

Olivia skimmed through the message, which read: *"Hey, Livie, what's up? Do you suspect Crystal bumped off her husband? I looked through the files going back to Kenny's disappearance, but there's no record of Crystal marrying anyone else. It's always possible she remarried in another jurisdiction. If Kenny hadn't been declared dead, and there's no evidence he was, Crystal had to be divorced from him in order to remarry legally. To get him declared dead, she would have gone to court and shown that Kenny was in peril when he disappeared—you know, like his ship sank or his plane went down, something like that—and even then, it usually doesn't kick in for seven years. I got curious, so I checked a few other courthouses—I've been at this a long time, so I know people—but I got no hits. I have an older cousin who used to be a friend of Crystal's. I gave her a call, and she said Crystal liked to complain, especially about men, but she was lazy when it came to follow-through. She always had to have a man in her life. That's all I've got, but I'll keep my ears and eyes open."*

"Well, that's a letdown," Maddie said. "It's time to move on to the town gossips."

"Actually, it's time to get back to work," Olivia said, glancing at the clock over the kitchen sink. "The Cookie Cutter Collectors Club members swooped in and cleaned off our shelves. We have about an hour to help Bertha restock before the lunch crowd hits."

As Olivia entered the sales floor, she heard the tinkle of the bell over the front door announcing the arrival of a customer. Her mother stood framed in the doorway. At least, the petite figure looked like it belonged to Ellie, although her costume indicated she'd recently escaped from a harem. Curling ribbons festooned her long, gray hair, and a white veil covered her nose and mouth. Pale blue balloon leggings draped from just below her waist and gathered at her ankles. Her loose silk top, pale blue and decorated with embroidered flowers, left a sliver of bare midriff.

"Mom?" Olivia took a step forward. "Isn't it a bit chilly for that outfit?"

"Don't be silly, dear," Ellie said. "Exercising keeps me warm." She raised her hands in the air and crossed the sales floor by way of three perfect cartwheels, landing a few feet away from Olivia. "Such fun. I haven't turned cartwheels since I was a young girl. I searched online and found some excellent directions. Of course, I'd much rather attend a class, but that will have to wait until we get the arts and crafts school up and running. I do hope we can get back to work soon."

"Hasn't Del given you permission yet?" Olivia asked. "All he has to do is secure the room where the bones are."

"You're a bit behind on the news, dear." Ellie gave her daughter a solicitous pat on the arm. "You really need to communicate more with Del. It would enhance your relationship. As we speak, Del and a team of forensic types are packing up the entire contents of that ill-fated wall. They wanted the place to themselves. They should be finished shortly. Del asked me to tell you that he might be a few minutes late for your date at Pete's, but lunch is on him."

"Good," Olivia said. "I'll order a couple appetizers while I wait for him."

"That's fine, dear, but do remember to increase your exercise to compensate for the extra calories." Ellie twirled around, her hands swirling gracefully above her head. "Now, I have some shopping to do," she said. "Alicia wants to bake cookies for the workers. I suspect she'd prefer to stay in the kitchen for now. She is still in some shock. You and Maddie have the most wonderful supply of colored sugars and other delightful decorations. I thought it would be fun and distracting for Alicia to have more to work with than icing alone."

Olivia scanned the sales floor. A few customers had wandered in, but Bertha and Maddie were taking care of them. "Okay, Mom, I'll tag along while you select the decorating add-ons. I have a few questions, and I suspect you're the only one in Chatterley Heights who might have all the answers."

"Of course, dear. Meet me over by the sugars." With an ease and flexibility that Olivia found irritating, Ellie executed two cartwheels and landed like a feather within reach of the decorating sugars.

Olivia sighed audibly and joined her mother. While Ellie held a jar of lavender sanding sugar up to the light, Olivia quietly asked, "Mom, have you heard anything about a feud between Sam Parnell and Binnie?"

Ellie's hazel eyes widened. "I have indeed. I'm surprised it hasn't reached more ears already, though I'm certain it will in no time." She picked up a jar of multicolored nonpareils, shook it briefly, and put it back on the shelf.

"What, Mom? What hasn't reached more ears?"

"Hm? Oh, just the usual thing, dear. They are so very alike, after all." Ellie smiled as she shook a jar of sapphire blue sugar.

"Are you talking about Binnie and Sam? Mom, are you saying those two are having a lover's spat? Because that's so—"

Ellie threw back her head and laughed, drawing smiles from all corners of the sales floor. "Oh, Livie, you do have your father's delightfully ironic sense of humor." Several of the long ribbons in her hair began to slip. "Oh dear, I need to secure these ribbons," Ellie said. "Let's adjourn to the cookbook nook, shall we?"

Once they had settled on the large armchairs in the relative privacy of the cookbook nook, Ellie rolled onto her knees and began to disentangle the ribbons from her long, gray waves. "When I said that Binnie and Sam are so alike," she said from behind a curtain of hair, "I merely meant that they have a similar, shall we say, interactive style."

"They both irritate people?"

"Blunt," Ellie murmured, "yet precise." Her hairdo repaired, Ellie tossed back her mane and settled cross-legged in her chair. "Much better," she said. "Now, about Sam and Binnie . . . I suppose it was inevitable. They are both terrible gossips, of course, though quite different in their techniques. Sam is more honorable, in an odd way. At least he digs for gossip before he resorts to making it up."

"Ah," Olivia said, "and Binnie skips right to making it up. That would explain why I find Sam marginally easier to tolerate, though I wouldn't want to find myself locked inside a vault with either one of them."

"What a dreadful thought." Ellie hugged her knees to her chest. "Don't forget that Sam has access to the mail, and he doesn't balk at sneaking a peek. In this instance, he allegedly steamed open a letter to Binnie from her niece, Nedra. I do have trouble calling her Ned."

Olivia's interest piqued at once. "I thought Ned was taking another photography course in DC. Is something else going on? Has she run away from home . . . I hope?"

"No, nothing like that, Livie. Not yet, anyway. Apparently, she has met a young man, also a photographer, and things are getting serious."

"You're kidding. I've never heard Ned utter a word. How do they communicate? No, don't answer that."

Ellie giggled like a teenager. "Oh, Livie, there is someone for everyone. The problem is Ned wants to stay in DC permanently. Well, you can imagine how Binnie must feel."

"Must I?" Olivia leaned back in her leather chair. "All right,

Binnie must be feeling sad. She loves that mute, skinny kid like a daughter. So I'm gathering that Sam steamed open Ned's letter and is spreading the news around Chatterley Heights simply to torture and humiliate Binnie?"

"Exactly," Ellie said. "He has been broadcasting Binnie's misery. Her blog has hurt a number of Chatterley Heights folks, so you can imagine how gleefully the news has spread. Binnie hit back hard, of course. Normally, I wouldn't concern myself with such a cruel and rather silly feud, but its talons are reaching through town. I'm worried . . ." Ellie began to braid a segment of her beribboned hair, a sign of anxiety.

"Worried?" Olivia prodded.

Ellie shook loose her braided hair and began again. "I'm worried about Alicia."

"*Alicia*? How on earth did she get involved in this? She's just a kid."

"She is nineteen, dear. And she is vulnerable because of her family situation. She is so determined to find out what happened to her father, which could lead her into danger. As I'm sure you've gathered, Alicia was quite attached to her father." Ellie's braiding picked up speed. "Perhaps she knows more about his disappearance than she realizes."

"That is a possibility," Olivia said, remembering how she, as a teenager, had picked up subtle clues about her father's illness before she was told he was dying. "And how, exactly, does Binnie's misery relate to Alicia's situation?"

"I wasn't referring only to Binnie, dear. It's true that Binnie is intrigued by those bones in the wall. She has her nose to the ground, following any scent she can find. I realize that sounds overdramatic, but in this instance, it is apt. She is trying every trick she can think of to draw out leads. Those dreadful photos . . ."

Olivia nearly hopped out of her chair. "The ones she took of Lenora? Have you seen them, too?"

"Yes, dear, I'm afraid so. They came to our computer, which

Allan uses for work. There was no message attached, although they were sent from Binnie's email address. We forwarded them to Del, naturally. We've heard no more about them."

Olivia sank into the comforting softness of her armchair. "Maddie and I got them, too. Now I'm wondering if Binnie sent those photos to anyone else. I'm meeting Del at Pete's for lunch. I'll ask him."

"I'll be interested in what Del has to say." Ellie checked the time on her cell phone. "My theory is that Binnie hopes a good dose of scandal and mystery will draw Ned back to Chatterley Heights to stay, with or without her new boyfriend. There's no telling how far Binnie would go to make that happen." Ellie unfolded from her chair and stretched toward the ceiling. "I should meditate before my yoga class."

"Oh no you don't," Olivia said. "Sit right back down and tell me what you meant when you said Alicia might know more than she realizes."

Ellie curled into a corner of her chair with her legs tucked underneath, as if she were seeking protection. "It's something I heard from an old friend of mine. You remember Jane, don't you? She is my age but much taller. She used to have the most gorgeous long, jet black hair. It's still lovely, of course, but streaked with gray and cut—"

"About Alicia . . . ?" Olivia prodded.

"I'm merely setting the stage, Livie. Oh dear, I'm beginning to sound like Lenora. Anyway, Jane and I hadn't gotten together for a while. We both love yoga, so we met at her house for an impromptu session. I'd never visited her lovely new home. She and her husband built it a couple years ago, so everything is fresh and new. She has the perfect floor for yoga and a wonderful new DVD with dozens of yoga—"

"Not to pressure you, Mom, but I do have this store to run." Olivia tried to keep the sarcasm in her voice to a minimum. She really did want to hear what her mother had to say.

"Of course, dear," Ellie said. "When Jane and I finished our session, we had some tea and chatted. Naturally, she wanted to know all about those bones we found in the boarding house wall, and I saw no harm in telling her what I knew. When I mentioned Kenny Vayle as the probable victim, Jane looked troubled." Ellie captured a lock of her hair and absently braided.

Olivia's frustration evaporated. "Your friend knew Kenny Vayle?"

Ellie nodded. "She knew the whole family. She had lived next door to them for some time, specifically the years right before and after Kenny's disappearance. Well, when I asked Jane what disturbed her, she said her husband had suggested they build their new house because their neighborhood had become more dangerous, or so he felt. She agreed. She mentioned one episode in particular that deeply disturbed them. It happened during a birthday party Crystal and Kenny threw for Alicia when she turned fourteen and a half."

"Wait, Mom . . . the Vayle family celebrated half birthdays?"

"No, Livie. It was sadder than that, believe me. On Alicia's actual fourteenth birthday, Crystal had ordered Kenny to leave the house. They'd had a screaming match. Jane and her husband, unfortunately, heard it all. Instead of a party, Alicia lost her father. After six months, her parents tried to reconcile. They managed to pull off the party before they split again. That was ongoing life at the Vayle household."

"How sad," Olivia said.

"Indeed."

Olivia peeked out at the sales floor. "No customers. My business is doomed, but at least you can finish your story. What was this incident your friend described?"

"Relax, Livie." Ellie gave her daughter a consoling pat on the knee. "Businesses go up and down. One light afternoon does not a foreclosure make."

"That's so comforting, Mom. I think."

"Now, back to my story," Ellie said, with perhaps too much enthusiasm. "Kurt crashed Alicia's birthday party.

Apparently, the two of them had dated briefly a couple years earlier. Alicia broke it off, or that's what Jane heard later."

"Whoa, wait a minute." Olivia bolted upright in her seat. "Alicia would have been twelve, maybe thirteen, and Kurt was . . . what?"

Ellie nodded emphatically. "You nailed it. Kurt was about nineteen."

"Ick."

"Indeed." Ellie leaned toward Olivia and lowered her voice. "Jane and her husband overheard an argument that took place outside their open bedroom window. It was between Kurt and Kenny. Jane said she'd never heard Kenny so angry. He ordered Kurt to stay away from Alicia, said that she didn't want to see him ever again. Kenny said he'd kill Kurt if he even approached Alicia. Kurt said, *'Don't count on it, old man. I never go anywhere without my switchblade.'* Jane heard a metallic sound. Her husband said it was a switchblade opening up. He called the police, but Kurt was gone by the time they arrived."

Olivia was silent while she processed her mother's information. Finally, she asked, "Mom, do you have any idea when Kenny disappeared? Was it very long after that evening?"

Ellie relaxed against the soft back of her armchair. "I asked Jane that very question. She didn't know the precise answer, but she said it was about two, maybe three months later. Jane and her husband were working out in their yard, and Kenny passed their house, acting very excited. He waved to them and said he was heading to a job interview. He never returned."

Chapter Fifteen

Olivia was well behind schedule by the time she headed out to meet Del for lunch at Pete's. The diner was filled to capacity, and Del had already arrived. He made a show of checking his watch as she passed the front window, where he'd snagged a table.

"Sorry I'm a bit late," Olivia said as she slid onto her chair.

"No problem," Del said. "You've saved me a bundle on appetizers."

Olivia shrugged off her jacket and let it fall back on her chair. "I have a good excuse. Mom and I were discussing matters of import, such as Binnie's recent bad behavior. I'm assuming you got my email?"

Del's eyes rolled heavenward. "I tell myself that every small town has a Binnie. I had a quick chat with her early this morning. Binnie blamed Sam Parnell for her foul mood, so I had a talk with him as well. I told them both that I'd throw them in the same jail cell for a week if they didn't stop behaving like spoiled brats."

"Wow, that was . . . forceful." Olivia felt a twinge of uneasiness. Del was usually so even tempered. "Aren't you afraid they might take revenge on you?"

"How? By trashing me in a blog or steaming open my mail?" As Del shook his head in disgust, an errant lock of sandy brown hair fell across his brow. His tone softened as he added, "I do worry they might turn on you, though."

Olivia shrugged. "I'm used to it. Neither of them has the clout to damage my business, and that's the only way they could hurt me. Binnie is forever blogging derogatory comments about The Gingerbread House and my humble self, but really, no one pays any attention. So don't worry about me."

Del reached across the table, captured Olivia's hand, and gave it a quick squeeze. "Thank you for tolerating me," he said softly.

Olivia squeezed his hand in return. "It isn't all that difficult," she said with a grin. "My ex-husband, now there was a man who strained my tolerance. I contend that if there were a contest for most irritating small-town character, our Binnie would win hands down." Olivia picked up one of Pete's tattered, ketchup-stained menus, even though she always ordered the same meal for lunch or dinner.

"Lucky us." Del ran his fingers through his hair. "I took a chance and ordered for you," he said. "I promise I'm not taking you for granted. It's just that I know what you always order, and I thought it would give us more time to talk."

Olivia opened her eyes wide. "What if I had my heart set on something entirely different?"

"Did you?" Del asked with the slightest twinge of uncertainty in his voice.

Olivia decided she'd better let him off the hook, given she was about to request information that he probably ought to keep to himself. "Don't be ridiculous," she said with a smile. "I can never get enough of Pete's special meatloaf."

Ida appeared at the table, bearing an extra-large tray crammed with plates. "Hey, you two, stop canoodling and clear the table so I can dump these serving plates." She groaned as she plunked the tray down between Olivia and Del. "Pete is trying to kill me," she said. "I'm too old to be carrying around my own weight in food." She wandered off, muttering to herself.

Olivia stared at the array of food on the tray. "Del, what on earth made you order all this food?" In addition to their usual meatloaf, potatoes, and salad, the tray held a pitcher of extra sauce, a basket of rolls, two barbecued beef sandwiches, a bowl of potato salad, and half an apple pie.

"I didn't order it," Del said. "Except for the two meatloaf meals, that is."

Ida reappeared at their table with a full pot of coffee. "I'm leaving the pot with you two," she said. "I can't keep up with this crowd, so you'll have to pour your own refills. Don't know why I keep on working here. Run off my feet all day long, no appreciation . . ."

"Ida, why all this extra food?" Del asked.

Ida rolled her eyes toward the ceiling. "Pete, that's why. He'd better hang on to enough money to pay my salary, that's all I have to say. Giving away free food . . ."

"But why?" Del asked.

An impatient customer waved his menu in Ida's direction. "Gotta go feed the bears," she said. "I'll come back later, when you've stuffed down all that free food." Ida seemed to be in no hurry as she headed toward the insistent customer.

Olivia filled her plate with small servings of everything except dessert. "This is overwhelming," she said as she picked up her fork. "I can't figure out where to start."

Del regarded his own fully crammed plate, and said. "I'm thinking of going around in circles, starting with the tried and true." He poured an extra dollop of Pete's special sauce over his serving of meatloaf and took a bite.

Olivia followed his example. As she tasted her meatloaf, she thought about her mother's attempts to reproduce Pete's recipe. They'd all been good, especially the last one, but this . . . She took a second bite, just to be certain. Yup, Pete's meatloaf was better. She took one more bite and put down her fork to savor the taste experience. Then she moved on to her barbecued beef sandwich.

After a period of tasty silence, Del filled their nearly empty coffee cups and pushed the cream closer to Olivia. "I believe a break is in order," he said. "Did you remember to bring along that note?"

"Ah, thanks for reminding me." Olivia reached into a canvas bag she'd slung over her chair. She pulled out a manila envelope and handed it to Del. "I can assure you that my fingerprints will be all over that paper. It was windy last night— or rather, this morning—and I was pretty irritated that someone had shoved a tack into my beautiful and expensively restored front door."

"Yes, I remember that wind and your worries about the door," Del said as he opened the envelope. Using a clean napkin, he extracted the sheet of paper and placed it on the envelope to keep it safe from Pete's meatloaf sauce. "Huh," Del said. "This is both puzzling and interesting."

"I figured it was a practical joke," Olivia said. "I suppose you read Binnie's blog this morning? Also, Sam stopped by, angling for more information about that note. As you already know, Sam is feuding with Binnie, so I'm guessing he wants to one-up her." When Del said nothing in response, Olivia said, "You have that intent frown you make when something intrigues you. What do you see in that note?"

"Hmm?" Del glanced up at Olivia. "I'm puzzled, that's all. I assumed this would look more like a joke, given the odd message, but the handwriting is . . . Well, it looks hurried, almost desperate." Del took a tiny flashlight from his pocket and shined it on the paper.

"You're killing me here," Olivia said. "What do you see? Do you think this note is for real?"

"Possibly." Del shrugged. "I'll hand it over to forensics

and maybe a handwriting expert. It looks to me like whoever wrote this was using a hard pencil that needed sharpening. You don't see many pencils around anymore." He held the paper so Olivia could see it. "See this?" He pointed toward the small "r" at the end of the note.

Olivia squinted at several marks following the letter. "I see what you mean. If a pencil point is really worn down, I can imagine the wood making marks like that as the writer tries to get enough lead to make a letter." Olivia settled back in her chair. "I wonder if the writer was in a big hurry for some reason. That might explain why he or she didn't take the time to find a pencil sharpener or a pen." She leaned closer to the note. "Maybe the writer intended to add more but couldn't get the pencil to work."

"We'll have to see what the experts come up with." Del slipped the paper back inside its envelope. "When they have time to look at it, that is. They might not take it too seriously."

As the lunch crowd began to thin, Ida arrived at their table with a fresh coffeepot, which she placed at Del's elbow. "I'm on break, so you're on your own." Nodding toward the serving plates, Ida said, "Don't make me tell Pete you didn't like the food."

"Not a chance," Del said. "We intend to savor it for the next several meals, except for the meatloaf, which I suspect we'll manage to finish off."

"Oh yeah," Olivia said. "Not a problem."

Ida sighed and shook her head. "I'll bring out some takeout containers after my break. You can box it all up yourselves."

"So why did Pete give us such a generous meal?" Del asked. "Is he trying to buy off the police for some reason?"

Ida snorted. "Pete can fight his own battles." She dragged over a chair and sank onto it. "Pete wanted to thank you for coming so quick and arresting that Kurt fellow, the one who took a swing at him. Not that Pete was scared of the little pip-squeak," Ida said. "Only he was worried he might have to slug the kid to get rid of him. Mostly, Pete wanted to protect Alicia. I don't suppose you can keep Kurt in jail for a year or so?"

Del chuckled. "Sorry, no can do. I've already had to let him go with a stern warning to stay away from the diner and from Alicia. I made it clear to him that if he ignores my warning, I'll ask a judge to issue a restraining order. I'm afraid that's the best I can offer."

"He won't pay any attention to you," Ida said. "That kid is bad news."

"Do you know him personally?" Olivia asked.

"Oh yeah." Ida pulled her chair closer to the table and lowered her voice. "My youngest boy, the one who lives in DC, had a run-in with Kurt a few years ago. My son found out his daughter was dating Kurt. She was only fourteen at the time. Kurt was twenty-three."

"Did your son report this to the police?" Del asked.

"Ha!" Ida shook her head so vigorously that a lock of iron gray hair escaped from her hairnet. "That boy of mine was always a stubborn hothead, just like Kurt, only not as crazy. He threatened to go to the police if Kurt didn't leave his little girl alone, but what he really wanted was to pound Kurt into the pavement."

"Did he get that chance?" Del asked.

Ida shook her head. "Nah. Kurt's a lot braver when he's hiding behind that computer. Of course, my son is bigger than Kurt and has just as quick a temper."

Olivia lifted a forkful of meatloaf and hesitated, puzzled. "Ida," she asked, "do you have any idea what Kurt does for a living? He must have some means of support, but he seems to spend his time writing trashy blogs and posting insulting comments about anyone who crosses him."

"Never thought about it," Ida said. "Maybe people pay him to write some of that stuff." She checked her watch. "Break's over. Back to the salt mines. You two want anything else?" Her tone suggested they'd better answer in the negative. They complied. Ida shuffled off, muttering about aching feet and kids who want to put their mothers in nursing homes.

"Is it my imagination," Olivia asked, "or is Ida even crankier than usual?"

"Everyone is crankier than usual," Del said. "I've had a stream of complaints from Chatterley Heights citizens who want me to shut down Binnie's blog. Apparently, she is now aiming lies and innuendos at everyone in town. Personally, I can't bring myself to read the stuff."

"I've been wondering if Binnie has finally lost her last ounce of sanity." Olivia sipped her coffee and added more cream. "Mom's current theory is that Binnie is upset because Ned has a serious boyfriend in DC, someone she met in one of her photojournalism classes. She might not return to Chatterley Heights."

Del's forkful of meatloaf paused halfway to his mouth. "Is it too much to hope that Binnie might move to DC to be closer to her niece?"

"In your dreams. Binnie would much rather stay here and make the rest of us miserable."

"At least she has a sense of purpose," Del said.

Olivia took another bite of meatloaf and closed her eyes to better appreciate the experience. Before she forgot everything except Pete's meatloaf, she put down her empty fork, and asked, "While we're on the subject of Binnie's behavior, did you say anything to her specifically about that empty email with the attached photos? Mom said she got the same email and forwarded that to you, as well. As far as I can tell, Binnie seems to have backed off, at least for now."

"Well, I made a stab at handling the situation before she sicced me on Sam," Del said. "We'll see if it has any effect. I told Binnie that sending those photos amounted to blackmail, and blackmail is illegal. Between you and me, if she simply posted the photos, there wouldn't be much I could do. I'm assuming Lenora was, indeed, drunk?" When Olivia nodded reluctantly, he said, "Then Lenora put herself at risk of exposure. The law can't protect her from herself. However, emailing the photos to you and Ellie could be interpreted as an attempt to coerce both of you into offering her something, like money or information, to keep her from making them public. Although my interpretation might be more convincing if Binnie had included a written demand along with the photos. By saying nothing, she left room to argue that she was merely sharing the photos with you, perhaps to warn you that Lenora has a drinking problem."

"So do you think Binnie took your warning seriously?" Olivia asked.

Del shrugged. "Time will tell. If I were Herbie and Gwen, I'd try to get Lenora some help for her drinking."

"I'll talk to them, but I know they've tried," Olivia said. "Herbie even gave up his wine cellar. Actually, Lenora accomplished that for him by consuming every bottle in it. And still she finds more. I'm amazed she discovered that bottle of sherry behind all the boxes and pans we store on top of our refrigerator."

"Lenora is remarkably adept at scavenging," Del said. "If she were here, she would pick at our plates of extra food until there was nothing left for us to take home."

"It's a survival skill." As Olivia poured herself more coffee, she recalled how frequently Lenora had pilfered food from her companions' plates while protesting that her appetite was too tiny to require a full meal. "Her husband, Bernie, was a well-known producer, but apparently they spent every dime he earned on lavish living."

"I suppose it was good while it lasted." Del reached toward Olivia's plate. "If you aren't going to finish that last bite of meatloaf, I could—"

Olivia's left eyebrow arched in warning as she curved a protective left arm around her plate. Her right hand hovered over her silverware "I wouldn't try it, if I were you. I have a fork, and I know how to use it." Olivia became aware that conversation had ceased at two nearby tables. She slid her last morsel of meatloaf onto her fork and ate it.

"Well, that was fun," Del said as he filled their two cups with coffee.

"Back to bleak reality," Olivia said. "I still wonder why Binnie chose to send those photos only to Mom and me. It felt personal."

Del's mouth was full of potato, so he limited his response to a shrug.

"I guess I'll have to wait and see." Olivia dreaded the prospect. If those photos appeared online, might they hurt business? Maybe. On the other hand, a number of customers had witnessed Lenora's behavior, and so far no one seemed to be boycotting The Gingerbread House. Olivia decided to worry about business later. She was nearly out of lunch hour and still had questions. "So according to rumor," she said, "you and some crime lab folks have finally carted off those bones for analysis."

"Word gets around fast," Del said with a lopsided grin.

"I suppose eons will pass before the crime lab finds time to do . . . whatever it is they'll do?" *Nicely phrased, Livie. I need to pick up some professional jargon.*

Del chuckled. "Yes, we took everything down to the dust. As for how long before forensic analysis gets under way, I'm guessing they will start at once. We found a few surprises." Del drained the last of his coffee. "I might as well tell you. If it isn't all over town now, it will be very soon. I wouldn't want you to be the last to know."

The diner was emptying fast, so Olivia assumed they weren't likely to have an audience. However, Ida was heading toward their table bearing a stack of takeout boxes. "Pete wants me to box everything up for you. Easy for him. I ran myself ragged serving all those customers. You'd think they hadn't eaten in a week. My feet hurt, and my back don't feel so good neither. But don't you dare tell that to my kids. They'll use it as an excuse to shove me into an old folks home. I'll go to an old folks home when I'm dead and not a minute before." She sighed heavily as she began to fill the first container with Olivia's leftovers.

Olivia grabbed the plate and to-go container away from Ida. "Sit down, for heaven's sake. I'll do that." Olivia pushed the coffee carafe toward her. "Help us finish off this coffee. Pete won't mind, and you know it." She took a clean cup from a nearby table and handed it to Ida.

Del poured the steaming liquid into their three cups. As he passed around the sugar and cream, he asked, "I suppose both of you intend to take this opportunity to pump me for privileged information?"

"Good idea," Ida said. "First off, I'd like to know if it's true there was more in that wall than poor Kenny Vayle. I heard you found two, maybe three heads, plus a big pile of arm and leg bones, all sorts of sizes. So what was going on in that old flophouse? Some sort of devil worship? Maybe one of those serial killers we keep seeing on television?"

Olivia started to laugh, then stifled the urge when she saw the serious look on Del's face. Ida saw it, too. "I thought so." She crossed her arms over her skinny chest and nodded smugly.

Del topped off his coffee and added more cream. He chewed a forkful of apple pie, then another. To Olivia, Del's silence suggested there might be some truth to Ida's wild speculation. Olivia sipped her own coffee and waited for him to decide how much information to reveal with Ida present. She could always try to get more details out of him later.

Ida planted her elbows on the table and leaned in, as if she were about to share a secret. "When I was a girl," she said, "my mama told me a story about that old boarding house. Of course, it was in better shape back then, but the Great Depression had already started to wear the place down before I was born. Mama told me that men down on their luck would go out looking for work during the day. Once it got dark, they'd gather in that boarding house and sleep on the floor, sometimes ten or more to a room. Mama used to say the place was haunted, too. When she was twelve or so, she and her brothers would sneak out after bedtime and hide in the bushes around that building. They'd peek through the windows to see what was going on inside." Ida leaned in even closer and lowered her voice. "One hot summer night they heard screams coming from one of the rooms on the top floor. I wouldn't be surprised if there's bones in every one of those rooms."

Olivia realized she'd been holding her breath.

Ida glanced up at Pete's Audubon wall clock. "Well, I can't sit around gossiping all day. I've got too much to do before we have to get ready for the dinner shift. Pete wants me to run some errands." She lumbered to her feet, grabbed her coat off the nearby rack, and shuffled toward the diner door without clearing the table.

"Well, well," Olivia said, once the door had shut behind Ida. "That was an interesting story. Although I doubt those screams of agony came from poor Kenny Vayle, given he hadn't been born yet. Oh, and by the way, congratulations. You managed to avoid telling Ida anything about what you actually discovered."

Del barely smiled. He stared toward the diner's front window as Ida shuffled past. Olivia felt a prick of concern. "Del? Are you feeling all right?"

Del leaned against the back of his chair, a thoughtful expression on his face. "Livie, if you were to hazard a guess, would you say that Ida made up that story about her mother hearing screams from the second floor of the boarding house?"

"I'm not sure my guess would be worth the hazard," Olivia said. "I don't agree with Ida's kids that she is ready for the old folks home, but she is in her mid-seventies. She heard that story from her mother many decades ago, so she might be misremembering or embellishing. Besides, Ida's mother might have fabricated the entire story simply to entertain her young daughter. Is it important?"

"Maybe." Del went silent again.

"Del, you're driving me nuts. I can't stand the suspense. What are you not telling me?"

Del shifted his chair closer to hers. "You have to promise me, Livie . . . Promise you'll keep this to yourself at least until tomorrow. I may have more information then. The crime lab folks intend to work all night, if that's what it takes."

"The crime lab . . . ?" Olivia slumped down in her seat. "Yes, all right, I promise. We'll be busy working at the store this afternoon, and Maddie can bake alone tonight, if that's what it takes for me to keep my mouth shut."

Del scanned the nearly empty diner and seemed satisfied he wouldn't be overheard. Lowering his voice, he said, "When the crime lab removed those bones from the boarding house wall, they found a couple surprises underneath."

"Surprises? Like what? Was there a weapon?"

Del shook his head and leaned closer to Olivia. "The first surprise is right up your alley. In fact, we'll want to draw upon your expertise, as well as Anita's."

"Anita? Are you saying you found some antique cookie cutters while you were removing those bones?" Anita Rambert ran an antiques mall and was a leading local expert on vintage and antique cookie cutters. Olivia felt a shiver of anticipation. "Please, I beg of you, let me see them before Anita does. She'll know more about their worth, but I'll be more excited."

Del's smile came and went in a flash. "I'll take it under advisement," he said. "There was a second surprise, as well . . . a more sobering one."

Olivia held her breath as Del shifted his chair closer to hers. "We found more remains."

For an instant, Olivia wondered if Del might be setting her up for a joke. He'd never played such a trick on her before, but . . . No, the look in his eyes was serious, even somber. However, she tamped down on her excitement and asked, calmly, "When you say remains, do you mean . . . ?"

"Human bones. To be specific, an extra skeleton. There were two bodies in that wall. And both were human." Del sank against the back of his chair as if he'd just finished running a marathon.

"Whoa," Olivia whispered. "Did they find any clues as to whose remains they might be?"

Del shrugged one shoulder. "We're not sure. They believe the extra skeleton to be older than the bones presumed to have belonged to Kenny Vayle."

"How much older?" Olivia asked.

"Yet to be determined."

"This case just gets more and more intriguing," Olivia whispered. "I don't suppose there was another cookie cutter necklace."

Del shook his head. "But we did discover something else. "The second skull had what looked to be a bullet hole in it."

"Wow." Olivia touched his arm. "Del, do you realize how difficult it will be for me to keep this from Maddie?"

"Nevertheless," Del said. "If it would help, I could put you in protective custody."

"It may come to that."

Chapter Sixteen

Following lunch with Del, Olivia hurried back to The Gingerbread House, distracted by her growing list of questions about the startling information he had revealed to her. The discovery of a second skeleton—with a bullet hole in the skull, no less—intrigued her. Olivia salivated at the thought of those antique cookie cutters the forensic team had uncovered. But she had promised Del to keep that information secret, at least for a while. It wouldn't be easy. Surely Maddie would notice the sparkle in her eyes. However, a promise was a promise, and Olivia was touched by Del's willingness, finally, to trust her with inside information about a murder investigation. She wouldn't break her word, even if she had to glue her mouth shut and communicate through sign language. If only she knew sign language . . .

It was nearly one-thirty p.m. by the time Olivia climbed the steps up to her front porch. Once inside, she paused in the foyer to compose herself before entering The Gingerbread House. Maddie might sense her excitement, so Olivia tried to focus on a depressing topic, like the coming of winter. She envisioned short days, frigid winds, cold and flu viruses . . . but soon her thoughts drifted to holiday baking, colorful decorations, and carols. Well, there was always Del's offer of protective custody.

Olivia took a deep breath and grabbed the doorknob. It didn't turn. She stepped back to get a look in the front window and realized the heavy curtain was drawn shut. *That curtain should be open.* Why would The Gingerbread House be closed up tight at one-thirty on a Wednesday afternoon?

Olivia dug into her jacket pocket for her key. When she unlocked the front door, she found the foyer empty and the Gingerbread House door shut. She turned the knob. It, too, was locked. There was no note on the door. Her heart pounding, she slid her key into the lock, opened the door, and quickly scanned the sales floor. There was no sign of life. Spunky's chair by the window was empty.

"Spunky?" Olivia's voice squeaked. She took a deep breath to quell her anxiety. "Spunks, are you there, boy?" The little guy came trotting out of the cookbook nook to greet her as if nothing were wrong. Once she realized Spunky wasn't upset, Olivia's heart rate began to drop closer to normal. She scooped the little Yorkie into her arms, and said, "Hey, Spunks, what's up around here? Are we in an alternate universe? Where is everyone?"

Spunky launched a volley of yaps, which revived Olivia's apprehension. "Hey, slow down, kiddo. What's going on here? Where's Maddie?" Spunky licked her face. She tucked his small, wriggling body under her arm and strode toward the kitchen door. As she reached for the knob, the door opened. Bertha's plump, worried face peeked out.

"Oh, thank goodness." Bertha's face disappeared, and Olivia heard her say, "Livie is finally back. What? Oh, of course." The door opened wide, and Bertha pulled Olivia into the kitchen. Spunky squirmed eagerly as he entered forbidden territory. "I'm so sorry I didn't hear you arrive, Livie," Bertha said. "I guess we were all talking at once."

Olivia paused to take stock of the scene in the crowded kitchen. Her mother, her legs tucked under her petite body, occupied one of the two kitchen chairs. Ellie's husband, Allan, stood next to his wife's chair, a protective hand on her shoulder. The other chair had been pushed back from the table, perhaps when Bertha left to find out why Spunky had been yapping. Maddie sat on the kitchen counter, swinging her legs and leaning against her lanky husband, Lucas Ashford.

Olivia was most surprised by the kitchen's sixth inhabitant. Polly Franz, the indomitable force behind the Chatterley Heights Homeless Shelter, stood near the sink, a full glass of water in her hand. "Hey, Livie," Polly said. "I guess you're wondering why we're all gathered together in the kitchen. Oh dear, that sounds like a line from a murder mystery—you know, where the sleuth is about to reveal the killer?" Polly's good-natured face lost its ruddy color. "I didn't mean . . . I'm sure everything will turn out fine."

Ellie's small hand reached back to touch Polly's arm. "We must all pull together to make certain of that," she said. "Now that Livie has joined us, perhaps we can make some progress. Livie is quite the planner, aren't you, dear?"

"What the heck is going on here, Mom?" Olivia handed her pup to Ellie. "Hang on tight," she said. "I'm not eager to scrub down the kitchen again."

"Of course, dear. We'll be fine, won't we, little one?" Spunky settled on Ellie's lap, content to observe the babbling humans.

Olivia noticed that Mr. Coffee's carafe was almost empty. "I need coffee," she said. "While I make a fresh pot, will someone please explain to me what this is all about? Why is the store closed? And if it's closed for a good reason, shouldn't we tape a sign on the door?" Olivia gave Maddie a questioning look.

"I leap up to obey," Maddie said. "Or rather, I leap down." She slid off the counter and headed toward the small desk that Olivia kept supplied with paper and pens. "I shall return in a trice," Maddie said as she headed into the sales area.

"Mom, what's wrong? It must be serious for Maddie to close the store without warning." Olivia rinsed out the dregs in Mr. Coffee's carafe and refilled it with fresh water.

Ellie straightened in her seat and closed her eyes. An instant later, she reopened them, and said, "There, I am about as centered as I can manage at the moment. I called everyone together, Livie, because I'm quite worried about Alicia. She has disappeared."

"Now, Ellie," Allan said, "let's not go overboard here. The truth is, she simply went off without telling us where she was going or when she'd return. She did leave us—"

"Allan, I sense danger." Ellie's firm tone silenced her husband. With a good-natured shrug, he yielded the floor.

"Thank you, dear." Ellie again closed her eyes and took several deep breaths before continuing. "Livie, we're so sorry to interrupt your working hours, but we do have a dilemma. You see, Allan and I went out for breakfast this morning and then to do some grocery shopping, and when we returned home, Alicia was gone. We checked her room and found some of her clothes missing. A few hangers had fallen on the closet floor, as if she'd been in a hurry. On the kitchen counter, we found this . . ." Ellie pulled a small square of folded paper from the pocket of her size two jeans. "Read it, Livie."

Maddie slipped back into the kitchen as Olivia unfolded the paper, and read aloud: "*Ellie and Allan, thanks so much for helping me, but I need to leave right now. I can't explain yet, but it's really important. There's someone I have to talk to right away. I promise I'll be back, though I'm not sure when. Don't worry about me. If this goes well, I'll have someone to help me. Alicia.*" Olivia skimmed through the note again before handing it back to her mother. "Do you have the slightest idea what Alicia is talking about or who this someone might be?"

Ellie exchanged a quick glance with her husband. "I think we might," she said. "This is where Polly has been so helpful.

You see, Allan and I had breakfast this morning at the Chatterley Café, and we ran into Polly. She told us an interesting story. Tell her, Polly."

"Of course," Polly said. "You see, the Chatterley Café donates the most delicious food to the shelter, which is so generous and much appreciated by our guests. It's simply wonderful of them to—"

"I should explain," Ellie said, "that Polly always brings along a shelter guest or two to help transport the food back to the shelter."

"They are always volunteers, of course," Polly said. "I wouldn't presume to—"

"Certainly not, dear." Ellie softened her second interruption with a smile. "Yesterday evening, Polly's volunteer helper was a man named Jack, who'd appeared at the shelter a few hours earlier. He told Polly he had lived in Chatterley Heights some years ago. He was down on his luck but said he wanted to come back to town only because his stepdaughter lives here."

"I see," Olivia said. "And you think the stepdaughter might be Alicia, and that Alicia disappeared to be with this man? Did he disappear, too?"

"Well, yes and no," Polly said. "He was gone this morning, but he'd left his few belongings behind, along with a note asking me to save them for him until he returned from a job interview. He signed the note with only his first name, just like he signed the shelter register. So many of my guests are reluctant to give their last names, and I don't push."

"Perhaps Jack actually did have a job interview," Olivia said. "Maybe he wants to settle down near family. This all might be one big coincidence."

"Oh my, I suppose that's true." Polly began to tear up. "I do get carried away with the sad stories I hear from the poor dears who come to the shelter. My guests have gone through such terrible times. The last few years have been so—"

"Here's an idea," Maddie said, a shade too cheerily.

"Let's assume, for now, that your guest might be a 'person of interest,' as the cops on television say. That means we should be prepared to question him if and when he returns for his belongings."

Maddie shot Olivia a look that said *This might be important. We don't have time to dither.* Olivia gave her a faint nod of assent, then asked, "Polly, could you describe this man for us?"

"Yes, of course." Polly's plump cheeks bunched as she smiled. "Well, Jack is tall, at least six feet, maybe more. Quite thin, too, which so many of my guests are, especially the ones who lost their jobs early in the recession." Polly blinked rapidly. "But we don't have time to dwell on such things now," she said in a soft voice. "Jack looked to be about midforties, although his skin was roughened by being outdoors so much in winter. His hair was mostly gray, with some brown streaks, a bit long but not shaggy. Rather a good-looking man, all things considered. Kind eyes . . . blue, I think. He was very polite and respectful, which is why I chose him to help me with the Chatterley Café food donations. Does that help?"

"Perfect," Olivia said. "Did you notice what Jack was wearing?"

Polly nodded vigorously, sending a lock of straight gray hair swinging across her cheek. "Worn jeans and a flannel shirt with red and white checks—what I would call working clothes for a man who has worked in construction. I'm so pleased to see that construction is picking up again. Perhaps you are right that Jack had a job interview somewhere. Wouldn't that be lovely?" Polly's smile faded. "Except then we'd have no clue where Alicia might have gone off to, would we?"

"Let's not worry about that right now," Ellie said. "We have a lead, as the police detectives say, and that's what counts."

"Speaking of the police," Olivia said, "why aren't we talking to Del about all this?" When no one answered, she added, "I'll take care of it when we're finished here. Polly, we packed a box of cookies for you to bring back to the shelter. There are several dozen. It's our treat. All we ask is that you call

Del and us at once if Jack returns, with or without Alicia, or if you hear from either one of them. Don't ask him about her. Del can do that. We'll take care of the rest."

"I will," Polly said. "Bless you both for the cookies. We do have more children at the shelter than usual. You'd be surprised what a difference it makes when we can offer them delicious treats. They just ooh and ah over your cookies."

Olivia wasn't at all surprised. She knew the power of decorated cookies.

"Maybe I ought to reopen the store," Bertha said. "I'm worried that rumors might start flying. You know what Chatterley Heights is like. If you need me for anything, just poke your head out the kitchen door and holler." She straightened her dress and fluffed her short hair.

Holding Spunky against her shoulder, Ellie unfurled from her chair with the smooth grace of an awakening flower bud. She handed Spunky to Bertha, and said, "Perhaps you might return this sweet creature to his rightful place out on the sales floor. Customers will be disappointed if he isn't there to greet them."

"I do so love your company, little one." Bertha cuddled Spunky against her ample bosom. "You and I will mind the store together." Spunky didn't even whimper when she opened the door and carried him out of the kitchen.

"I noticed your faucet is dripping again." It was the first time Lucas had spoken, which wasn't unusual. "Lucky I brought a few tools. I'll just fix it while I'm here. It won't take but a minute." Maddie gave her husband a thank-you kiss on the cheek, which made him smile and blush.

"Shouldn't we let Crystal know what is going on with her daughter?" Ellie asked. "I would certainly want to be informed if one of my children might have disappeared with a strange man."

"Let's hold off for a while," Olivia said. "Crystal isn't you, Mom. And Robbie . . . well, I suspect Robbie would say 'good riddance' to Alicia. He clearly despised Kenny, and he probably considers Alicia as weak and useless as her father. I'm beginning to wonder if this Jack fellow was Crystal's second so-called husband. Maybe Robbie didn't come along until later."

"Well, um . . ." Lucas Ashford drew his head out from under the faucet he'd been working on. When he turned to face the group, his chiseled features registered concern and a touch of shyness. "About Robbie," he said. "He's a regular customer at the hardware store. We supply most of the tools and materials for his construction projects because, well . . ."

"Because Heights Hardware is the best hardware store ever," Maddie said. "And you know everything there is to know about construction and . . . related stuff."

Lucas grinned at his bride. "It's the only hardware store nearby," he said, "and we've been around for generations, so we know lots of suppliers and construction companies."

"That, too." Maddie hiked herself up onto the kitchen counter and wrapped an arm around Lucas's broad shoulders.

With the merest show of pink on his cheekbones, Lucas said, "This might not mean anything, but I witnessed an argument between Robbie and Kenny that happened shortly before Kenny disappeared five years ago. I was delivering a load of lumber to a construction site Robbie was overseeing. Robbie and I were unloading when Kenny showed up. He was red in the face, really angry. Robbie can be hotheaded, too, but this time he held back and tried to keep things under control. Kenny was so mad he didn't care who heard him. He threatened to kill Robbie if he didn't stay away from Crystal."

"I'll bet Robbie lost it right about then," Maddie said.

"Nope," Lucas said. "I expected a fistfight, maybe worse, so I signaled my guys to back away. Robbie was mad, I could see that, but he just stood there and stared at Kenny. Finally, Robbie said, 'The booze is making you imagine things. Now go away and don't ever come near me again.'

"Kenny said, 'Or what? You'll kill me? If you come near my wife and daughter, *I'll* kill *you*.' Then Kenny turned around and walked away." Lucas slumped against the edge of the counter as if reciting his story had worn him to the bone.

Maddie gave her husband a quick squeeze around his shoulders. "You remembered that really precisely, honey," she said.

"Yeah, I guess it made an impression," Lucas said, apparently to the floor. "Only I totally forgot about it until just now. Mom always said I could remember really well when I paid enough attention, but sometimes my memory needs a jolt to wake it up."

Maddie caught Olivia's eye and raised her pale eyebrows, conveying a message that Olivia understood perfectly— *Robbie stays on the suspect list.*

For the next hour, a steady stream of visitors kept Olivia, Maddie, and Bertha busy on the sales floor. Chatterley Heights Elementary School had freed their prisoners early for a teachers meeting, so clusters of giggly girls used the free time to drop by their favorite stores on their way home. In The Gingerbread House, their preferred activities included playing with the cookie cutters in the cookbook nook, poring over cookbook photos of luscious desserts, and eating the free cookies.

When the girls had all left the store, Olivia took the opportunity to straighten up the cookbook nook before actual customers returned. She had to use one of their large Gingerbread House bags to collect all the cookie cutters strewn around the nook. This time, Olivia also found several small containers of nonpareils, jimmies, and sparkling sugars left on the seats of the two large armchairs. One jar of sapphire blue sparkling sugar had been opened and its inner seal broken. Olivia wondered how Del would react if she asked him to pull fingerprints and identify the little culprit. She decided to swallow the loss as part of the cost of doing business. Next time, she would ask Bertha to keep an eye on those little budding criminals.

Maddie poked her head into the cookbook nook, and said, "Okay, Livie, before the next herd arrives, tell me instantly what you learned from Del during lunch. I figure he must have told you something interesting about those bones, or your date wouldn't have lasted so long."

Caught off guard, Olivia hesitated. Maddie would hear her discomfort and know she was hiding something. Olivia grabbed a pile of cookbooks and began to shove them back on the shelf. "Maddie, if we don't get busy and *do* our actual jobs, we won't have jobs at all. I've been going over the books, and they aren't pretty." Olivia hadn't planned to say that; it just popped out. And she wasn't exactly lying. She really had been looking over the books.

"Oh," Maddie said. "Is it really bad?"

The alarm in her best friend's voice sent a bolt of shame through Olivia's heart. Terrific, she thought, now I've kept my promise to Del by frightening Maddie. "Nothing we can't weather," she said. "It was a tough summer, that's all. Remember, there were days when hardly anyone was willing even to think about heating up the kitchen to bake cookies." She peeked out at the sales floor, where Bertha was trying to help three women at once. The after-work crowd had begun to arrive. "See, Maddie? We have customers again. And Bertha needs us." Olivia charged out to the sales floor, vowing she'd never again promise Del to keep information from her best friend since age ten.

Once the influx of customers had slowed to a crawl, Olivia sought out Bertha and Maddie and asked them to mind the store long enough for her to take Spunky outside for a bathroom break. In fact, Olivia wanted to make a private phone call, but she kept that to herself. With luck, she'd return with her unbearable burden lifted.

"Come on, Spunks." When Olivia dangled his leash, the little Yorkie leaped off his chair and raced toward her. "Good boy," she said as Spunky followed her into the empty foyer. She closed the store door behind them. "An extra treat will be available for cooperative dogs who refrain from yapping at squirrels while I'm talking on my cell phone." Before heading out to the front porch, Olivia felt in her jacket pocket to make sure she had, in fact, remembered to bring her cell phone. It was there, fully charged.

While Olivia followed Spunky around the side yard, she punched Del's speed-dial number with her thumb and held her breath, willing him to answer. He did, on the second ring.

"Livie, I'm glad you called," Del said. "I need to set up a time when you, Anita Rambert, and Maddie, if she's interested, can come to the station and look at those cookie cutters I mentioned. I did get permission to bring the actual cutters, by the way, though my life will be forfeit if anything happens to them. They didn't yield much in terms of forensic information, so we're hoping for insight at this point. How about we all meet right after your closing time? Anita said she could come then."

"Anita would skip her mother's deathbed to see those cutters," Olivia said.

"Are you aware that you said that out loud?" Del asked with a chuckle.

"I meant to. Could we make it later and meet at Aunt Sadie's house? She knows a lot about vintage and antique cookie cutters, and she won't have a vested interest in underestimating their value."

"Good idea," Del said. "Frankly, I'll feel safer with Aunt Sadie around to keep the peace. I'd hate to have to use my gun. See you then."

"Wait," Olivia said. "I'm the one who called you, remember? I have a couple things to say to you, starting with . . . Don't ever again ask me to lie to Maddie. I mean it, Del, I can't take it."

"To be fair, I didn't ask you to *lie*," Del said, "merely to keep certain information to yourself. So I—"

"I'm serious, Del. Maddie is my best friend. We've always shared important information with each other. When the topic is as serious as . . . Hang on a sec." Olivia led Spunky to the backyard, which was farther from the windows. "When the topic is really important," she said in a more subdued voice, "Maddie naturally expects me to be open with her. It wouldn't occur to her that I might hide information from her. She asks questions, and if I refuse to answer or try to change the subject, she'll know I'm hiding something. So I end up lying. It's the only way I can avoid making her suspicious. I hate lying to Maddie. Can you understand what that feels like?"

There was a moment of silence on the line before Del said, "You're right, Livie. I shouldn't give you important information and then order you not to share it with Maddie. And I can understand your feelings, because I have them, too. I hate keeping important information from you. Frankly, it gets harder every day. And anyway, in this case, silence is creating problems rather than preventing them. The rumors are worse than the truth."

"Really?" Olivia almost lost her balance as Spunky lunged toward a squirrel. "Stop that," Olivia yelled.

"Livie? Are you okay?"

"I'm fine, Del. Although I'm glad Yorkshire terriers are little critters. If Spunky were a Labrador, I'd have a dislocated shoulder. Now, what were you saying about rumors being worse than truth?"

"I'm referring to the items the crime lab extracted from the boarding house wall. The whole town knows we found more than we'd expected, but, miraculously, the details haven't become common knowledge. Believe it or not, the rumors are even more incredible than what we actually found. I can tell Ida has been talking, because the satanic ritual theory has made the rounds. Some versions include human sacrifice. The most recent speculation I heard involved a serial killer who kidnapped random strangers and walled them up alive."

"Yikes." With her free arm, Olivia grabbed Spunky around his middle to keep him from leaping toward another squirrel that appeared to be taunting him. "You're right, the rumors are worse than the truth. So may I tell Maddie what you really did find?"

"You may," Del said, "though I'd appreciate it if you waited until you've closed the store. And please don't tell anyone else."

"That goes without saying." Olivia checked the time on her cell phone. "Del, I need to get back to the store, but I wanted to let you know that Alicia has gone off somewhere. She left a note for my mom and Allan saying she was going to talk to someone about her father's death. Mom is really worried that she's putting herself in danger. Apparently, there's a man at the homeless shelter who told Polly he came back to town because his stepdaughter lives here. His name is Jack." Olivia repeated Jack's description as best she could recall. "Mom thought the stepdaughter might be Alicia, so she called together a rescue posse that met in the Gingerbread House kitchen. They hope to find Alicia through this man."

"Sounds like quite a long shot to me," Del said, "but let me know if it leads to anything. If you have reason to believe Alicia is in danger from this man, let me know. Otherwise, there's not much I can do. Alicia is nineteen. She can go off anywhere she wants. And I really can't declare her missing after only a few hours. I'd rather she didn't try to investigate her father's death on her own, of course. That can get dangerous. I can't stop her, though. If Cody were here, I'd have him talk to Polly, get a full description of Jack, hunt down his full name, see if he has a record, and keep an eye out for him. On an unofficial level, all I can do is keep my eyes and ears open. That's the best I can offer at this point. But if anything changes . . ."

"I'll let you know if mom's posse comes up with anything," Olivia said, "especially if it appears that this homeless man did know Kenny Vayle."

"And definitely inform me if Alicia disappears altogether, particularly if the homeless man never returns to claim his belongings," Del said. "Meanwhile, I can share with you one more tidbit about the evidence we took from the boarding house. In fact, I'll need your help. We didn't find another cookie cutter necklace. However, underneath the bones, cookie cutters, and dust, we found a fair amount of detritus, all of which we scooped up and carted back to the lab. I just got a call from the lab folks to tell me that they found a bullet. Not just any bullet, either. This one was old, certainly from well before Kenny Vayle disappeared. The lab techs are pretty excited. They think it might have been fired from an early twentieth century pistol. Also, the bullet appears to be a decent match to the hole we found in the second skull."

"That's fascinating." Spunky squirmed to escape Olivia's arm, so she lowered him to the ground and began walking him around the backyard. "In other words, it's true that the owner of the skull was murdered. Is it possible he shot himself?"

"I doubt it. The bullet hole was in the back of his skull. I'll let you know what the forensics reveal . . . if they can learn anything. Anyway, they should be able to determine how old the skull is. DNA testing could prove difficult without more clues." When Olivia didn't answer him, Del said, "I should let you go back to work. I'll call Aunt Sadie and arrange the meeting this evening at seven."

"Wait, Del." Olivia hesitated a moment, thinking back to Tuesday night. "When you mentioned Aunt Sadie, it made me remember a story she told us yesterday. I wonder . . ."

"Now I'm curious," Del said.

"Well, you know how knowledgeable Aunt Sadie is about Chatterley Heights history, not to mention cookie cutters, life, death, and the universe. Anyway, the other evening Maddie and I brought her dinner, and we talked about finding those bones. Aunt Sadie began reminiscing about the boarding house itself . . . you know, its history. She told us a marvelous story about Horace Chatterley, who actually built that boarding house at the behest of his mistress-of-the-moment, whose name was Imogene Jones. Aunt Sadie told us that Horace lost his fortune in the stock market crash and ended up living in his own boarding house. I'm sure she said Horace simply 'disappeared,' some years later."

"Interesting," Del said. "It's a place to start, anyway. I'll mention the story to the crime scene techs and see what they say. They might have some leftover Chatterley DNA."

Olivia knew he was referring to a previous murder in Chatterley Heights that had occurred after she had moved back to town. "Thanks for keeping me in the forensic loop," she said, "and for releasing me from best-friend purgatory. Speaking of which, I'd better get back to the store, or Maddie will be assembling a second search party. I'll keep you posted."

"See you tonight," Del said. "I wish it were under more romantic circumstances."

"Romantic is nice, but it isn't every evening I get to look at potentially antique cookie cutters. I'm glad we'll be able to see them up close and personal. I know Aunt Sadie can tell a lot more from actually holding a cutter in her hands."

With a light laugh, Del said, "I aim to please. I also aim for the most accurate information I can get."

Olivia sighed audibly. "You say the sweetest things."

Chapter Seventeen

Visions of dancing cookie cutters swirled in Olivia's head Wednesday evening as she and Maddie closed The Gingerbread House and headed toward Aunt Sadie's house to see what might be antique cookie cutters from the fabled Chatterley collection. Olivia shivered in her light jacket as the wind picked up. But even the coming of winter wasn't enough to quell her excitement. By the time she and Maddie bounced up the steps to Aunt Sadie's porch, Olivia had already unzipped her jacket.

Olivia tried to maintain adult composure as she settled next to Maddie on Aunt Sadie's living room sofa. As always these days, Aunt Sadie remained in her wheelchair, seated between Del and Anita Rambert, who were relegated to folding chairs. The rest of Aunt Sadie's living room furniture waited in Maddie and Lucas's garage for the completion of their new mother-in-law suite. Lucas had spent nearly every evening working on the project, hoping to finish before the arrival of winter.

Del held a box on his lap. "These cookie cutters have

been thoroughly examined by our forensics team," he said as he removed the lid.

"Ooh, what did they find?" Maddie clapped her hands like an over-excited child.

Anita raised a sculpted eyebrow. "Enjoying yourself, Maddie?"

"What, too much enthusiasm?" Maddie grinned. "Fine, Anita, play it cool. We know better. You are every bit as excited as we are about these cutters." Maddie's fingers twitched as if she could barely keep herself from snatching the box from Del's lap. "What if they really are part of the Chatterley collection?"

"The *mythical* collection, you mean." Anita flipped her sleek black hair over one shoulder. "The Chatterley *cooks* might have used cookie cutters, but I suspect the Chatterley wives were far more interested in balls and fancy gowns than in menial labor."

Before Maddie could retort, Olivia said, "Let's move on, shall we? I'd much rather discuss these cookie cutters than the culinary habits of the Chatterley women. Maddie is right. These might be genuine antiques."

"I'll be the judge of that." When Anita crossed her long, slender legs, the creases in her ruby red slacks remained obediently centered.

Anita was, as Olivia well knew, an expert on antique cookie cutters. However, her interest in these particular cutters would depend, ultimately, on how much money she could make by selling them. She might be tempted to undervalue them. If the cutters turned out to be genuine antiques, Olivia hoped they wouldn't disappear into private collections. She wanted them to stay in Chatterley Heights, where they belonged.

"Now, now," Aunt Sadie said. "We are so lucky to be allowed a peek at these cutters. Let's leave it at that." No one objected.

Del had observed the bickering with a look of resigned patience. "Whether or not these cutters once were used by Chatterley wives or their cooks isn't really my concern right now," he said. "I'm more interested in why, when, and by whom they were deposited behind a wall in a boarding house once owned by Horace Chatterley. If possible, I would like to know the approximate age of the cutters, as well as which Chatterley family member might have obtained them, and so on. We've taken care of the forensics. Now I want a sense of their history, which might help answer some questions we have."

"And those questions are . . . ?" Anita asked.

"Not relevant for purposes of this discussion," Del said.

Olivia could have kissed him, but that would have to wait. While Anita scowled at Del, Olivia contented herself with a quick glance at Maddie, who half winked one sparkling eye.

Del opened the small box he'd been holding on his lap. He removed five cookie cutters, and arranged them on the inside of the box lid. The forensics process had cleaned them of dust and dirt. At first glance, they looked remarkably free of rust. However, Olivia noticed dents and discoloration that pegged the cutters as old and well used. Of course, some damage might have resulted from the rough treatment the poor things experienced following the end of their culinary lives.

"Only five?" Anita complained. "I heard you found at least twenty-five cutters in that boarding house. I need to see all of them." She crossed her slender arms over her chest. "Now I'll have to arrange a private viewing. Tomorrow morning will work for me, as early as possible."

"That number is somewhat exaggerated," Del said with an affable smile. "And I'm afraid it won't be possible to see the others at present. They are all exhibits in an active murder investigation. Two investigations, in fact. They will be out of circulation indefinitely. I selected these five cookie cutters because our forensics experts and I were most curious about them," he said. "They aren't necessarily the best preserved specimens, but the shapes intrigued us. We thought maybe their uniqueness might make them easier to trace." Del shrugged, and added, "We could be wrong, of course."

"Once the case is concluded, how will you handle the sale of the collection?" Anita asked. "I doubt you have antique cookie cutter experts on your forensics team."

"The sale?" Del's blank face gave nothing away, though Olivia sensed he was stalling for time to think. He must know he needed to keep Anita engaged. She was more knowledgeable even than Aunt Sadie. "These cutters belong to the town of Chatterley Heights, not to the police. After we've completed the investigation—and trial, if it comes to that—we'll determine when or whether these items can be released."

Anita groaned. "We'll all be dead by then."

Aunt Sadie reached over the side of her wheelchair to pat Anita's arm. "Now dear, don't fret. If these are Chatterley cookie cutters, then the town must preserve them. But, Anita, think how your help with this case will enhance your reputation. Why, everyone will be so impressed when they learn the police called upon you to help crack a cold case. Two cold cases, in fact."

Olivia could swear she saw a glint in Anita's dark eyes.

Aunt Sadie turned to Del, and asked, "Might we be permitted to hold the little darlings? I can tell so much more about a cutter if I feel its weight and examine those little nicks and bruises. My eyes are not as sharp as they used to be. Anita will know more about their authenticity and value, of course, especially if you allow her to examine the cutters closely."

Anita's shoulders relaxed against the back of her chair. Following Aunt Sadie's lead, Del said, "I thought I'd start by having each of you choose a cutter to examine. Then you can pass them among yourselves however you want. Anita, why don't you start." By now, Anita was almost smiling. She looked carefully over the five cutters before selecting one that looked like a flower. She handed the box lid to Aunt Sadie, who selected a little girl with one arm slung out to her side. Maddie picked up an unusually fat pig. "This is to remind me not to eat too many cookies," she said as she passed along the remaining two cutters. Out of curiosity, Olivia picked a shape she couldn't identify. That left one lonely cookie cutter, a little boy, which Del offered to Anita. Now that she had been shown proper respect for her expertise, Anita focused her full attention on the two cutters she held.

"Del, dear," Aunt Sadie said, "would you mind fetching the coffee from the kitchen? You can pour it into the empty carafe I left on a tray, along with cups and spoons. Cream is in the fridge, and sugar should already be on the tray."

Del looked confused and a bit alarmed.

"I can promise we won't discuss the cutters behind your back," Anita said. "I want complete silence during my examination."

"Aunt Sadie and I won't give anything away," Maddie said. "This room is teeming with competition."

Del hesitated. Taking pity on him, Olivia said, "I'll help you." She handed her yet-to-be identified cutter over to Maddie and followed Del into the kitchen, closing the door behind them. "Del, if you've already done all the forensic stuff, what do you really hope to learn from us about those cutters? If you're willing to tell me, that is."

"Are you kidding, Livie? I owe you big time for passing on that story about Horace Chatterley. We do have access to Chatterley DNA, and we've already begun testing the skull."

"I aim to please," Olivia said. "What if it isn't a Chatterley skull?"

Del shrugged. "At least we'll know that much. If it is a Chatterley, the forensic folks will try to estimate the age of the skull. That will help us determine if it's Horace Chatterley. Incidentally, I checked your story, and you were right. After the Stock Market Crash of 1929, Horace was destitute. His family kicked him out, so he moved into the Chatterley Boarding House. The place was well built, but without upkeep it must have declined steadily. Apparently, Horace remained arrogant even after his dramatic downfall. He treated nearly everyone with equal disdain, so he might not have been particularly popular with the other boarding house inhabitants." Del peered into the refrigerator and selected a container. He frowned at the contents before handing the container to Olivia. "Is this the right stuff?" he asked.

"Looks like cream to me." She sniffed it. "Fresh, too. Before we return to the living room, were you planning to tell me what we're supposed to look for as we examine those cutters? Are you hoping to learn about anything in particular? I'd rather not appear too ignorant in front of Anita."

Del chuckled and kissed Olivia on the tip of her nose.

"Was that it? That's the thanks I get for telling you about Horace?"

"Not enough, huh." Del sighed and shook his head. "About those cutters, I'm hoping for ideas, impressions, connections . . . anything to jumpstart our thinking about this case. Our top priority, of course, is the more recent murder. The plywood nailed over the hole wasn't more than twenty years old. We think Horace's killer patched the wall after depositing Horace inside. This is all still speculation, of course."

"Was there any sign of the original patch?" Olivia asked.

Del leaned back against the kitchen counter. "Some nail holes. The original patch was probably just as obvious as the second one, so I suspect Kenny Vayle's body was deposited behind that temporary wall as a matter of convenience." Del's eyes appeared to sparkle as the overhead light caught the gold flecks in their brown depths. "You know, if that skull belonged to Horace Chatterley, I'd get a real kick out of determining what happened to him."

"I get that." Olivia filled the cream pitcher and put the

container back in the refrigerator. "I'd love to know how and why those cookie cutters wound up in the wall. Are they clues, or were they planted to incriminate someone? Did Horace have them with him when he died, and if so, why? Did Kenny Vayle rip out that wall and find the skull and the cookie cutters, or was he already dead before the wall was reopened?"

"Good questions," Del said. "This is a complex case, which is what makes it so fascinating. Are we really dealing with two completely separate murders, or are they somehow connected? All we know at this point is that both men were probably murdered."

"Well," Olivia said, "that's something. How was Kenny murdered?"

"Probably blows to the back of the neck and base of the skull, given the damage to some of the neck bones."

"Blows . . . Does that mean—?"

The kitchen door opened and Maddie poked her head inside. "The natives are getting restless." Del picked up the tray and Olivia followed him back to the living room. She noticed at once that Anita had collected all five cookie cutters and arranged them in a row on the coffee table. She picked up one cutter and examined it under a small magnifying glass. Intense concentration made her lovely face look tight and angry. Olivia and Maddie poured coffee in silence.

Anita lowered the magnifying glass to her lap and sat up straight. "These cutters," she said, "are the real deal. They are genuine antiques, almost certainly dating back as far as the late seventeen or early eighteen hundreds. Four are tin, hand-made by experienced tin workers. You can tell from the soldering, which is neat and precise. The fifth cutter is more recent—I'm guessing late nineteenth or early twentieth century. It is made of copper, rather than tin, and the design is most unusual. These five alone would fetch perhaps thousands of dollars in a bidding war among serious collectors." Anita took a deep breath and released it slowly. "I can't believe I'm saying this, but these pieces should not be allowed to leave Chatterley Heights. They are museum quality. When the time comes, I would like to be involved in tracing their histories and arranging their display. They should be kept secure at all times. Above all, avoid damaging them any more than you already have." Anita gave Del a pointed look.

"Thank you, Anita," Del said. "That was most helpful. I'll relay your concerns to the mayor. As long as the cutters are in police custody, I will keep them in our safe." He took a sip of coffee, and said, "I'd like to hear from everyone else, too." When no one responded, Del added, "I asked you four to take a look at these cookie cutters because I was hoping to hear different perspectives. I feel more confident that these might be part of the Chatterley collection, but I also need to understand why they were left in that wall."

Aunt Sadie touched Maddie's arm, and said, "Dear one, would you take my cup? I'd like to see those darlings again, if I may. I might have an idea or two." The slight tremor in Aunt Sadie's hand caused the cup to rattle on its saucer. Maddie quickly rescued it, while Anita, with delicate care, transferred the cutters to Aunt Sadie's lap. Olivia felt the hushed anticipation in the room. One by one, Aunt Sadie held the cutters in the palm of her hand and closed her eyes. A gentle smile played across her face as if each cutter were sharing its story with her.

After several minutes of silence, Aunt Sadie nodded and opened her eyes. "I don't know if any of my wanderings will be helpful, Del, but here goes. I have always been fascinated by our Chatterley origins. Many years ago, I spent several summers helping to catalog items in the mansion. I do so hope the research can be completed someday."

Much as she loved Aunt Sadie, Olivia wished she would skip the background and spill what she knew about those cutters. She hadn't felt this impatient since her tenth birthday party, when her parents made her wait to open up the ice skates she'd so wanted.

"I'm an old lady now," Aunt Sadie said, "but I still remember a great deal of what I read so many years ago. I'm surprised by how much more returned to me as I held these cutters." Aunt Sadie gently stroked the metal shapes on her lap before moving them to the table, where everyone could see them.

No one else spoke. Even Anita's dark eyes widened with interest as Aunt Sadie pointed toward one of the cutters.

"Now," Aunt Sadie said, "this sweet little three-petaled flower shape appeared in one of the diaries kept by Chatterley wives. You see, I was at loose ends after tutoring steadily during the school year, so every summer I volunteered to help sort through the contents of the mansion. The town had no funds to pay me, of course. This was after the last Chatterley had passed on. Or so we thought. Anyway, at the time, I was cataloging the contents of the mansion's master bedroom."

Aunt Sadie chuckled softly. "Bless those Chatterleys, they never parted with anything. I spent an entire summer on that room alone." Aunt Sadie ran her index finger along the outline of the flower. "We discovered Charlotte Chatterley's diary, which she'd written over the course of one year, 1859. During that period, she became pregnant and delivered triplet daughters." Aunt Sadie picked up the cutter and held it up for everyone to see. "Charlotte commissioned this three-petaled flower from a local tin worker to commemorate the safe arrival of her daughters. Can you see the tiny curve at the top of each petal? It was meant to be a curl. Charlotte wrote in her diary that she was delighted with her curly-haired daughters, though her husband was greatly disappointed because she hadn't produced three sons." Aunt Sadie returned the flower cutter to her lap.

Olivia did some quick math in her head. "Aunt Sadie, did Charlotte live long enough to know Horace Chatterley?"

Aunt Sadie nodded. "Yes, indeed. She was his aunt, though not an especially fond one. In a much later diary, she described Horace as arrogant and rude. She predicted misery for his future wife."

"I wonder if Charlotte would have predicted his murder," Olivia said.

"The thought might have occurred to her," Aunt Sadie said, "though she died well before Horace left his family for a string of younger women." She selected two more cookie cutters, the boy and the girl. "I should point out that all five cutters are almost certainly one-of-a-kind." She gave Anita a questioning glance.

Anita nodded. "Several are similar to common designs, but each has a unique aspect."

Aunt Sadie placed the boy and girl shapes on the coffee table. "These two cutters go together." When she slid the cutters toward each other, their outstretched hands interlocked.

"Ooh, how adorable," Maddie said. "Who are those two?"

"These sweet little ones are very old. During my summer research, I found no mention of who first commissioned them, or when they were made. Dear old Frederick P. wasn't much of a record keeper, and neither was his long-suffering wife. After a few generations, though, I started to notice irregular references to these cutters. Finally, I realized they were being passed down to the first-born Chatterley son on the occasion of his marriage."

"Chatterley husbands tended to favor philandering," Olivia said. "Maybe their wives weren't so fond of those particular cutters. Did anyone mention their disappearance after Horace moved out of the family mansion?"

A cluster of wrinkles gathered between Aunt Sadie's pale eyebrows as she thought back to her summer in the Chatterley mansion. "Not that I remember," she said. "I wasn't able to read all the family diaries, and there were other writings, as well. If it's important, I believe many of those papers are still stored upstairs in the mansion's attic." With a wistful sigh, Aunt Sadie said, "Someone really ought to finish reading all those fascinating journals."

Anita squirmed in her chair, impatient to move on. "What about those last two cutters?" she asked, nodding toward the remaining shapes. "One looks like a pregnant pig, and the other is beyond my comprehension. I'm usually quite good at identifying cookie cutter shapes."

Aunt Sadie clapped her hands like an excited child. "I saved those two for last. I must admit, I was rather proud of myself when I identified these shapes so many years ago." She picked up the portly pig. "This guy was commissioned by Caroline Chatterley in 1805. What looks like pregnancy is actually meant to represent the portly figure the Chatterley men often achieved as they entered middle age."

"Whoa," Maddie said. "Pigs are naturally portly. This fellow is downright bloated. I'm guessing Caroline had issues with her husband. Now I think of it, I don't remember ever hearing about a Chatterley wife who actually liked her husband."

"Oh, I do believe that Imogene truly loved Henry Chatterley," Aunt Sadie said. "Although it's true that Henry was not a typical first-born Chatterley man. In fact, when I ran across references to him elsewhere, it was clear he'd always maintained his slim figure."

Olivia flashed back to Aunt Sadie's story about Henry Chatterley. "He actually changed his surname to Jones, right? So in a sense he rejected the Chatterley legacy. I wonder . . ."

Del snapped to attention. "Remember, I didn't grow up in Chatterley Heights, so I've never heard anything about Henry Chatterley. Tell me." He listened while Aunt Sadie repeated her story about Henry's marriage to Imogene Jones. "So Henry Chatterley became Henry Jones," he said. "Jones is a common name. Aunt Sadie, do you know what happened to Henry after he took his wife's name? Did he disappear? Is that what you were wondering, Livie?"

"Partly," Olivia said. "I was also wondering if Henry might have had anything to do with his father's murder."

"Oh, I'm sure that isn't true." Aunt Sadie sounded genuinely alarmed. "Henry was such an honorable man. He became a successful attorney, and he used his earnings to help his mother and siblings after Horace lost what was left of the family fortune in the stock market crash. I can't believe he would murder his own father, no matter how irresponsible Horace had been. What would he gain, after all?"

Del shrugged. "Rage can make people do things they wouldn't even consider under other circumstances."

"Well, I'll never believe it," Aunt Sadie said.

Del wisely dropped the subject.

Aunt Sadie picked up the last of the five antique cookie cutters, a confusing combination of curves, corners, and stemlike protrusions. "I'll admit, I would never have identified this shape without help from Abigail Chatterley's personal diary."

"Abigail?" Maddie took the strange cutter from Aunt Sadie's palm. "Wasn't Abigail the first Chatterley wife, the one married to Frederick P.? That would mean this cutter dates back to the early 1700s, and it doesn't look anywhere near old enough."

"No, Maddie, dear." Aunt Sadie retrieved the cutter. "This is a much newer cutter, commissioned by a second Abigail Chatterley. She traced the outline in her journal, but she neglected to mention what it was. I thought perhaps she was simply doodling. Abigail was artistic, you see. She did lovely free-form embroidery. We found her work in a cedar chest in one of the mansion bedrooms. As I remember, we moved that chest to the attic. I assume it was preserved with care during the mansion's more recent renovation."

"Lucas would have seen to that," Maddie said. "I'll ask him. But, Aunt Sadie, who was this second Abigail? Would she have known Horace?"

"Oh, didn't I say?" Aunt Sadie reluctantly handed the

cutter to Del. "She was Horace's mother. Poor woman. She must have been mortified when Horace deserted his wife and children for a younger woman."

"A *scarlet* woman, too," Maddie said. "At least, that's what Abigail must have thought."

"Oh, I'm not so sure." A tremor slowed Aunt Sadie's hand as she tried to push an errant lock of gray hair off her forehead. "Remember, it was Henry, Abigail's grandson, who took care of the family his father had abandoned. And he did so with Imogene's full approval. In the end, the family Horace left behind fared far better than he did. There's a certain justice in that, don't you think?"

Chapter Eighteen

Olivia and Maddie practically floated across Aunt Sadie's porch after the fascinating evening they'd spent discussing cookie cutters from the Chatterley collection. They didn't notice the chill until they began their walk back to The Gingerbread House. The moment they left the shelter of the porch, a forceful wind nearly knocked them sideways.

"How long did that meeting last, anyway?" Maddie had to raise her voice to be heard over the rustling trees. "It feels like winter out here."

Olivia pulled up the collar of her jacket. "We should have dressed warmer. No walk for Spunky this evening. He gets nervous in high winds."

"Not fond of them myself," Maddie said. "Let's fire up the computer and do some research. Maybe the wind will die down later. I hope Alicia has found shelter. If she's with that Jack guy, she's probably okay. From Polly's description, he sounded like a reasonable fellow."

Olivia buried her hands in her jacket pockets as they walked past the closed businesses along Park Street. "Del doesn't seem too worried about Alicia. Maybe there's been progress, and Del thought we knew about it. We should check our emails when we get back to the store."

As they came in sight of The Gingerbread House, Maddie said, "Jeez, this wind is bad. Let's run." She took off, and Olivia followed behind, swearing to herself that she would go back to regular runs around the park to get her muscles in shape. Spunky would benefit, too. He might work off a few of those extra treats he got from customers and . . . well, just about everyone.

By the time Olivia dragged herself up the front steps to the porch, she was thoroughly winded, although warmer. Maddie had run ahead and reached the porch, where she was staring at the front door. Olivia paused to catch her breath, but Maddie didn't move. "Don't you have your key?" Olivia asked. She reached into her jacket pocket. "If you'll move aside, I'll unlock the door."

"Interesting," Maddie said.

"Not the response I was expecting." Olivia looked around Maddie's mass of windblown hair. "Oh no, not again," she moaned. "Another tack hole in my lovely door . . . What does the note say?" Maddie pulled out the tack and handed over the note. "At least it's easier to read this time," Olivia grumbled. Written with blue pen in neat cursive, the note read: *Please tell everyone to stop worrying about me and leave us alone. Jack is nice. He's been telling me stories about my dad and helping me find out what happened to him. Alicia.*

"Livie, please tell me we were never that young and dumb." Maddie produced her own key and unlocked the front door.

"Of course we were." Olivia scurried into the foyer and slammed the door behind them. "We were once naive teenagers, too. On the other hand, there's a chance Alicia is right that Jack is trying to help her."

"Then why won't he show himself in public like a person

whose face isn't on a wanted poster?" Maddie unlocked the door of the store, reached inside, and flipped on the sales floor lights.

Olivia ran a hand through her wind-tangled hair as she followed Maddie into the store. "I don't understand why they need to deface my lovely antique front door with tacks. Why couldn't Alicia have left a cell phone message like a normal person?"

"Maybe she didn't want to deal with talking to you in person." Maddie led the way into the kitchen.

"I guess I can understand that." Olivia nodded toward the kitchen phone. "We have several messages on the landline, but they're probably all from my mom. I don't have the patience to listen to them right now. I need to brush my hair."

"Yes, you do," Maddie said. "I'll leave mine alone. Brushing would only encourage it." She pointed to the red tangle of curls, which was twice its normal height. "I'll check the messages."

"Shout if you hear anything interesting." Olivia headed for the tiny kitchen bathroom, where she kept a supply of toiletries. Leaving the door open, she worked a brush through her tangled auburn hair, then lightly dampened it to help the waves recover from wind shock.

"No important phone messages," Maddie called from the kitchen, "but Binnie has gone bonkers again."

Uh-oh. Olivia quickly smoothed some moisturizer on her wind-chapped cheeks and rejoined Maddie, who had fired up the laptop. Olivia requisitioned a chair and joined her. "I don't see any incriminating photos on the screen," Olivia said. "What has Binnie done this time?"

Maddie opened Binnie's nefarious blog. "She seems to have lost interest in publishing her weekly rag. I kind of miss *The Weekly Chatter.* It was more carefully written, plus it appeared only once a week. Binnie goes overboard on this blog. She thinks she can write anything about anybody, no matter how nasty. In her newspaper, at least she mostly stuck to innuendo. Also, she used punctuation, so a person could make sense of the snide remarks."

"When this investigation is all over," Olivia said, "we must have a forceful talk with Binnie. I'll see if I can get in touch with Ned. Maybe she can help."

"Does Ned actually talk?" Maddie's fingers began to fly around the keyboard. "Ah, there it is."

"There what is?" Olivia sat back for a panoramic view. "Oh, I see. It's a photo collage. Is that Ned's work? It's really very good. How on earth did you—?"

"Simple," Maddie said. "And I didn't have to hack. I found a photojournalism contest sponsored by American University. Ned is taking classes there. Let me check something." Maddie clicked in silence for a few moments. "Oh wow," she said. "I knew Ned was good, so I figured she might have placed in that contest, but hey, she actually won first place. No wonder she is trying to distance herself from her crazy aunt."

"Her crazy aunt is paying for her education," Olivia said. "I can't believe I'm defending Binnie Sloan."

"I think I'll print this collage. I like it." Maddie pressed a key, and the color printer sprang to life.

"I wish I'd thought to make a copy of that first note I found tacked to the front door," Olivia said. "Although the writing was so light and scratchy, it might not have copied well."

"It copied beautifully." Maddie grinned as she opened a drawer used for storing towels. "I forgot about this until now. That note sat around until you left for lunch, so I scanned it into the computer and made a couple copies. Ta da!" She handed a copy to Olivia, who squinted at it under the lamp on her desk. She could see the scratches following the last letter of the note, the "r" at the end of the word "cutter." "Do we have a magnifying glass?" Olivia asked.

"We do." Maddie rummaged through the junk drawer and produced what looked like a glass stick with a small, round magnifying glass on the end. "Aunt Sadie needed a more powerful one for her embroidery, so she gave this one to me. I use it when I need to be precise about placing a tiny decoration on royal icing. It's important to be compulsive," Maddie added.

"Especially when you *are* impulsive," Olivia mumbled under her breath.

"What was that?"

"Thanks!" Olivia took the magnifier from Maddie's hand. "I'll let you know if I have a eureka moment."

"And I shall begin creating dozens of amazing cookies for all those lovely events we've been scheduling. We are going to be insanely busy as the holidays approach," Maddie said. "We need to wrap up this mystery soon."

"Uh-huh." Olivia squinted at the scratches, an idea forming in her mind.

"You're so cute when you lose touch with reality," Maddie said as she opened a container of sugar.

"A flashlight might help," Olivia muttered to herself.

"Jeez, and they say I'm the one who gets lost in my own little world." Maddie added butter to the mixing bowl.

"I'm sorry, what did you say, Maddie?"

"I said there's a flashlight in the storage closet, bottom shelf, right-hand side." Maddie put in her earbuds and began to hum off-key as Olivia left the kitchen.

When Olivia returned, flashlight in hand, the slapping sound of butter and sugar blending together drowned out Maddie's musical attempts. Olivia settled at the little kitchen desk, where she hunched over the copied note, flashlight in one hand and magnifier in the other. When she'd examined the original note, the marks after the last letter had barely been visible. They'd appeared to be random. Del had assumed the author was trying, perhaps frantically, to expose more pencil lead. Presumably he had wanted to add another line or two of explanation to his cryptic note. That had made sense at the time.

Olivia held the magnifying glass closer to the paper to look for minute details. She realized there were many more scratches than she'd thought. They were tiny, thin, and relatively close together, as if they were meant to form a pattern. She examined the entire surface of the note and saw no other marks.

If the author had wanted to expose more pencil lead, rubbing the wood on paper was more likely to tear the paper. And Jack might have had a pocketknife. That would have worked much better. What am I missing?

What if those marks weren't random? What if they'd been added for a purpose?

Olivia abandoned the flashlight and magnifier. *Mom would tell me to stop trying so hard . . . to let it come to me.* She leaned against the back of her chair and closed her eyes, hoping for quick clarity and insight. What she got was clutter. She could almost hear her mother's voice telling her to let the clutter drift away. *Easy for you, Mom.*

"Livie?" It was Maddie's voice. "Is it past your bedtime?"

Olivia scraped back her chair and twisted around. "I was trying to clear my mind, like Mom is forever suggesting." As Olivia turned back to her desk and reached for the mysterious note, she heard a tiny ping, like a muted bell; only it came from inside her own head. Olivia knew at once what she'd been missing. "I'm an idiot," she said.

"Really?" Maddie abandoned her mound of freshly made cookie dough and joined Olivia. "Does this mean I get to feel superior, or are you about to reveal a profound, eternal truth that I probably won't comprehend?"

Olivia laughed, though mostly at herself. "I've been struggling to find meaning in those scratches at the end of this note. It doesn't make sense that they'd accidentally cluster this way. But I've been too close to it. And by that I mean too close physically, holding a magnifying glass in one hand and a flashlight in the other. I was seeing the trees quite clearly, but I totally missed the forest."

"I have no idea what you're talking about," Maddie said as she dragged a kitchen chair next to Olivia.

"Then you won't be disappointed. Watch." She picked up the magnifying glass, but instead of holding it close to the paper, she backed it away.

Maddie looked through the glass and shrugged. "I still don't get it."

Olivia opened the desk drawer and rooted around until she came up with a pencil. "Watch this," she said. "If you connect all those little scratches, this is what you get." Using the pencil, she traced a light "S" that was several times the size of the other letters.

Maddie tilted her head as she studied the note. "You get a gigantic squiggle?"

"Um . . ." Olivia felt a pinch of self-doubt. She had to admit, it did look rather like a big squiggly line. Was she making something out of nothing? Were the scratches meaningless?

"Ooh, wait, I get it!" Maddie's wild red hair fluffed in all directions as she bounced up and down with excitement. "You're right, it's a forest and trees thing. If you read the whole note now, it says '*If you want to know what happened to Kenny Vayle, follow the cookie cutterS*.' It must be referring to those antique cutters the police found under Kenny's bones. "So that means . . ." Frown lines gathered between Maddie's flour-dusted eyebrows. "Do the police know for sure who wrote that note, or are we just assuming it was the mysterious Jack? Would a drifter have heard of the Chatterley cookie cutter collection? If we didn't have a clue that part of the Chatterley collection was hiding inside the boarding house wall, how would . . . Oh." Maddie's already pale skin lost any hint of color. "The person who wrote the note must have seen those cutters. Are you saying that Alicia has gone off with the man who killed her father?"

"I'm saying we shouldn't rule him out, although if we assume this Jack fellow did write that first note, he has to be considered a suspect. Alicia thinks he's 'nice,' but can we trust her assessment? At the very least, he must know about those extra cutters. On the other hand, it seems unlikely that

Kenny Vayle's killer would have volunteered any information that would tie him to the death. It was such a strange, indirect clue, though. I can't help but wonder . . ." Olivia ran a hand through her hair. "Why would Jack take the risk of leaving that note?"

"And why would he go to such pains to hide its true meaning?" Maddie asked. "He must be really, really afraid of someone."

A t eleven p.m., Olivia stood up to stretch. She had been hunched over her desk for two hours, catching up on paperwork. Maddie had spent the time baking cookies in puppy and kitten shapes for an upcoming fund-raising event at Chatterley Paws. As she removed the last sheet of playful puppy-shaped cookies from the oven, a cloud of orange-scented warmth permeated the kitchen.

"I must be hungry," Olivia said. "Those cookies smell delicious."

Maddie deposited the sheet on a cooling rack. "They smell delicious, my friend, because they *are* delicious. Try one." Maddie handed Olivia a cooled sleeping kitten cookie.

Olivia took a bite and sighed with pleasure. "Cookies do make everything better."

"How true." Maddie began to gather bowls and pans for washing. "I've baked more than enough animal-shaped cookies for the event at Chatterley Paws on Saturday evening. She glanced up at the kitchen clock. "In an hour, it'll only be Thursday, so I'll have plenty of time to get these little guys decorated." She pointed to a rack of cooled, sleeping kitten-shaped cookies. "I'm thinking of piping multicolored stripes on those little guys. You know, like pale green and teal, or maybe hot pink and purple."

Olivia arched an eyebrow at her friend. "Cats don't appreciate insults to their dignity."

Maddie shrugged one shoulder. "The little critters are

napping. They'll never know." She began to fill a cake pan with cooled kittens. "Hey, what should we do next? I'm bursting with pent-up energy."

Olivia rolled her stiff shoulders. "I've been sitting at a computer for too long. At least I've caught up on actual store tasks, like ordering supplies and responding to customer emails." Olivia picked up the copy of the note. "I should tell Del my theory about what this note really says, but . . ."

"But you don't want him to leap to the outrageous, yet true conclusion that we plan to investigate on our own?" Without waiting for an answer, Maddie added, "Because I completely agree. We wouldn't want Del to worry. Worry is one of the major causes of premature aging." Maddie snuggled the last sleeping kitten into the cake pan and slid the cover shut. "I'll store these cooled cookies in the freezer," she said. "I can put the others away afterward."

"Afterward? You mean tomorrow morning?" Olivia lifted the laptop lid and clicked the email icon. She had two new emails, one from Del and the other from her mom.

"It's almost tomorrow now," Maddie said.

"Uh-huh." Olivia clicked on Del's email.

"Livie, you really aren't tracking well. You should probably leave the multitasking to me."

"Del says the forensic team is finishing a DNA test on the skull right now," Olivia said. "Del is so excited, he's decided to stick around for a while. He says the lab folks can't stand the suspense. Neither can he. He borrowed someone's laptop so he could let me know. That's sweet."

"That's probably because poor, patient Del tried to text you and discovered your phone is, as usual, dead." Maddie wedged the cake pan of cookies into an already well packed freezer. "So Chatterley Heights is without police protection tonight— by which I mean police interference, of course."

"What? Oh, Del says that Twiterton will handle any 911 calls." Olivia blinked her eyes, which felt dry from staring at the computer screen. "He has decided to stay at the lab until he hears the DNA results. Then he'll head straight home. I wish he wouldn't drive when he hasn't had any sleep." Her fingers hovered over the keyboard. "I'm sorry, Maddie, what were you saying?"

Maddie hiked herself onto the counter next to the laptop. Olivia barely had time to yank her hands off the keyboard before Maddie closed the lid. "Livie, we need to go to that boarding house. Now. There's a good chance Alicia is in there with this Jack person, who might or might not be a thoroughly nice guy."

"Maddie, I gave the key back to Mom, and it isn't all that easy to break into that building. Those new locks are solid. You should know that—after all, Lucas installed them. Also, the windows are boarded up on the ground floor. Besides, the police have been in and out of the place so much lately. All things considered, it doesn't seem like a very tempting place to hide out."

Maddie's eyebrows shot up. "Not a tempting place? Are you kidding? Part of the famous Chatterley cookie cutter collection was recently discovered in that boarding house. The kitchen is the only room Calliope and her workers have finished renovating. They were just getting started on all those rooms upstairs. Who knows what secrets lurk behind those old walls?"

"I do not intend to go out in the cold and spend the night tearing down boarding house walls. We're more likely to find mice than Chatterley cookie cutters. Mom has the key, and she is frantic to find Alicia. I'm sure she checks regularly for any signs that Jack and Alicia might be using the building as a hideout. Mom will be thorough beyond what is normally considered human. It's more likely Jack has taken Alicia some-where far away from Chatterley Heights. Personally, I suspect Alicia went with Jack willingly and is safe with him."

"Poop head."

"Besides, I have more emails to write," Olivia said. "I

want to get the Binnie situation under control before she humiliates poor Lenora with those photos."

Maddie fit another covered pan of cookies into the packed freezer. "Good luck controlling Binnie. She's likely to smack Lenora even harder, if only to get back at you."

"That's why I'm turning the project over to my mom. She can handle Binnie much better than I can. I figure Mom can get away with gushing about Ned's work, if that's what it takes to soften up Binnie." Olivia downloaded Ned's prizewinning photo and attached a copy to the email to her mother. "The photo is really quite good, but Binnie would never believe that coming from me."

"Ellie is amazing, that's for sure," Maddie said. "Not that you don't have your own gifts, Livie. You write a really stunning business plan, and no one can equal your paper-work skills."

"Um, thank you?" Olivia copied Ned's email address and added it to the text of her email. "I wish I had your gift with decorated cookies."

"You do okay." Maddie began selecting gel icing colors to use on her shelter animal cookies. "I mean, you haven't ruined a batch of royal icing in years."

Olivia hit send, and her email whooshed off to her mother. "Okay, Maddie, what's with the passive-aggressive act? Are you mad at me just because I'd rather not wander around outside after dark on a cold, windy night?"

Maddie took a deep breath and released a noisy sigh. "Well, since you ask . . . Lately you've been so, I don't know . . . so *adult*. Here we have a lovely mystery to investigate—two mysteries, in fact, one even colder than the other, both of them utterly fascinating. I'm way ahead on the baking for the week. You've placed the orders for supplies. Your mother will use her wiles to save Lenora from the wrath of Binnie. Yet the most totally intriguing puzzles are the ones you don't seem truly interested in solving. Livie, my friend, you have lost touch with your inner Nancy Drew and become all grown-up Business Woman."

"Well, I did solve the riddle of the cryptic note. That was Nancy Drewish." Olivia thought of several more retorts, but they all sounded equally defensive.

Maddie stared wide-eyed at her best friend since age ten. After several seconds, a faint chortling sound came from her throat. Then she began to laugh. Olivia joined her.

When they'd caught their breath, Olivia asked, "You really want to go out and look for Alicia, don't you? Because it's frigid and windy out there, not to mention dark. She and Jack might be anywhere, including another town. Or is finding Alicia an excuse to search for more cookie cutters in the Chatterley Boarding House?"

"The two are not mutually exclusive," Maddie said. "I'll admit, the thought of finding more of the Chatterley collection makes my heart go pitter-patter. Don't tell me *you* wouldn't love to go antique cutter hunting, because I wouldn't believe you for an instant."

Olivia yawned. She wasn't really tired, simply tired of sitting. A walk might help. Maybe the wind had calmed down a bit. And she could take Spunky along. He'd been cooped up for quite a while and undoubtedly needed a visit to that doggie bathroom called the great outdoors. "Mom did mention a board covering one of the ground floor windows was loose," she said. "In a sense, we wouldn't really be breaking in . . . exactly."

"Yippee!" Maddie pumped her arm in the air.

"However, I draw the line at breaking windows or tearing down walls. Even if Mom didn't notice, Calliope would, and she'd tell Mom."

"Understood," Maddie said. "We've seen only the kitchen and room eight. We could check the other rooms for signs of tampering or repair. There's probably a cellar, too . . . and maybe an attic."

"Then we'd better get moving." Olivia turned off the

laptop. "I do not intend to be out all night. We have to work tomorrow."

In under ten minutes, Olivia returned to the kitchen, dressed warmly and toting an eager Yorkie. She found Maddie, wrapped in a long sweater, loading the last soiled coffee cup into the dishwasher. "Are you sure you'll be warm enough in that sweater?" Olivia asked.

"I'll freeze to death." Maddie pulled a set of car keys from her sweater pocket. "My little VW is parked in the alley. We should drive to the boarding house, at least most of the way. We can park out of sight and walk around the perimeter first. I'm pretty sure I could survive that much exposure to the elements. Spunky will find plenty of tempting smells to guide him to his doggie bathroom."

"Okay, I'll be right behind you. Spunky's leash didn't snap on right, so I need to fix it. Hold still, Spunks." Olivia held the squirming Yorkie under one arm as she tried to attach the leash firmly to his collar. Finally, it snapped into place. "There, that should do it." She started toward the back door . . . and froze. Maddie stood framed in the open doorway facing Olivia, the pitch-black alley behind her. The look on Maddie's face told Olivia that something was very, very wrong.

"Maddie?" Olivia realized she was whispering.

Maddie slewed her expressive eyes down and to the side. Olivia followed Maddie's silent instructions but could see only darkness in the alley behind her. Maddie jerked as if she'd been poked in the back. Spunky growled and strained at his leash so hard it pulled him up on his hind legs. Olivia understood at once. Although she saw nothing, someone must be right behind Maddie, holding a weapon against her back. Olivia scooped up Spunky, while her eyes swept the kitchen, searching for a knife, anything . . . but Maddie had cleaned too thoroughly.

Olivia considered releasing Spunky. No, that was too risky. He had no clue how tiny he was. He could be hurt or worse. It was too late, anyway. Maddie jerked again and took a step into the light of the kitchen. The partial outline of a figure appeared behind her. The intruder's shoulders were broader than Maddie's, but he or she must be shorter, since Olivia couldn't see the top of a head. Maddie's wild hair hid the face.

In a matter of seconds, Olivia's questions were answered. Maddie's captor pushed her inside and slammed the alley door behind them. Clutching Spunky under one arm, Olivia rushed forward to stabilize her friend, who teetered as if she might lose her balance. "Who are you? What do you want?" Olivia had to shout to be heard over Spunky's ferocious yapping.

The intruder stepped into view. He wore a knit face mask, as if he'd been out for a mid-winter walk in an arctic climate. He appeared to be a short, thin man, although dark clothing covered him from head to toe. "Shut that mutt up, or I'll kill him."

"Maddie, are you all right?" Olivia's question came out hushed and squeaky.

Maddie gave her a faint nod. Her translucent eyes seemed to darken against her ashen skin.

Spunky squirmed to escape his mistress's right arm, wrapped firmly around his small body. Olivia gripped his collar with her left hand. The frustrated Yorkie snarled at the intruder with a fierceness Olivia had never heard before. The intruder stepped backward. Sensing fear from his quarry, Spunky wriggled mightily, paws flailing. Olivia struggled to hold on to him as he strained forward. She didn't want to squeeze too hard and hurt the little guy. Maddie rushed forward to help, but Spunky was wriggling too much.

In the midst of chaos, Olivia had a sudden, clear thought. Without loosening her hold on Spunky, she studied the intruder. He hadn't moved. In fact, he appeared frozen in place, his empty hands hanging at his sides. Despite the threatening mask, he seemed . . . The word "uncertain" popped into her mind. At once, it hit her. Either he was afraid of a five pound dog . . . or he wasn't armed.

Olivia lowered Spunky to the floor. Keeping a firm grip on his leash, she released her enraged protector. With the aggressive stance of a much larger dog, Spunky lunged forward, nearly yanking the leash from Olivia's hand. The intruder stepped backward. Again, he did not reach for a weapon . . . but he didn't run out into the alley, either.

"Who are you?" Olivia had to raise her voice to be heard over Spunky's yapping. "What do you want?"

Maddie took a step toward the man. "Hey, I felt you poke me in the back. I thought you had a knife," she said. "Where is it?" When the man neither responded nor produced a weapon, Maddie strode toward him. "That's what I thought. You're nothing but a faker." She reached toward his head as if to yank off the knit mask. The intruder spun around and grabbed for the alley door, but Maddie was too quick for him. She snatched at the top of the face mask and whipped it off his head. With her free arm, Maddie seized his shoulder and spun him around to face her. "You're Kurt Kurtzel, aren't you?"

Kurt shrugged one shoulder. "Tell me where Alicia is hiding."

"We don't know," Olivia said. "We believe she is safe."

"She's with that old guy, isn't she? Where did he take her?"

"You're wasting your time, Kurt," Maddie said. "We have no idea where Alicia went. Besides, she's an adult. She can go wherever she pleases."

Maddie might not feel threatened by Kurt, but Olivia wasn't so sure. Now that she'd seen his face, she had mixed reactions. She knew he was in his midtwenties, but his sullenness made him seem younger. With his fine-boned face and dark blue eyes, she could see why young girls might find him attractive. Kurt had thin, hunched shoulders that practically screamed "computer nerd," but his hands, with their long fingers, might be described as elegant. Those fingers looked strong, too. Kurt's hands tightened into fists.

Maddie reacted quickly. She grabbed Kurt by his upper arm and dragged him over to the kitchen table, where she shoved him into a chair. "If you aren't armed, what did you use to poke me in the back?" she demanded. "I definitely felt a sharp point."

Before Maddie could stop him, Kurt slid his hand into the pocket of his faded black jeans and pulled out a jack-knife. Maddie snatched it from his hand. "That's nothing but a little pocketknife," she said.

Narrowing his eyes, Kurt said, "I left my switchblade at home. Didn't figure I'd need it with you two." Kurt's nasal voice made the statement sound more whiny than threatening, but Olivia shivered at the intensity in his eyes. She lifted the folded knife from Maddie's hand and tossed it in the kitchen junk drawer.

"Hey, give that back!" Now Kurt sounded like an aggrieved ten-year-old whose mother had just confiscated his favorite toy. Olivia was beginning to understand why he appealed only to much younger girls. It was reassuring to know that Alicia had outgrown him . . . assuming she truly had, that is. "Fine, then," Kurt said with a shrug. "You can keep it. I'm expecting a shiny new shipment tomorrow, anyway."

"You order your weapons in bulk?" Olivia asked.

Kurt smirked. "You'd be surprised what I can get online. No one can trace me, either."

Maddie shot an amused glanced toward Olivia. "Well, Kurt," she said, "maybe no one has really tried. Yet."

Kurt relaxed against the back of the kitchen chair. "I am very, very good at what I do," he said. This time he sounded calm and sure of himself. "That's why I know you aren't going to call the police."

Over Kurt's head, Olivia exchanged a quick, puzzled glance with Maddie. "Why on earth wouldn't we call the police?" Olivia said. "You hid outside our kitchen and threatened my friend."

"That's not the first time I've hidden outside your kitchen." Kurt looked pleased with his cleverness. "It was funny, really. You two never caught on, and neither did that dimwitted husband of yours." He grinned at Maddie, whose eyes narrowed dangerously. "It never occurred to him that anyone was messing with those bulbs he kept having to change. He'd replace one, and I'd just shimmy up the pole and shake it to break the filament. You girls aren't nearly as smart or safe as you think you are."

Olivia saw her own shock reflected in Maddie's eyes, and in that split second, Kurt jumped up, knocking his chair to the floor. Slipping past Olivia before she could grab even a pinch of his shirt, he flung open the alley door. Kurt turned to face them and, for a moment, stood framed in the doorway. "I will find Alicia," he said. "Don't even try to stop me. You can't. Alicia *belongs* to me." He stepped backward and disappeared into the black night.

Chapter Nineteen

❦

Olivia's eyelids slid open. Given the thumping of her heart, she expected to see a ravenous tiger leaping toward her, but there was only darkness. She sat up and tried to orient herself. Once she understood she was in her own bedroom, the covers no longer felt like restraints, but her heart kept right on pounding. She'd had a nightmare, that much was clear. From her physical reactions, Olivia decided the content of her dream was best left unexamined. As she fell back on her pillow, Spunky emerged from under a fold in the blanket and crawled onto her stomach.

"Hey, Spunks. So what just happened here?" Olivia's voice sounded raspy, as if she'd been screaming in her sleep.

Spunky's fluffy tail wagged in comforting response. Settling his fuzzy face on his paws, the little Yorkie fixed trusting brown eyes on Olivia as if he expected her to answer her own question. Olivia reached over and ruffled the silky hair between his perked ears. "Unfortunately," she said, "it's beginning to come back to me. It was only a dream, but a scary one. You and I were playing catch in a room in the boarding house when a hole opened in the wall. Only this time there weren't any nice, quiet bones inside. Thousands of tiny knife-shaped cookie cutters rose up en masse and spewed into the room, heading right for us. I was reaching out to grab you when the cutter knives flew between us. Suddenly I couldn't see you anymore. I called your name and tried to push through the cutters, but . . ." Olivia's breath caught in her throat. She pulled Spunky to her chest and held him so tightly he squirmed and yapped.

"Oops, sorry, little one," Olivia said. "It was that wretched young man, Kurt. He must have scared me more than I realized." She released Spunky, who retreated to the end of the bed, where he watched his mistress warily for further signs of insanity.

"I don't blame you one bit." Olivia pushed herself up on one elbow and felt along her bedside tabletop for the lamp switch. She checked her cell phone, which told her it was two a.m. She'd been asleep for only an hour and a half. The nightmare had receded, allowing her heart to resume its normal rhythm. Spunky tilted his head and whimpered as if he were leery of his mistress's mood. Olivia gave his ears a quick rub before melting back into her soft pillow. Spunky snuggled into the crook of her arm. Within moments, he was snoozing.

Olivia was not so lucky. She kept thinking about those flying cookie cutters. On the whole, she preferred comforting dreams about cookie cutters dancing in the moonlight. However, the thought of those angry, swarming cutters did trigger a thought . . . or rather, a question about the antique cutters Del had found under the skull that might or might not have belonged to Horace Chatterley. Those cutters were probably connected in some way with Horace Chatterley's murder, but how? Were they meant to convey a message? Olivia couldn't shake the suspicion that those lovely, abused antiques might somehow lead her to Kenny Vayle's killer.

Olivia sat up so quickly that Spunky yapped in alarm. "It's

okay, sweetie." Olivia felt his little body relax as she massaged the soft hair behind his ears. "I need to go over my suspect list again." Olivia disentangled her legs from the covers. "You can stay here, Spunks, and have a nice snooze."

Spunky had other ideas. He leaped off the bed and headed toward the hallway. At the doorway, he paused to yap at his mistress. "Oh, all right," Olivia said. "I'll give you one extra Milk Bone, but that's it. Then you hightail it back to bed. Understood?" Spunky yapped again. "I'll take that as a 'yes,'" she said, though Spunky had already disappeared.

It would be cold downstairs in the store, so Olivia pulled on an old pair of jeans and a scruffy sweatshirt. She left the bedding tangled. With any luck, she'd be diving under those covers again soon. A dreamless sleep awaited once she had removed the whirling thoughts from her mind and recorded them on paper. Her father had called the exercise a "brain squeeze," and he had taught the skill to Olivia.

The apartment kitchen was empty when Olivia entered it. Spunky had failed to stop for his promised treat. Such behavior was unprecedented. A sharp yap called her down the hallway to the front entrance, where she found a determined little Yorkie barring the door with every one of his five pounds. Olivia gave up without a fight. She knew Spunky would fret if she went downstairs alone in the middle of the night. "Okay, fine." Olivia opened the deadbolt. "You can sleep on your chair out on the sales floor, and that's my final offer. If you try to sneak into the kitchen, I'll turn you over to the health department myself."

Once downstairs, Olivia unlocked the Gingerbread House door and held it open for Spunky. He entered with an air of ownership and, Olivia thought, smugness. However, he stopped to look back as if worried his human might be planning to lock him inside, alone. He relaxed when Olivia followed him to the sales floor, flipped the lights on low, and locked the two of them inside.

Ever hopeful, Spunky followed Olivia to the kitchen door

and stared up at her with eyes that begged to be allowed to go inside. "I'm sorry, little one." Olivia crouched down to rub his ears. "Not even your melting gaze could convince me to let you into the kitchen." Spunky accepted defeat and headed toward his chair, his claws clicking on the tile floor.

Olivia slipped into the kitchen and flipped on the lights. She eyed the clean, empty coffeepot with longing. After the shock of Kurt Kurtzel's late night appearance, she and Maddie had reported the incident to the Twiterton police and then decided to call it a night. Maddie had already cleaned Mr. Coffee, so Olivia had no dregs to reheat. She wasn't sleepy at the moment, but coffee always helped her think. In the interests of alert sleuthing, she brewed half a pot before settling at the kitchen table to skim through her original list of suspects and questions.

"Well, this won't help much." Olivia's voice sounded eerie in the empty kitchen. She wished Maddie were there, baking cookies and humming off key to her earbuds. A gulp of sweet, milky coffee comforted Olivia. She returned to her list and began to jot notes next to her questions. The first two seemed to have simple answers. The mysterious Jack was probably one of Crystal's post-Kenny companions, but almost certainly not legally married to her. That might explain why Jack had told Polly, when he'd arrived at her homeless shelter, that he had come to Chatterley Heights to see his "stepdaughter"—presumably Crystal's daughter, Alicia. Olivia had found no evidence that Crystal ever bothered to marry or divorce any of the men who'd followed Kenny. Nor had she divorced Kenny or had him declared dead. It followed that Crystal's marriage to Robbie Quinn was a sham.

Olivia's next question now had an answer, as well. Robbie and Kenny once were, if not friends, at least drinking buddies. According to the story Lucas had told, Kenny had publicly warned Robbie to stay away from Crystal, which implied they were involved before Kenny disappeared. It probably wasn't Kenny's drinking that ended his so-called friendship with Robbie, though it might have driven Crystal into Robbie's arms.

That left Kurt Kurtzel. He had developed an unsavory attachment to the much younger Alicia Vayle. Kenny, whatever his other failings, had loved his daughter, and he had ordered Kurt to stay away from her.

"Kurt Kurtzel has one mean temper," Olivia told her nearly empty coffee cup. Kenny got between Kurt and Alicia, so Kurt took revenge on Kenny by posting a photo of him looking drunk. Olivia poured the last of the coffee into her cup, shivering at the memory of Kurt's midnight visit to the Gingerbread House kitchen. His behavior had struck her as staged, like an online persona designed to appear mysterious and threatening. Still, his obsessive pursuit of Alicia sent a chill down Olivia's spine. She imagined him lurking in the alley behind The Gingerbread House, disabling their light, watching them come and go . . . Then he had forced his way into their kitchen, terrifying Maddie in the process. True, Kurt hadn't produced a real weapon, but quite possibly the police did confiscate his switchblade. In fact, finding such a weapon on him might have convinced the police to arrest Kurt for trying to slug Pete.

Olivia took a sip of warm coffee as she pondered the final question on her list: on the day he disappeared, who had Kenny Vayle gone to meet about a job? Olivia wondered if this meeting, if there was one, had taken place at the Chatterley Boarding House, perhaps in the very room where Kenny's bones were found.

So far, no one had mentioned how Kenny might have heard about a possible job opportunity—a phone call, a note, over a beer in a nearby bar? If Del knew the answer, he hadn't shared it with Olivia. He was too busy salivating over an old skull with his forensic buddies. Olivia dropped her pen on the table and rubbed her eyelids. She still wasn't sleepy, but she was certainly getting cranky. More discouraging, she wasn't any closer to a breathtaking breakthrough.

Olivia was tempted to call Del. She'd left him a message about Kurt's invasion of the Gingerbread House kitchen, but Del hadn't called back yet. Maybe he was schmoozing with the lab staff while they analyzed DNA results. She picked up her cell phone and checked messages. Nothing. Del might be catching some shut-eye before driving back to Chatterley Heights. She could only hope he wasn't actually driving home exhausted. No, she thought, he would have called her at once if the DNA results were available.

Tired or not, Olivia decided to head back upstairs to her apartment. She could brainstorm more on her own sofa, slouching comfortably while Spunky snoozed on her legs. Olivia wedged through the door to the sales floor to keep Spunky from sneaking into the kitchen. She needn't have worried. No clicking Yorkie claws rushed toward her. Maybe he hadn't heard her open the door. She flipped on the light. Spunky's chair was empty.

"Hey, Spunks, where are you?"

A furry face poked out from under the heavy curtain that covered the large front window. With an air of urgency, Spunky scurried toward the store's front door, where he turned in tight circles and whined.

"Oh no you don't." Olivia was well aware of Spunky's manipulative tactics when in pursuit of nocturnal quarry. "You do not need to go outside. I'll bet you've had your eye on a squirrel, haven't you?" She opened the store's door. Spunky shot into the foyer and flew toward the front door. Olivia cringed as he scratched at the door and whimpered.

"Oh, Spunky, must you? It's the middle of the night." But Olivia knew she had no choice, unless she was willing to clean up a mess. "All right, but make it quick. Hang on while I get the extra leash." She always kept one stashed in a small bureau in the foyer, just in case. When she'd snapped it on and opened the front door, Spunky raced across the porch and down the steps. Olivia stumbled after him, clutching the leash. They reached grass without a moment to spare.

"That was well and quickly done," Olivia said. "Now let's go to bed." Spunky's ears perked up, though probably because he'd heard a squirrel. Then a full choir began to sing "Stille Nacht," in German . . . outdoors . . . at three o'clock in the morning. Well, Maddie did like to begin celebrating the holiday season early. She also enjoyed playing with Olivia's ringtone. Restraint, however, was not in Maddie's vocabulary.

As the musical onslaught began again, Spunky yapped in alarm and took shelter against Olivia's ankle. She picked him up and felt his little heart pounding. Her cell phone went quiet, so she didn't check her caller ID. Maybe Del had called with the DNA results. She'd insisted he do so as soon as he knew anything. Well, Del could wait until she was back in her apartment.

Spunky had regained his nerve. He wriggled free of Olivia's loose grip and landed on his feet. As "Stille Nacht" once again shattered the silence of the night, Spunky lunged toward a nearby squirrel. He hadn't a hope of catching it, but he did yank Olivia off balance. She managed to right herself, hang on to Spunky's leash, and put her phone to her ear. Her mother would never believe her capable of such a triumph of coordination.

"Hi," Olivia said, gasping for breath. "Did you get the test results?"

"Yes, Livie, and I'm not pregnant."

"*Maddie?*"

Olivia heard Maddie's distinctive chuckle. "Well, that was fun, Livie, but we don't have much time. Did I hear Spunky's squirrel yap? Are you in the store?"

"We're outside." With her free arm, Olivia scooped up her pint-sized hunter. "I forgot to buy puppy pads."

"Which turns out to be a good thing," Maddie said, "because it means you are outside, more or less dressed, and ready to be picked up."

Olivia heard a squeal in the background. "Why?"

"No time. We'll meet you at the curb in front of the store. Be ready to fling yourself into the back seat."

"But Spunky—"

"We'll have to bring him along," Maddie said. "He might come in handy, in case . . ." The sound of murmuring voices came through the connection.

Olivia had a bad feeling. When she had a bad feeling, it was usually correct. "Maddie, is my mother with you? What are you two up to now? Because I refuse to be . . ." Olivia realized she was talking to air. At that moment, she heard squealing tires. Maddie's little yellow Volkswagen screeched to a halt at the curb in front of The Gingerbread House. Olivia had never felt so grateful to be the only nighttime resident at the north end of the Town Square.

The driver's side window lowered, and Maddie's head poked through. "Come on, Livie, move those legs. It'll be dawn before we know it."

Spunky yapped happily as he and Olivia slid into the backseat. "This better be really important," Olivia said as the little car took off.

Maddie turned on her bright lights. "Ellie will explain. I've got to concentrate. We need to get there fast."

Ellie twisted backward to face Olivia. "We're heading for the boarding house, Livie. Something is going on there. I saw two lights, you see." Ellie nodded emphatically.

"Two lights . . . Okay, but I don't see. And, Mom, bear in mind it's a short trip to the boarding house, so be concise."

"I'm always concise, dear, but apparently I'll need to start from the beginning." Ellie loosened her seatbelt so she could turn more easily. "You see, it all started with Ida. She was on her way back to town for her evening shift at the diner when she saw a car hit a cat. The car drove on, but Ida stopped, of course. She's hard as an over-baked cookie, but she loves animals."

"Sure, Ida's a softie. Whatever you say, Mom."

"No need to be sarcastic, Livie. However, in the interests

of time . . . The cat was injured but alive, so Ida took it to Chatterley Paws for emergency care. It wasn't far out of her way. Ida was walking back to her car when Lenora caught up with her and begged a ride to Pete's Diner. Business is business, Ida told me, even though she suspected Lenora would wangle a free meal out of Pete."

Olivia bit her tongue to keep herself from interrupting.

"Dear Lenora . . ." Ellie rolled her eyes heavenward. "She neglected to mention to Ida that she hadn't told Herbie and Gwen where she was going. Naturally, they would have been horrified."

Olivia couldn't stop herself. "Horrified at the thought of Lenora eating at the diner?"

"In a minute, Livie, all will be clear. You see, Lenora was, in fact, responding to Binnie's afternoon blog post, which I suspect you haven't had time to read."

Olivia shook her head.

"Well, Ida had read it, of course, so she got suspicious when Lenora began to prattle about her play. Ida wondered if Lenora had some wild notion about hunting for more bones or maybe treasure. When Lenora left the diner, it was dusk. After that, the diner was so busy Ida forgot all about the blog and Lenora."

"The blog, Mom?"

"Yes, of course, the blog post is vital," Ellie said. "Binnie hinted . . . well, actually she came right out and insisted that the old boarding house was full of hidden treasure. Well, not treasure as in gold and silver, but she did mention the Chatterley cookie cutter collection . . . and maybe another skeleton or two. No one takes Binnie seriously, of course."

Spunky yapped as Olivia sank back against the seat. "No one except Lenora. Are you sure she hasn't finagled a ride back home by now?"

"Positive," Ellie said. "I called Herbie and Gwen to check. They are frantic. They had no idea she'd left until they'd finished surgery and begun to prepare dinner. By then, it was well past dark. So they called me, and I told them that Ida had given Lenora a ride to the diner. So they called Ida. She said Lenora had left the diner an hour earlier, alone."

"So you think Lenora sneaked off to the boarding house to search for the Chatterley cookie cutter collection?" Olivia tried to visualize the tiny, elderly woman ripping down a wall.

"I hate to interrupt," Maddie said, "but we have arrived." She slowed the Volkswagen to a crawl as it crunched over the disintegrating remains of a private road that once had led around to the back of the Chatterley Boarding House. Calliope and her workers had cleared away much of the debris around the abandoned property. However, they'd yet to tackle the trees that had sprouted behind the building and grown tall over the decades. Maddie killed the engine. "This is as far as the car can go," she said. "We'll have to walk the rest of the way."

"Wait a minute." Olivia scooted forward to poke her head between the front seats. "I want to be sure I understand what we're getting ourselves into here. You said you saw two lit windows, right, Mom?"

Ellie nodded. "At opposite ends of the top floor, which consists of a corridor between two rows of rooms. There's a bath in the middle of each side. Come on, I'll show you." She stepped out of the car and signaled to Olivia and Maddie, who followed behind, cracking small branches along the way. Olivia kept Spunky close to her chest. There had to be dozens of squirrels nearby. It was a miracle he hadn't yet gone berserk.

With the aid of a small flashlight, Ellie led them along a circuitous route through dense trees. They soon arrived at an opening several yards from the building's back entrance.

Olivia saw the two lighted windows on the second floor. "Are you sure no one can hear us?" she whispered. "What if Spunky starts yapping?"

"The windows are closed, dear." Ellie doused her flashlight. "They are good, thick windows. Dear Imogene made sure that Horace provided the very best construction materials for the Chatterley Boarding House."

Olivia loosened her stranglehold on Spunky's little jaw. "Good for Imogene, but doesn't that mean we can't hear anything? What can we possibly accomplish out here? In fact, why are we here at all? Are we sure Lenora is even in there? The workers might have left those lights on."

"You forget, Livie . . . I've been here once already this evening, looking for Lenora." Ellie pointed toward the upper left corner of the building. "When I arrived, only that one light was on. I figured it had to be Lenora, and I was just about to go into the building when the other light went on."

"But, Mom, haven't you been checking the building at night for Jack and Alicia? They might be sneaking in to stay warm. They probably think no one would be out looking for them at night." Olivia couldn't keep the exasperation out of her voice.

"Olivia Greyson, I'll thank you to remember that I am not an idiot. "

"I didn't call you an—" Spunky silenced Olivia with a whimpering yap. "Okay, that's it," Olivia said. "I'm locking you in the car, young man. Maddie, I need the keys."

"We might need Spunky's protection," Maddie said as she handed Olivia her car keys. "Take another look at the boarding house windows." She pointed toward the upper floor of the building.

"Oh, my," Ellie said. "Now there are lights on in *three* rooms. Is the entire town of Chatterley Heights planning to tear down my walls?"

Chapter Twenty

Olivia felt uneasy about locking Spunky in Maddie's VW. His sad brown eyes pleaded with her through the closed window. He would yap unhappily for a while, afraid he'd been abandoned, but at least he would be safer. Olivia pulled her sweatshirt tighter as she made her way back through densely packed trees to rejoin her mother and Maddie behind the Chatterley Boarding House. A wet leaf plopped down on her head, quickening her heart rate. She was relieved to find Maddie and Ellie where she'd left them. As they watched, a light appeared and disappeared in a corner window.

"Maybe it was a trick of the moonlight," Olivia said.

"No," Ellie said. "I think someone with a flashlight just left the kitchen."

Maddie said, "I'll bet that was Jack and Alicia. They were probably hungry."

"Then I'm glad I restocked the refrigerator," Ellie said. "I wonder if they realize they aren't alone. I'm not sure how far sound carries inside the building. The original construction is quite solid."

Olivia glanced up at the two lighted windows on the second floor. She saw no movement, but the windows were high, and those rooms were generously sized. "Okay, then. Let's start with the kitchen."

"You want to go in there?" Ellie's eyes seemed to widen in the moonlight. "Shouldn't we call Del or . . . or someone?"

"It might be a good idea to let Del know there's something afoot at the boarding house." Olivia whipped out her cell phone and punched in the code for Del's number. She was sent directly to voice mail. "Del, it's . . . Well, I'm not sure what time it is, but it's dark. Mom, Maddie, and I are in the woods behind the boarding house. It appears to be occupied, perhaps by several people. Otherwise, all is—"

"Livie, look up there." Maddie pointed to the top floor of the boarding house. The light had gone out in the corner room. Within moments, the room next door lit up. "Someone is moving from room to room. What do you want to bet it's Lenora searching for the treasure Binnie mentioned in her blog post?"

Olivia scanned the building's upper level. "So who is in the room at the other end?"

"I realize you two are more experienced in these matters, but isn't it time to alert the Twiterton police?" Ellie asked. "I do own the boarding house, and no one has my permission to be in it right now."

"That's no fun." Maddie checked the time on her cell phone. "If you're scared, we could call it a night and leave Lenora to fend for herself, but that wouldn't be right. I vote we go inside and find out what's going on. Livie?"

"I think it's too early to call in the cops," Olivia said. "Most likely it's some gullible readers who fell for Binnie's silly post."

"Won't they all discover each other at some point?" Ellie asked. "The promise of treasure can turn decent people into greedy monsters."

"Or they might have a treasure hunting party," Maddie said.

"Let's find out what's going on." Olivia signaled them to follow her. "Luckily, we can use your key to get inside, Mom. We should start with the kitchen. If Jack and Alicia have been eating our sandwiches and cookies, they owe us an explanation."

"Yippee!" Maddie whispered.

The three women tramped through wet weeds toward the building. As they approached the kitchen, Ellie whispered, "Stop a moment. I've been wondering how all these people got into my tightly locked building. There might be an answer just ahead of us." Ellie pointed toward steps leading below ground to a small door. "I haven't had a chance to replace this door, so I padlocked it, thinking no one would even see it." She grabbed the door's primitive handle. "The padlock is missing. I should have checked more often."

"Well, then," Olivia said, "let's join the crowd, shall we?"

"The hinges are rusty, so the door doesn't fully open." As Ellie slid through the narrow space, Olivia and Maddie exchanged a doubtful look. Maddie cringed as she scrunched herself through the opening, and Olivia, who was taller, barely made it. "I think part of my shoulder scraped off," Olivia whispered. "I intend to leave by the front door, like a normal person."

Maddie nodded in agreement. "We will look back on this as an adventure . . . eventually."

"Where are we, Mom?" Olivia smelled earth and mold.

"This is an old earthen cellar below the kitchen." Ellie switched on her flashlight and aimed it toward the ground. "Be quiet and follow me." She took Olivia's hand. Olivia reached back with her free hand and felt Maddie grab hold of it. Ellie must have explored every inch of the building because she seemed to know exactly where she was going and how to get there.

"Will we reach the kitchen soon?" Olivia didn't like the scratching sounds she was hearing.

"We're almost there," Ellie said. "Livie, do you happen to have a gun with you?"

"You know I don't own one, Mom. I'd only shoot myself in the foot."

"You could get professional training, dear. You might want to think about it."

"Couldn't I just take martial arts at your new school?" Martial arts sounded painful but potentially less fatal.

"I have a black belt, Livie. A gun is faster and more efficient." Ellie sighed audibly. "I suppose you are right, though. You'd probably trip and shoot yourself in the foot. Okay, here we are. I oiled the hinges on this door, thinking I might want to use this cellar for storage. That was before I got a good look at it."

The door opened so quietly that Olivia was surprised when a sliver of light shone on the stone steps below. Her mother poked her head into the kitchen. "No one is here. Follow me." She held the door for Olivia and Maddie.

Olivia glanced around the room she and Maddie had organized and tested on Monday, only three days earlier. "I'm sure we didn't leave this room looking so neat. Mom, did you clean up after everyone left last Monday?"

"Don't be silly, Livie. I had too much to do. I didn't even think about it."

Maddie felt the towel hung neatly near the sink. "This is damp. Looks like you were right, Ellie. Alicia and Jack must be hanging out here. I'll let Lucas know this place isn't as secure as he thought."

Ellie opened a cabinet door to find nonperishable items organized by category. "My goodness, I'm certainly not responsible for such precision and order, and I didn't observe such a quality in Alicia, either. When this unpleasantness is all over, perhaps I'll hire Jack as building caretaker."

"Good idea," Olivia said. "Always assuming Jack isn't an ax murderer."

Maddie put a finger to her lips. "I hear something," she whispered, pointing toward the kitchen ceiling.

Olivia heard pounding, then a cracking sound. "I think

someone is taking down a wall, and I doubt it's Calliope. I'm going up there. Maddie?"

"I'm in. Ellie, why don't you stay here and call someone. If you can't find Del, call Lucas."

Ellie's hazel eyes darkened. "You forget, Maddie, that I'm the black belt here. Someone is vandalizing my future craft school, and I'm going to stop them."

They heard a loud thud above their heads. Ellie sprinted toward the kitchen door. Olivia and Maddie were close behind.

"Any idea what room is directly above us, Mom?"

"Room seven." Ellie poked her head into the hallway and signaled the others to follow.

Olivia led the way up the rickety staircase. She chose speed over stealth, hoping the racket on the second floor would drown out the inevitable squeaks and groans from the old steps. As they neared room seven, Olivia realized the door was slightly ajar. She put her finger to her lips. As she reached toward the door, it slammed shut.

Olivia whispered, "Do you think they heard us?"

"There are no working locks on these inner doors," Ellie said. "Perhaps we should—" Her next words were drowned out by a piercing shriek that trailed off with . . . The phrase "dramatic precision" came to Olivia's mind. "Was that *Lenora*?"

"Such a distinctive voice," Ellie said. "Lenora so excelled as the captive maiden in horror films." As if she'd heard Ellie's compliment, Lenora performed an encore, followed by a feeble cry for help. Ellie's eyes narrowed as she twisted the doorknob and opened the door.

Five startled inhabitants stared at the intruders. Alicia stood in a corner of the room near the window, her pale face framed by tangled long hair. A tall, thin man stood next to her, a protective arm around her shoulders. Olivia assumed he must be the mysterious Jack. Robbie and Crystal Quinn stood together. Pale blue bits of plaster dotted Crystal's honey-brown hair. Robbie's powerful hands opened and closed repeatedly, as if he were preparing to make a fist. They stood in front of a jagged hole in the wall, which the broken plaster had once covered.

Dressed in black, Lenora perched on a wide ledge that might once have been a window seat. She reached out one thin hand as if she needed help getting down. When no one budged, she curled into a tight ball. "Oh, Livie," Lenora said in a stage whisper, "I'm so glad you've come. I knew you would rescue me." Olivia wondered if she had downed a fortifying tumbler or two of Pete's merlot before making the trek to the boarding house.

Olivia stiffened as Robbie lifted the nasty looking hammer he was holding. She didn't know the implement's proper name, but she'd heard Jason call it a brick hammer. He'd used the sharp end to break up an old stone walk at Calliope's farm. As a weapon, that hammer might not be as quick as a gun, but it could do as much damage. The powerful muscles in Robbie's upper arm tightened and bunched as he took a step toward Olivia.

"Robbie, no." Crystal's tone reminded Olivia of her own mother's voice when she had reached her wit's end with her children. Robbie made no response, angry or otherwise. Crystal reached out to him, one small palm upturned as if to receive the weapon.

Robbie frowned but said nothing.

"Come on, honey, we can share with these good people." Cajoling now, Crystal made it sound as if unexpected guests had shown up at their private picnic. "We probably won't find any antique cookie cutters in there, anyway."

Robbie hesitated a moment before his angry expression dissolved. "Sure, honey, why not." He lowered the hammer.

"How utterly delightful!" Lenora clapped her hands. "Now I'll be able to finish my play. I'll just peek inside this wall to make sure there's no—"

"There is no treasure in there," Robbie said.

"You might get your lovely outfit all covered with dust and dirt," Crystal added.

When Lenora slid off her window perch and tiptoed through the plaster, Olivia realized the aging ingénue was wearing black silk pajamas and a flowing black scarf around her neck. Olivia shivered as she imagined Lenora trekking over to the old boarding house in such thin clothing.

"Isn't it exciting, Livie?" Lenora clasped her hands together under her chin. "This evening is turning out even better than I'd hoped." She poked her head through the hole in the wall and withdrew it quickly. "Ugh," she said. "Nothing but dust and broken wood. So disappointing. However, I shall persevere. We will simply try another room. I'm so glad I won't have to search for the Chatterley treasure all by myself. It would have taken me all night with only my little hammer." She waved a dismissive hand at a small hammer on the floor. Olivia wondered if it had come from Lucas's hardware store.

"All right, then, it's settled." Crystal clapped her hands like a kindergarten teacher calling her noisy class to order. "Robbie will clean up in here, while we explore another room."

No one moved. Robbie raised his more substantial hammer enough to suggest a threat. Jack's protective arm tightened around Alicia's shoulders as she snuggled closer to his chest.

"Do hurry, everyone," Lenora begged. "Dawn will be here before we know it. The Chatterley collection is in these ancient walls. I can sense it." She strode toward the door, pajama legs flapping. "If I must, I shall unearth the collection all by my—" As Lenora flung open the door, her silk scarf unwound from her neck and slithered downward. She made no attempt to fling it back over her shoulder. Instead, she stumbled back as Kurt Kurtzel stepped into the room.

Kurt was dressed all in black, minus the knit face mask he had worn when he'd forced his way into the Gingerbread House kitchen. Kurt's confidence was understandable given the weapon in his hand—a knife with a long, thin, and undoubtedly lethal blade. Olivia was fairly certain it was a switchblade, though she'd never seen one before. How did he manage to obtain a weapon like that on such short notice? Just hours earlier, he'd had only a pocket knife.

Kurt stepped into the room, slamming the door behind him. "Don't anyone move." His eyes darted about as if he expected weapons to come flying toward him. "Alicia, come over here and stand next to me."

"No," Alicia said.

"Not a chance, kid," Jack added. Olivia heard a quiet firmness in his voice, as if he were accustomed to dealing with hotheaded delinquents.

"You belong with me," Kurt said.

"You stay away from my daughter," Crystal said. "You killed her father."

"Oh, come on, everyone," Lenora pleaded. "Let's please get into the spirit of our treasure hunt."

Kurt gave Lenora a disdainful glance up and down. "What are you supposed to be?"

Lenora straightened to her full five-foot-three-inch height and planted her fists on her prominent hip bones. "I, young man, am Lenora Dove, star of stage, screen, and television commercials."

Kurt stared at her, his dark blue eyes nearly black against his pale skin. "You're nothing but an old has-been. Nobody will miss you." He aimed his knife at Lenora's throat.

Evidently, Lenora had mistaken Kurt for an actor with whom she was sharing an impromptu scene. Resting her right hand at the base of her throat, Lenora said, "I have but a little neck."

Only Olivia heard Maddie's faint chortle. "Lenora thinks she's playing Ann Boleyn," Maddie whispered. "We must save her from herself. Diversion time."

Several chunks of plaster lay at Olivia's feet. She scooped up two pieces and quickly tossed one. It hit the wall behind Kurt's back. When he spun around, knife at the ready, Maddie rushed toward Lenora. Olivia threw the second hunk of plaster, hitting the wall above Kurt's head. As he looked up, bits of plaster fell on his face. Maddie had just enough time to grab Lenora around her tiny waist and yank her out of reach. Lenora, thank goodness, was too startled to make a sound, melodramatic or otherwise.

They had rescued Lenora for the moment, but Olivia had no idea how to subdue Kurt. Robbie would be no help. He leaned against the wall near the door, his arms crossed over his thick chest, seemingly content to let the intruders exhaust themselves until only he and Crystal were left standing.

Kurt had dropped his knife but quickly scooped it up. Olivia was out of ideas, as well as handy bits of plaster. However, her petite, exercise-addicted mother took the reins. Ellie stretched her arms toward the ceiling and executed several perfect forward flips while managing to avoid the clutter dotting the floor. Her acrobatics brought her to Kurt's side. His lower jaw went slack. Without hesitation, Ellie kicked her leg straight up and whacked Kurt's extended arm. His knife flew from his grip and landed amid the detritus on the floor.

Kurt, however, had come prepared. He reached into the pocket of his black jeans and produced a pocket knife. His face twisted with rage as he lunged at Ellie. Olivia's peripheral vision caught movement on her left as Jack raced past her. Jack was a full head taller than Kurt and far stronger. His upper arm muscles bunched impressively as he grabbed Kurt's wrist and twisted his arm behind his back. Kurt cried out in pain and dropped his knife. Jack kicked the knife toward Olivia. Robbie lunged toward the knife, grabbing it before it could reach her.

"Well," Lenora said, clasping her hands together like a delighted child, "I'm so glad that's all settled. Now, can we all move on?"

Jack's weather-beaten forehead furrowed in confusion. "Shouldn't we call the police and wait here for them?"

"Oh, don't be such a spoilsport." Lenora waved her claw-like hand dismissively. "That silly boy only had a knife."

"What if he used a knife to kill my father?" Alicia shivered. Jack held Kurt's upper arm and searched his pockets for more weapons. He found none. Kurt yanked his arm free and ran from the room.

"There, you see?" Lenora said. "He's merely a silly boy showing off. I'm sure the real killer is long gone, my dear. You must move on with your life. Now we really should explore more rooms. I simply *know* there's a fortune in antique cookie cutters hidden throughout this old monstrosity of a building."

"Yes, why don't we at least take a look around?" Crystal sounded chipper, as if she were proposing a pleasurable excursion. She shot a quick glance at her husband.

"Excellent idea." There was more than a hint of command in Robbie's voice. "I suggest we split up. We'll clean up in here while the rest of you wait for us in another room of your choice. However, to make sure no word of the treasure leaks out, please hand over your cell phones."

"Keep your hands off my cell phone," Lenora said. "That's my private property."

"She is correct." Ellie, still a sixties radical at heart, pumped her fist in the air. "We know our rights!" More angry voices joined in as Ellie began to chant, "Hands off our phones!" Olivia was familiar with her mother's tactics. Ellie was creating a diversion.

Red blotches spread across Robbie's face. His fists tightened. Crystal touched his arm. Robbie shook off her hand. When he picked up the brick hammer he had brandished earlier, Olivia punched 911 into her cell phone. The call didn't go through. She searched frantically but saw nothing that might serve as a weapon.

Lenora showed no interest in the battle escalating around her. Tilting her head like a curious sparrow, she peered through the hole in the wall. She reached inside with both thin arms and lifted out a piece of wood about a foot and a half long. It looked as if it might have been split lengthwise, leaving a splintery, jagged edge. Lenora shrugged and slid the wood back through the hole.

"Why aren't you joining the riot?" Maddie whispered in Olivia's ear. "It might be our only chance to overpower those two."

"Keep up the good fight," Olivia whispered back. "I might have a couple ideas."

Maddie nodded and rejoined the chant.

Olivia turned her back and tried her cell phone again. Still no signal. She'd been able to call from the kitchen, but maybe the tree branches outside were dense enough to interfere with the signal. So much for that idea.

Robbie and Crystal were arguing with each other, so Olivia sneaked away to join Lenora at the damaged wall. "Mind if I take a look at what you found inside that wall?" Olivia asked.

Lenora shrugged. "This is just a broken board or something. There's no treasure in there."

Olivia peered through the hole in the wall and saw nothing but broken plaster. The piece of old wood Lenora held might make a good weapon, though. Olivia assumed she was looking at the back of room eight's closet area. It seemed odd to find open space between the plaster wall and the back of room eight's closet, but she knew nothing about construction.

Lenora's thin, penciled eyebrows pinched together as she studied a darkened area along the broken edge of the wood. She shrugged, and said, "I hoped to find a secret message carved into this board, but this is probably just an old water stain."

"May I see that board for a moment?" Olivia asked.

Lenora released an Oscar-worthy sigh as she handed the wood to Olivia. "In a movie, everything is important. Life simply cannot compete with the theater."

While Robbie and Crystal argued, Olivia quickly examined the wood. As a weapon, it might be awkward. Robbie's hammer would easily smash it. The stain looked old, so

Lenora was probably right. Only in fiction were puzzling details important.

Despite Ellie's efforts, the protest had begun to wind down. Olivia slid the board back through the hole in the wall. As she turned around, she saw Crystal watching her.

Robbie opened the door to the hallway. "The fun is over," he said. "Time to leave."

"Hah!" Lenora said. "You want all the treasure for yourself."

"There is *no* treasure." When no one budged, Robbie's jaw worked as if he were grinding his teeth.

Ellie stared him down. "I own this building," she said. "You are the ones who must leave."

"You want to bet on that?" The brick hammer was still in Robbie's hand. He lifted it. "Get out of this room, all of you," Robbie yelled. "I don't care where you go, but don't let me see you again. Search the other rooms, tear the building down, I don't care. Just leave."

Drained of her adrenaline-fired energy, Olivia felt confused. Something seemed off to her. Robbie wanted them gone from the room, that was clear. However, why wasn't he chasing them out of the building? What was he trying to accomplish?

"Well," Lenora said, "I, for one, intend to search other rooms before the night is over. There's nothing in here." She sashayed toward the door as if adoring fans were watching her. Jack and Alicia followed.

Olivia frowned at the damaged wall. Why had Robbie smashed a hole in it? The narrow enclosure had looked empty except for the stained board, which was probably accidentally walled inside during construction. Unless . . . Olivia glanced toward Robbie and saw him check his own cell phone. He smiled and slid the phone back into his pocket. She guessed he might be relieved to find no signal. Was he hoping to disappear?

Ellie had plunked down cross-legged on the floor. With

his free arm, Robbie grabbed her around the waist and carried her out the door.

Maddie sidled up to Olivia. "What just happened here?" she asked quietly. "Robbie gave up on confiscating our cell phones too easily."

"Just what I was thinking. Come on. We won't have much time before they realize we stayed behind." Olivia hurried over to the hole in the wall and pointed to the board. The narrow wall cavity was backed with strips of plywood. Why was there a cavity in the first place? Calliope might know, but that would have to wait. "We must be looking at the back of Horace Chatterley's closet."

Before Olivia could stop her, Maddie lifted the broken board out of the enclosure. "What's this?" she asked in a whisper.

Crystal poked her head into the room. "What are you two still doing in here?" She blanched when she saw the board in Maddie's hand. "Where did you get that? It shouldn't be—"

"What's going on in here?" Robbie pushed past Crystal and closed the door behind them.

"Robbie?" Red splotches appeared on Crystal's ashen face. "Robbie, you promised you'd gotten rid of—"

"Be quiet!" Robbie grabbed Crystal's frail upper arm and shook her.

Crystal struggled fiercely and broke his grip. "You *promised*. You said you'd protect me, that you would fix everything so I'd never be blamed. You said you'd take care of everything so . . . so we could be together."

"Stop talking, Crystal." Robbie spoke in a low, firm voice, as if he were hushing an excitable child. "You need to trust me." Crystal quieted down, though fear and confusion showed in her eyes.

Olivia's mind raced as she tried to understand what was happening . . . and what to do.

"I'll take that," Robbie said, reaching toward the board.

"Sure." Maddie handed the board to him. "I was just

curious to see the other side of Horace Chatterley's closet."
Her cheeks flushed as Robbie studied her face.

The snake tattoos on Robbie's arm slithered as his muscles tightened. "This is just some junk that got left behind
when this place was built. No builder is perfect," he said
with a faint smile. He turned the board in his hands until he
saw the stain.

"Robbie?"

"It's too late, Crystal," he said. "They know. Leave the
room. I'll take care of things. I always do."

"Robbie, no, please." Crystal touched his arm with her
fingertips. "Can't we just disappear?"

"And leave my construction company? Don't be stupid.
What would we live on? Trust me, Crystal. Haven't I always
taken care of you?" Robbie headed toward the door of the
room. On the way, he scooped up his hammer. A shiver of
dread coursed through Olivia's body as she watched Robbie
take several long nails from his pocket. He nailed one end of
the stained board to the door jamb and the other end to the
door. He had nailed the four of them into the room together.
But why? Did he intend to kill Maddie and her and then disappear with Crystal?

Olivia suspected Robbie had blocked the door behind the
others as well. Eventually, they would break out, but it might
be too late.

Crystal's words echoed through Olivia's mind. One
phrase, in particular . . . something about Robbie promising
to make sure Crystal wasn't blamed . . . *for Kenny's death*?
"That board . . ." Olivia pointed toward the blocked door.
"Is that what killed Kenny? Is that the stain from Kenny's
blood?" She watched Crystal's face blanch.

"Don't say anything, Crystal," Robbie said.

"Kenny must have done something unforgivable," Olivia
said. "He wasn't careful with money, was he?" Her sympathy
felt strained, but it seemed to work. Crystal nodded as tears
filled her eyes.

"Those stupid schemes of his . . ." Crystal's delicate features twisted with resentment. "He was always on the verge of getting rich from some scheme or other, but he always lost money . . . money that *I* earned."

"It would sure make me furious if Lucas did that to me," Maddie said.

"I was furious, all right." Crystal's fingers curled tightly. "What's worse, he was turning our daughter into a dreamer like him. Alicia loved him more than she ever loved me, even though I was the one trying to feed and clothe her." Crystal swiped at a tear with her fist. "I *despise* cookie cutters. I wish that wretched Chatterley collection never existed."

While Crystal vented, Olivia surreptitiously watched Robbie. His silence puzzled her. The hint of a smile softened his features as he listened to Crystal vilify her dead husband. Perhaps it stoked his ego to hear her lambaste his predecessor. Did he believe Kenny's murder was justified? Is that why he'd gone to such lengths to protect her?

"Did Kenny really think he could track down the Chatterley collection?" Maddie sounded genuinely aghast at the thought.

"Oh yeah," Crystal sneered. "That was Kenny all over. You know what really made me mad?"

Maddie shook her head, wide-eyed.

"Kenny told me he'd already found the Chatterley collection." Crystal tossed up her hands in angry despair. "He wanted me to come here with him and see for myself," Crystal said. "His plan was for us to dig those beat-up old things out of the wall at night, and then we'd find a way to sell them to rich collectors. It didn't occur to him that we'd be seen . . . or that we'd have to leave Alicia alone at night. She was still a kid!"

Maddie nodded in sympathy. Robbie, Olivia noticed, had begun to look impatient.

"I was at the end of my rope with Kenny," Crystal said, "but he wouldn't drop it. He'd gone to the boarding house to sleep off a drunken bender, as usual. He woke up in the middle of the night when he heard noises, probably mice. There was a hole in the wall, covered with plywood. It was attached with some sort of old, disintegrating adhesive. Kenny took it down so it wouldn't fall and wake him up. He was using a flashlight, which shone on the cookie cutters inside the wall. Then he found bones."

"Crystal—"

"I need to tell them, Robbie. They have to understand." Crystal turned back to Maddie. "I didn't believe Kenny, but he wouldn't back down. He said he'd found the Chatterley cookie cutter collection, that we'd be rich. He'd brought one home. I told him I was leaving him for good. I'd had enough of his schemes. Kenny begged me to stay. He came back here to collect more of the cutters to prove he was telling the truth." Crystal took a shaky breath. "After Kenny left, I looked over the cutter he'd brought home. It was tarnished and dented. I figured it was just some junk he found at a flea market. I was so mad, I followed him back to the boarding house." Crystal shivered and hugged herself. "I found him collecting a bunch of old, dirty cookie cutters. Then I saw the pile of bones in that closet. It creeped me out seeing Kenny pawing through dust for cookie cutters while that skeleton lay there watching him."

"It's getting late, Crystal," Robbie said. "I need to find a safe place for you. I'll come and get you when . . . when everything blows over." There was a chill in Robbie's quiet, rational voice. Olivia shivered.

"Just let me finish explaining, Robbie." Crystal ran her fingers through her tousled hair. Olivia noticed dark roots had begun to show. "I want them to understand why I . . ." She turned again to Maddie. "I didn't mean to hit Kenny so hard. He just . . . He could be so *stubborn*, especially when he was caught up in one of his crazy get-rich-quick fantasies. I needed to get away from him and make sure he never came back."

Olivia glanced sideways at Robbie, expecting him to silence Crystal. He stared at the floor, expressionless.

Crystal grabbed Maddie's hands. "You understand, don't

you? I couldn't take it anymore. Kenny destroyed all my chances at life. He refused to be a responsible husband and father, even though Alicia adored him. I was so angry, I . . ." Crystal broke into sobs and threw herself into Maddie's arms.

Olivia held her breath and instinctively moved closer to Crystal and Maddie, hoping for safety in numbers. Robbie hadn't moved. His face gave nothing away.

Over Crystal's shoulder, Olivia met Maddie's worried eyes. Olivia thought she heard pounding sounds in the distance. If she and Maddie could keep stalling for time . . .

"We need to leave now, Crystal," Robbie said. He patted the right pocket of his jeans, where Olivia assumed he carried a weapon . . . perhaps a knife, since his jeans were too snug to conceal even a small caliber gun.

Crystal pulled away from Maddie and wiped at her eyes. "I want you to understand why I . . . Well, I couldn't take it for one more minute."

"You were miserable," Maddie said.

"Yes, yes." Crystal's relief was palpable. "Kenny was incapable of being a responsible adult."

"Didn't he have a job interview the day he disappeared?" Olivia asked. "Did that fall through, too?"

"Oh . . ." Crystal's shoulders drooped. "It wasn't a real job offer, but I can't blame Kenny for that. The call was just a ruse we used to get Kenny out of the way when we—"

"Crystal." Robbie sounded like a stern father.

"Well, it was, Robbie. We have to take some responsibility. Kenny only went out drinking that day because he didn't want to come home and tell me there wasn't any job interview. He knew I wouldn't believe him. And then he came back here because he wanted to prove himself to me."

The pounding down the hall sounded like several bodies heaving themselves against the door.

Crystal lifted her chin and spoke directly to Maddie. "There was a broken board lying on the floor. Some tramp probably meant to burn it. Anyway, I picked it up. Kenny was lifting something out of the closet to show me. He had his back turned and I . . . I just lost it. I swung that board and hit him hard near his neck. He fell forward, right into the closet. I guess the board was sharp because he was bleeding." Crystal hugged herself again as tears rolled down her cheeks. "Alicia loved Kenny so much. She'll never forgive me."

Olivia's mind was whirring. Something didn't feel right. As if she were following an online trail, Olivia flipped through every detail she could remember hearing about Kenny's death.

A distant sound like cracking wood broke her train of thought. Robbie grabbed Crystal by the arm and yanked her toward the door. "We need to leave now, Crystal."

"Just one more minute, Robbie."

"Crystal, I've always fixed everything, haven't I? I can still fix this if we leave *now*."

"No, Robbie, I already told them. I'm the one who hit Kenny."

Olivia flashed back to her conversation with Del in Aunt Sadie's kitchen. Del had mentioned Kenny's injuries. She couldn't remember his exact words, but she was nearly certain he'd said Kenny had suffered *two* blows, both in the neck area. One had hit the neck directly, and the other was higher. Olivia was willing to bet that the lower blow had been Crystal's, which meant it had come first. And then she'd left the scene.

"Wait." Olivia reached her hand toward Crystal. "Was Kenny alive when you left?"

"He groaned as I went out the door." Crystal flinched at the memory.

"Did you hit him again?"

"What?! Of course not. I just called—" Another loud crack drowned out Crystal's voice. But Olivia watched her lips and recognized the name—*Robbie*. Fists began to pound on the door. The board nailed to that door was almost certainly the weapon used to finish off Kenny Vayle.

Out in the hallway, the pounding turned to thuds as one

or more bodies threw their weight against the door. Olivia wasn't hopeful for a quick rescue. Robbie had done an expert job of securing the board. Olivia remembered her mother mentioning recently, with pleasure, that no one made doors that solid anymore.

Robbie reached into his jeans pocket and produced a penknife, which he opened and handed to Crystal. He whispered in her ear. With a grimace, Crystal took firm hold of Maddie's left arm from behind and touched the tip of the penknife to her back. "I'm sorry," she said. Robbie lifted one pants leg to reveal a closed switchblade strapped to his calf with a rag.

Olivia heard a thud as their rescuers hit the door again. The wood inched away from the wall. From behind, Robbie grabbed Olivia's left upper arm and squeezed hard. She felt nothing against her back, but she knew the closed switchblade was in his right hand. The moment the door flew open, their rescuers could become unwitting killers. Robbie undoubtedly counted on shock for Maddie's and her welfare to slow their reaction time and allow him, at least, to get away. Olivia felt certain he didn't expect Crystal to escape. He might love her, in his own twisted way, but he had shown himself more than willing to sacrifice her to save himself.

With Maddie behind her, Olivia couldn't communicate with her eyes. If she tried to break free before the door opened, would Maddie react quickly enough to save herself? Would Crystal freeze? Or would Robbie simply push the lever on the switchblade and send the knife into her back, then calmly take Crystal's place behind Maddie? Crystal . . . Crystal was the weak link.

Another thud. The board loosened a bit more. One more blow might do it. There was only one choice. Olivia figured she had nothing to lose. She spun around to her left. She felt her shoulder give, but adrenaline kept her going. As Robbie turned to face her, the switchblade shot open. With her free right hand, Olivia grabbed Robbie's bare wrist and dug her fingernails into his skin.

Maddie's strong, shapely leg shot straight up. Her shin caught Robbie under the elbow. Olivia heard a snap. Robbie dropped the switchblade and clutched his elbow.

"Crystal, *do* something," Robbie cried.

Crystal did something—she dropped her penknife. "Oh, Robbie, you're hurt." Crystal wrapped her arms around his chest. In the process, her arm whacked Robbie's elbow. With a cry of pain, he fainted.

The door burst open. Jack rushed in and bent over Robbie's prone figure. "Out cold," Jack said. He left Crystal to sob over the man who was willing to let her take full blame for killing her husband.

Olivia's mother appeared at her side. "Well," Ellie said, "all's well that ends well."

"You don't know the half of it." Olivia pointed toward the penknife and switchblade on the floor. "Those were aimed at our backs while you were breaking through the door."

"Ah." Ellie's cheeks blanched. "I see."

"Is that a siren I hear?" Olivia asked. "Did you call the police, and if so, how?"

"Jack is so handy. He broke a window so I could lean out. I had to sit on Jack's shoulders, but I finally got cell phone reception. I called 911." Ellie glanced across the room, where Jack had tied Robbie's ankles together with a rag and thoughtfully propped him against the wall. Crystal sat next to him, hugging her legs to her chest. Alicia knelt down and wrapped her arms around her mother. Crystal leaned her head on her daughter's shoulder.

Del appeared in the open doorway, his service revolver drawn. He took in the scene and lowered his weapon. "Well, well. Apparently, I'm no longer needed here."

"Del!" Olivia ran to him and threw her arms around his neck.

Del wrapped his free arm around her waist and held tight. "I was on my way back from the crime lab when the

Twiterton police called to tell me about your mom's 911 call. You gave me quite a scare," he whispered.

Olivia whispered back, "I won't tell." She released him and pointed toward the prisoners, one unconscious and the other exhausted. "Those two are responsible for Kenny Vayle's death."

Alicia pulled away from her mother when she heard Olivia's pronouncement.

"It's complicated, though," Olivia said. "I'm reasonably certain that broken board near the door is the murder weapon. You'll want to test it for blood stains, if that's possible."

Del gave her a lopsided grin. "Yes, ma'am." His eyes darkened. "You sure you're okay? What about Maddie and Ellie?"

"We're all fine, Del, really," Olivia said. "Robbie might have a broken elbow, though. That was Maddie's work."

"I'm impressed," Del said. "I hear sirens heading this way. We'll want to interview all of you, so don't leave town."

"I assume you meant me." Jack put his arm around Alicia's shoulders. "Don't worry, I'll be sticking around for some time. Alicia needs my support."

Ellie beamed at Del, whose arm encircled Olivia's waist. Raising an eyebrow at her mother, Olivia said, "Just so you know, Mom, if you say 'all's well that ends well' again, I'll have to gag you."

"Perfectly understandable, dear."

Chapter Twenty-one

On a dreary Saturday afternoon in mid-November, Olivia and Maddie sprawled on a forest green velvet settee in the front parlor of the Chatterley Mansion. Spunky snuggled on Olivia's lap. Her mother, Ellie, her eyes closed, sat cross-legged on the rose velvet seat of a small parlor chair. Her ramrod straight spine barely touched the padded back.

"This is the life." Maddie stretched her stocking feet toward a crackling fire.

Aunt Sadie sat in her wheelchair, her knitting on her lap. While she watched the flames frolic among the logs, her fingers looped raspberry red yarn over and around the needles as if they needed no guidance.

"On the other hand," Maddie said, "being a Chatterley wife doesn't sound like fun to me. Most of them didn't even get to decorate their own cookies."

"Plus they were married to Chatterley men," Olivia said.

Ellie's eyes opened. "I hear Del and Lucas banging around up in the attic. I do hope they don't knock a hole in the wall when they turn that corner in the staircase."

"I've had my fill of holes in walls," Maddie said. "Speaking of which . . . Ellie, is Lenora still pestering you about turning your craft school into a theater?"

With a tolerant smile, Ellie said, "Yes, dear, of course she is. However, I've decided to use dear Lenora's enthusiasm as a way to, shall we say, guide her toward sobriety."

"Exactly how does that work, Mom?"

With an impish grin, Ellie said, "I have promised Lenora the opportunity to teach a small acting class. Calliope is designing an intimate stage for the class. Herbie and Gwen are thrilled."

"But how exactly will teaching keep Lenora sober?" Maddie asked.

"I'm not promising a miracle." Ellie rolled her shoulders back to achieve perfect posture. "But we will try to keep Lenora well-nourished and busy, happily doing what she loves . . . with subtle oversight, of course. And did I mention our no-alcohol policy? Calliope will be enforcing that rule."

"That should do the trick," Olivia said. "Well, we'll still have Binnie to torture us day and night."

"Not to worry, Livie, dear. I believe I've taken care of that little problem as well." Ellie's smile seemed—to Olivia, at least—a bit smug. "In a week or so, Ned will be returning to Chatterley Heights to stay. Her special friend will be coming with her."

"I see," Olivia said. "That's sort of a good news, bad news thing, isn't it? Do you know anything about this special friend?"

"I didn't pry, dear. It will be what it will be."

"We are doomed," Maddie said, rolling her eyes toward the ceiling.

The sound of grunting announced Del and Lucas's arrival. Between them, they carted a small, though clearly heavy leather trunk. "Where do you want this thing?" Del asked.

"Over here between Maddie and me," Olivia said. "We'll dig through the diaries and try to find the ones Aunt Sadie needs. Do you have the list, Maddie?" Maddie produced a folded paper from her jeans pocket and handed it to her.

"I'm so excited, I won't be able to concentrate on knitting." Aunt Sadie's needles kept on clicking.

Lucas waved good-bye as he left to return to his hardware store, and Del moved a carved walnut rocking chair next to Olivia's end of the settee.

"I can't wait another second." Maddie opened the lid of the unlocked trunk. It was filled to the rim with leather-bound diaries in a variety of shapes, sizes, and colors. "Wow, those Chatterley women were prolific. Either that, or they needed to unload a lot about their husbands. Hand me the list, Livie. It'll be more efficient if I do this alone. This will take a while, so feel free to talk among yourselves." Maddie lifted a journal from the open chest. "And by that, I mean you, Del. I want a blow-by-blow account of your investigation. We deserve that after all we went through to capture your suspects for you."

"Yeah, like my dislocated shoulder." Olivia rubbed the injury she'd sustained while dodging Robbie's switchblade. "You've been way too closed-mouthed about Kenny Vayle's murder investigation since you arrested Crystal and Robbie. You owe us."

"And if I don't pay up, you'll hold it against me forever, right?" A corner of Del's mouth quivered as he stifled a smile. "Okay, as it happens, Crystal, at least, has finally begun to weaken after two weeks of stonewalling. They blame each other, or Kurt, for Kenny's death. Mind you, Kurt isn't entirely blameless. Once her father's remains were discovered, Alicia became suspicious of Robbie, so he wanted her gone."

"How did Kurt fit in?" Olivia asked. "Robbie wanted an excuse to kick Alicia out of the house, so she wouldn't hear or observe something that pointed to Robbie's guilt, right? Is that how Kurt fits in?"

Del nodded. "Crystal told us Robbie hoped to portray Alicia as unstable. That's why he visited your store. To further his plan, Robbie told Kurt a lie about Pete's intentions toward Alicia. He hoped Kurt would react violently and that Alicia, in turn, would react hysterically. He also supplied

Kurt with an array of his favorite weapons. When Pete fired Alicia, it fit right into Robbie's scheme."

"Switchblades," Olivia said. "Scary. Did Robbie consider the possibility that Alicia might have been hurt?"

Del shook his head. "Robbie didn't care. He was more concerned with protecting himself. He'd already convinced Crystal that she was solely responsible for her husband's death. He hoped she would confess if the remains were ever discovered. He hung on to the murder weapon without Crystal's knowledge, thinking it might come in handy as further evidence against her."

Ellie shivered. "What a horribly controlling man."

"Robbie hadn't read enough murder mysteries," Olivia said, "or he'd have known more about forensics. But I suppose he was arrogant enough to think he already knew everything."

"Well, Robbie still hasn't confessed," Del said, "but the forensics will get him when he goes to trial. Crystal is convinced she killed Kenny with one blow. She didn't even try to make it sound like an accident. However, the blow that struck Kenny's neck didn't kill him. He'd have fallen to the floor, head first, probably knocked unconscious. Crystal thought he was dead or about to die. By her own admission, she didn't think to check his pulse. She just ran to find Robbie."

"And Robbie took care of everything?" Olivia asked. "Just like he always did?"

"That's our conclusion," Del said. "The second blow was higher and broke Kenny's neck."

Olivia thought back to Crystal's tearful confession. "I suppose Robbie might continue to stonewall, but it seemed clear to me that Crystal hit Kenny only once, and she believed she'd killed him. She seemed genuinely shocked and confused when I asked if she hit him a second time. Robbie was cool and controlling, as always."

"So very sad," Ellie said. "Crystal never learned to stand up for herself, so she became prey for men like Robbie."

"I'm confused by one thing," Olivia said. "We ran up to room seven when we heard a crash. When we arrived, we realized that Robbie had smashed a hole in the wall right where he'd hidden the murder weapon. Why would he do that?"

"Interesting question." Del chuckled. "Naturally, Robbie told us he'd had no idea the board was behind that wall."

"I wonder . . ." Ellie tilted her head like a curious bird. "Lenora can be so single-minded, you know."

"Okay, Mom, so that means . . . what, exactly?"

"Oh, Livie, dear, I was remembering you as a toddler. You wanted to taste everything, which kept your father and me on our toes. One day your father was making a mustard and cheese sandwich when he saw that you were about to taste a toothpick you had found on the kitchen floor. He quickly put a spoonful of mustard in your little open mouth, while he snatched the toothpick from your hand. So clever of him."

"That explains why I'm not fond of mustard," Olivia said. "Now back to Robbie and the hole in the wall . . . ?

Maddie looked up from her perusal of a diary. "Oh, I get it," she said. "Robbie wanted to distract Lenora from pounding her little hammer into that part of the wall. Maybe he also hoped to cover the murder weapon with plaster to make it less visible."

Del shrugged. "It's a working hypothesis, anyway."

Maddie plunked a stack of four journals on the coffee table. "Fascinating as our discussion has been, are we ready to move on? Because these are the journals on Aunt Sadie's list, and I can't wait to see what they have to say about those antique cookie cutters."

The fire had begun to die down. Aunt Sadie pulled her sweater more tightly around herself, and said, "Maddie, dear, would you read the passages to us? My eyesight is not what it used to be."

Del hopped up to add another log to the fire. Olivia smiled her thanks as he returned to his chair.

"This will be fun." Maddie picked up a journal with a tan

leather cover and opened to a page she had marked with a scrap of paper. "Okay, this was written by Charlotte Chatterley in 1859. That three-petaled flower cookie cutter was hers. Charlotte wrote, *My new little girls are the delights of my life. They are healthy and beautiful, with strong lungs and lovely curls. I am thankful I did not contribute three more Chatterley sons to the world. I must teach my innocent little daughters to be careful whom they marry.* Should I read more?" Maddie asked.

"Thank you, Maddie." Aunt Sadie sighed. "That passage says enough, I think. You see, Charlotte's husband already had a mistress when he married, and he saw no reason to change afterward. Those little curly-haired girls gave Charlotte three good reasons to go on."

"Next," Maddie said, opening a journal with a black cover. "This one was written in 1833 and belonged to Harriet Chatterley. I don't remember anything about her."

"Oh yes, Harriet," Aunt Sadie said. "She was one of several Chatterley wives whose journals mentioned the little boy and girl cookie cutters whose hands interlock. Such a lovely image. Do read us the passage, Maddie."

Maddie opened the journal and began to read. "*I wish my dear mother-in-law had buried those hand-holding cookie cutters in the garden instead of passing them to me. Now I must give them to my lovely daughter-in-law, who deserves someone better than my first-born son. I shall try to help her through the difficult years to come.*" Maddie closed the journal. "That was disturbing. Any idea what happened to that lovely daughter-in-law, Aunt Sadie?"

"I'm afraid she died giving birth to a son. I suspect her husband shed no tears. As I remember, he quickly replaced her." Aunt Sadie blinked rapidly, fighting tears of her own.

Picking up the third journal, Maddie opened to a passage which she skimmed quickly. "This one is powerful," she said. "It was written in 1805, by Caroline Chatterley. *I have asked the tinsmith to create a cookie cutter to my specifications. I did not tell him why I wanted such a shape, but when he met my husband, I believe he understood. It will be a secret to which only we Chatterley wives will be privy, and our hearts will be lighter for it."* Maddie closed the journal. Grinning, she said, "I think we can all agree that Caroline commissioned the portly pig cutter."

No one spoke as Maddie picked up the fourth journal. She held it up so everyone could see the intricate flowers, embroidered in shades of purple, clustered on dark green vines that curled around the surface of the pale green cloth cover. "Isn't this journal gorgeous? It belonged to Abigail Chatterley. Oh, I remember now. Aunt Sadie, didn't you mention that Abigail did free-form embroidery? She was Horace's mother, right?"

"Yes, indeed," Aunt Sadie said. "Poor Abigail was a sensitive soul. Her journals are filled with bits of her own poetry. I must ask Lucas to look in the attic for a trunk filled with her embroidery. Oh, I do go on, don't I? Please read her words to us, Maddie."

Maddie silently skimmed the page. "Abigail is the one who commissioned that odd cookie cutter with the geometric design. None of us could figure out what it was supposed to represent." Maddie turned the page. "Here's Abigail's drawing, too. My, my, she certainly wrote some scathing comments about her own son, Horace. Listen to this: *Recent stories of my son's appalling behavior have so saddened my heart. If only Horace were more like his dear father, may he rest in eternal peace. Horace has a good and loyal wife at home, and children who need a better example. Though perhaps they are better off without his presence. Their mother, bless her, does her best, and I help when I can with food and clothing. All this while Horace lavishes gifts on other women. May God forgive me, I often wish it had been my son taken from me by influenza, rather than his kind and loving father."*

Maddie had finished all the diary readings. No one spoke for some time. Olivia watched the dying fire, letting the words of four Chatterley wives meld together in her mind. As the last log turned to ash, she said, "I sense a theme in those passages."

"Yeah," Maddie said. "Being a Chatterley wife wasn't all it was cracked up to be."

"That could be said of many wealthy families." Ellie rolled back her shoulders to restore her posture. "And of less well-to-do ones, too. Sadly, it is nothing new."

"Yes, but most disgruntled wives don't express themselves through cookie cutters," Olivia said. "Think about it. Those four Chatterley women, from different generations, turned to cutters to handle rejection, neglect, betrayal by their husbands . . . which makes me wonder if Abigail Chatterley's oddly shaped cutter had a special meaning. Her embroidery work was so flowing and beautiful. Why would she draw a geometric design and go to the trouble of having a cookie cutter made in that very shape? And I find it even more intriguing that all five of those cutters were found with Horace Chatterley's remains. I wonder why."

"We wondered the same thing, Livie." Del took a small notebook from his pants pocket and leafed through it. "The placement of those cutters, when we found them, indicated they might have been arranged on top of Horace's body after he was placed inside the closet."

Olivia jumped up and began pacing the parlor. "Del, I never asked . . . Why didn't I catch sight of Horace's bones when we were trying to see Kenny's cookie cutter necklace? Kenny and Crystal did."

"Because the bones had been covered by a cloth of some sort," Del said, "possibly by Kenny. The material was coated with dust, but not enough to date it from the 1930s. Remember, that closet had been in use when Horace died. He had stored shoes, clothing, even some books in there. We figured Horace's killer shoved him toward the back of the closet, covered him, and left the other items scattered around him. Kenny found him, but he wouldn't have been eager to let anyone else in on the secret."

"Yet you said the cutters had been arranged on top of

Horace's body?" Olivia ran her hand through her hair, frustrated by her confused thoughts.

"That's right." Del checked another page in his notebook. "Okay, here it is. Forensics indicated remnants of a tarp among the bones. So the cutters were arranged on the body, and the tarp was then spread on top. The cloth was added later."

"So, that might mean . . ." Olivia sank onto the settee and stared into the dying fire. Spunky reclaimed her lap.

"What?" Maddie demanded. "Livie, I'm dying here. What does all this mean?"

Olivia shook her head. "We'd never be able to prove it."

Del touched Olivia's arm. "Livie, are you thinking that Horace's wife or children might have killed him, then for some reason buried him with those cookie cutters."

Olivia shook her head. "No, Horace had already squandered the family fortune. His wife and children knew he was living in squalor, and his eldest son was already taking care of them. What would they gain from murdering him?"

"Then who?" Del reached over the arm of the settee to take Olivia's hand. "What are you thinking, Livie?"

"I can't be sure." Olivia stroked the soft hair on Spunky's head. She saw Aunt Sadie pull a length of yarn from a skein and smile as her hands resumed their rhythmic knit and purl. A little *ding* sounded in Olivia's head. "I'm thinking Aunt Sadie didn't have you and Lucas cart that box of journals down from the attic merely so we would empathize with those unhappy Chatterley wives."

All eyes focused on Aunt Sadie, whose innocent expression blossomed into a grin. "I hoped you would feel empathy, of course," she said. "But after all these years and generations of anguished Chatterley wives, is it truly necessary to assign guilt?"

"It's just human curiosity," Maddie said. "Livie is right. We can't prove anything now."

"Exactly." Aunt Sadie resumed her knitting.

"Lucas will be here soon to take Aunt Sadie and me home." Maddie nestled the journals into the trunk, while Del stirred the ashes of the dying fire to cool it more quickly.

Olivia found herself wondering about Imogene Jones. Unlike her husband, Imogene had a colorful history. She'd demonstrated a ruthless streak. Driven by her zeal for social reform, she had reputedly been a mistress to several wealthy, powerful men. They had been willing, in exchange for Imogene's favors, to finance her schemes to help the downtrodden. Olivia wanted to believe that Imogene's marriage to Henry had been a love match. After all, Henry saved his mother and siblings from abject poverty, which would have impressed Imogene. Henry also provided substantial funding for Imogene's reform projects. But what if Henry had wanted to help his own father? What if Horace, lacking his son's compassion but willing to use it to his own advantage, had begged more and more money from Henry? Wouldn't Imogene have been angry the old reprobate was draining the family coffers? Might she have been furious enough to—

"Livie?" Del touched her arm. "What are you thinking?"

Olivia started, even though he had spoken softly. "Sorry, Del, I was following a convoluted and wildly speculative train of thought. Probably not important." She stared at the cooling logs and smiled to herself.

When the doorbell rang, Maddie hopped up to open the front door for Lucas. While he and Maddie wrapped a heavy shawl around Aunt Sadie's shoulders, Del took Olivia's hand and entwined his fingers with hers. "We should sit by a fire to discuss long-ago murders more often."

"I agree." Olivia gave Del a quick kiss on the tip of his nose. "Thank you."

"For what?"

Olivia grinned. "Thank you for not being a Chatterley son . . . and for being you."

Recipe

Pete's Meatloaf

  1½ pounds lean ground beef (or lean ground turkey)
  2 large eggs, beaten
  2 tablespoons dried (or 3 tablespoons fresh) rosemary,
      finely chopped
  freshly ground pepper, to taste
  1-2 dashes Worcestershire sauce
  ½ cup dry oatmeal
  1 tablespoon olive oil, divided
  5 large shallots, finely chopped
  ¼ cup bell pepper (any color), finely chopped
  1 small clove garlic, finely chopped
  1 cup chili sauce (Heck, I use the whole bottle. Pete)
  ⅓ cup petite diced tomatoes, well drained
  2-3 tablespoons brown sugar (to taste)
  1-2 tablespoons Dijon mustard (to taste)
  ¼ teaspoon horseradish (if desired)

Preheat oven to 350°F. In a large bowl, mix together beef or
turkey, eggs, rosemary, pepper, Worcestershire sauce, and
oatmeal.

Heat the olive oil in a frying pan. Add the shallots and sauté lightly. Add to the turkey mixture. Add more olive oil to the frying pan, if necessary, and lightly sauté the chopped bell pepper and garlic until softened but not browned. Add to turkey mixture.

In a small mixing bowl, combine chili sauce, diced tomatoes, brown sugar, horseradish, and Dijon mustard. Mix well.

Pat the turkey mixture into large loaf pan or casserole. Spread topping evenly over meatloaf. Bake for one hour or until done.